When President Franklin Roosevelt choked to death on a chicken bone in 1933, it signalled the start of a brave new world – a world in which America would ally with the USSR against the threat of the Anglo-Chinese Alliance . . . a world where the death on the Moon of rock superstar Bitch Alice sparked a Wracker explosion that would obliterate America's space programme and leave Straight and Wracker alike at the mercy of their enemies' nuclear bomb-loaded station.

And now, years after the deaths that forever changed the course of history, Earth's future is about to be altered again . . .

Wrack and Roll

Bradley Denton

HEADLINE

British Library Cataloguing in Publication Data

Denton, Bradley
    Wrack and roll.
    I. Title
    813'.54[F]   PS3554.E5/

ISBN 0 7472 0016 5
ISBN 0 7472 3009 9 Pbk

Printed and bound in Great Britain by
Collins, Glasgow

Headline Book Publishing PLC
Headline House
79 Great Titchfield Street
London W1P 7FN

For Barbara

Contents

Prelude

We goin' up to Moscow
Got our rifles in our hands.
Yeah, we goin' up to Moscow
Got our rifles in our hands.
Well, we goin' up to see ol' Uncle Joe,
So he an' Gen'rl George can be friends.

Well, when we get there Joe'll be sorry
For all the bad things that he done.
Yeah, when we get there Joe'll be sorry
For all the bad things that he done.
He been messin' round with Cousin Adolf,
But now we gon' have us some fun:

We gonna wrack an' ruin—
Yeah, gonna roll right over you.
Gonna cut you down, Joe,
Ain't gon' be nothin' you can do.

Say now,
What's this here thing blazin' in our soul?
Just some of Gen'rl George's sonofabitchin'
Wrack an' Roll.

     —Pvt. Eddie Dixon,
      "Goin' up to Moscow," 1945

Hysterical Perspective I: *Dallas, Dallas, Do You Read?*

Bitch Alice died on the Moon in 1967. She was standing in front of a TV camera in the *Mare Tranquillitatis*, about to sing "Race You to Hell" with a taped accompaniment, when a fuel valve exploded on the lander thirty yards away.

There was no chance that she and the other four astronauts of *Conquistador 18* could be rescued. History does not record how many of them committed suicide before their twelve remaining hours of oxygen were expended.

* * *

The former Alice Pendleton was survived by an illegitimate ten-year-old daughter, seven platinum albums, and millions of pissed-off Wrackers.

Forty thousand of the latter, give or take a few hundred, honored her memory by carrying out her last wishes.

"If I'm gonna die," she had said before anyone at the National Organization of Space Science (NOSS) had the presence of mind to cut off the worldwide transmission, "those jewbaiters are gonna pay."

A half-second of silence had followed, and then came the Bitch's last two publicly-heard words:

"Trash Dallas."

So they did. Not the entire city, but all of the suburb that was NOSS.

America's manned space effort, which had taken twenty years to build, took only three hours to be destroyed.

Almost before the riot was over, the Anglo-Chinese Alliance (still miffed over being stuck with the ravaged Eastern and Western Trust Territories in 1946 while the United States had taken the relatively undamaged Central) saw its opportunity. Thus, by the mid-Seventies, the Lemon-Limeys had not only established a Moon outpost,

1

but had constructed Churchill-Chiang Station in Earth orbit.

They made no secret of the fact that their goal was to gain economic and political ascendancy over the United States.

Still, the scrod didn't really hit the slinger until December 1979, when (1) the British invaded the island of Concepcion in the Caribbean, and (2) the political war between Annabelle "the Squid" Kirk (J.D. Fitzgerald's secretary of state) and "Big Whig" Winton R. Wilson took a violent turn. Dealers and Whigs had been bitter enemies ever since their creations in 1933 (after Garner succeeded the short-lived Roosevelt), but never before had they been so brutal with their pawns. . . .

In retrospect, it seems funny that the Whigs expected results from Pissant Jackson. It must be remembered, however, that Wilson was used to getting what he wanted from people—and if he didn't, he got rid of them. Painfully.

Also in retrospect, the fact that Kirk tried to manipulate the Bastard Child seems ludicrous. But since when did Straights ever understand a skagging thing about Wrackers?

Or even about Straights? *Nobody* foresaw the minor but necessary role of the Hack—my personal hero even though he was a jagoff.

But, as Bitch Alice wrote:

> *You're a slice of putrid scum.*
> *You screw and cheat and lie;*
> *You're nothing but a human rat—*
> *Hey, baby, so am I.*

Man, ain't it the glorious truth.

—Lorna P.N. Chicago-deSade,
*A Brief, Biased History of
Postwar America, 1945–
1995, Complete with Nude
Photographs*

(New Miami: Purple Press,
2019), pp. 245–46. [Sound-
and Visi-tracks Available on
Barsoom Chips & Discs.]

1

Rock & Ruin

A man break in my room,
Say he got a gun.
    Singa gimme gimme bang bang
    Gotcha you're gone.
Say he want me to love him
'Fore I next see the sun.
    Singa gimme gimme bang bang
    Gotcha you're gone.
Well the sun don't mean that much to me.
I ask if he'd like to watch TV.
He got the gun but I got a knife.
He turn his head I take his life.
    Singa gimme gimme bang bang
    Gotcha you're gone.

—Lieza Galilei,
"A Song About Flowers," 1975

Thursday, December 20, 1979. Washington, D.C.

The good pain didn't come until the seventy-eighth sit-up, but then it hit all at once in a warm rush. Lieza paused for a second, grinning at the mirrored wall, and watched the flush move up from her slick abdomen to her breasts. The upper third of her appendectomy scar burned violet over the waistband of her leathers.

Her forehead, cheeks, and neck tingled under wet strands of black hair. Sweat stung her right eye, but she didn't let herself wipe it away. Instead she concentrated on the lovely sharp stink of muscle balm and the prickle of the carpet on her back. She had seventy-two more sit-ups to go in this set.

The buzz of the phone on the table beside the bed broke her concentration, and she barely managed to get back into rhythm without losing count.

Sputzing hotel. She'd never been bothered when the old Madison had been here, but the fricking Straights running this new beast seemed to have a collective death wish. She hadn't minded doing without a suite, but she'd meant it when she'd told them no calls, no bugs, no nothing.

She glanced at the clock beside the phone and saw that it was only 4:00 P.M.; it wouldn't be time to leave for another three hours. She'd have to tell Cherry, Fug, and Joel to trash their rooms.

Not to worry about Tycho's, though. He never waited to be told.

The phone was still buzzing when she got to a hundred and twenty. All this sensation to savor—pain, strength, muscle, sting, wrench, stink—and she'd lost it somewhere around a hundred and seven. She'd finish her set, and if the phone hadn't stopped by then, she'd rip it out of the wall, throw it through the window, and watch it fall eighteen stories.

But first she'd find out who was calling. There might be an opportunity here to make a Straight miserable.

At a hundred and fifty she fell back, unhooking her feet from under the barbell. The effort of the final thirty had calmed her a little, so for a moment she was able to enjoy the contradictory hot-and-cold sensations created by having exercised while wearing black leather jeans and no shirt. The room's ventilator kicked on, and she felt as though her nipples had become as hard as pebbles.

Lieza liked the simile. *Teats of stone*, she thought, and decided it would make a good song title.

The first line was almost complete in her mind when the buzz went up an octave.

Her jaw muscles tightened. Messing up a workout was bad enough. Messing up a song was Death.

She stood, kicking the jar of muscle balm across the room, and went to the table. She stared at the phone for several seconds before picking up the receiver, imagining hot blue beams shooting from her eyes.

The beige plastic felt cold and utterly Straight as she pressed it against her ear and waited for a voice. Too bad this wasn't a visiphone. Faces were easier to hate than sounds.

"Lisa Pendleton," a flat male voice said.

The plastic creaked in Lieza's fist. Nobody called her that. Nobody who wanted to keep his teeth and at least one of his eyes.

"No Straight here, skaghead," she said in as even a voice as she could manage. She hoped she didn't sound as feral as she felt, because she didn't want to scare off this scrod-sucker before she found out who he was.

"Lieza Galilei, then," the voice said.

Probably a Wrack-lusting Jack who'd paid the desk clerk for her number. Going with that hypothesis, she said, "My name ees Babette, sojerbwah. Who be you?"

"Are you or are you not Lisa Pendleton, stage name Lieza Galilei?"

Her face and hands felt as hot as flame. "Go sputz, jagbreath. You've probably got it in your hand, oui, oui?"

She slammed down the receiver, and the buzzing started again.

Lieza overturned the table, knocking the phone, lamp, and clock to the floor, then tried to yank the plastic-sheathed telephone wire from the wall.

"United States government business," a faraway voice said from the receiver on the floor. "Special Agent Dodson speaking. Urgent. The President wishes . . ."

Lieza sat on the floor, braced her feet against the wall, and pulled, straining until her muscles felt like knotted cables. This time she managed to get the wire out, and when she hammer-threw the phone, the floor-to-ceiling window shattered into beautiful silvery fragments. The only disappointment was that the plastic bomb just missed a parking-lot preacher who was loudly denouncing the minions of Satan, more popularly known as Blunt Instrument.

She couldn't tell whether any of the glass shards got him or not, but she felt better. To celebrate, she took a quart of French vanilla ice cream from the room's tiny refrigerator. After eating, she did another hundred sit-ups, went into the bathroom to vomit, and put on a thin camisole.

"Bleached cotton, black leather," she said aloud while looking at herself in the bathroom mirror, and realized that she had another song title. She went back into the main room, set the table upright, and got to work with pen and paper. A freezing mist had started to fall outside, and wisps of it blew in through the jagged hole where the window had been.

* * *

She had lyrics and most of a melody worked out by seven o'clock, when Tycho broke down the door with an ax.

"Am I early?" he asked as he came in.

Lieza smiled. Tycho looked like a six-foot-four personification of Hell, which meant he was anxious to play even though tonight's show was only the warm-up for tomorrow. He was wearing a cowboy vest without a shirt and had managed to find his zircon-studded pink kneepants. His long blond hair and beard were knotted and tangled, and his chest was crisscrossed by random scratches. His silver nose was dulled by what appeared to be a greenish blob of grease.

"Right on time," Lieza said, glancing at the blue numerals of the clock on the floor. "I was just working on a new song."

Tycho put the ax over his shoulder and crawled across the bed to look at what she'd written. "Jag-ass great," he said after a minute. "Best thing you've cranked in months. Maybe work it up for tomorrow?"

"If we have time. Cab here?"

"Yeah, but we better hurry." He shook his head and exhaled cloud of steam into the cold air. "Center's sending over a limo. Sputzin' D.C.'s gettin' more dink every year."

Lieza nodded and looked out the hole. The sun had gone down, but she could see the bright shaft of the Washington Monument a half mile to the south. Lights glowed everywhere, illuminating the mist that was rapidly changing to snow.

"You got that right," she said. "At least about this part of town." She stood up and jammed her new song into a hip pocket. "Let's go."

Tycho grunted absently. He was staring out into the mist.

"Teek? Dallas to Teek, over."

"I was just thinkin'," he said without looking at her. "That George Washington musta been some lover."

Lieza half-laughed and headed for the doorway. "Wouldn't know."

"Why else would they build him a monument like that?"

Lieza made her way out of the room over the scraps and splinters that had been the door.

Tycho caught up with her at the elevators and brandished his ax at an overweight Straight who hurried off down the hall.

"How you figure he can run so fast bein' so fat?" Tycho asked.

"Wouldn't know," Lieza said again, punching the down button with her thumb.

"Pretty dink to leave without me. You coulda got hurt."

Lieza looked up at him and curled her upper lip back from her teeth.

Tycho shrugged, then glared at the numbers above the elevator doors. He had a twitch in his cheek that Lieza knew indicated impatience.

"We're not gonna beat the limo at this rate," he said, and axed the panel containing the up and down buttons.

"Let's take the stairs. That's where I found Bert." He started down the hall at a trot.

"Bert?" Lieza asked, dashing past him.

"Bert, the Fire Emergency Ax!" Tycho bellowed as he chased after her.

Lieza hit the stairwell door first, but Tycho beat her to ground level by three floors.

"No fair jumping at sixteen and seven," she said at the first-floor landing, doubled over with her hands on her knees.

Tycho used Bert to push open the door. "I think I broke my sputzin' foot," he said, and limped out.

Lieza followed him down a short hallway into the huge blue-carpeted lobby. At Lieza's suggestion, Tycho paused beside a velveteen bench and asked Bert to whack it to pieces. Bert did so. The numerous Straights who had been milling about began to disappear.

While Tycho and Bert were occupied with the bench, Lieza went to the desk and crooked her left index finger at a pair of red-jacketed Straights.

"You there," she said. "Jack and Jackie."

The male said, weakly, "Yes, ma'am?"

Lieza smiled a smile of mock sweetness. "Eyeam no ma'am, sojerbwah," she said, fluttering her eyelids. "Eyeam, ah, howyousay, a hoor."

"Um," the man said.

"That's how I've been treated," Lieza said, all sweetness, mock or otherwise, instantly gone. "It was essential that I be left to myself this afternoon. Yet I was disturbed. Do you see the gentleman with the ax?"

The man and woman behind the counter nodded.

"Good. He's rearranging the components of that exceedingly tacky piece of scrod in order for it to serve as a reminder to you to be nice to paying guests no matter what their sociopolitical persuasion or lack of same. Any questions?"

"Ah," the Jackie began, and reached into her blazer.

Immediately, Tycho was there, holding Bert high, ready to split Jackie's skull.

The woman made a gagging noise and stumbled backward. A record album, still in its plastic wrapping, fell from her blazer.

Lieza leaned over the counter and saw that the album on the floor had a cover photo depicting a church sanctuary full of parishioners. The view was down the central aisle, and the priest at the far end was holding a dagger over a naked baby.

After four years, *Critical Mass* was still selling. Not bad for a second effort, Lieza thought. The third and fourth were better, but *Critical Mass* held a special place in her heart because it had been the first time she'd worked with Blunt Instrument instead of her mother's band.

Or maybe it was because it contained the first song of hers to start a small riot: "Bonzo's Blood." Now there was The Music.

Tycho leaned over beside her. "Oh," he said, lowering Bert. "Autograph time." He reached down with his free hand and retrieved the album, then offered it to Lieza.

"To Maureen, please," the red-jacketed woman said hoarsely.

Lieza laughed. "Got no pen, Jackie." She took a corner of the album cover into her mouth and bit down hard. Tycho took the opposite corner.

Then they dropped the album onto the counter. Two sets of teeth marks were pressed into the parishioners.

"Pretty good," Lieza said. "Last time I nearly busted a tooth."

Tycho hefted Bert onto his shoulder and headed toward a row of gray-tinted glass doors. "You're supposed to break the record, not your teeth. Now c'mon or we'll be late if we ain't already."

Lieza started after him, then paused and turned back toward Jack and Jackie. "By the way," she said, "the door to my room is broken. Wouldja mind having it repaired before I get back? Likewise for the window. The elevators are jackbugged, too. Some hotel you're running here."

She jogged for the doors, wondering why upscale hotels always smelled like piles of synthetic fiber coated with kerosene.

* * *

Cherry, Fug, and Joel were leaning against the cab and sharing a bottle with the driver when Lieza and Tycho came outside. Lieza looked them over and grinned. They were ready to play.

Cherry towered over them all, wearing a red jumpsuit with an empty bandolier, the cartridges having been glued to the ends of her spiked Afro. Fug had shaved his head but otherwise looked as he usually did—raggy, doggy, scruffy, lovable, and homicidal. Joel, as pale and suave as ever, had on his typical top hat and tails, complemented tonight by a pair of hip boots.

After dealing with Jack and Jackie, Lieza was glad to see that the cab driver, a woman who appeared to be in her late thirties, was a fellow Wracker, dressed in a copper mesh blouse and lavender hot pants with bicycle-chain garters and pink stockings. The outfit couldn't be comfortable in winter weather, but that was the point.

"Buggers," Tycho said, pointing down the icy drive toward M Street. A black limousine with opaque windows had just turned in. "They've seen us."

Lieza frowned. "So? What're they gonna do, kill us if we don't ride with them?"

"This is the Truman Center for the Performing Arts we're talking about. They goddamn well might."

The cab driver squinted at the approaching limo. "Hobnails?"

"Naw," Tycho said. "Cross between Hobnails and sheep."

"I always thought that was just a rumor," the cabbie said thoughtfully.

Joel coughed. "I say, Leez. Hadn't we best be off?"

"Quite so, jagbreath. Ladies first?"

"Thank you," Joel said, and got into the vehicle. The others followed, and Tycho, as usual, took up slightly more than half of the back seat. Lieza sat on his left thigh.

There was a slight problem when both the cabbie and Fug tried to get behind the wheel.

"Fug always drives," Lieza explained.

The cabbie frowned. "S'okay by me, but the beast

ain't mine. The frickin' owner's Straighter'n Eisenhower, an' what with this weather..."

"Fug wrecks it, I buy the owner two."

The cabbie scooted over against Cherry in the front seat. "Rammin'," she said. "I'm Bazz Watson."

"Rollin', Bazz," Lieza answered. "I'm—"

"Know you, babe."

Joel, sitting next to the left rear door, coughed again. "Pardon me for interrupting," he said, "but that rather large black vehicle has stopped directly behind this rather smaller and yellower one. A grim-looking gentleman wearing mirrored sunglasses and an exquisite tie has just emerged. The lump under his overcoat may be a plaque of appreciation, a cluster of bananas, or an automatic weapon."

"Maybe he's just glad to see you," Cherry said in terrible Mae West imitation.

"Fug," Lieza said.

Fug grunted, and the cab's rear wheels spun on the ice for a few seconds before burning through to pavement.

"You have a bony ass," Tycho said into the back of Lieza's head.

"You have a pointy nose," she said. "And if it's still got that green blob on it, you can keep it out of my hair."

"That's antirust compound."

Cherry looked back with an exasperated expression. "Silver doesn't rust, scrodbrain. It tarnishes. You ought to get to know your body parts better."

Tycho made a metallic snorting noise. "Hell, I'm still tryin' to figure out the original equipment."

The cab lurched over a concrete island and into the street, where it fishtailed ninety degrees.

"A little slick out today," Bazz observed.

Fug spun the steering wheel until the cab skittered down the street in more or less the right-hand lane.

"Jolly good work," Joel said, reaching up to scratch Fug's stubbled head. "I feel I should point out, however, that we are traveling east. The Truman Center is west and south of here, on the riverbank. Oh, look, here's one of those delightful circular traffic thingamabobs. What fun."

Fug cranked the wheel, and the cab spun a hundred

and eighty degrees as it slid into the traffic circle. The
black limo, which had been trying to follow, braked and
skated across three lanes, finally colliding with the aluminum shaft of a streetlight.

"Anybody in that thing get hurt?" Tycho asked. "I
can't see around this greaseball Leez uses for a head."

"We can only hope," Cherry said solemnly. "By the
way, Leez, 'greaseball' ain't far off the mark, peesh? You
smell like an operating room in a stable. Got no respect for
my nose?"

"No," Lieza answered.

"You need one like mine, Cherry-mash," Tycho said.
"Can't smell doodoo."

Fug stomped on the accelerator, and the cab shimmied
back and forth, going nowhere. Fug grunted unhappily and
took his foot off the pedal.

"The gentleman with the lump under his coat has
emerged from that vehicle again," Joel said, pointing.
"From the cut on his forehead and the set of his mouth, I
surmise that he is upset, and—oh, my, I see that the automatic weapon hypothesis was correct. The lump has
emerged, and it appears to be a machine pistol."

Lieza leaned forward and whispered in Bazz's ear.
"Tell me this heap is bulletproof," she said.

"OK," Bazz said agreeably. "It's bulletproof."

Both front-door windows crumbled.

Tycho shoved Lieza's head toward the floor.

"We needn't be alarmed," Joel said. "A single shot can
often be interpreted as a mere warning. The fact that the slug
traveled the breadth of the car without striking anyone would
seem to lend strength to this hypothesis. The gentleman
must be an excellent shot. Or perhaps a lousy one. The difference won't matter if he switches to full automatic."

From her cramped position under Tycho's massive
hand, Lieza strained to look out the window and glimpsed
a crew-cut blond man with a burp gun. His free hand was
reaching for the cab's right rear door handle.

"Well, sputz, if they want us to ride with them that
bad—" Cherry began, and then Fug hit the accelerator
again.

The cab fishtailed and knocked the crew-cut man to the ice. His weapon slid across a lane and under a truck.

"Oh, my, that was fortuitous," Joel said.

The tires finally found pavement again, and the cab rumbled west through the traffic circle in the wrong lane. After a few clever maneuvers, Fug had the vehicle back on M Street, this time heading toward the Potomac and the Truman Center for the Performing Arts.

Tycho let Lieza up. "Don't worry," he said. "He wouldn't have gotten to you. I would've had Bert cut off your head first."

"Who's Bert?" Cherry asked.

"I say, Bazz," Joel said before Tycho could answer Cherry, "would you mind terribly if I partook of some of this vehicle's store of ethanol?"

"Your guts, babe."

Joel pulled a length of rubber tubing from his right hip boot, rolled down his window, and began to unscrew the cap on the left rear fender.

"Gonna play good," Fug said as the cab spun through a curve. "Gonna play till they all jag."

"Hey," Bazz said. "He talks."

"Don't spread it around," Lieza said. "It'd spoil the mystique."

* * *

It was ten minutes to eight when the cab shot past the last row of cars in an immense field of automobiles and slammed up against a concrete column. The enormous blue dome of the Truman Center rose above the asphalt like a frosted glass eye, and two double-doored stage entrances waited like tiny brown teeth.

The cab's right side was crumpled against the column, and Fug had managed to jam the driver's door, so they all crowded out through the left rear doorway. Joel emerged first and began wandering off toward Baltimore, his tubing dangling from his mouth. Lieza was second, but she didn't bother to go after Joel. He hadn't missed a show yet.

Something thumped inside the cab's trunk.

"Jeez, I forgot about him," Cherry said.

Bazz unlocked the trunk and pulled out the parking-lot preacher Lieza had nearly hit with the telephone. He was a chubby, wild-haired man who was waving his Bible and giggling.

"Bless you, kidlings!" he yelped. "Let Preacher Bob show you the Way!"

"He seemed upset with us," Cherry explained, "so we gave him something to calm him down. Then he insisted on crawling in there. Something about returning to the womb, being born again. Go figure."

The center's Patton Week programming director, a nervous little Straight named Deaver, emerged from the center stage door and came scurrying up to Lieza looking as if he were wired on amphetamines.

"Hey, Deavie, give this guy a backstage pass," Lieza said, gesturing toward the preacher.

But Deaver didn't seem to hear her. "OhdearMizzGalilei I'msosorry it'sreallyallmyfault," he said, wheezing. "Thelimousineservice calledandsaidtheirdrivers refusedtodrive foryouandIdidn'tknowhowIwas goingtogetyouhere. Itriedtocall butyoudidn'tgivemethenumber andthehotelwouldn'tbelieve IwaswhoIsaidIwasand—"

Lieza clamped her right hand over Deaver's mouth. "Take a couple deep breaths, peesh?"

Deaver wheezed through his nose a few times, and his skin began to turn bluish.

While he was doing that, Lieza considered what she thought he'd said. "You didn't send a black limo with one-way windows?" she asked, taking her hand away from his mouth.

"NoMizzGalileiwhatblacklimousine theysaidthey-wouldn't butyouseethat'swhatcomesfromnot showingupatleastafewhours inadvancelikemostperformers it'sstandingroomonly the—"

Tycho stepped up beside Lieza and pressed Bert's cold head against Deaver's lips. "If that car wasn't from this frick, then who the skag was it?"

"Hobnails," Cherry said as she went past them toward the stage doors. "Roly holers come to get Preacher Bob there. Didn't want him to partake of the juice."

Lieza shrugged and headed toward the stage doors herself. "Maybe sputzed-up fans."

"Ain't no fans carry tommies," Tycho said.

Blunt Instrument's two roadies, Dude Reineman and Ellyn Flacke, met Lieza just inside the doorway. They were wearing body stockings and denim jackets, and Lieza noticed that Ellyn's pregnancy was beginning to show.

"Got a dink problem," Dude told Lieza. "Never should've stashed stuff here yesterday. Some jewbaiter locked up our equipment until about fifteen minutes ago, so we aren't set up yet. Ellyn can't lift heavy scrod in her condition."

"She could if you hadn't been too cheap to buy love-gloves," Lieza said. She was joking; Dude and Ellyn had planned the baby. Just why they had done that, though, she couldn't figure.

"Skag you, Leez," Ellyn said. "We got seven minutes and only three amps set up. Can Fug help?"

"Gotta tune."

"Then the show's gonna be late," Dude said. "It ain't kosher to let you down, but motherbear, what can we do?"

Lieza opened the stage door and leaned out into the cold. Out by the crumpled cab, Bazz Watson was smoking a joint and laughing at Preacher Bob as he tried to baptize a Volkswagen.

"Hey!" Lieza yelled at the cabbie. "You want a new job?"

Bazz looked toward her. "Doing what?"

"Whatta you care?"

Bazz took another drag off the joint, then flipped it away and trotted toward the stage doors. Preacher Bob dove for the joint and disappeared under a bus.

"Here comes help," Lieza told Dude and Ellyn, then went down the hallway to where Tycho, Fug, and Cherry were waiting. She could hear the crowd stomping and clapping.

Her skin tingled. She was going to play The Music.

* * *

The arc lights flared on, and the voices of thirty thousand mingled Straights and Wrackers exploded simultaneously with the sweat that broke out on Lieza's face and chest.

"IN THE NAME OF EDDIE DIXON," she cried, "WE ARE BLUNT INSTRUMENT!" By the last syllable she could no longer feel the mike taped to her throat. The answering roar washed over her like a hot sea, and all she felt was The Music, the words and sounds that were to come. She might even be able get into trance tonight, even though the energy level would be limited because of all the Straights in the audience.

"ONE! TWO! THREE!" she screamed, and slammed into the first notes of her mother's "Tomorrow Is the Day." She usually preferred to start with her own work, but she'd agreed with the rest of the band that "Tomorrow Is the Day" was the most appropriate song for opening a Patton's Eve concert. Besides, the long opening riff gave her a chance to get introductions out of the way.

"CHERRY ANGOLA!" she called, and the tall mulatto stepped into the glare to Lieza's right, clawing at her red bass as if it were a lover's back.

"THE RESURRECTED ONE, TYCHO!" Lieza looked behind her at the platform where the wild man crouched, flailing at stretched membranes and golden circles of metal. The insistent, shuddering beat of his bass drum was like an electric charge throbbing up her spine.

"THE INCREDIBLE STINKING FUG!" A piercing shriek split the air, then slid down three octaves until the stage resonated and rumbled like an approaching tornado. A series of rapid triplets ripped back up the other way, and then Fug was standing with Cherry, the fingers of his left hand a blur on the Stratocaster's neck.

"JOEL H. RODSTEIN THE FOURTH!" White beams stabbed down onto a raised island to Lieza's left, and in her peripheral vision she saw the pale, small man bent over backward inside a circle of assorted wind instruments and keyboards, blowing a wail on soprano sax up to the darkness beyond the lights. She had no idea when he'd finally made it to the stage. His life, more than that of any other Wracker she'd ever known, was incapable of tolerating gaps that could only be filled with waiting around.

"AND I—" Lieza began, waiting for the mob's shouts to subside. "I—"

The waves of sound rose again, like water rushing from a burst dam, and she touched a floor switch with her right foot to boost her mike amplification. Even then, she screamed so loud that her throat burned:

"I AM THE BASTARD CHILD!"

The roar lifted the world, and Lieza pinwheeled her left arm, smashing her thumb into her black guitar's strings over and over again while her right hand slid up and down the slick neck.

She didn't have Fug's skill and never would. But then, Fug wouldn't be so good if it weren't for her. Something in her fired the others and made them better than they could have been without her. Each of them, even Tycho, was only a particle. She was the unifying force that bound them into Blunt Instrument.

Such were the physics of The Music. It had been that way for her mother, too, which was why the death of the Bitch had produced the same violence as the splitting of an atom.

Lieza hoped she would never die. She hoped The Music would keep her alive forever.

"To-mor-row," she sang, "is-the-day!"

"The day!" Cherry and Fug shouted.

"He-will-take/Our-pain-away!"

"Pain away!"

"He-will-bring/The-Holy-Fire!"

"Holy Fire!"

"And-fulfill/Our-heart's-desire!"

"Heart's desire!"

Lieza threw back her head and closed her eyes, trying to fill the next lines with as much power as her mother had. "He - will - bring - the - fire - down - on - Berlin/And - wash - away - its - wretched - sin/He - will - light - the - skies - of - To - Kee - Yoh/Till - rapture - makes - our - skin - and - teeth—"

Sixteen hard, fast beats, and then every mouth in the auditorium shouted the final word of the line:

"GLOW!"

The lights changed in that instant, and Lieza couldn't decide if the color she and her friends bathed in was that of fire or of blood.

In the final analysis, she thought as she slipped closer to trance, maybe there wouldn't be much difference.

* * *

Her hotel room had a new door, but they hadn't managed to replace the broken window. A sheet of clear plastic was taped over the hole.

Lieza didn't care. The five-hour show had drained her, and if she was going to be ready for the Patton Day concert in eighteen hours, she'd have to sleep at least ten of them. Preferably twelve.

"Maybe we should stay," Tycho said. He and Bazz had come into the room with her. "You know how those Straight pseudofans can get after a show. This door wouldn't stop 'em."

Lieza stripped off her soaked camisole and fell onto the bed, where she lay supine and looked up at her drummer.

"Piss off, scrodface," she said hoarsely. "I can take care of myself. Always have."

Tycho shook his head. "Long shows jackbug you worse than the rest of us. I think we oughta stay."

Lieza groaned. "Listen, I'm crazy for both of you, but I gotta sleep, which I won't if you and Bazz are in here jazzing all night. Peesh?"

Bazz grinned. "Well, yeah, babe, that's the plan."

"Wish you joy, but I'm too blasted to want to be in the same room. Forget participate."

Tycho nodded uncertainly, and he and Bazz went to the door.

"Don't like you being alone when you're so skagged," he said, turning back toward Lieza after Bazz had gone out.

"Dink," she said, yawning. "I'll double-lock, and you're only three rooms away. If I need you I'll yell."

"He might not hear you," Bazz said from the hall. "I tend to yell a little myself."

Lieza forced herself up from the bed and shuffled over

to the door. "Have fun, Teek," she said, shoving him out. Then she shut the door and locked it.

Her skin was coated with sweat and muscle balm, and even though her olfactory nerves didn't seem to be working, she knew she stank. A hot shower waited just beyond the bathroom door, but she was so tired that she only had three buttons on the left hip of her leathers undone before deciding to wait until she'd slept.

So she stank. So what? There was nobody here to smell her.

She hit the button to kill the room lights, then went back to the bed and collapsed again. As she rolled onto her side, she thought she could see the Moon through the plastic window patch.

But the sky had been thick with clouds when they'd returned to the hotel. It must only be one of Washington's myriad lights. . . .

"G'night, Mama," she whispered to be sure, and closed her eyes.

* * *

The hum that rose up to envelop her was composed of tens of thousands of voices, all loving her, worshipping her, wanting her. She could see no faces, could not tell who was Wracker or who was Straight, male or female, old or young.

It didn't seem to matter. All were members of her Church. She was the High Priestess, set above them, out of their grasp, yet washed with their moist breath.

Her followers were like a single vast creature that lived only to adore her, to devour her.

"But I'm no one," she tried to say. "I'm skinny, I'm ugly, I'm scarred. It's my mother you want. I'm only her bastard child."

* * *

Light blazed above her, stinging her eyes.

"I'm only—" she said again, and then screamed: "THE BASTARD CHILD!"

"We know," a voice like crunching gravel said.

Lieza tried to sit up, but was pushed back down.

She felt as if she were trapped inside her own skull,

trying to swim up through gray jelly so she could see what was happening outside.

Was she awake? Should she be? Was the light . . .

A flashlight. She could see the outline of gloved fingers holding it, but that was all. The hot white circle was so bright that even the lights that had to be shining through the window hole had disappeared in its glare.

"You're a hard person to get in touch with, Mizz Galilei," Gravel-Voice said.

The gray jelly was beginning to dissolve. Lieza still couldn't see who was behind the light, but she was awake enough now to know that she was in deep shit.

She tried to take in a breath to call for Tycho, but the hand that had pushed her down covered her mouth.

"No sound, slut," Gravel-Voice said.

"Please, Mizz Galilei." This was a second voice, smoother, but also male. Whoever owned it was standing behind Gravel-Voice, to Lieza's left toward the door. "We only want to give you a message. We tried to contact you earlier, once by phone and once in person, but you were so reluctant to speak with us that we resorted to hiding in your bathroom. Please accept our apologies. I assure you that we have no wish to harm you."

"Not officially, anyway," Gravel-Voice muttered. The leather-covered hand slid off Lieza's mouth. "But if you yell or even breathe too loud, I can hit you so you'll feel like you have needles in your throat."

Lieza scooted back until her hair brushed the bed's headboard. The intruders' speeches had given her time to bring herself to full consciousness, and she was able to think clearly now. She remembered the techniques Tycho had taught her for fighting in the dark. She remembered how she had used them when that geek had tried to rape her in '75.

"OK if I sit up?" she asked in a half-whisper.

"Certainly," Smooth-Voice said. "Zackman, why don't you back off? That light must hurt her eyes."

"I'm fine where I am," Gravel-Voice said angrily.

Lieza suppressed a smile. So Smoothie and Gravel-mouth didn't get along. Good. She didn't know if

Smoothie had a gun or not, but he didn't sound as if he wanted to shoot. "Zackman," however, didn't have a gun in either hand but didn't seem to like her at all.

She sat up slowly and braced her back against the headboard, then raised her knees until she was almost in a fetal position. She tried to look vulnerable as she put her right hand up to her throat. Both Smoothie's and Zackman's eyes would follow that movement, and the light was trained on her face, so they wouldn't notice her left hand sliding down the leather that sheathed her calf.

Don't jag around with us lefties, man.

In one motion, she brought her razor up from its pocket, slashed behind the flashlight, and rolled off the bed to her right. The flashlight hit the floor beside her, and Zackman's scream told her that she'd managed to cut through his glove.

"Teek!" she shouted, even though Zackman's shriek would get Tycho there in a few seconds. She wanted the big drummer to know she was alive, because otherwise he'd go as berserk as his Viking ancestors had on occasion.

"Quiet, idiot," Smoothie said. But Zackman kept screaming, and the next sound Lieza heard was a muffled thump, followed by a louder thump as a body hit the floor.

An odd silence followed, and Lieza held her breath.

Then Smoothie's voice continued: "I'll turn on the light, Mizz Galilei. Once you see that I have no weapon pointing at you, I can deliver my message and be done with it."

She heard footsteps heading toward the light button beside the door, then a yell and a splintering crash.

"Go, Bert!" she heard Tycho bellow. "Kick ass!"

The light came on, and Lieza risked looking over the bed.

Tycho was smashing through the door with Bert. A stocky, bald man in an overcoat was backing rapidly toward the bed, and his shoulder movements indicated that he was reaching inside his coat with his right hand.

Another man, with a square face and close-cropped blond hair, was lying on the floor. He had a bandage on his forehead, and blood was soaking into the carpet under his right wrist. The muzzle of a machine pistol protruded from under a corner of his coat.

That gun had to be exactly the sort of thing Smoothie was reaching for under his own coat.

The Bastard Child still held her razor, so she somersaulted across the bed, came up behind the bald man, and slashed down hard enough to cut into his right deltoid. His hand twitched out of his coat, empty.

Then Lieza grabbed Smoothie's wrist with her right hand, pinned it between his shoulder blades, and touched the tip of the razor to the soft skin just under his left ear.

Smoothie froze.

Tycho gave a final roar and burst through what was left of the door.

"Oh, shut up," Lieza said.

Tycho blinked twice and then put Bert over his shoulder. He looked hurt. "Well, excuse me for living."

"As long as it took you to get in here, I might not be living myself," Lieza said, and pressed the tip of the razor a half-millimeter farther toward Smoothie's medulla oblongata. "By the way, oh jagoff of the shiny pate, not living will be exactly your condition if you so much as piss your pants without my permission."

Tycho walked past them, hitching up his kneepants, and sat on the man on the floor. "I'm sorry, Leez, but these Hobnails picked the worst possible time to sputz around. I was right in the middle of something."

"Yo," Bazz said from the ragged doorway. She had a crumpled bedsheet wrapped around her torso. "I hate to interrupt, but I was kind of interrupted myself, peesh?"

The man on the floor moaned and tried to move out from under Tycho. Tycho tapped him on the head with Bert's flat side, then reached for Lieza's hundred-and-thirty-pound barbell with his free hand. He positioned the bar over the prone man's neck, pinning him to the floor.

"I recognize this jewbaiter," the drummer said, peering at the left side of Zackman's face. "This is the guy who shot out our windows."

"He exceeded his authority when he did that," Smoothie said.

Lieza twisted Smoothie's arm up farther and nicked his earlobe.

Bazz came in quickly, reached into Smoothie's coat, and removed his machine pistol. "Hey, Leez," she said, backing away, "none a' my biz, maybe, but . . . if you gotta kill the piece of scrod, kill 'im. Torture's Hobnail."

Lieza stared at the other woman. Who did this middle-aged, jag-headed, skew-titted frick think she . . .

But the rage died before it could reach her mouth, and then she felt the way she imagined a Ranger shooting Russian peasants would feel if he were able to feel at all.

She'd had to slash Zackman to protect herself, and Smoothie to protect Tycho, but now they were down. Cutting Smoothie's ear was chickenshit. Either he was still a danger, in which case she should waste him neatly and rapidly, or he wasn't, in which case he'd been hurt enough.

Lieza nodded to Bazz. "Peesh. But these skagasses roused me up like they were the sputzin' Gestapo. Pissed me off. I get that way sometimes."

"Bet your sweet nips she does," Tycho said, shifting his weight. "Damn, Leez, this frick's butt's almost as bony as yours."

* * *

The paper was thick, elegant, and golddusted, but the words embossed on it were economical:

The President of the United States requests your presence in the Oval Office of the White House at 11:00 A.M. on Friday, December 21, 1979. Transportation from your hotel will be provided.

Bazz, reading simultaneously with Lieza, said, "Now, that's about as openly threatening as I've ever seen a Dumbass get."

Lieza rubbed the back of her neck and yawned. "Nothing threatening about it. Big propaganda op, he thinks. Give me some scroddy award for the flacks. Lots of pictures. Popularity rating jumps twelve points. I ain't goin'."

Bazz chuckled. "You see that second sentence? That

doesn't say RSVP. That says, 'You *will* come if we have to drag your little ass . . .'"

"*Bony* little ass," Tycho interjected.

"'. . . your bony little ass here with a half-track.'"

Lieza tossed the note onto the bed beside where Smoothie, alias Special Agent Dodson, was sitting.

"I decline the invitation," she said.

"You can't," Dodson said.

"You won't," Zackman said from the floor. Tycho was no longer sitting on him, but he was still pinned by the barbell, and he looked terrible.

Lieza ignored them both. She walked around the bed, pulled the plastic away from the hole in the window, and tossed a handful of .45-caliber bullets down to the parking lot.

"You don't understand," she said, watching the bullets pepper car roofs in the glare of mercury-vapor lamps. "Even if I wanted to go, and I'd have to be pretty frickin' dink to want that, I couldn't." She glanced at the clock on the floor. "It's after three. I've got to sleep until at least eleven-thirty. When I do get up, I've got a new song we've got to rehearse. That's gonna take the rest of the day up to the concert."

She went back around the bed and looked down at Dodson. "Peesh, bozo?"

Dodson took his hand away from the bandage Bazz had put on his ear, stood up, and kicked Zackman in the ribs until the other agent managed to push the barbell off his neck and get to his knees.

"You don't look so good," Bazz said to Zackman. "Get that wrist looked after right away, Jack."

Tycho shook his head. "I can't believe you two are Secret Service. If the rest of the bunch are as good as you, it's skaggin' amazing that Fitzgerald ain't had his nuts shot off by now."

Zackman's eyes flared, and his uninjured left hand darted to his coat pocket. It came out with a .357 and instantly grew a switchblade handle between the knuckles of the index and middle fingers. Zackman screamed, and the .357 fell to the floor.

Lieza, who had been reaching for her razor, stared at Tycho. She'd never known him to carry a knife; he was more of a Bert man.

Tycho was staring too, at Bazz, whose bedsheet had slipped down from her breasts.

"Where'd you hide the pig-sticker?" the drummer asked.

Bazz looked at Lieza with an expression of mock indignation. "He always ask such personal questions?"

Dodson yanked the switchblade from his partner's hand, pulling him to his feet and provoking another scream in the process, and handed the weapon back to Bazz.

"This isn't your day, Zackman," Dodson said, and pushed the bleeding man toward the doorway. Then he winced. He had used his right arm. "Mine either."

Lieza sat down on the bed, yawning. "You should've knocked first."

Zackman stumbled into the hall, but Dodson paused and looked back. "I'll tell the President you don't feel you can make it."

Lieza raised her left index finger in a wait-a-minute gesture, then took the gilded invitation and rolled it into a tube.

She found her jar of muscle balm against the wall and stuck the invitation into it, twirling the tube until it was coated with orange ointment.

Then she went to the doorway and handed Dodson the result. "Don't bother to tell the President that I 'don't feel I can make it,'" she said. "Just say I'm returning his invitation so he can put it to better use. Peesh?"

Dodson stared at the greasy thing in his hand for a few seconds. Then he half-grinned, shook his head, and left.

Lieza looked at the jagged wood chunks and splinters on the floor.

"Can't sleep here now," she told Tycho and Bazz, "and I won't go to your room. Guess I'll see if Cherry'd mind some company."

Tycho put his ax's business end against his ear and cocked his head.

"Bert says to take a shower first," he informed Lieza. "Either that or sleep with Fug."

Lieza went into the hall, knowing that Tycho would follow. Dodson and Zackman had disappeared, but as she shuffled toward Cherry's room she had a cold, tight feeling in her neck that made her feel as though something much worse was coming for her.

She hoped whatever it was would wait a day or two. She was tired, and all she wanted in the universe was a place to rest.

For the first time, she envied her mother the peace and quiet of the Moon.

2

The Difference Between Literature and Physics

Teach us, Herr Professor.
Put some numbers on the board.
Be our Father Confessor;
We'll be your loyal horde.

They say the math is hard to do.
Hey, we don't care at all.
Build a bomb or fly to the sun;
You'll catch us when we fall—

But who'll catch you?
Baby, who'll catch you
When you take your ship too high?
Baby, when you're through—
When you're good and through—
Will you just lie down and die?

—Bitch Alice
"The Learned One," 1958

Thursday, December 20, 1979. Lawrence, Kansas.

Liberal Arts mixers sucked.

It was bad enough that he'd had to shake the hand of the weasel-faced neo-Nazi whom the Regents had been stupid enough to name Chancellor, but now he found himself standing elbow-to-elbow with pseudoartistic queers from the—Jesus H. Christ—Art History Department and pedantic wiseasses from the—double Jesus H. Christ stuffed into an eggroll—English Department. If he got near enough to Professor What's-His-Butt Lightman to hear the seven principles of modern poetry again, he would surely puke all over the Alumni Center's whorehouse-red carpet, which might not be a bad idea.

Not that anybody from the sciences was any better. Looking around, he saw only jagheaded, brownnosing scrodbrains. Not a decent researcher in the bunch. They were all here either to suck up for tenure, or if they already had it, to debase themselves for a deanship. Even Worthing, his own department chairman, was snuffling at the Chancellor's metaphorical tush—and what else could be expected? The only worthwhile paper the son of a bitch had ever produced had been swiped from a grad student's thesis.

Speaking of grad students, there was quite a bunch of the snotnoses here. Cow-eyed girls and sleek faggots from the humanities; pimple-faced nervous wrecks like that idiot Thomas from everywhere else. Didn't they have families to go home to between semesters? Or had they all been cultured from the bits of fungus that grew between the tiles in the physical science building's first-floor restrooms?

That wouldn't apply to the artists and humanists, of course. Their origins were far less distinguished.

And then there were the alumni. Holy bat piss.

Put them all together, and you had a torture chamber of body odor and cigarette smoke. It was enough to gag a maggot.

So much of what Jackson saw and smelled at this "College of Liberal Arts and Sciences Christmas Break Chancellor's Reception" (or whatever the hell they called it) disgusted him that for a moment he wondered why he himself had come. Then he glanced at the empty highball glass in his hand and remembered:

Free booze.

Someone plucked at his sleeve and said, "Excuse me, Doctor Jackson. I must speak with you." But Jackson twisted away and escaped into the crowd. He had no time for being chewed out by superiors or hounded about the past by alumni.

He headed for the bar and wedged his way in between a fat chemist and a blue-suited PR slut who was talking to a dried-up old futz he didn't recognize.

"So, how are the alumni blowjobs going?" he asked the PR woman, but she didn't seem to hear him.

Jackson pushed up his eyeglasses from where they'd slid halfway down his large, veined nose and peered at the woman. Christ's Blessed Whickerbill if she wasn't wearing an impervious layer of makeup that made her look like a K-Mart mannequin.

"You got a face under all that?" he asked, leaning closer to her ear.

She heard this time. He could tell by the way her shoulders clenched up under the polyester. But she was dry-ice cool, and wouldn't even look at him. Instead she took the old futz's arm and steered him toward an alcove.

"Give him a lick or two for me," Jackson called after them, but the noise of a hundred conversations was so loud that he doubted she heard him. The fat chemist beside him did, though, and snorted in contempt.

Jackson swallowed a mouthful of air, let it mix with his half-digested Mexican meal, and belched in the chemist's face. The chemist went away, and Jackson had the center of the bar to himself.

The bartender, an acne-scarred young man with a rivet in his left earlobe, leaned across the bar and rapped a fingernail against Jackson's glass.

"More of the same, sir?"

Jackson grinned, knowing that his smile looked like a snaggletoothed grimace. "You know it, Bud. Say, your name isn't really Bud, is it? Been calling you that for an hour and you haven't griped."

The bartender took the glass, dropped in four ice cubes, and filled it with Johnnie Walker Black. "Names mean nothing unless they match the observer's perception, sir. If I look like Bud to you, then I'm Bud." He pushed the glass back across the bar.

Jackson took a big swallow of the Scotch, trying to savor the burning sensation that slid past his deadened taste buds and down his numb throat.

But his mind wasn't on it the way it usually was. Something about Bud had caught his attention.

He smelled burning ethanol and tried hard not to blink, afraid of what he might see if he closed his eyes. He heard himself asking, "You a Wracker?"

Bud looked away for a moment, nodded at someone at the end of the bar, and began drawing a beer. "Does it show when I'm wearing this thing, sir?" He touched his chin to the shoulder of his white bartender's jacket.

Jackson pushed his right hand back through his thin, rat-brown hair and breathed deeply. His eyes were stinging, and he couldn't help closing them for an instant. He saw a flash of blood and glass.

The only way to avoid it was to drink at home, which ensured that he didn't run into anybody like Bud. But free booze. . . .

"Tell you what," he said, swirling the ice cubes in his drink to mask his hand's quivering. "You're letting me call you what I like. You do the same for me."

Bud delivered the beer and then looked up and down the bar, apparently hoping for more customers.

"Go ahead," Jackson said. "Call me what I look like. What I am."

Bud's eyes focused on the ceiling. "I need this job, man. I need the cash so I can get out of this fricking Straight hole. Would I be working on Patton's Eve if I had a choice?" He looked down at Jackson again. "I don't want to get sacked, sir."

Jackson laughed and took two quick swallows of Walker, nearly choking himself. When he'd recovered, he grinned at Bud and leaned farther across the bar.

"Kid, I can't get anybody anything. Sacked, hired, promoted, pregnant—doesn't matter; I can't do it. Now, what's my name gonna be? Scrodbrain? Jewbaiter? Skagface? Dink-Dink? Jagoff?"

The left corner of Bud's mouth pulled up in a half-smile. "Something like that, sir."

"Knock off the 'sir' shit. You don't have to dance around the flopheap like those waste cases." He waved in a gesture that took in everyone in the room. "Come on. Which is it?"

Bud excused himself for a moment to make a faculty wife a Tom Collins. When he returned, Jackson said, "Well?"

The rivet in Bud's ear seemed to gaze at Jackson like a silver eye as the bartender turned and stared into the crowd.

Jackson thought he saw a wet drop of red in the silver eye's pupil.

He turned away quickly to stare in the same direction as Bud. "Who're you lookin' at?" he asked weakly.

"I'm trying to find which one was you.... There." Bud pointed.

Jackson followed the imaginary line extending from the bartender's finger and saw a tall, thick-haired, tanned chemical engineering professor who'd crashed the party and whose name he couldn't remember. The chem e. prof was talking with a good-looking woman Jackson had often seen going into one of the biochem labs.

"That's me? Tan-Man?" Jackson took another drink. "Damn, boy, you flatter me. That woman wouldn't've spoken to me even when I was capable of caring whether she did or not."

Bud nodded. "Yeah, that's you, all right. You used to be on top of everything. Her too, if you'd wanted to. You used to be The Man. Write your own ticket, get it validated anywhere you frickin' wanted."

Jackson looked down at his drink. The numbness in his mouth, he realized, must be wearing off, because he was tasting something moldy and poisonous. He tried to wash it away with more Johnnie Walker.

"So you've heard of me," he said, not looking up.

Bud poured more whiskey into Jackson's glass. "I got no idea who you are, namewise. But you ain't no alum, 'cause you got an attitude toward this party like it was scrod, which it is. Ain't no dean, 'cause you ain't stickin' your tongue up no alum's crack. Ain't no up-and-comer, 'cause you're too old, and you couldn't afford to pull some of the shit I've been watchin' you pull with these jew-baiters. So you gotta be tenured, and the only way a ten-ured prof'd need to get so jackbugged would be if he'd fallen from grace. All adds up to that stud over there: used to be you, ain't now, and you're pissed about it."

The taste in Jackson's mouth was getting worse, and he was beginning to lose the affection he had felt for Bud earlier.

"Skag you, kid," he said. He didn't look up.

"Kiss a frick, Icarus," the bartender answered.

Jackson's head snapped up. "What'd you call me?" He was surprised at how hoarse his voice sounded. What had he swallowed?

"Icarus," Bud repeated. "You flew too high and burned the sputzing hell out of your fine, fine feathers."

Jackson glared. *Goddamn punk.*

The bartender's expression changed, and he backed away, waving a rag. "Man, did you fart?"

At those words, Jackson's irritation disappeared. The kid was too sharp to dislike, and it took too much energy to stay mad anyhow. Besides, he really had farted.

"You Wrackers sure lay it down," he said.

"Well, jeez, that was frickin' horrible."

Jackson shook his head and took a crumpled handkerchief from his jacket pocket. "I was referring to the name you gave me."

Bud shrugged. "Seemed appropriate."

Jackson blew his nose hard, and the sound rose above the din of conversation and clinking glasses. He could feel people turning to look at him, but he didn't care.

"Appropriate," he said, thinking about the word. "No, I don't think so, Bud. You see, although Icarus was fool-ish, he's a symbol of man's noble striving for the un-known, the unattainable."

"You didn't do that, huh?"

Jackson gave a sardonic half-laugh. "Oh, I did, I did. I *intentionally* tried to fly as high as Icarus did accidentally. No, the reason Icarus is inappropriate for my name is be-cause it's one of honor."

He spread his arms out, hitting the face of a woman approaching the bar, and looked down at himself. His suit was wrinkled and drink stained. "Do you see here such a one as should have an honored name?"

Bud made a face. "Honor. Hobnail word."

"Nevertheless," Jackson began, and then he had a thought that amused him. "You ever read Melville, kid? *Moby Dick?*"

"When I was fourteen," Bud said.

Jackson picked up his highball glass and struck a statuesque pose. "Call me Pissant," he said dramatically. Then he took a long drink and winked at Bud. "That's what she called me, you know."

But seemed to almost smile a full smile. "Fem involved, huh? Shoulda known. Somebody else's wife?"

Jackson nodded and raised his glass high. "To the beautiful Moon Lady," he bellowed.

A hand clamped on his shoulder. "You're making a royal ass out of yourself," the voice of the Physics Department chairman hissed behind him. "Get away from the bar while you can still walk. Damn it, you're a full professor!"

Jackson turned and glared at Worthing's round, red face. "Well, you're a *stuffed* professor." He let his head loll back until he could see an upside-down Bud. "See you later, Bud," he said, and then walked into the crowd, raising his arms to part the bodies as if they were the Red Sea.

"Later, Pissant," he heard the bartender say.

* * *

Getting clear of Worthing wasn't difficult since the department head couldn't abandon his ass-kissing for long. Pissant wandered among the various clots of conversation, smelling perfume and sweat, listening to lies and inanities.

"Excuse me," someone said, grasping his elbow.

Too tired to bolt away, Pissant looked down and saw a small man wearing an immaculate suit. The man's face, dominated by a sharp nose, looked as if it were carved from wood.

"Do I know you?" Pissant asked.

The wooden face remained expressionless. "No, Doctor Jackson. But I hope we shall be working together soon."

Pissant stuck out his tongue. "Yuccch. No way. Thomas was the last graduate student I'll take on. Talk about your blind leading the blind."

As if responding to a summons, Thomas, a skinny giant who looked as if he had four elbows, walked by on his way to the bar, talking earnestly to another student whose name Pissant couldn't remember.

"That's him now," Pissant said, pointing with his free hand. "Ugly jackbugger's working with Shaw now, I think. Not my fault he blew his Qualifyings. Told him two-body problems were over his head—which is pretty damn deep considering how tall he is."

Pissant laughed until the sound became a cough. It felt as if his throat lining were peeling away. He suppressed the hacking breaths with an effort and tossed back three swallows of Walker to make his esophagus feel better.

"I'm not a student," the stranger said. "I have a message for you." He held out a small white envelope.

Pissant squinted. "Who from?"

"The letter inside will explain."

Pissant took the envelope and wondered why it immediately began quivering. "Why didn't you mail it?"

"I was asked to deliver the letter today, in person, and to be sure that you read it. I was unable to find you at your office or apartment. Would you be so kind as to read the letter, please?"

Pissant drained his highball glass and held it out. "Hold this," he said. The stranger took it.

The envelope was tricky, Pissant discovered as he examined it. Every corner looked alike, and he couldn't tell which diagonal line was the one under which he should try to slide his fingernails.

"It isn't sealed," the stranger said.

Pissant tossed the envelope into the air. "Too damn complicated," he said, and walked away backwards, bumping into several bodies before getting himself turned around.

Worthing was nowhere in sight, so he headed for the bar again, forgetting about his highball glass, the envelope, and the wooden-faced stranger.

He found himself passing a table where four people were having a heated discussion over whether it made any sense to be a Christian existentialist. One of them had just sat down with a fresh glass of what looked like something strong on the rocks.

"A philosophical question," Pissant said loudly. "That is what I have for you, gentlemen."

He picked up the glass of something strong and drank half of it in three swallows.

"Now, good sirs," he said, holding the glass up to the light. "Is this glass half-empty or half-full?"

One of the men at the table said something Pissant didn't understand.

"Well, if that's the case," Pissant said, pausing to drain the glass, "is it now completely empty or one-over-infinity full?"

The man who'd brought the drink to the table glared at him.

Pissant did a double take, looking at the empty glass in his hand as if seeing it for the first time.

"Your whiskey has evaporated," he said mournfully. "Allow me to replace it." He resumed his search for the bar.

* * *

Somehow, he wound up across the room from where Bud and salvation lay, but he didn't let himself panic. Instead, he stole another drink.

Then he heard Satan's challenge.

"There is a great difference," a honey-dripping voice was saying, "between the teaching goals of a humanist— say, an English professor such as myself—and an instructor in the sciences, say, a physicist."

Pissant felt as though an iron rod had been jammed up the length of his spinal cord. That voice belonged to What's-His-Butt Lightman, the biggest prick in a university full of them.

So this side of the room was hell. Pissant had strayed from the path of righteousness that led to the bar, and now he was going to pay for it, because he couldn't avoid listening to whatever sewage Lightman was spouting. There was something terminally fascinating about being in the living, breathing presence of something that natural selection couldn't possibly have allowed to survive. By all logic, the thing's mother should have devoured it at birth. Lightman was a paradox, and Pissant was a sucker for paradoxes.

He looked around, squinting to see through the smoky air, until he spotted Lightman standing in a circle that consisted mainly of young female graduate students, one of whom was no doubt already committed to going home with the mealworm for the night. There were a few others in the circle, too—portly men in three-piece suits and soft dowagers in pastels and pearls—but Pissant paid no attention to them. It was a sure bet that Lightman wasn't.

"You see," Lightman was saying as Pissant came up behind him, "the physicist deals with cold facts—numbers, wires, and little steel balls. A humanist, on the other hand—a person teaching great literature, for example—must go beyond facts. A humanist breathes life into words and ideas to help his students soar beyond the classroom. A humanist attempts to help his students become better human beings, and he does so by shining the light of his soul onto that which is to be learned. A physics professor can't afford to teach from the soul; a good literature professor can't afford not to. Therein lies the difference, and therein lies the lack in the education of the student who devotes herself solely to the study of a science—someone such as yourself."

Lightman gestured at a woman across the circle from him, and Pissant saw that it was the same biochemist who had been talking to Tan-Man, the chemical engineer.

"Well, professor," the woman said in a tired voice, "I'm sure you know more about the soul than I do. But science is more than numbers and symbols. Numbers have meanings beyond themselves, you know, just as words do."

Lightman shook his head vigorously. "No, no, no, I

didn't mean to suggest otherwise. All I meant to suggest, in my roundabout way, was that you might get more out of a course entitled, say, Poetry and the Human Spirit, the one I teach, than you might imagine. The physicist—"

"I'm a biochemist," the woman said. "And I took a poetry course as an undergraduate, thank you."

Lightman waggled an index finger. "Liberal education shouldn't end with your bachelor's degree. And as for physics, I'm merely using it as an example, seeing as it's the most blindly empirical of the sciences. Now, as I was saying, the physics professor teaches facts, but he hardly ever helps his students *learn*."

Pissant took out his handkerchief and blew his nose so hard that his head buzzed.

Lightman turned at the noise, leaving a small opening in the circle. Pissant slipped into it.

"God*damn*, that's deep," Pissant roared.

A look of horrified recognition crossed Lightman's face. There wasn't anyone in the College who didn't know Daniel P. Jackson, if only by reputation.

"Well, thank you, I—" Lightman began, but Pissant cut him off.

"The soul!" he shouted. "So *that's* what makes you different from me! I had it wrong all this time. Hell, I had a completely different explanation."

All eyes in the circle were focused on him now. It gave him a marvelous feeling of control that even Johnnie Walker failed to give him, and although an infinitesimally small sphere of reason buried beneath stratified layers of Scotch told him to back off, that he was going too far just to deflate a fatass, he knew he wouldn't give up the impending moment of triumph in hell for anything. It would be brief, and Satan would have his revenge—but the moment was all that mattered.

He looked knowingly at the young biochemist Lightman was clumsily trying to seduce, and at the other young women in the circle Lightman already had seduced or would try to seduce in the future. Oh, and the others too, others who would witness his victory: an alumnus, rich and blubbery; a dean, thin and greedy-eyed; Worthing . . .

Jesus shit, Worthing.

For an instant Pissant thought of listening to the small sphere of reason, but then a larger, hotter sphere flamed over it, blasting it out of existence.

The Physics Department chairman had been standing and listening to Lightman spout his dickheaded idiocies. He'd been listening, and—*smiling*.

Now, of course, Worthing's expression was one of sheer terror, knowing that the falling Icarus was going to take out as many gulls as he could during the tumble to the sea.

Pissant took a swallow from the drink he had stolen, then breathed deeply and grinned.

"Yes, folks," he said, looking straight into Lightman's eyes, "I've always seen the humanist/scientist dichotomy a little differently. From what I've observed, the main difference between teaching physics and teaching English is that the physics professor hardly ever tries to fuck his students."

In the brief calm that preceded the tempest, he saw his old student Thomas and thought, *Or wants to, either*.

Then judgment came swiftly. The angels and archangels—Worthing, the Chancellor, the deans, Satan (for Satan was an angel too, wasn't he?), the alumni—all turned their terrible visages upon him.

For an instant, he thought he saw Bud across the room, nodding approval, and the smile of the biochemist, also approving, but he couldn't be sure. He'd lost his drink, so he couldn't be sure of anything except a faulty fuel valve, blood, fire, and broken glass—things these demon-mannequins knew not at all.

His defeat had come long ago, so it didn't bother him that it was now being played out on the stage of the palace Lucifer. This was only playacting, an anticlimax, whether it took place in hell or heaven or Lawrence, Kansas.

The others, though, would see it as the true Fall. That was all right, because they would also see it as being simultaneous with a brief moment of triumph.

Just as it had been for Icarus.

A divine voice pierced him, saying:

Flap your naked arms, Pissant. Flap them until you reach the Moon, Mars, the Sun.

And burn.

3

Hello Muddah, Hello Faddah

Pretty Jack and Jackie,
Ain't they a beautiful pair?
Incredible contortionists:
Head up ass, nose in air.
They know just what's tacky,
They do it all the time—
They slip the screws to me and youse,
But they won't drink Jewish wine.

"How about new clothes?
How about a car?
Gotta get a tax break;
Have a church bazaar.
How about cocaine?
How about a whore?
Gee I'm glad Mum and Dad
Invested in the war."

Pretty Jack and Jackie,
How are new ones ever made?
You'd think that either one of them
Would rather hump a grenade.

—Bitch Alice
"Jack and Jackie," 1963

Friday, December 21, 1979. San Jorge, Concepcion, the Caribbean.

The Journal of Clifton Bonner:

Patton Day. Dear Mother and Father—

A problem. If I die, I'll want Mom and Dad to have this, sort of as my way of saying goodbye. But in that case, it'd be better if I left out some things.

On the other hand, if I make it back to Prairie Village, I'll want to have everything down, because this could be my break. An eyewitness account, guaranteed publication.

Hell, if I'm dead what do I care what Mom and Dad think? Go for the money.

Oh, Lieza, don't despise me for that. You're glaring down at me from the wall like an angry goddess, saying you piece of scrod, trying to make money off death and dying—

OK, OK. I love you; I want you. Maria has been only a momentary temptation of the flesh. Tell you what: I'll write this just to be doing it, and then if it makes money, well, what do I care? Like you make The Music just to be doing it and what do you care if people buy the records or not?

Jeez, you probably made a mint off the Patton's Eve concert last night.

Yeah, I know. Tonight's is free. Wish I could be there. Maybe I could get close enough to the stage to see if your leathers really do have a zippered crotch like *Wrackweek* says.

Bill just came in and asked what I "broody fink" I'm doing. I told him I was writing of him and his comrades, and he told me to let him read it when I'm finished. Then he went off down the hall to bang into more rooms. Some of the others must be afraid of him, but he's OK. It's his sergeant that scares the shit out of me.

Better do this from yesterday. Less to rewrite later.

Or from the beginning, since readers will want to know who's telling the story:

I was born February 12, 1956, of middle-class Kansas City parents, and I—

Holy God somebody just got shot outside. Shouts, a scream, then machine-gun fire, then nothing. I want to look out the window, but if I do they might shoot me too. Jesus I've got to piss but I've got to wait until Bill comes back in an hour or so to escort me to the john. Better empty my jar of peanuts in case I can't wait that long. Any more screams and shooting and you can bet I won't, either.

Try again:

God, I know I'm an agnostic but please don't let me get killed. There was just now more gunfire. I'm underneath my desk now, scrawling and unable to keep the words on the line.

Try again:

I was packed and ready to go yesterday morning, to get on the bus that would take me the short hop down to the airfield, where I would board the plane that would take me home for Christmas break.

Long mother of a sentence. Need something shorter, more powerful. Like a news story:

Yesterday, Patton's Eve 1979, Gurkhas invaded the tiny Caribbean island of Concepcion. My name is Clifton Bonner, and I'm an American medical student here.

"Who cares?" the fat slob watching the evening report growls. "Get to the blood and guts!"

I haven't seen much of that yet, only one big islander who was shot in the leg. I've heard quite a bit more.

From what I've been able to tell from in here, some of the locals are resisting, which is worse than suicidal. When you try to commit suicide, there's always a chance you might botch the attempt. But when you spit in a Gurkha's face, you're dead, baby, and all that's left is to bury you.

What I should have done was check up on the history of this place before applying to med school at San Jorge. But no, I waited until I got here to find out where I was.

Not only does this scrap of green rock have a history of violence reaching almost all the way back to Columbus, but back in 1950-something it decided to give Great Britain, the colonial landlord, the big kiss-off. They even changed all the place names to Spanish, just for spite. Britain sent troops, but the United States set up a blockade consisting of something like two Marines in a rubber dinghy, and the Limeys turned tail.

Back then, still licking their wounds from the war, the Brits wouldn't have had the guts to take on a troop of Camp Fire Girls. But 1979-going-on-1980 is another matter. Now, pissing off Mother England is a big mistake, so—

Who do I think I am, blathering about politics? All I know is what happened yesterday and what's happening today:

The Gurkhas invaded yesterday at about seven-twenty in the morning. My guess is that true-blue Caucasian Limeys piloted the harriers and helicopters in from the carrier or carriers, but the only actual troops I've seen have been Gurkhas in khakis.

From everything I've heard and read (and I've seen nothing to prove it wrong), Gurkhas would make Hitler's SS troops look like choirboys. Which is a funny way to put it, because they're about the size of little boys themselves. I doubt that there's any soldier among them that weighs more than a hundred and thirty-five pounds.

Doesn't matter. Gurkhas are the wolverines of humanity. When the Brits want something bad enough, they quit messing around with the tall, propah gents who were raised on tea and scones, and they send in the pintsized badasses.

So Mother England has reclaimed this dirt clod, and I and the other six-hundred-and-some-odd Americans on campus are under house arrest. Each building, from what I've been able to see from my window, has a guard of at least five lean, mean, bloodthirsty Nepalese killers. Here at the dorm, we've got maybe fifteen or twenty—eight or nine downstairs, and two apiece for each of the other floors (I think): one sentry, one rover.

Bill's third floor's rover. I have no idea what his real name is, and I don't expect to. He's Bill to me.

He smiles a lot, which seems odd. I've never thought

of Gurkhas as being the smiling type. Except when they're disemboweling somebody, that is.

From some of the screams I've heard outside, that must be what they're doing.

So, anyway, yesterday again: I was here, in my room, waiting for bus time, and I heard something going thumpa-thumpa-thumpa in the distance. Didn't think anything of it at first; there're a couple of locals who use helicopters for tourist charters. But the noise grew louder and louder and then multiplied, and superimposed over it was a hiss/scream of jet engines.

A troop-transport chopper set down right on the lawn. I watched it from my window. Six feet before the wheels touched the ground, a huge door in the side slid open, and umpteen soldiers with assault rifles, grenade belts, and longknives leaped out.

My first thought was that the U.S. was conducting a whacked-out troop exercise. Then I saw the squinty, leathery, merciless faces, and I knew that British colonialism was back. In force.

They spread out, a unit of about twenty-five heading this way, and I thought I saw one of them look up and point his rifle at me.

I dropped to my hands and knees, crawled across the room, and locked my door. After that I cowered under my desk for a minute or so, right where I'm cowering now.

When I heard shouts and running footsteps in the hall, I came to my senses and unlocked the door. They'd only have kicked it down or shot it to pieces.

Bill and a friend burst in a few moments later, holding their guns ready to spray me onto the wall if I tried anything. I obeyed their gestures, which were accompanied by grunted commands (most of the Gurkhas seem to understand English, but they prefer to communicate in guttural noises), and went into the hallway. There, Bill put a circular sticker with the number 52 on it onto my forehead. His partner stuck an identical sticker onto my room door. Other Gurkhas were following the same procedure with other students up and down the hall.

I and the rest of the third floor's inhabitants (all male, as is fifth floor—second and fourth are women) were herded downstairs into the cafeteria, where we were told to sit down at the tables.

I saw Maria across the room and started to go to her, but one of the Gurkhas looked at me and tapped his finger on his rifle's trigger guard. I stayed put and gave Maria what I hoped was a well-I-tried smile.

Maria didn't smile back. I think she saw me, but she had other things on her mind. She looked both frightened and furious, in yet another manifestation of her remarkable ability to express multiple emotions simultaneously. The first time we went to bed, she looked mildly amused even when she was coming. I've kept my eyes closed at that point ever since.

Funny how thinking about sex can take your mind off damn near anything, even bullets.

None of us sitting in the cafeteria spoke. Nobody was willing to find out if talking was punishable by death.

All I could think of was something I think was called the Bombay Massacre. Gurkhas under the command of a British officer slaughtered hundreds of Indians who were gathered in a walled-in square . . .

In the eyes of the Gurkhas I saw no compassion, only obedience and blood lust. Bill seems nice enough now, for a trained killer, but yesterday morning he was only one of many butchers waiting to hack me into bite-size pieces. I imagined them wasting us, then devouring our bodies. We were, after all, in the cafeteria.

A Gurkha with sergeant's insignia on his sleeves jumped onto a table and looked out over us with an expression of satisfaction. "You are students," he said loudly. His voice was thick with a strange combination of Oriental and Scottish accents. "You have no involvement in the criminal actions of the government of this island against Her Majesty the Queen. Nevertheless, as citizens of the United States of America, which has assisted this government in its mistreatment of the Crown, you must remain under house arrest until your departure can be arranged."

Then he got into the nitty-gritty:

"After you are returned to your rooms, you will not leave them for any purpose without a military escort. Anyone attempting to leave his or her room without an escort will be shot.

"You will not attempt to communicate with anyone in any other room or with anyone outside this building. Any person who does so will be shot.

"Any person who interferes with the duties of military personnel in any way whatsoever will be shot.

"Meals will be brought to your rooms twice a day. Anyone who complains about the food will be shot."

He grinned, then threw back his head.

"Ha ha ha ha ha ha ha," he said.

"Ha ha ha ha ha ha ha," the other Gurkhas said in unison.

Apparently, the last injunction had been meant as a joke.

My breakfast this morning was a bowl of some horrible sort of gruel and a paper plate full of runny scrambled eggs. I'm not complaining, and I'll bet no one else is either.

"At this time," the sergeant went on, "your rooms are being searched for contraband. All weapons and drugs, as well as any objects that could be converted into weapons or drugs, will be removed. When this process has been completed, you will be returned to your rooms. Some of you may be questioned about items that have been found there. And oh yes, do not remove the adhesive numbers from your foreheads until you have been returned to your rooms. Anyone attempting to remove or alter his or her number before that time will be shot."

The guy sitting next to me was Peter Somethingor-other, who has an oily complexion. I noticed that his number was starting to peel off all by itself.

I didn't know what to do. If I told him, I might be shot for talking, or he might be shot for moving when he tried to press it back on. And I sure as hell wasn't going to try to fix it for him myself. God only knew what the

Gurkhas would do to someone who looked like he was trying to switch numbers with somebody else.

I wanted, more than anything else, to scoot far away from good ol' Pete, but I was afraid that the penalty for scooting would be the same as for everything else. I also realized that I had a serious need to urinate, just as I do now.

Hell with it. I'll use the peanut jar.

Now what? My immediate thought is to tell Bill it's apple juice. But my guess is that the penalty for getting your guard to drink piss is being shot. Maybe tortured with a longknife first.

Back to the cafeteria:

Pete's number was curling off his head with alarming rapidity, and I was sure we'd both be dead as soon as it fell. The machine-gun spray directed toward him would doubtless get me too.

God, but I hated him. Greasy bastard. Deserved to die for getting me killed.

The sergeant was explaining more rules, something about respect and courtesy and making a difficult situation easier for everyone, but I didn't catch it all. My attention was riveted on that sticker. I was silently begging it to stop curling. I was praying for the hand of God to come down and slap it so hard that it'd be permanently embedded in Pete's slimy head.

But God always wants a sacrifice before He'll answer a prayer.

Remember Cain and Abel? I'd never say so in front of my parents, but I was always on Cain's side. He worked his ass off to grow all that stuff, and all Abel had to do was sit on his butt on a scrodding hillside and watch his sheep eat.

But God didn't care who had worked harder. He cared about blood.

I prayed for God to save me from the doom that would be brought about by Pete's excess facial oil, and God heard me.

And sent forth an islander from the kitchen. A man I've seen every day for four months, but whose name I never learned. He looks a little like Sam in *Casablanca*.

"You must use your time of confinement to contemplate your country's sins," the sergeant was saying. "Thus when you return home you will be able to explain why our actions have been made neces—"

"Hey, mon!" Sam was standing behind the cafeteria counter, in the doorway of the kitchen. "What d'yell goin' on outyear?"

I don't know how he'd avoided hearing all the noise outside, or how he'd managed to escape the notice of the room-to-room rousters. Maybe he was asleep in a pantry. I don't know; I've never been in the kitchen.

He came out around the end of the counter.

"What you doin'?" he said loudly. "No breffus today, mon. You all s'posed to fend f' y'selves and get on t' where you goin'."

Then Sam looked to his right, and he saw the Gurkha on the table.

"Mon, who d'fock you tink—"

The sergeant drew a pistol and shot Sam in the left thigh. Sam screamed and went down.

Most of the rest of us did, too. Pete did. Maria did.

I didn't. I was paralyzed. I had never seen a man shot before. There wasn't any blood at first, but the white tiles began to be smeared with red as Sam writhed.

None of us made a move to help him. My impulse here is to try to justify that, to list the many reasons why trying to help Sam would have been foolish. But I won't. Suffice it to say that we let him writhe. And bleed.

"Return to your seats!" the sergeant shouted in staccato syllables. "If any student or faculty member is not back in his or her seat within ten seconds, I shall instruct my men to open fire."

Those who had dropped to the floor got back into their seats. Quickly. Some of them were shaking and crying. I smelled urine.

Maria looked strange. For a few seconds I didn't know why, and then I realized that she had a little of Sam's blood on her right cheek. He had been shot right next to her table, and she must have landed practically on top of him. I wondered why I hadn't realized his proximity to her until then.

It reminded me that the worst guilt I feel about our relationship isn't over the way I use her, but over the fact that I don't love her, not even a little bit. She has a good body, and I like to be next to it. That's it. At other times I don't pay much attention to her.

Not that she feels anything more for me than I do for her. The difference is that she's been honest and told me that I'm fun, "sort of." Coming from her, that's praise.

At the moment in the cafeteria when I saw that tiny smear of blood on her face, I didn't want to be next to her ever again.

Now I'm not so sure. If thinking about sex can take my mind off bullets, maybe the real thing could take my mind off what the Gurkhas are said to do with their longknives. Or maybe it would only make me think about it more.

In the cafeteria, I thought about nothing but what I saw and smelled: blood and piss.

"Lack of respect will not be tolerated," the sergeant said, holstering his pistol.

Sam's screams had diminished to whimpers in the span of about twenty seconds, and a few seconds after that he was quiet.

He's passed out, I told myself. Nobody dies from a thigh wound, not right away. He's only passed out.

I glanced at Pete. The sticker was flat on his forehead.

Thanks, God. You son of a bitch.

What a sputzing hypocrite I am. I was glad, glad, glad that the sticker was no longer in danger of coming off! I was glad, glad, glad that Sam had drawn the guards' attention away from my area!

I am not the best of people, although I often pretend to be. I'm pretty good at it. Especially around Mom and Dad.

I'm also not the best of students. I blew at least two exams. First semester of med school down the toilet. Dad must've pulled strings to get me in here in the first place.

I'm thinking now that this invasion may work out to my academic advantage, particularly if the Gurkhas torch the administration building.

What a shit.

Face it: I'm not cut out to be a physician. I saw blood yesterday, and I felt sick. Worse than that, after another minute or so I realized that the urine I smelled was my own.

What I'd really like to be is a wrackwriter. Follow the circuit, maybe get a chance to talk to Lieza in person.

Fantasies. Lord, I love 'em. Beats reality...

The sergeant ordered a couple of the faculty M.D.s to see to Sam. They and two guards took him out. It wasn't easy because Sam is a big man, and one of the guards had to stay ready to shoot rather than help carry. A half-minute later, my peripheral vision caught a glimpse of movement outside the cafeteria windows. It looked like they were dragging the wounded man to the infirmary.

I haven't heard whether he's still alive or not. I tried to ask Bill this morning, but he just looked at me as if I were an insect on flypaper.

I think I'll save my peanut jar for a few days, and if I get to the point where I absolutely have to take out my frustration, I'll try to get Bill to drink the contents after all. Of course, he might confiscate it before then anyway. I'll wait until that happens to decide whether to tell him or not.

By my watch, we were in the cafeteria for two hours and forty-three minutes. Seven or eight of the two hundred (a guess) of us there fainted. An M.D. was allowed to revive them, but I'm not sure that was a kindness. Sometimes unconsciousness can be the best thing in the world.

When the room-searching detail finally reported to the sergeant with a list of numbers, about thirty-five of us were separated from the rest and taken out of the cafeteria. I was one of the Chosen Ones; so was Maria. When one of the Gurkhas that came out among the tables put his hand on my shoulder, I had a vision of myself on the floor, screaming.

We Chosen Ones were herded down the hall and into

the television room, where we were told to sit on the floor. Then, one by one, we were taken into the hall to be interrogated.

I managed to sit beside Maria. She had wiped the blood off her face with the sleeve of her blouse.

"What's that on your pants?" she whispered, nodding at my crotch.

"Spilled a glass of water when they came into my room," I lied.

"I was half-naked," she said, shaking out her long, dark-blonde hair. "You should've seen their eyes. You'd think they'd never seen boobs before."

"There will be no conversation!" a Gurkha shouted.

"Asshole," Maria hissed at him, and I wished I *hadn't* managed to sit beside her.

I'm positive he heard her, because he turned toward us. But when he saw where the epithet had come from, he looked confused and even, unless I imagined it, embarrassed. I felt certain that this particular soldier had been one of the lucky ones who'd burst in on Maria in the first place.

"Queer bait," she said. I elbowed her. Embarrassment has its limit, particularly among Gurkhas.

He stared at her the whole time we were in there, but I had the feeling that I'd be the one to get shot if he lost his temper. I was actually glad when the sergeant looked in from the hall and called my number.

That gladness lasted exactly the length of time it took to get from my spot on the floor to the doorway. Then I froze.

What had they found in my room? Was it bad enough that they'd kill me? Hadn't I smoked the last of my dope a month ago? Even if I hadn't, why should they care?

Why, indeed? Any excuse will do. Witness what happened to poor Sam.

I wasn't able to make my body move into the hall until I was prodded in the back with a bayonet.

"Ah, Mister Number Fifty-two," the sergeant said once I was in the hallway. He and three other Gurkhas formed a circle of inquisition just outside the TV room.

I felt dizzy, and began to see the pattern of black dots that precedes unconsciousness. Then I was prodded in the back again, and this time my shirt ripped. At that point I couldn't tell if I was cut or not, but it hurt. The pain wiped out the black dots and propelled me two steps closer to the sergeant.

He smiled up to me (he's about a foot shorter than I am, and I'm only five-ten), but it felt as if he were glaring down on me with the eyes of a rabid twelve-foot-tall Doberman.

"It is customary," he said, "to respond with 'Yes, sir,' when addressed by one such as myself. We will try again. 'Ah, Mister Number Fifty-two.' "

"Yethur," I said. My tongue had become too dry and thick to move properly.

The Gurkha didn't seem to notice. "We have found items in your room we would like you to explain to us. Would you be amenable to this?"

"Thurtenlee, thur," I said, or tried to say.

This time he noticed. "Speak intelligibly," he said. "If I cannot understand you, I shall be forced to have you shot for lack of any evidence in your favor."

"Yes, sir," I said. I shouldn't have been able to speak at all, but apparently my survival gland knows just when to kick in.

He held out his hands, palms up. Lying in one of them was a scalpel; in the other was my green plastic water pistol.

"Explain the purpose of these and why they are in your possession," he said crisply.

"Um, well sir, that one," I said, pointing to the scalpel, "is a surgical instrument I borrowed to use as a letter opener. I've also used it to cut articles from journals."

"It could also be used to attack a member of Her Majesty's Royal Army, could it not?"

I shook my head, probably too vigorously. "No, sir, not by me, sir," I insisted.

His eyes moved to my crotch. "I believe you," he said

after a moment. "And this?" He indicated the water pistol.

I told him what it was.

"I see," he said, obviously skeptical. "And this fluid in it is—?"

"Water, sir."

His eyes narrowed. "You are positive it does not contain a caustic chemical that could be used to blind or kill a member of Her Majesty's Royal Army?"

"Yes, sir."

He smiled. "We shall see."

He squirted me repeatedly. I didn't mind; it gave me an explanation for my pants in case anyone else asked.

Finally, he was satisfied. "Very well," he said. "You will be taken to your room as soon as an escort is free. You will not be punished for owning these items. However, they must be confiscated. You will please stand against the wall until your escort arrives."

One of the soldiers in the circle slammed me back-first into the concrete-block wall.

This particular soldier also gave me a look that told me where he'd shoot me if I so much as blinked before I was told to.

Maria was brought out next and was shoved, without benefit of bayonet, into the circle.

"Ah, Mizz Number Seventy-eight," the sergeant said.

"Skag you," Maria said.

Sometimes in the dark, I've fantasized that Maria was Lieza Galilei. For that brief instant in the hall, I almost thought she really was, and I almost loved her.

But then my brain's hearing center recognized Maria's curse for what it was: an obscene pout.

She's a spoiled brat like me—hell, yes, I admit it; there'd be no point in denying it when it's so pitifully obvious—who thinks the world should cater to her. And spoiled brats pout when they're unhappy. A Wracker vocabulary doesn't make a Straight a Wracker. I know, because when I was nineteen I tried to make the transition that way. It didn't work.

And it didn't work for Maria, either. If she'd really been Lieza, she'd have probably skipped the "Skag you" and smashed her knee into the little jagoff's pea-sized balls.

"It is customary to respond with 'Yes, sir,'" the sergeant said. "We shall try again. 'Mizz Number Seventy-eight.'"

"Skag you, sir."

It would've been admirable if her lower lip hadn't been sticking out and her tone hadn't been whiny. As it was, she sounded like a seven-year-old rug rat daring the babysitter to spank her.

Unfortunately, when Gurkhas give spankings, they give them with longknives.

Knock it off Maria you goddamn better knock it off, I thought, and considered praying. But I didn't, because I was afraid that this time God might require *my* blood for the sacrifice.

The sergeant smiled a rattlesnake smile. "You are upset. This is understandable, and there will be no punishment. However, if you attempt any resistance of a physical nature, I shall give you to my men and allow them to decide your fate. You have no aversion to sharpened steel, I hope?"

It was at that point that I named him Genghis Khan.

I don't love Maria, but she's a friend, sort of, and a good lay. We come from the same mold; the only thing that differs is our sex. When Genghis threatened her, he threatened me.

Too bad I'm a coward.

Now hold on, Cliff. That isn't fair. What were you supposed to do, slapped up against the wall with wet clothes and a bayonet cut in your back? Singlehandedly kung fu five Gurkhas armed with several varieties of deadly weapons?

Other than sinking a little closer to the floor, I stayed put.

Maria had turned pale, and she didn't seem inclined to insult Genghis anymore. She isn't creative, but she does have enough imagination to figure out what being "given" to a squad of Gurkhas would be like.

One of Genghis's underlings handed him something, and Genghis held it out toward Maria.

"You will explain, please, the purpose of this object," he demanded.

It was her vibrator. A ten-inch model.

"Um," Maria said weakly. Her eyes were wide.

I had a pretty good idea of what she was thinking. If she told them what it was, they might demand a demonstration.

Genghis's eyes narrowed until it must have been almost impossible for him to see.

"Is it a weapon?" he said in a low voice. "A communicating device? An explosive?"

"Nngg," Maria said, which I interpreted as "No."

Genghis sneered, revealing crusty, yellowish-gray teeth. "You will answer freely within five seconds, or under torture within five minutes."

Maria looked paralyzed. Her face, which normally holds multiple expressions, was blank. Her lips trembled slightly, but no sound came out.

"Two seconds," Genghis said.

Maria's eyes seemed to cloud over.

Genghis shrugged. "Very well," he said, gesturing to one of his men, who began to step toward Maria.

"It's a tartar remover," a voice blurted.

I was stunned at the spontaneous generation of the words. Maria's lips had stopped moving altogether, and certainly none of Genghis's men had said anything. It was as if the voice had been magically produced out of empty air.

So why, I wondered, was everybody looking at me?

Genghis took three quick steps toward me and slapped my face on both cheeks, onetwothreefourfive.

"Do you wish to die?" he shouted. "You were not given permission to speak!"

I didn't see how the voice could've been mine, and I still don't. Maybe God was speaking through my mouth.

Hardy-har.

The magic voice, whatever its origin, didn't seem to know when to shut up.

"She's too frightened to answer," it said. "I thought it would be better for me to tell you what that thing is rather than for her to be hurt just because she can't get the words out."

Definitely not my voice. I'd never speak to Genghis Khan like that, not me, boy, huh-uh, never.

On account of I knew Genghis wouldn't like it, and sure enough, I was right. He slapped me five or ten or thirty more times and then jabbed three fingers into my solar plexus. I doubled over, seeing black dots again, and he gave me one on the back of the neck. I went down, and my face bounced off the floor.

All I could think of was the summer when I was nine years old and had to take swimming lessons at the employees' club of my dad's firm.

See, Mom used to drop me off and then go shopping or whatever. There were these two older kids who always waited for me in the showers, where they'd shake me down for my pop money. I only resisted the first time, which was the time they not only pushed my face down against the hair-clogged drain, but also punched and kicked me. Eventually I got fed up and told Mom, who told Dad, who did something, and then I really got it. They pulled off my suit and pushed me out, naked, in front of everybody, including my bikinied swim instructor, my first crush. My tiny nine-year-old pecker shrank to nothing and didn't come back until I was fifteen.

Worst three months I ever had, and I relived every second yesterday morning about 11:10. Genghis had my face in the drain again, breathing wet, tangled hair.

"Get up, dirty Yankee," he said, kicking me in the ribs. Not too hard; I didn't quite fall over.

After a few more kicks, I made it back to my feet. I was coughing and could hardly breathe, but goddamn if that voice didn't come back.

"I'm telling the truth, sir," it said. "That device is designed for dental hygiene. It vibrates tartar off the teeth."

For a second or two, Genghis looked ready to hit me again. Then he thrust the vibrator at my face.

"Demonstrate," he said.

My right hand came up involuntarily and took the vibrator.

"It's simple," the magic voice said. "You turn it on with this switch—"

Three assault rifles drew beads on my head.

My thumb flicked the switch, and the vibrator hummed happily. Genghis looked at it curiously.

"Then," the voice continued, "you insert the rounded end in your mouth and bring the teeth down on it gently, taking care not to bite too hard. Ten minutes a day of this, and I guarantee that all grunge will disappear from the old pearly whites."

My hand brought the vibrator up and stuck it in my mouth. An interesting sensation, but one I couldn't fully appreciate because of the other vibrations Genghis had already set in motion in my head.

After a little while, Genghis reached up and took the vibrator from me. He flipped the on-off switch a few times, buzzclickbuzzclickbuzzclick.

"This device truly does as you say?" he asked, sounding surprisingly nonthreatening.

It was only then that I remembered how bad his teeth had looked when he'd bared them. My survival gland had been working hard, and I hadn't even known it.

"Check out the young lady's teeth if you don't believe me," I said, in control of my own voice again now that I consciously knew what was going on.

Maria opened her mouth and pulled her lips back with her fingers. Her teeth are perfect; three orthodontists got rich off her parents, and she flosses frequently, particularly after sex.

As Genghis peered into her mouth, Maria's eyes were fixed on me. The terror had disappeared from them and had been replaced by a combination of exhilaration and amusement. As if she'd just had an orgasm.

There was no gratitude there, but I didn't really expect any. I didn't expect anything at all, and what I got didn't surprise me:

It turned her on to see someone kick the shit out of me.

Bill and two other Gurkhas joined the group, apparently returning from a trip upstairs, and Genghis nodded to them.

"These two may be returned to their rooms," he said, and then looked at Maria. "This must remain with me." He indicated the vibrator. "A violent person might turn it into a bomb."

One of the Gurkhas who had come with Bill jerked his head at Maria, and she coolly stepped out of the circle.

"As for you," Genghis said, looking at me, "if I ever encounter you again, and you speak to me without being spoken to first, I shall have your genitals sewn to your nose."

I didn't risk saying anything in response. Bill gestured to me, and I went down the hall with him. My legs felt as if the bones had turned to pizza dough.

We went up the stairs behind Maria and her guard, which gave me a view of the lovely tush I had saved from slicing and dicing. As the buttocks flexed and relaxed, flexed and relaxed under the sky-blue material of her bodypants, they seemed to be saying Ha ha ha ha ha ha ha.

Maria didn't look back at me, and she and her guard continued on to the fourth floor when Bill and I left the stairwell at three. That was about twenty-four hours ago, and I haven't seen her since.

Funny: although I know her face can hold multiple expressions, I can't picture any of its physical features. I've been trying to compose a description of her for this account, but all I can see in my mind's eye are those laughing blue buttocks.

As for a description of myself—

"You one lucky bwah," Bill told me when we'd reached my room.

"Oh yeah?" I asked, shuffling in and bracing myself against my desk so I wouldn't fall over.

"Yeah, bwah. You fink Sarge always let off back-talkers? You fink again, bwah."

Then Bill left, and I made it over to the bed. It's across the room from the closet, which has a full-length mirror screwed to the door.

My nose looked as though somebody had stuffed it with an apple. The skin under my eyes was beginning to blacken. The bayonet cut in my back was throbbing. I managed to get the fingers of my right hand to it, and they came away bloody.

But hey, my nifty light-brown, blow-dried hair still looked great.

My face is still pretty bad today, but there's nobody to see it but Bill. It doesn't hurt much, unless I forget and try to scratch my nose, as I just did. Goddamn.

More shots outside. What bothers me about them this time is that they hardly bothered me at all. Somebody was just now getting killed out there, and I didn't even flinch.

My own death, I know, would be another matter entirely. I'm more glad than ever that Genghis let me off, as Bill says. Yesterday, with my face in the drain, I didn't feel let off at all. Today, after hearing all the gunfire outside, I do.

The past twenty-four hours have been uneventful for me. The highlight was when Bill escorted me to the showers this morning and let me wash off the dried blood. When we came back here, he pointed at my poster of Lieza Galilei and Blunt Instrument and told me that he loved their stuff.

Can you believe that, Lieza? A Gurkha loves The Music. Goddamn, the world is strange.

But then, strangeness is what's keeping me alive. The past day has been fine, and the days to come will also be fine, no matter how many weeks pass before I make it home.

What's going to get me through, you see, is the thought of Ghenghis Khan spending ten minutes every morning with an electric dildo in his mouth.

Hysterical Perspective II

Before Dallas, the United States had been the only nation to send human beings to the Moon. They'd even started sending up celebrities to boost public support (which, ironically, was how Bitch Alice got there in the first place). By early 1967, a permanent lunar base was only a few flights away.

After Dallas, the Anglo-Chinese Alliance moved in.

Also before Dallas, NOSS had been drawing up plans for a large Earth-orbit space station. Seven months after Dallas, a former NOSS employee gave photocopies of those plans to a Scottish girl in exchange for what, he realized later, didn't amount to much in the long run.

At about the same time, the rinky-dink dictators of the Fourth World realized that whoever controlled the high ground might someday decide to roll rocks down on the town bully, hitting his sidekicks in the process.

Thus the United States began to feel a certain loss of power. It began to feel an even more certain loss of money.

By 1976, bigshot Whigs and Dealers alike began saying that something had to be done about getting back into space. As usual, however, they disagreed on how to do that.

Briefly and incompletely stated, the Dealers felt that the United States's reentry into space should be accomplished by *kissing* Alliance ass, the theory being that if a child is nice to a bigger child, the bigger child will give the nice child part of his candy.

Briefly and pretty much completely stated, the Whigs felt that the United States's reentry into space should be accomplished by *kicking* Alliance ass, the theory being that the best way to get a bigger child to give you his candy is to sneak up and cave in his skull.

However, J.D. Fitzgerald's victory in 1976 indicated that things weren't yet bad enough for the Straight public to want a war. (Yankee blood lust was satisfied every evening when the TV news ran the latest clip of "subversives" being shot in the Central Trust Territory.) So "Big Whig" Winton R. Wilson hung back until 1979—by which time all could see that Fitzgerald was getting nowhere—and then began blitzkrieging for the 1980 election.

Wilson was smart enough not to publicly advocate violence this time around. Instead, he advised the American public to forget about the Moon and the space station.

Mars, he said, was the place to be. Surely, if God had wanted America to be satisfied with Earth alone, He wouldn't have given her all those German scientists.

Records of the period indicate that the Great Straight Public actually thought he meant it.

> —Lorna P.N. Chicago-deSade,
> *A Brief, Biased History,*
> pp. 251-52.

4

Patton Day Brunch

Say Hail to the Chiefs,
Gonna give all the world relief.
Running day after day,
Majority bought him; minority pays.

All of them sing:
"I ain't no dictator; I ain't no king."
All of them pray:
"Give us our daily dead today."

Say, elect a winner
With the style to pull off state dinners.
Hey, what do you think?
Which of these dudes can put the screws
      to the Chinks?

So many seem to die—
Call your local Secret Service; ask 'em why
Frankie Roosevelt choked on a chicken bone,
Then Garner answered an exploding phone.
Later Truman took one in the skull—
Don't go on; my stomach's full.

—Lieza Galilei
"Hail to the Chiefs," 1978

Friday, December 21, 1979. Washington, D.C.

> *Lieza crawled on a gray plain with black ice for air. When she cried, her mother appeared, wearing a moonsuit with an open faceplate.*
>
> *Her mother picked her up from the dust, cuddled her, cooed to her. Milk shot from a blue nipple on the suit.*
>
> *She opened her mouth to catch the stream, but when it entered her mouth it tasted like frozen plastic.*
>
> *A sharp pain stabbed into her right arm, and she saw that her mother had bitten her with a single long, bright fang.*
>
> *She tried to cry out, but the stuff in her mouth wouldn't let her.*
>
> *As the fang withdrew, her mother's face crumbled into sand, leaving the moonsuit empty.*
>
> *The fang remained, hanging in space, glittering.*

* * *

"Let's get going," the smooth voice of God said, and then Lieza saw the translucent tube behind the needle.

She tried to fight, but her muscles were flaccid and numb. It was as if she had been separated from her body.

As her vision cleared, she saw gloves, buttons, stubble, a mustache . . . and Cherry lying prostrate on the bed, one long cocoa arm hanging over the edge of the mattress, the fingers bent against the carpet.

If you've hurt her, Lieza tried to say, *I'll kill you all.*

But there was a stiff plastic thing in her mouth, and tape over her lips.

"Find a shirt," the voice of God said. "Christ, I wonder if she ever takes these pants off?"

She was lowered to the floor and found herself staring at the ceiling, unable to turn her head.

"Is she conscious?" a second voice asked.

"Hard to tell. Here, give me that."

Gloved hands dressed her in one of Cherry's pullover sweatshirts. She felt as if she were being placed in a shroud.

She saw the face of one of the men for the first time. It was Special Agent Dodson, grimacing.

The shoulder must be hurting him. Good.

Dodson hooked his arms under her knees. "Let's get to the roof before the goon with the metal nose shows up."

Hands grasped her under her armpits, and she was carried backward past where the window should have been onto a narrow metal platform. Cherry's body sank away, and Lieza saw herself in mirrored glass, being held by two figures in long coats. The Washington Monument wavered behind them, almost invisible against the gray shell of the sky.

* * *

By the time they put her into a leather chair in the Oval Office, the muscle relaxant had worn off enough for her to kick at Dodson. Her bare toes grazed his knee.

Dodson raised an eyebrow and spoke to his new partner. "What'd I tell you, Fred? Be careful taking the gag out. She'll eat your fingers if she can."

Fred, a swarthy man with a mustache, squatted beside the chair. Then, with a quick, darting movement, his hand shot to Lieza's mouth and ripped off the tape. Her cry forced an egg-shaped chunk of black rubber out of her mouth, and it rolled under the enormous mahogany desk she was facing.

"Oh, boy, wouldn't the President like to find that," Fred said, getting down on his hands and knees. While he was groping under the desk, he crawled directly in front of Lieza.

"Fred—" Dodson began.

The man's buttocks were raised high, giving Lieza the opportunity to aim a kick precisely where his scrotum had to be.

The agent howled, hit his head on the underside of the desk, and fell flat.

It was at that moment that the President of the United States and five other people entered the room.

Four were men who were obviously Secret Service agents. Lieza was beginning to recognize the telltale walk of someone wearing a machine pistol in a shoulder holster.

The fifth was a blonde, gunmetal-blue-eyed woman wearing a maroon suit. She looked like the TV pictures

Lieza had seen of Secretary of State Annabelle Kirk.

The agent named Fred, groaning, crawled out from under the desk.

President J.D. Fitzgerald looked bewildered.

"Is there something I should know about?" he asked.

Fred got to his feet and stood doubled over with his hands on his knees. He seemed unable to answer.

"He was dry-humping the rug," Lieza said. She felt thick-tongued, and her mouth still tasted like plastic.

Dodson coughed. "Uh, Mister President, sir, I recommend that we place Mizz Galilei in restraints."

Fitzgerald walked around the wheezing Fred and settled into the huge chair behind his desk.

"I hardly think that will be necessary," he said. "I have six armed agents here. Even if she could hurt me, I doubt that she'd want to risk federal prosecution for attacking the President."

Lieza studied the man across from her. Eyes the color of weak tea; a complexion created by sunlamp and lotion; mouse-brown hair that looked like it was covered by a coat of acrylic spray. Fitzgerald was soft, pretty; a Dumbass Jack if ever there was one. She was surprised that he'd been tough enough to have her kidnapped, tough enough to . . .

Her chest muscles tightened as she thought of Cherry's limp body.

"You're half right," she said. "I wouldn't attack a President, not even if he'd ignored my constitutional rights. However, if Mizz Angola was killed in the course of my abduction, I'll waste whoever was responsible. I won't give a skagging damn who he is. Peesh?"

Fitzgerald looked worried. "Um, no one was supposed to be harmed . . ."

Dodson cleared his throat. "No one was, sir. We introduced a tranquilizer into the room via the air conditioning system in order to ensure that we wouldn't be discovered while removing the window glass. Once inside, we injected both Mizz Angola and Mizz Galilei with a relaxant. As you can see, the effects are temporary."

Lieza coughed loudly, mocking Dodson's throat-clearing. "My arm hurts, and Cherry's must too. If we can't play tonight, there're going to be a hundred thousand Wrackers on Roosevelt-Patton Island who're going to be upset. There were only forty thousand in Dallas in '67."

"That sounds like a terroristic threat," Fitzgerald said.

Lieza shrugged her shoulders. "A sociological prediction. If I can't play, I won't tell them to trash anything. But I'll tell them the truth, and they'll make up their own minds."

The agent named Fred, who was still doubled over, moaned.

Lieza smiled at him. "You look a little queasy, jag-brain. Helicopter rides don't agree with you?" She turned toward Dodson. "What happened to the sputzer you liked so much? Zackman, wasn't it? He go running home to mommy?"

Her peripheral vision caught a change in the posture of the secretary of state, a stiffening of the spine.

President Fitzgerald slapped the top of his desk. "Now see here, Mizz Galilei. I realize you maintain a certain image for the public, but you're not in public now. Here you must display a little respect. Don't you know where you are? Look up and tell me what you see."

Lieza tipped back her head and saw the Presidential Seal molded into the ceiling plaster.

"Art deco?" she asked.

Fitzgerald's features molded into Pat Expression Number Eight: The Grim, Determined World Leader.

"That's the symbol of the power vested in me by the people of this nation," he said theatrically. "It's the symbol of a responsibility I cannot take lightly and that I must fulfill using every means at my disposal."

Lieza looked around in mock curiosity. "Hey, where're the cameras?"

Fitzgerald leaned across his desk, peering at the Bastard Child. "I regret that I had to have you brought here by force, but I must speak with you, and it must be in person. Since we each have a busy day ahead, I'll come right to the point. London and Peking, among many other abuses, have stolen our rightful place on the Moon and have constructed a permanent space station in Earth orbit—"

"Old news," Lieza interrupted. "You're a few years too late to do anything about that, and even if you weren't, it has nothing to do with me."

Annabelle Kirk spoke for the first time. Her voice reminded Lieza of dry leaves being crushed.

"It has everything to do with you, Mizz Galilei," the secretary of state said. "Were it not for the incitement of the Dallas riot by your mother, the United States flag would be stenciled on the bulkheads of those outposts."

"Whoop-te-do," Lieza said, clapping her hands.

She didn't feel as defiant as she pretended. Something about Kirk's voice and expression told her this wasn't someone who played nice.

If the secretary were capable of having a lover, she decided, it would have to be someone like Zackman. It was probably a safe bet that the kidnapping hadn't been Fitzgerald's idea after all.

Kirk, flanked by a Secret Service agent, came closer to Lieza until she was standing over her like an inquisitor about to apply torture.

"Laugh if you like," Kirk said slowly, "but you might not be laughing if you knew how serious the situation is. We have reason to believe that the socialistic leaders of the Anglo-Chinese Alliance will soon be using their off-Earth bases for military purposes. There is evidence to suggest that they're constructing an electromagnetic launcher on the Moon, and we're certain that Churchill-Chiang Station is armed with between ten and fifteen high-yield nuclear devices. Do you have any idea—"

Lieza leaned back in her chair, affecting boredom. "Yeah, yeah. They might clobber us with Moon rocks or drop bombs on us if we don't lick their buns occasionally. Natural selection strikes again. What else is new?"

Fitzgerald's actor's mask dissolved into confusion. "Natural selection?"

"Sure, Prez. Survival of the fittest. He who holds the high ground wins."

Kirk pointed a long, bony index finger at Lieza. "Exactly. And the United States would be holding the high ground were it not for your mother."

Lieza's hands knotted into fists. "Were it not for the fact that you killed her."

Fitzgerald slapped his desk again, and Lieza saw that his face had returned to Pat Expression Number Eight. "No one here is responsible for that," he said. "It happened nearly thirteen years ago. An entire nation shouldn't be made to suffer in perpetuity because of one malfunction."

Lieza made a sardonic noise through her nose. "You're getting pretty frickin' good at the righteously indignant speech, Fitzy. You must be studying Wilson's technique."

She was pleased to see that the jab was effective. Fitzgerald's mask crumbled a second time.

Kirk's acrid perfume cut into Lieza's nose as the secretary of state leaned closer.

"Eau de Baboon's Ass?" the Bastard Child asked mildly.

The secretary's lips pursed for an instant before she spoke. "I don't know to what you're referring, but it doesn't matter. Winton R. Wilson has nothing to do with this. He is a private citizen. Our problem is a national concern."

Lieza looked around again. "There've *gotta* be some cameras in here somewhere, because you can't be talking to me. The Great Straight Public might swallow this King Kong turd, but my throat won't stretch far enough."

Kirk's eyebrows raised. "You find it hard to believe that we see the Anglo-Chinese off-Earth outposts as threats to national security?"

"You see them as threats to *your* security, since Wilson's been harping on them for the last several weeks. He's taken a situation that's been in existence for a decade and turned it into an election-year crisis. You're afraid the voters will panic and rally behind him because of it. Every administration confuses its own well-being with that of the nation, doesn't it?"

Fitzgerald looked incredulous. "You listen to Wilson's shows?"

Lieza grinned at him. "I tune in to your speeches and press conferences too, sir, and with a great deal of enthusiasm. True comedy has been rare on the airwaves ever since 'Lum 'n' Abner' was cancelled."

Kirk made a warning gesture with her hand. "That's enough. All we require from you is a simple answer to a simple question. Will you help us or not?"

Lieza pushed herself up from the chair to face Kirk in a standing position. The Secret Service agents' hands snaked inside their coats.

"Please stay calm, everyone," Fitzgerald said nervously.

Lieza ignored the agents and the President. She glared at Kirk and said, "Help you do what? I'm no politician."

Kirk glared back. "You have a duty to serve your country. You must use your music to alert your listeners, Wracker and Straight alike, to the cause our nation must take up."

Lieza backed away a few steps on half-numb legs, pushing her chair aside. The back of her neck tingled.

"You want a war," she said, staring. "You want me to help you recruit cannon fodder. With all due lack of respect, Madame Secretary, you can go shtup yourself with a hot crowbar. Or do you have one of your SS men serve that purpose?"

Annabelle Kirk's powder-white complexion turned the color of blood.

"You perverted slut," she said in a quavering voice. "We could have you put in prison for the things you've done here today. How would you like to visit a camp in Siberia for the rest of your life? All four years of it?"

The tight lines of the secretary's face made it clear that she meant what she said.

Lieza tried to suppress the contractions she felt beginning in her abdomen. Fear was sometimes a useful emotion, but it had to be controlled. "Well, Madame Secretary, how would you like a third of the nation, minimum, vying for the honor of putting your head on top of the Empire State Building's radio tower?"

The President made a whimpering noise and said, "Now, now, none of this is necessary. Mizz Galilei, I assure you we aren't thinking of starting a war with Britain and China. Madame Kirk and my Chiefs of Staff tell me that such a conflict would inevitably escalate into a worldwide nuclear battle. We'd destroy them, but they'd destroy us too. We'd gain nothing. No one is asking you to recruit soldiers."

Lieza looked at the President skeptically and tried to read past his mask. He seemed sincere, but if Kirk was running the show, Fitzgerald might not know the truth.

Whatever the truth was, Lieza was determined to continue being uncooperative. A Dumbass like Fitzgerald didn't deserve anything better, and Kirk, apparently a Hobnail masquerading as a Dumbass, deserved worse.

But the Bastard Child's curiosity was piqued. If they weren't planning a war, then what?

"You're not going to try to get back the Moon?" she asked, unsure of what she was groping toward.

"Not by violence," Kirk said, coldly. "Not at this point."

"You see," Fitzgerald said, putting on Pat Expression Number Thirteen, The Optimistic Good Guy, "we feel that breaking new ground would be more profitable. We're going to go to Mars."

Lieza stared at the President for a few seconds, then laughed at the ceiling's sculptured plaster. These pitiful jagoffs couldn't even come up with their own *shtick*; they were trying to steal Wilson's.

"We're not joking, Mizz Galilei," Kirk said. "The United States is going to send the first humans to another planet, and eventually, we are going to colonize that planet. America is going to expand across the solar system."

An Oriental-looking man in a white coat and black slacks entered the Oval Office, pushing a silver cart laden with covered trays. He was accompanied by yet another Secret Service agent.

Lieza looked at the servant in mock horror and screamed. "Aaagggghhh! You've got one! A Martian, complete with spaceship! And wouldn't you know it, the little jackbugger looks like a Chink! Exterminate all the brutes!"

The servant looked up from the cart with a worried expression. "Mister President? Sir? You did say to bring in brunch at eleven-thirty, didn't you, sir?"

"Um," the President said, obviously confused.

"Yes, Earl, thank you," the secretary of state snapped. "That will be all."

"Sputzing Christ!" Lieza yelled as the servant left the Oval Office. "Aren't you gonna make the poor guy taste the food first? Can't be too careful about those slant-eyes, you know. Might put cyanide into the marmalade. Or worse, saltpeter into the muffins."

Kirk sneered. "We'll leave the tasting to you, Mizz Galilei. The President was afraid you'd be hungry. But apparently you don't appreciate his concern. You don't seem to feel anything at all except pleasure in your own obscenity."

Lieza went to the cart and took the cover off the largest tray.

"Obscenity is a relative term, Madame Secretary," she said. "For example, certain persons might consider these little sausages with toothpicks in them dreadfully obscene. Here, Dodson, have some." She threw several at the Secret Service agent, who lunged to catch them.

"Perhaps we should take Agent Dodson's suggestion after all, Mister President," Kirk said. "Restraints for Mizz Galilei would, if nothing else, prevent some nasty stains."

"Um, well, I . . ." Fitzgerald began.

Lieza turned away from the cart to give the President a look of disgust. "If you're going to let the Bride of Stalin here make up your mind for you, at least have the sense not to look silly by pretending to do it yourself. You're not *that* good an actor."

Fitzgerald looked confused for another instant, then straightened in his chair, affixing Pat Expression Number Four, I Am In Charge, to his face.

"There's no need to place our guest in restraints at this point in time," he said with artificial firmness. "However, if she throws any more food, the secretary of state's suggestion will be implemented."

Lieza's immediate impulse was to toss ham slices at the eagle on the ceiling, but she stopped herself. Being tied down would not be a good thing.

What would be a good thing, she decided, would be to get out of here. She had to make sure Cherry was all right, and then Blunt Instrument had to get ready for the General George S. Patton Memorial Music Festival and Goat Sacrifice.

She raised her hands as if she were a captured enemy soldier. "OK. I shall endeavor to cooperate." She went back to her chair, bumping into Secretary of State Kirk on the way, and sat down.

Kirk gave her a thin-lipped smile. "I've seen videos of you in concert, Mizz Galilei, and I know you're not clumsy. You collided with me on purpose."

"Excussa moi, Madame," Lieza replied with a single-fingered flourish of her right hand.

Kirk kept on giving her the same unsettling smile. "I wonder if you realize how close you came to being shot. If it had been the President standing here instead of me, you probably would have been."

Lieza made a clicking noise with her tongue. "Some days I have no luck at all, Madame Secretary. Now, to paraphrase your earlier words, let's cut the scrod. I'm going to try to be polite, even if it makes me sick, which it probably will. Tell me what I have to do to get out of here and back to my hotel. My friends must be going bugsputz by now."

"We've already told you, Mizz Galilei," Fitzgerald said, the tone of his voice revealing his desire to prove that he was indeed in charge. "We want you to undo the damage your mother did, to reaccustom Americans to the idea of manned space exploration. I've been told that the technology exists to get us to Mars. All we need is public support."

Lieza couldn't help laughing again. "In the first

place," she said when she was able to, "I don't do requests. I write what I write, I sing what I sing. It has to come from inside, or it isn't The Music. I might be able to crank some made-to-order song that'd fool most of the Straight population, but ain't no skaggin' way it'd get by Wrackers. They'd feel the lie in a second."

"We aren't asking you to lie," Kirk said angrily.

Lieza briefly closed her eyes and bit her lower lip. This Hobnail-in-Dumbass-clothing wouldn't even know the difference between a lie and the truth.

"Maybe," she said slowly. "Maybe you're not, by your definition. But anything I sing has to come from my soul, or from the soul of someone I can get into. If I sing anything else, it won't go with Wrackers. And it's Wrackers you've got to sell, isn't it? You can have most Straights in your pocket within a month if you use the right advertising. You don't need me to get to them, and you *can't* use me to get to Wrackers, because they'd know it."

Fitzgerald looked nervous again. "What are we to do, then?"

Annabelle Kirk looked at the President with a condescending expression that made Lieza feel sorry for him.

The emotion was uncomfortable, and she got rid of it by concentrating on her dislike of Kirk.

"Quite simply, Mister President," the secretary of state said, "we have to convince Mizz Galilei of the rightness of our cause. Then she'll feel it in her, ah, 'soul,' and her music will ring true."

Lieza had a vision of herself doped on sodium pentothal, listening to a tape that said, "President Fitzgerald wants to go to Mars. Mars is good because he says so. It would be very nice to go to Mars for President Fitzgerald. And even nicer to go for Secretary of State Kirk."

The President's hands wandered across the top of his desk, fiddling with paper clips and pencils. "Well, um, do we have time for that?"

Before Kirk could answer, Lieza stood up again. "Not today. Tell you what, though: you pitch whatever let's-beat-the-Lemon-Limeys-to-Mars campaign you want to, and I won't say anything against it. To tell you the truth, I don't care. My mother died a long time ago, and, hell, maybe she shouldn't have done what she did about it. Now, may I please get back to my hotel?"

The secretary of state shook her head. "Not good enough. Simply promising not to speak against our project won't prevent Wracker opposition. And if we can't prevent Wracker opposition, we won't have the general public behind us either. They'll be afraid of what the hoodlums might do, and what the public fears, Congress fears. I don't think you're so dense as to believe that we can send people to Mars without Congressional support."

Blood throbbed in Lieza's temples. She felt sick at Kirk's hypocritical manipulativeness and Fitzgerald's basic stupidity.

She didn't believe for a second that Kirk really thought America should go to Mars. Fitzgerald might, if Kirk told him to believe it, but Kirk was only out to get the Fitzgerald administration a third term. She wanted to beat Winton R. Wilson at his own game, and to do that she had to show the public that Fitzgerald, not Wilson, was the man who could go to Mars.

It would take an idiot to buy it. How could going to Mars have any effect on a military threat from the Moon or Churchill-Chiang Station?

Fortunately for the politicos, the Great Straight Public consisted almost entirely of idiots. They'd buy it wholesale. Then, whichever of the candidates came out on top next November, the wind of electoral victory would blow Mars away like so much chaff.

Why couldn't the sputzing politicians ever fight over things they really intended to do something about? Like a new sauna for the White House?

"All right, Madame Secretary," Lieza said, feeling tired. "Final offer. Instead of saying nothing, I'll say I don't care. If a reporter asks me what I think of your Mars project, I'll say I don't give a rat's ass one way or the other. If a Wracker on the street asks, I'll say the same thing. It'll be nothing more or less than the truth."

Kirk shook her head again. "Still not enough."

"It'll have to be. Look, Madame Secretary, Mister

President—you called me in here because you think Wrackers listen to me. So if I don't care one way or the other, will any other Wracker? What do you do about something when you don't care? Nothing. Zippo. Exactly what you should want."

President Fitzgerald smiled. "If we can take your word, and I think we can—"

Annabelle Kirk interrupted him. "Mister President, I'm not convinced of the wisdom of believing this woman."

Fitzgerald looked up at the secretary quizzically. "What else can we do? We can't very well torture her, now, can we?"

Kirk pursed her lips.

Lieza grinned at her. *There's nothing you'd like better than to rip off my skin with a pair of hot pincers, is there, you dried-up old squid?*

She saw hate in the secretary of state's eyes, and she knew that she and Kirk understood each other.

Enemies.

She exhaled loudly and half-shrugged. If that was the way the Squid wanted it, that was the way it was. It wouldn't be the first time she'd had to guard her back against a pissed-off Straight.

"Am I free to go?" Lieza asked, directing her question at the President to further antagonize Kirk.

It would be smarter, she knew, to avoid twisting the knife. But she couldn't help it.

Fitzgerald stood, smiling. "Certainly, Mizz Galilei. Agent Dodson will return you to your hotel."

"Oh, good. Dodsie and I are getting to be real pals, ain't we, Dodsie?"

Dodson responded in the same tone of voice. "If you say so, Leezie."

She was beginning to like him despite his unfortunate choice of lifestyle and profession.

Annabelle Kirk's face looked as though it had been carved from limestone. "We may need to see you again, Mizz Galilei. If so, we'll expect less trouble than we encountered this time. But we'll be prepared for more. Do I make myself clear?"

"Like a crystal toilet. Do yourself a favor and get your hormone levels checked, OK?"

The Bastard Child turned away before Kirk could react. Dodson hurried ahead, apparently anxious to get her out of there.

They were still ten feet from the door when it opened and three more men rushed into the Oval Office.

"Mister President," the leader said, puffing. "Sorry to interrupt, but your phone's on lock."

"Of course it is," Kirk snapped. "We wanted it that way. You'd better hope this is a crisis, Hornon."

Lieza recognized the name as that of the national security advisor. The title didn't seem to fit the overweight, wheezing man who had just come in.

"It is," Hornon gasped. "Oh, boy, you're damn right it is. The Brits invaded Concepcion yesterday. Gurkhas, if our information is correct. Our people were captured, and so far radio broadcasts have been deceptively normal, so that's why it's taken us so long to realize what's—"

Kirk cut him off with a shout. "Idiot! Look around you!"

Hornon did so, and his gaze fell on Lieza for the first time. He looked infinitely puzzled.

"Who are you?" he asked. "And why aren't you wearing any shoes?"

"Get her out of here *now*, Dodson," Kirk ordered.

Dodson reached for Lieza's arm but stopped when she raised a warning finger.

The Bastard Child looked back at Fitzgerald and said, "Have a nice day, Mister President, and take a downer or two. Looks like you're gonna need 'em."

Then she walked out of the Oval Office ahead of Agent Dodson, relying on her memory to retrace the path to the helipad. The last thing she heard as she entered the hallway was the voice of the Commander in Chief of the United States Armed Forces asking where the heck Concepcion was, Africa or something?

Lieza smiled as she looked down at the wine-colored carpet of the hallway that led away from the Oval Office. Everything here looked so perfect. The place even *smelled* of plushness and power.

What a comfort to know that it was a sham, that even here, especially here, blessed Chaos reigned.

Her leather jeans felt wonderfully hot, and she walked faster until she could no longer hold back her joy. Then she ran.

5

The Wracker's Creed

Look at you sittin' there
Wonderin' just what's real.
Call up the Devil,
Try to make another deal.
The Devil, he can't help no more,
His calendar's booked up.
And Jesus, He won't speak to you,
Friend, looks like you been stuck.

But hey, don't you feel
Like there's something in the air?
A fission chain reaction
To the bullshit everywhere?
Stop and breathe it in
Until your lungs are good and full.
Then prepare yourself to fight
And cause as much trouble
As humanly possible.

—Bitch Alice
"Cause Trouble," 1964

Friday, December 21, 1979. Washington, D.C.

The destruction of the hotel lobby was nearly complete by the time Lieza made it down from the roof. Slivers and cubes of glass were scattered across the blue carpeting like sunsparkles on water.

Tycho was roaring incoherently and using Bert to demolish everything that was breakable and a good number of things that shouldn't have been. The drummer's torso had far more scratches than the day before, and drops of sweat flew from his hair as he whipped his head back and forth.

A red-jacketed male clerk writhed on the floor several yards away from where Tycho was axing a potted palm. Otherwise, the lobby appeared to be deserted.

That, Lieza thought, was hardly surprising.

She took in the whole scene as soon as the elevator doors opened, and as she stepped out toward the destruction, she wondered if the best course of action might not be to let Tycho keep going until he ran out of steam.

Trouble was, that might take a couple of weeks. His Viking genes had kicked in.

Cherry, Joel, and Fug were standing against the wall to the left of the elevator doors.

"Staying out of the way?" Lieza asked.

"Damn right," Cherry said.

Lieza joined them and pointed at the writhing Jack in the center of the lobby. "What's with him?"

Joel pushed his top hat back off his forehead and said, "Well, you see, Leez dear, that gentleman endeavored to explain to our colleague that breaking windows, chairs, tables, and vases would be unlikely to ensure your safe return. I don't believe, however, that yon tall, blond berserker even knew that the Straight gentleman was there. He simply walked over him on his way to that large planter. Or, rather, to the large planter that used to be there."

Lieza nodded. "And what are all of you doing here when you ought to have taken cover?"

"Trying to make sure the asshole doesn't hurt himself," Cherry answered. "Or to give him first aid if he does." She frowned and looked at the clerk. "Too bad we can't get to Jack. I think he's just got a broken ankle. Maybe a cracked rib or two."

The Jack was still squirming. "As long as he's able to move," Lieza said, "he's OK."

"By the by," Joel said, "if you're wondering why we didn't go after you, it was because Cherry was sure you'd been taken to the White House, and we had no desire to be riddled with bullets for our lack of embossed invitations."

Lieza had guessed as much. But Tycho, knowing he could do nothing, had needed to do *something*, and this was it.

There went this month's album royalties.

She decided to ask the White House to pay for the damage. They would refuse, but the bill would irritate the Squid. That alone might be worth the price of the lobby.

Tycho began whirling in a mad dance, extending Bert so that man and ax became a tornado of demolition.

In its way, Lieza thought, it was a beautiful thing to see. Unfortunately, the whirlwind was spinning back across the littered floor toward the hotel employee.

"Jack's about to get trampled," Cherry observed.

Fug grunted enthusiastically.

Lieza bit her lower lip. This time, without meaning to, Tycho might actually kill an innocent—well, as much an innocent as a Straight ever got—by stomping him into the broken glass. It presented a problem.

"Any suggestions?" she asked the band.

"Purchase some popcorn, perhaps?" Joel asked.

At that moment, Bert flew out of Tycho's hands, arced across the lobby, and caromed off the wall over Fug's head. The ax landed on the floor several feet in front of Lieza.

"Yah-yah!" Fug shouted, his eyes wide with joy.

"A close brush with death always did turn you on," Cherry said.

Lieza raised her left arm to get their attention. "Hey! Now's our chance."

Joel looked at her quizzically. "Our chance to *what*, pray tell?"

"To avoid hiring a new drummer while Teek's in the can for manslaughter," she said, and ran at the bellowing Viking.

The back of Tycho's massive right hand caught her on the ear. She landed on the hotel employee.

"Sputzing hell," she said.

"Aaaaaaahhhhhh," the hotel employee yelled.

As Lieza started to get to her feet, she saw Tycho tackled by the other band members. They hit him low, around the ankles, knees, and thighs, but once he was down he began kicking.

Joel came loose and collided with Lieza, knocking her onto the Jack again.

"Oh, dear," Joel said into Lieza's stomach.

"Scrod it," she said angrily.

"Unnng," the hotel employee groaned.

"You know," Joel said as he stood and stumbled back toward the battle, "if you fall on that gentleman many more times, you may be the one to go to, as you put it, 'the can for manslaughter.'"

Lieza struggled to get up. "As long as he's making noise, he's all right," she said, inadvertently driving her elbow into the Jack's stomach.

"Muahhgg," the man said.

By the time Lieza reached the others, Tycho was thrashing on the floor with a bouncing body attached to three of his limbs.

"Where the skag are the roadies?" Lieza shouted as she grabbed the drummer's left arm and tried to sit on his chest.

"Coffee shop," Cherry gasped. "Took one look at Teek and decided they were hungry."

"We should all be so smart," Lieza said as she grasped Tycho's hair in her left hand.

He looked even worse than during a show. His skin was splotchy, his eyes were rolled back, and his beard was soaked with saliva. His nose was covered with condensation and looked as if it had been knocked slightly out of position.

If he's hurt himself, Lieza thought, *somebody is most definitely going to pay, Madame Secretary.*

She pulled on his hair and yelled. "Teek, it's me! You can knock off the Erik the Red act!"

"Yaarrrgggggghhhh!" Tycho roared.

"I say," Joel said brightly. "We should introduce him to the gentleman with the broken ankle. They should have quite a lot to talk about."

Lieza hit Tycho's head against the carpet. "Come out of it! It's me!"

Tycho's body convulsed, dislodging Cherry and Fug from his legs. Then he began to roll.

Just as she was about to be crushed, Lieza saw Dude, Bazz, and Ellyn approaching. Each was carrying a pitcher of water mixed with crushed ice.

"Jagging great," Lieza said sarcastically, and then all three pitcherfuls hit Tycho in the face.

The drummer roared again and gave a tremendous shake, sending Joel and Lieza tumbling across the floor. Then he was on his feet, breathing heavily and dripping ice water.

He blinked, and Lieza saw that his eyes were no longer rolled back.

"Jesus Fricking-Eddie-Dixon Christ," Tycho bellowed. "That's *cold!*"

Bazz grinned at Dude and Ellyn and raised her empty pitcher high. "What'd I tell you? Just like the sputzin' Three Musketeers. All for one, one for all, save the day, all that horseshit."

"More like the sputzin' Three Stooges," Cherry said. "What if you'd made him mad?"

Lieza's peripheral vision caught a red movement. The Jack on the floor was crawling toward the registration desk.

Tycho squatted beside Lieza and watched the Straight's progress. "Who's that guy?" he asked.

Lieza stood up and brushed bits of potting soil and broken glass from her wet clothes and hair. "That's the guy you nearly killed when you went into berserker mode."

Tycho looked upset. "Damn, I didn't mean to. Hey, listen, Jack, I'm sorry..." He stood and started toward the hotel employee.

The Straight saw him coming, jumped up, and ran. When he reached the registration desk, he dived over it.

"Nothin' wrong with that ankle after all," Cherry observed.

Fug grunted, a little unhappily.

* * *

The stage had been built in 1970 between the statues of Theodore Roosevelt and George S. Patton. Fifteen acres of the surrounding forest had been cut down, and now, in its place, rough-hewn benches rippled away from the stage in concentric arcs. The original benches had been made from the wood of the forest itself, but those had disappeared during the first Memorial Music Festival.

Lieza taped a mike onto her throat and looked out over the empty amphitheater, her breath rising before her like steam from a waiting geyser. A five-acre half-disk of frosted earth separated the stage from the first rank of benches. She tried to imagine it full of jostling, screaming bodies, but it looked too barren, too dead.

Yet she knew that in a few hours it would be transformed, as would the whole island. The benches wouldn't last long this year. The passengers of any airplane, helicopter, or zeppelin passing over the Potomac tonight would see the golden lights of bonfires blazing below, pockets of energy cutting hollows into the night.

By morning, the people and their fires would be gone. The island would be cold again, but it would never return to precisely the state it was in now. Just as it was different now than it had been before last year's concert.

Lieza smiled at the thought and blew on her fingers. She liked coming here. The island's constant transformation appealed to her.

A thing that was perfect, she had read once, could never change. If that were true, then she lived in the most imperfect of worlds.

It was a pain in the ass. It was fun.

Dude was kneeling on the stage in front of her, hook-ing up a sound monitor. "Motherbear," he muttered as he fumbled with a jackplug. "It's too dinking cold to do a show. Everything's gonna sputzin' freeze up."

Lieza nudged him in the ribs with the toe of her boot. "Hey, man, you think Patton's troops were toasty-warm during the march on Moscow? You think Washington's militiamen sunbathed at Valley Forge?"

Dude looked up at her and mock-snarled. "How should I know? I don't watch TV."

Behind Lieza, Tycho hit five rapid-fire rim shots. "Hey, scrodheads, we gonna rehearse or not? I'm freezing my skaggin' jewels off up here."

"Can't be," Bazz yelled from the doorway of the equipment trailer behind the stage. "I already bit 'em off, remember?"

"Perhaps we should purchase him some silver ones," Joel said.

Tycho growled, and Fug joined him, harmonizing.

Ellyn's voice boomed out over the amps. "I need more sound from Cherry and Joel. You first, tall, dark, and fat-rumped."

Cherry thumped on her bass and sang, "I'll bet that trailer's warm inside/You pregnant little shit./You're all nice and cozy/While I'm freezing off my tits."

Lieza laughed. Cherry and Ellyn loved each other like sisters, which meant they also hated each other like sisters. The relationship was a wonderful affirmation of the way the cosmos was structured.

"Oh my, that was vicious," Joel said. He had drunk a pint of ethanol on the way over from the hotel, and now he was lying on his back and staring up at the gray sky. "If we're having a poetry contest, I want a turn:

> There once was a lady named Cherry
> Whose friend, name of Joel, was a fairy.
> She pulled a mean trick
> When she gave him a lick
> The night she said 'Hi; call me Larry.'"

Lieza was surprised. She hadn't known about that particular relationship. Or difficulty. Or whatever.

She glanced sidelong at Cherry, who looked uncharacteristically sullen.

Things weren't right between Cherry and Joel, she realized, and now that Joel had attacked, the subtle chemistry that allowed the band to create The Music might be disrupted.

It would be up to the Bastard Child to reestablish it, but she wasn't sure she could. She was tired from the struggles of last night and this morning, and she'd been counting on the energy of the other band members to boost her strength.

An abnormal silence followed Joel's limerick, surrounding them like a fog. Fug even refrained from grunting.

Lieza sucked in a sharp, cold breath, fully experiencing her fatigue. It'd be skagging great if they blew Patton Day, wouldn't it?

She exhaled explosively, and steam shot out like cannon smoke. There was nothing to do but roll over whatever Red Armies got in the way.

Her half-numb right-hand fingers squeezed the metal strands between the guitar frets, and her left thumb hit the chord. "Okay, jagheads. We got a song to work up. Wrote it last night. I'll start; you pick it up."

"I said I was sorry about that, man," Cherry muttered.

Lieza hit the chord again. "Sound check out, Ell?"

"Yeah."

The Bastard Child hit the chord a third time, then strummed. Electric harmonies, strangely gentle, drifted out to the distant ring of trees and came humming back to her.

She sang:

Mama's gone up to the Moon,
Won't be coming back very soon.
Left me down here all alone,
Feels like this world ain't my home.

A soft, tentative cry from Fug's Stratocaster melded with her chords, and a distant vibration rang in from Tycho's cymbals.

Lieza felt the absence of Cherry and Joel like an empty space in her chest, but she closed her eyes and tried to let The Music fill it:

Mama trained me up to be a whip.
I'll not be tempted by any fragile
*   crystal ship.*
You say my life of rage can never be enough,
But softness just won't do for me;
I've got to play it rough.

She took a deep breath to launch into the chorus, and in that moment she felt rather than heard the presence of the last two band members. The bass line was a heartbeat pumping life to the rest of the body, and the wail of an electric clarinet crackled in her brain with the energy of a tab of acid.

Her left hand struck the guitar strings hard, and the ballad became an anthem:

So piss off with your bleached-cotton love!
My softer nature died on that rock there
*   up above.*
No tie that binds is gonna strap my limbs together.
My life must be defined by freshly oiled
*   ...black leather!*

Blunt Instrument, oblivious to the cold and the emptiness of the amphitheater, blasted into an instrumental bridge with the energy of a nova. The band was a single organism, its components again following its leader, its brain, its soul, its unifying force.

Lieza, in one distant part of her mind, was aware of Cherry joining Joel on his platform. They meshed, reconciling, forgiving.

In that same part of her mind, she danced with Bazz and Dude on top of the trailer behind the stage, reverberated as Tycho struck her taut surface, floated with the fetus in Ellyn's womb.

All tiredness gone, she felt herself transforming so that she became The Music itself. It was like melting into the beautiful mass insanity that was the universe.

No doubt about it. This was one damn fine song she had cranked.

She let it take her.

* * *

When she became fully aware again, she saw fires burning and packed bodies slamming to the beat of "A Song about Flowers." That meant they were about halfway through the set.

She leaped high, screaming her triumph. She vaguely remembered shouting a greeting to the assembled mass, but otherwise she'd been in a trance with The Music for more than three hours.

The crowd screamed in response, sharing her victory.

She didn't have to worry about the rest of the show now. Even though she was out of the trance, the band had built up so much momentum that The Music would burst out Patton-powerful for at least another two hours.

Fug stepped up for a long solo, and Lieza danced across the stage, holding her guitar by its neck and whirling crazily, as Tycho had done with Bert in the hotel lobby.

She paused before the drum platform and leered up at the Viking. Steam was rising from his chest and arms as he pounded. He had seen her dance, and during a sixteenth-of-a-beat rest he managed to throw a drumstick at her. She ducked, and the stick went skittering across the stage and off into the crowd.

Lieza laughed and danced back toward the front of the stage. Fug's solo ended with a knife-edged wail, and Lieza leaned close to Cherry to harmonize the song's final chorus.

They ended with a concussive chord that had to rattle windows across town at the Capitol.

A few thousand members of the audience had brought fireworks, and explosions of red, green, blue, and purple hopped crazily above the dark sea of bodies.

A green flash illuminated the faces of those closest to the stage on Lieza's left, and she saw the square features of Secret Service Agent Zackman. He was wearing mirrored eyeglasses that blazed with the light, and his mouth was set in a thin line.

The flash was gone in an instant, and the crowd was faceless again.

Lieza gestured to Dude to key a spotlight where she'd seen Zackman, but it took the roadie fifteen or twenty seconds to understand what she meant. By the time the light began sweeping over the crowd, the green-eyed apparition had vanished.

She wondered if he'd been there at all.

Even if he had, what could he do to her? If he tried to point a weapon, a hundred Wrackers would swarm over him before he could get off a shot.

The thought didn't comfort her. In the brief instant that she'd seen him, she'd had the inexplicable feeling that he wasn't there to kill her. Not right away, anyway.

He was there to watch her. To wait. Like a snake

remaining perfectly still until the victim inevitably slipped into a moment of vulnerability. . . .

"How's everything so far?" she shouted, and the mob bellowed back its approval.

The light beam swept over the crowd like a brush held in the hand of a gargantuan artist. Lieza saw anonymous faces frozen in cheers, goats roasting over pits of red coals, a brief tableau of violence, another of lovemaking, a man wearing nothing but a headband despite the cold . . .

And a large black man with gray salting his short hair, a copper-colored tooth gleaming from his smile.

Then the light beam passed on, and she couldn't be sure that she hadn't imagined the face.

She felt warm breath on her right ear. "Leez, you okay?"

It was Cherry. Lieza flicked off her mike and looked up at the bassist.

"Dixon," she yelled. "I swear, I saw Dixon."

Cherry's eyebrows knitted in a frown. "You tranced?"

Lieza analyzed herself. She wasn't in The Music. This was realtime.

"It was just for a second," she said.

"Less than that, most likely," Cherry answered, adjusting the tension on one of her bass strings. "You know the Straights bought a ticket for Eddie in '63. Car burned to nothin'. Let's play now, huh?"

Lieza became aware that the crowd was clapping in unison and shouting, "LEE-ZA! LEE-ZA! LEE-ZA!"

She flicked on her mike and faced the mob, raising her arms in salute. The chanting and clapping dissolved into a roar again.

"We're about halfway," the Bastard Child cried, "and this is a good time to remind ourselves of where we came from. I just had a vision."

The crowd shouted back, unintelligibly.

"My vision was of a soldier," Lieza continued. "A man who was with Patton during the march on Moscow. I saw him here tonight, out there with you, where he would want to be. I think he wants us to sing his song."

Before she had finished talking, Fug had switched from the Stratocaster to a battered acoustic and had slipped a bottleneck over two fingers. By the time the crowd screamed their approval, Blunt Instrument had begun playing the slow blues strains of "Goin' up to Moscow."

Throughout the first two verses and choruses, Lieza tried to find the black man in the crowd again. But whatever he had been—spirit or flesh—he was gone, swallowed up in the dark sea.

Lieza couldn't help feeling that he'd been trying to tell her something, to force her into taking a path she couldn't see clearly. To have recognized two specific faces in the mob had to be more than coincidence, particularly since those faces represented such completely opposed forces. Zackman was the epitome of Straight bullshit, while Eddie Dixon—

Without Dixon I wouldn't be up here. None of us would be. We'd have gone on swallowing whatever the Hobnails and Dumbasses gave us. We wouldn't have known any better.

The band had reached the bridge between the two separate sections of "Goin' up to Moscow," and Lieza closed her eyes again as she began singing the verses that had been written after the Third Army had achieved its goal:

> *When Gen'rl George lay dyin',*
> *Commie bullet in his skull— Yeah,*
> *when Gen'rl George lay dyin',*
> *Commie bullet in his skull—*

We heard the news from Berlin,
Heard how Cousin Adolf had been gulled.

We heard about the fire,
Heard 'bout the East and 'bout the West.
Lord, we heard about the fire,
'Bout the East and 'bout the West—
How four million sudden dead folks
Had proven our brains was the best.

Oh Lord, we wracked and ruined—
Brought down a burnin' chunk of sun.
Must be just like the Krauts now,
Lord above, what have we done?

Say now,
Gen'rl George was meaner than Uncle Joe,
But he never woulda chosen hellfire over
Righteous Wrack an' Roll.

As she sang, Lieza thought of Dixon, the simple man from Alabama who had fought the Germans and Russians because he'd believed they should be punished for their murdering. He'd been with Patton's Third Army, one of only a handful of blacks in the March on Moscow, and he'd been wounded three times—twice by the Germans, once by the Russians. But he'd kept on coming back, burning with his fevered sense of justice.

As the Third Army had approached Moscow, Dixon had written the first part of his song, not knowing that he'd write more later. He'd found a guitar and harmonica somewhere and had sung for his buddies. Before long, men up and down the line, black and white alike, had taken up its chant.

They had been up. They had been mad. They had wanted to go get that Stalin son of a bitch.

drops on Berlin and Tokyo had come, and Eddie Dixon had been brought face to face with the fact that in just two quick blows the Allies had killed almost half the number of civilians that the Axis had murdered throughout the entire course of the war.

He had written the second part of the song then, and had been court-martialed.

Under normal circumstances he might have been shot for treason, but two days before his arrest, a CBS reporter had put a microphone in front of him. The world had heard the song, and while a great many civilians in the Allied nations had denounced it, a surprising number had praised it.

The court-martial had then sentenced Private Eddie Dixon to twenty years and had thrown him into a cell in Fort Leavenworth.

But over the next decade, the Wrackers had become a movement, and the Army had become too occupied with putting down rebellions in Russia to bother with a domestic subculture. By 1955 there were millions of Wrackers, and they had begun demonstrating on behalf of Eddie Dixon.

The Army had released him in 1956. He was only one man, after all. If the freaks wanted him free, what the hell. The military had rebellious peasants to worry about.

Yeah, what the hell, Lieza thought as her voice died to a whisper on the last word of the sing. *And if that wreck and fireball outside Montgomery were accidental, I'm a virgin.*

As soon as the song was finished, she looked out over the crowd, trying to see that copper tooth again. But it was gone, and Eddie Dixon was gone, and her mother was gone.

Maybe she herself was gone too and didn't have the brains to figure it out.

Maybe they were all gone, all the Wrackers who thought they meant something, that they made a difference by living as they did. Didn't the Straights always win in the end?

Of course they did. Look at Zackman. He'd been beaten, but only temporarily. Now he was back, probably on the orders of the Squid. No matter how good Tycho was at protecting her, or how good she was at protecting herself, there'd come a time when Zackman, or someone like him, would have an easy shot.

She rubbed her hands on her leathers and glared out at the mob.

I know you're out there. Maybe you're even disguised as a friend. Whatever, Herr Death, you sputzing Straight hero. You'll get me eventually, but I'll make you work for it.

The crowd was chanting and clapping again:

"Skag 'em ALL! Skag 'em ALL! Skag 'em ALL!"

Lieza felt her moment of melancholy wash away in a wave of delicious power that felt like a divine revelation.

She knew now why Dixon had appeared to her, and why she had thought back on what had happened to him.

Immediately after his release from prison, Eddie Dixon had been mobbed by reporters. But he had answered only one question from only one of them, the same CBS reporter who had broadcast his song eleven years before.

"Mister Dixon, there are a lot of people who are still angry with you," the reporter had said. "There are also a lot of people who see you as a hero, as a truly moral man. I'm sure both groups are wondering the same thing: What is Eddie Dixon going to do with his life now?"

The Founder had looked pensive for several long seconds, and then a slow grin had spread across his face. Even on the black and white tapes Lieza had seen, the copper-colored tooth had gleamed.

"Well," Dixon had said slowly, "whether I mean to or not, I 'spec I'll keep on causin' trouble."

That was why he had come to her tonight. That was why the crowd was chanting.

She joined them, as did the rest of Blunt Instrument. She knew exactly what she would do.

The band had three weeks free before the London show on January 11, and the others wouldn't mind if she added a concert date in that open time. Once she told them where and why, they'd love it.

Annabelle Kirk would burst an artery and probably

take part of her rage out on the national security advisor. In fact, she'd probably turn the White House upside-down and shake it.

Fitzgerald, as usual, wouldn't know what was going on.

Winton R. Wilson, though, would get good and pissed.

The Bastard Child looked out over her congregation and blessed them as they chanted their litany.

Firelight licked over the stone features of Teddy Roosevelt and General George S. Patton. Lieza couldn't tell if their expressions were condemning or approving.

It didn't matter. She'd made up her mind.

Blunt Instrument was going to play Concepcion.

6

Never Look a Gift Horse in the Wazoo

Deep in debt with government;
They've pushed until you can't feel.
Take heart, m'friend, it's not the end.
There's always one more deal.

"Do it for us this time,
And we won't forget you—
We'll pay you, you know that we will.
Here are your assignments,
A new gun, some bullets—
We'll give you a house on the hill."

There's no end in refusing them
With their medals and jackboots and drills.
Can it be so bad? Maybe you'll be glad
For that marble house on the hill.

—Lieza Galilei,
"House on the Hill," 1976

Friday, December 21, 1979. Lawrence, Kansas.

Pissant awoke eating carpet that tasted like dried sputum. He didn't think he'd thrown up yet, but he was pretty sure he was going to.

Guts and head churning, he managed to turn onto his left side, and the movement sent jolts of pain from temple to temple. He hoped to hell he'd enjoyed getting this way.

He couldn't open his eyes more than a few millimeters, but it was enough for him to see that he was in a small room with walls of cheap, cracked paneling. The only pieces of furniture were a decrepit desk piled high with papers, a pink plastic chair that had been fire-warped, and a mattress with a wad of dingy blankets in its center.

Gray light blazed through an uncurtained window, but Pissant tried not to look at that. Instead he focused on the mattress and blankets.

If there was a bed, what was he doing on the floor? Especially a floor covered with a thin, dirt-yellow carpet that smelled as if a hundred dogs had barfed on it?

Getting to his hands and knees was such a struggle that he nearly lost consciousness again. The black and red checkerboard that always preceded his blackouts began to form at the edges of his vision, but he was able to keep it from taking over completely by lowering his head and holding his breath for a few seconds.

He knew he should try to get to the toilet, but he didn't know where it was. Even if he had known, he didn't think he could raise his arm high enough to turn the knob of the finger-smudged door next to the desk. Until he felt better, he was trapped in the room.

The mattress would have to do. At least he'd be a little more comfortable when he got sick.

Slowly, concentrating on the individual movements of each limb, he began crawling toward the mattress plateau with its mountain of blankets, imagining himself as an explorer heading toward his lofty goal simply because it was there. The yellow carpet became a desert, and the buzzing and hissing in his brain became a sandstorm.

That wasn't right. If he were heading for a mountaintop, he should be struggling through a blizzard, not a sandstorm.

He *was* cold, but there was no way he could make the yellow carpet become snow. Even when he closed his eyes, the smell was still there, making him think of carcasses broiling under a merciless sun.

For the first time since coming to, he realized that he was painfully dehydrated. His tongue was like a mass of dry fiber, and the roof of his mouth felt like corrugated cardboard.

Something bitter crawled up his throat. At any moment it would burst forth and bring his liver up with it.

The mattress seemed to get farther and farther away, and he wondered what he was doing wrong. Had he forgotten how to crawl?

His remaining brain cells decided that they'd had enough. One by one, they began trooping down a spiral staircase that led to the base of his skull. The line became longer and longer, and as it did so, the cells began trooping faster and faster until the staircase was swept away in a whirlpool of panicked gray matter.

Pissant's elbows gave out, and he fell face forward onto the stinking carpet.

He was still on his knees. His soul drifted away to look at him and decided that his angular body was both hideous and hilarious. With his ass up in the air, his soul informed him, he looked like the Greek letter lambda.

"Lambda," he said, or tried to say. The whooshing sounds in his head made it difficult to tell whether he was articulating properly. "A baryon, null electric charge, can replace a neutron in a nucleus, but then the mess lasts less than a billionth of a second so who really gives a shit anyway..."

A horrific explosion battered his head.

Pissant collapsed and let his momentum roll him onto his back. Looking up through the small hole of clarity in the center of the black and red checkerboard, he saw an acne-scarred young man wearing torn jeans and a stained T-shirt. And who had a rivet in his ear.

"Bud," Pissant said weakly, and felt his stomach lurch.

It was coming now, and it would kill him. That was what happened to drunks who upchucked while lying on their backs. They sputtered, choked, and drowned in their own undigested failures. Hosanna in the highest, Amen.

The next things he was aware of were a cold wind on his right cheek and the eye-stinging sight of snow-covered earth two stories below him. The whiteness had been soiled in a most disgusting fashion.

Standing next to a tree and looking up at him was a small man in a brown suit. Pissant tried to make his eyes focus better so he could see if the man was anyone he knew, but the best he could do left him with the impression that the man's face had been carved from the tree trunk.

Pissant was pulled back inside, and he flopped onto the mattress.

Bud stood over him. "You empty now, Doc? 'Cause if you're not, we need to keep you hangin' out the window. This pit smells bad enough as it is."

Pissant tried to evaluate the condition of his body and found that he felt numb all over. Except for his head, which felt like it was in Topeka.

"I think," he said around an incredibly awful taste, "I'm through for now. I might need to empty my bladder in a little while, but not yet."

Bud shut the window. "Good. It's too sputzin' cold outside, and you're frickin' heavy. I nearly dropped you headfirst into the gnome down there."

The thick fingers of Pissant's right hand plucked weakly at the blanket-mountain. Bud squatted and shook out two of the blankets, letting them drift down over the physicist.

"Gnome?" Pissant croaked as the first blanket settled.

"Yeah. Little dink followed us home. I asked him if he was a friend of yours, but he wouldn't answer. Just ignored me. Far as I know, he's been down there all night. Must have antifreeze in his veins."

Even though it hurt to think, Pissant searched his memory for some clue as to who the wooden-faced man might be. IRS agent? One of Susanne's lawyers? He'd straightened all that out, hadn't he?

He couldn't remember.

Bud went over to the rickety desk, and Pissant's gaze followed. Nestled among the piles of papers were an aluminum coffeepot and two off-white mugs that hadn't been there before. Steam wafted up from the coffeepot's spout. Pissant tried to breathe in the good smell, but the carpet and his own breath overwhelmed it.

"Anyway," Bud went on, "he ain't been botherin' us, and there's no law against voluntarily getting frostbite, so I've been ignoring him, too." The rivet in Bud's left ear glinted at Pissant as the Wracker poured coffee into one of the mugs. "This is what I went to the kitchen for, Doc, but you can't have any until you're well enough to come get it yourself. You've got a royal scrodder of a hangover, and I don't want a mess. More than I've already got, anyway. Sorry about slamming the door, but that's the only way the jackbugged thing'll shut."

Pissant made a grunting noise of derision that nearly split his skull, but he covered up the pain as best he could and said, "You call this a hangover? I've felt twice as bad on days that I taught four classes in a row and sat through two colloquia."

Bud gave Pissant the half-smile that the physicist remembered from the night before. "You're just a regular dynamo, huh, Doc?"

"Bet your pockmarked ass. I can take care of myself. You had no goddamn right to drag me to this dump. I don't know what you've been doing on this floor, but I sure as hell know you haven't been cleaning it up afterward."

The Wracker poured coffee into the other mug, then wrapped his hands around the ceramic cylinder and leaned over to blow on the liquid. Steam shot up and surrounded his face for a few seconds. To Pissant, he looked like a god of heat.

Bud straightened up, holding the mug to his mouth, and sipped tentatively. "Shit's hot," he said absently, and then looked at Pissant again. "Guess I could've left you in the ditch outside the Alumni Center. All your academic pals seemed willing to. As for the smell, I inherited it. This was the only room I found that I could afford. Seventy bucks a month and the privilege of cooking in a communal kitchen that's been redecorated by cockroaches, not to mention whizzing in a john that'd make a cesspool look like a hot tub. Peesh?"

OK, OK, so I'm a foul-tempered old scrodhead, the physicist thought, but he didn't try to work up the energy to say it. If the kid wanted gratitude, he'd dragged the wrong guy home.

Pissant had too many other things to worry about. Getting rid of the horrible taste in his mouth, for instance, was a project that couldn't wait any longer. He stuck out his tongue and pulled it back across his front teeth to get rid of some of the accumulated scum, but it didn't seem to help. The mug of coffee on the desk might, though.

He tried to sit up, and a sledgehammer hit him in the forehead.

"Oh, you're sputzing great," Bud said while Pissant lay moaning. "We oughta go cross-country skiing."

Somewhere in all his pain, Pissant managed to nurture a spark of irritation. "You poured the stuff that did it to me. Any decent bartender would've seen I'd had enough."

Bud laughed, and the sound made Pissant's head throb so badly that he was sure his teeth were going to wiggle loose.

"I was about to cut you off," the Wracker said. "But you must've known it, because you stopped coming back and started swiping drinks from everyone else. I watched you, man. If I hadn't known better, I'd've thought you were a blitzed Wracker who'd crashed the party."

Pissant closed his eyes. "Do me a favor and shut up. Just let me lie here."

"Sure. But in case you forgot, the same dude who hassled you at the bar walked past while you were lying in the snow and said something like, 'My office tomorrow morning, ten-thirty. If you aren't there I'll be forced to call a University Judiciary hearing.' It's close to ten now. Thought you'd want to know."

Pissant squirmed down until his head was under the blankets. Worthing. Goddamn. What had he done this time?

He remembered something about fighting Satan on the

demon's home turf, but it didn't make much sense. Must have been a hallucination, he decided.

Whatever had happened, who cared? He'd heard that University Judiciary threat before, and it had never come to anything. He was a Famous Name, and he was tenured. The only way they could get rid of him would be if he seduced a coed, and he wasn't capable of that. It had been decades since he'd lusted for anything that didn't come in a bottle.

Skag Worthing. Skag 'em all.

Jesus H. Christ, maybe Bud's right. Maybe I might as well be a Wracker.

It was the wrong thought to have, because it made him remember all over again—the baby; the day Susanne had found out and left him; the day he had begun training to go up himself; the day it had ended in destruction and death.

A piece of flying glass had lodged in the right eye of a technician whose name he'd never known, and she'd stumbled around the control room, screaming and bleeding, while he'd dodged struggling bodies trying to reach her. He'd been grateful, actually grateful, for the chance to concentrate on her bloody face so he wouldn't think of the other blood that had boiled away, bloating and bursting its vessels and skin . . .

Ethanol bombs had exploded—one, two, three—and the technician had burned before he could reach her.

Just before her hair had flared, her face had changed into that of the sweet girl of 1955.

No no God don't let her—

ALLY!

"Hey! Doc! What the skag—"

The face crisped to ash. All that was left was the puke-smelling room.

Bud was holding him in a tight hug, pinning his arms. They were standing on the mattress, crammed into the corner like prison escapees hiding from a searchlight.

Pissant felt himself shaking and sweating. His hangover had disappeared and been replaced by something worse.

Once, he would have called it sobriety. But with all of

the warpage his universe had been put through, even that had changed.

Bud squeezed him until his ribs hurt. "It was only the door. Somebody knocking. Understand?"

Still quivering, Pissant tried to nod, but realized that it must look like part of his shaking. After another few seconds, he managed to say, "I understand," but didn't recognize his own voice.

Bud relaxed his grip. "I'll see who it is, all right?"

"Sure," Pissant said. The *s* sound came out in a long, wavering hiss. He was hyperventilating, so he began making a conscious effort to slow his breathing.

Bud turned away, leaving Pissant propped up in the corner, and walked four steps to the door. How was it, Pissant wondered, that the yellow desert had shrunk so much in so short a time?

"Yeah, what is it?" Bud said when he reached the door.

"I must see Professor Daniel Jackson," a monotonal voice said, and Pissant realized that he'd heard it before.

Bud looked back at the physicist. "Should I let him in?"

Pissant's breathing had almost returned to a normal rate, and he was able to say, "I think so."

Bud frowned skeptically, then shrugged and opened the door.

The man who stepped into the room was the wooden-faced gnome who had spent the night standing in the yard. He ignored Bud and walked across the room toward Pissant.

He stopped just as the toes of his shoes touched the mattress. "I still have a message for you, Doctor Jackson. I don't believe you read it last night at the Alumni Center, and my instructions are to ensure that you understand it."

The gnome reached into his coat and withdrew a small white envelope. "Would you like me to read it for you, Doctor Jackson?" he asked.

Pissant sniffed at an odd scent that knifed through the room's stink. It was a smell of utter cleanliness and slickness that reminded him of furniture polish.

He was almost able to laugh. The gnome even *smelled* like wood.

The strange little man's name had to be Pinocchio.

"I asked if you would like me to read this for you," Pinocchio said.

Pissant's throat itched, and he coughed violently. When he was finished, he stared in amazement. Pinocchio hadn't flinched, even though he'd been directly in the path of the foulest mucus-laden breath this side of hell.

Pinocchio opened the envelope. "I assume your answer is in the affirmative," he said.

Bud, who was leaning against the desk and holding his coffee mug again, laughed. It was a sharp, staccato sound. "This frick talks like an answering machine, Doc. Be careful. He may be a murderous attack robot."

Pinocchio didn't seem to hear the Wracker's comments. He withdrew a sheet of paper from the envelope, unfolded it, and read aloud in a voice that seemed even more monotonal than it had before.

"'Dear Professor Jackson: You may have heard of me. My name is Winton Ronald Wilson, and—'"

"Hey, you ain't Wilson," Bud said loudly.

Pissant coughed again and said, "He's right. Wilson's taller, with darker hair, saggier skin."

Pinocchio looked at Pissant with no trace of emotion in his features. "Mister Wilson is my employer. I am merely reading his words. I thought I had made that clear."

"You did," Bud said. "Just jagging you around, Hobnail."

The little man began reading from the paper again. "'My name is Winton Ronald Wilson, and I am deeply concerned for the future welfare of this great nation. For that reason, I campaigned for and won the Whig Party's nomination for President of the United States in 1976, and I intend to follow the same course of action in 1980.

"'That is why I am contacting you. In order to combat the threat posed by the space outposts of the Anglo-Chinese Alliance, my administration will once again make space exploration and exploitation a major goal of this country. I feel it is important to assemble the needed manpower now to ensure that delays in starting our new program will be minimal once I am in office.

"'You, Doctor Jackson, played a major role in this nation's first manned spacecraft program, and I hope you will take this opportunity to play an even more important role in the second. I have read your book, *To the Red World*, and it, along with other factors, has convinced me that we should make the exploration and eventual colonization of the planet Mars a top priority.

"'To begin this project, I would like you to join my personal staff. This would mean leaving your university position, but I am prepared to offer you a salary of seventy-five thousand dollars for the calendar year 1980. Then you will certainly be high on my list of candidates for the position of NOSS director-in-chief.

"'I would like to discuss details with you in person on Friday, December 21, 1979. I am currently staying in Kansas City, but I can arrange to meet you at the Lawrence Municipal Airport. Between ten and eleven in the morning would be best. Kindly make arrangements with my associate, Mister D. Claghorn. Sincerely, Winton R. Wilson.'"

Pinocchio refolded the paper and put it back into the envelope. "I am Mister Claghorn," he said.

"No shit," Bud said.

Pissant thought he saw a muscle at the corner of Pinocchio's left eye twitch. He wondered whether that was how the gnome expressed anger or if he just had a nervous tic.

He didn't give it much thought because of his own physical problems. His neck and shoulders were beginning to hurt horribly from leaning in the corner, and when he shifted his weight to try to relieve the pain, his right ankle folded. He fell down onto the mattress and found himself looking up at the stoic, wooden-faced messenger.

"What shall I tell Mister Wilson?" Pinocchio Claghorn asked.

"How about, 'Go diddle yourself?'" Bud suggested.

Silently, without changing expression, Pinocchio turned and walked swiftly across the room to the Wracker.

"Hey," Pissant said, struggling to get up, "don't get upset."

Bud threw his mugful of coffee in Pinocchio's face. The gnome didn't even slow down.

Pissant couldn't tell exactly what happened next, but it looked as if Pinocchio simply jabbed a finger into Bud's face just under the left cheekbone.

The Wracker's arms jerked, and he fell backward against the desk, knocking the coffeepot and stacks of paper onto the floor. Then his body twisted and pitched sideways, colliding with the warped plastic chair before hitting the carpet face-first.

The gnome turned back toward Pissant. He still had no expression.

Pissant stared at Bud, who was lying, unmoving, in a spreading stain of coffee.

"You've killed him," Pissant whispered, and the scene began to flicker back and forth with that of another Wracker lying on the floor of Mission Control in a smear of red.

* * *

Of course I killed him," the security guard said. "He jagged around with the wrong boy this time."

And then the second wave hit; the guard's gun was ripped from his hand, and he went down under leather and rivets and chains.

* * *

"Unlikely," Pinocchio Claghorn said, grasping Pissant's wrists and pulling him up. "Would you like a ride to the airport now, Professor?"

Pissant smelled coffee and furniture polish as the gnome dragged him over Bud and out of the room.

He began to tremble again. Everyone he had ever loved, no matter how briefly, had died. Everyone he had ever loved, he had killed.

The trembling became convulsive.

But his impotence had spread to his tear ducts, and he could no longer cry.

"I have to go to the bathroom," he told Pinocchio. It was the only substitute he had.

* * *

The interior of Winton R. Wilson's private jet reminded Pissant of the Alumni Center, and Wilson himself looked like a compilation of the worst traits of every rich old alumnus Pissant had ever met.

Even while sitting down, the politician appeared tall and broad shouldered, but the shoulders were enhanced by padding in the plaid sports coat. Wilson's hair was thick and dark, and his skin was a lovely tan color, but wattles hung beneath his jowls. His eyes were tiny, pale blue, and watery.

Wilson smiled a camera-pleasing smile and gestured for Pissant to sit down across from him at a collapsible table. Pissant, whose convulsions had diminished during the fifteen-minute ride to North Lawrence, managed to settle into the plush seat without falling down.

"Awfully good of you to come, Professor Jackson," Wilson said cheerfully. "It's a pleasure and an honor to meet you in person at last."

That, Pissant was certain, had to be a lie. He was hung over, unshaven, wearing rumpled clothes, and stinking. No one coming into contact with him could possibly consider it a pleasure.

He stared at Wilson's perfect-toothed smile for a few seconds and decided that he hated the son of a bitch.

"I was brought here by force," Pissant said in a voice so low it was almost a growl.

Wilson's plastic features instantly changed to an expression of shock, and he looked at Pinocchio Claghorn, who was seated across the cabin. "Dennis! Is this true?"

The gnome's expression remained impassive. "I don't believe so, sir. The professor must have misinterpreted my efforts to help him into the car. He isn't well today, you see, and I felt I should assist him."

Wilson's smile returned, and he turned back toward Pissant. "Dennis is a helpful man," he said smoothly. "I'm sure he didn't mean to offend you."

Pissant wished he hadn't already thrown up. He wanted desperately to ruin Wilson's plaid jacket.

"He killed a friend of mine," Pissant said, not knowing if it was true but enjoying the bitterness of the words.

"Dennis?" Wilson asked mildly.

"A Mister Theodore Albert attacked me while I was attempting to deliver your message to the Professor," Pinocchio said. "I incapacitated him in order to protect myself. He isn't dead, sir."

Pissant cleared his throat and spit across the cabin at Pinocchio, hitting a polished black shoe.

"You're a lying shit," he said. "Bud didn't attack you."

Pinocchio displayed no reaction.

Wilson reached across the table and patted Pissant's hand. Shuddering, feeling as if he'd just been touched by a corpse, Pissant pulled his hand away and pressed himself deeper into the red velour.

The briefest flicker of anger shot through the lines around Wilson's eyes, and then the genial smile was back.

"Please, Doctor Jackson," the politician said soothingly. "You and Dennis had a misunderstanding. Don't let that get in the way of an opportunity to regain the planet Mars."

Pissant felt cold despite the fact that a vent on the floor was directing hot air up his pants legs.

"I never had Mars in the first place," he said, trying to sound bolder than he felt. "So there's no way you can get it back for me, is there?"

Wilson raised an index finger in a teaching gesture. "Ah, but Professor, you almost had Mars. Almost, that is, until that filthy anarchist—"

Pissant stood and shouted. There were no words, only a broken roar. A red heat washed through his skull.

When he was finished, he collapsed into the seat again, feeling as though he'd been beaten with whips.

He was aware that Pinocchio had risen, probably to protect Wilson, and he wondered what the gnome would have done if he had gone for the politician's throat. Weakly, he turned to look at the little man, and he thought he saw a thin spike of steel being returned to a coat pocket.

"Very well, Doctor Jackson," Wilson said. "We won't mention that again. It isn't important now. What's important is that we get America back into space. That's where the future lies. That's where we'll find the lands that the next generation of American pioneers will settle and develop."

Pissant felt an odd sensation in his chest, and after a few moments he realized that he was chuckling. He'd written words awfully similar to Wilson's back in 1965, so it was clear that the Big Whig was merely regurgitating them to win him over. Beyond that, the politician didn't have any idea what he was saying.

"You must've enjoyed my book a great deal, Mister Wilson," Pissant said, still half-chuckling.

Doubt flickered across Wilson's face just as quickly as anger had a few moments earlier.

"Why, yes, Professor," he said enthusiastically. "I did indeed. In fact, it was what gave me the inspiration to create this bold new plan for the future. We'll no longer have to lag behind foreigners—not with your ideas and my ability to execute those ideas."

Pissant had the feeling that "execute" was a more appropriate term for what Wilson would do to ideas than the politician realized.

"Tell me," Pissant said. "Which of my books inspired you in this fashion?"

"Why—your book on Mars, of course."

"I wrote two," Pissant lied. "Which one?"

Wilson's facade began to crumble, and irritation showed through. "I wasn't aware you'd written two. I only came across one."

"Which was—?"

Pinocchio spoke. "It was *To the Red World.*"

Pissant scratched at the stubble on his left cheek. "I didn't know ventriloquism was among your many talents, Wint ol' boy."

Now Wilson was looking grimly at Pissant, all pleasantness gone from his face. "I don't know how we got off on the wrong foot, Doctor Jackson. Perhaps it was your misinterpretation of Dennis's actions. Whatever. I don't care. The fact is that I am deeply concerned about this nation's future, and you are a person with skills I feel should be used to ensure the greatness of that future. You were a vital part of our original space program, and I think you're the man to get it back on its feet again."

Pissant sneered. "You don't give a boar's hind tit about the space program. You're just looking for a political football that you can grab to make an end run around that wimp-ass Fitzgerald."

Wilson's eyes narrowed, and when he spoke, his voice was a low snarl. "Don't you dare say anything like that about me. Ever again. Do I make myself clear?"

Pissant felt Pinocchio standing close beside him. Death was a palpable presence, like cold needles in his neck.

His throat was raw. "I apologize," he said hoarsely. "Mister Claghorn was right about my not feeling well today. It's making me unnecessarily irritable."

As if at the wave of a magic wand, Winton R. Wilson's smile was back. "Of course, Professor. I should've realized. The fact is, I've been so intent on trying to convince you to work with me that I've been an extremely poor host. Dennis, would you get Doctor Jackson a drink, please? Once we've relaxed a bit, we can discuss plans for the future."

Pissant opened his mouth to protest, then closed it. Wilson probably wanted to get him drunk so he'd agree to anything, so he really shouldn't drink—

But he *was* thirsty.

And, hell, maybe he was being entirely too nasty. Jesus H. Christ and His Orchestra, he was being offered two and a half times his university salary, and he was looking the gift horse in the mouth!

But that's not the end that craps on you, is it?

A glass full of gold appeared before him. It smelled like every woman he'd ever wanted, every dream he'd ever had.

It smelled like the beautiful Moon Lady.

It smelled like Mars.

7

Weirdo in a Weird Land

Come out, Herr Professor.
Come on out and play.
Be my proud possessor—
For a night now, anyway.

They say that you can't fake it
With your wife and pure Straight home.
But I caught the look in your pale eyes—
You can't leave me alone.

But who'll catch me?
Baby, who'll catch me
When you're again the Learned One?
Baby's inside me
Deep down inside me
You've had your slummin' fun.

—Bitch Alice,
"The Learned One," 1958

Friday, December 21, 1979. Lawrence, Kansas.

Bud was lying on the mattress with a wad of blankets on his chest. His eyes were closed, but the blankets were moving up and down, so Pissant knew he wasn't dead.

The coffee stains on the floor looked like a Rorschach pattern. Two semicircular brown smears lay on either side of a yellow space shaped like Bud's torso. Pissant lay down on his back in that space and spread-eagled.

"Coffee angels!" he shouted, scissoring his arms and legs.

As a child, he had done this in the pure snow of Nebraska. It was appropriate, he thought, to be doing it now on a stinking rug.

At least he was warm, inside and out. Winton R. Wilson served the best Irish and Kentucky whiskies. (Scotch was out of the question, since it was made in Great Britain.)

Before Pissant was aware of the Wracker's motion, Bud was sitting on his chest and half-choking him with both hands. The fingers were cold on his throat.

"You came back," Bud said. "Why?"

Pissant gazed up at the young man's stringy brown-black hair, pockmarked skin, and angry eyes. He felt almost happy at the thought that he might be killed by this person. It would be just. It would be right.

"Do it," he said in a voice that sounded like a rusted hinge breaking.

Bud relaxed his grip. His expression had changed from anger to puzzlement.

"I mean it," Pissant said, giggling a little. "Do the world a favor."

Bud got off the physicist's chest and sat beside him on the floor. "You're seriously sick, Doc. No shit: you oughta be a Wracker."

Pissant stopped giggling and lay silent, staring up at the translucent plastic light shade that covered a single bulb in the center of the ceiling. A mass of black speckles was outlined inside.

"So many bodies," Pissant murmured. "And who is there to mourn for them?"

"I see you got fixed up with some stuff," Bud said.

Pissant let his head flop to the left so he could see the younger man more clearly. "More than that, Buddy Boy. I got fixed up with more than that."

"Great. Give me some."

Pissant didn't understand. "Come again?"

"This is Patton Day. I need to go into Kansas City tonight, but I don't get paid till the first, and I'm skaggin' flat."

Pissant struggled to rise to a sitting position and fell back three times before Bud helped him up.

"Tell you what," the physicist said once his dizziness had abated slightly. "You're broke and want to celebrate. I've got money, but nothing to celebrate. We can fill each other's needs. Take me with you, and I'll pay both our ways."

Bud looked away for a long moment, chewing on the inside of his cheek. When he turned back toward Pissant, he said, "I only need fuel to get my bug there. If you'll loan me ten, I'll pay you back in two weeks. You owe me that much, Doc. I bring you home to keep you from freezing your goobers off, and I get Hobnailed for my trouble."

Pissant felt like sobbing, but he couldn't tell if the emotion was real or the product of Wilson's booze. "It wasn't my fault," he whined. "I didn't know who Pinocchio was. And I made him bring me back to see if you were all right, didn't I?"

"Who's Pinocchio?"

Pissant searched his pockets for a handkerchief but didn't find one, so he blew his nose on his necktie. He noticed that it wasn't the first time he'd done it.

"That's what I call the guy who punched your card," he said, rubbing the tie on his coat sleeve.

Bud grimaced. "Pinocchio may be an accurate name for what the frick looks like, but it doesn't come close to his personality. Vlad the Impaler, maybe."

Pissant still felt like crying. "Did he hurt you?"

"My face is numb, and my brains feel like they've been run through a blender. That's worth ten, isn't it?"

Pissant sighed. "Sure. Sure, Bud. You don't have to pay it back. I'd really like to go with you, though."

Bud stood and went to the desk, where he shuffled and stacked papers in an apparently random pattern. "No, you wouldn't. Patton Day doesn't mean the same thing to you as it does to us. You couldn't handle it. You'd freak."

Pissant's emotions changed abruptly, as if a liquid in his chest had sloshed from one side to the other. He laughed bitterly. "Goddamn it, look at me. You think anything you dish out would freak *me*?"

The Wracker sat on the edge of the desk and stared at the physicist for what seemed to Pissant to be an awfully long time.

The wet redness appeared in the rivet again, and Pissant looked at the floor to avoid seeing it.

Take me with you, he begged silently. *I've fallen from grace, don't you see? I have to do penance if I'm ever to get back. I have to suffer. I have to bleed. I have to be scourged and wear a crown of thorns. Take me with you.*

Bud made a whistling sound through his teeth, then opened the bottom desk drawer. As he was taking out a tunic of copper mesh and a thin black jacket, he said, "I can't figure you. You ain't Wracker, but you ain't like any Straight I've ever come across. First I thought booze had made you something that wasn't either one, but there's a part of you that's separate from the alcohol. That's what I can't figure out—that skewed part that makes you whatever it is you are. It's something beyond what I said last night about you and that Jack who used to be you."

Pissant closed his eyes and heard shattering glass and his own scream. Tongues of fire licked at his hands.

But when he brought his head up and looked at the window, the panes were whole. He held his hands before his face and saw that they too were undamaged.

Except for the old scars. Thin white lines now.

"You hear that?" he asked Bud. "You OK?"

"Hear what? Why shouldn't I be?"

The whiskey was starting to wear off. Pissant was sure of that because he felt angry. "You're the goddamn prophet. You tell me."

Bud shrugged, took off his coffee-stained T-shirt, and put on the sleeveless tunic. The black jacket went on over that, and then the Wracker picked up the stacks of paper he had just arranged.

Pissant struggled to his feet and stood glaring. He pointed at the papers and demanded, "What's all that crap?"

"Subversive literature," Bud said. "Newsletters, song lyrics, surveys, dirty limericks, and other scrod for the Wracker grapevine. Have a look."

The sheet of paper Bud gave Pissant was labeled "Results of Gator Al's Survey No. 57: The Forty Biggest Skagheads of All Time."

Winton R. Wilson was second, right behind Paul Harvey. Hitler came in fifth, Stalin eighth. The great god Patton himself was twenty-fourth.

Pissant felt a tightness in his abdomen but forced himself to ignore it. He crumpled the paper and spat on the floor. "You'll take this junk with you, but you won't take me, right?"

Bud grinned. It was a weird, lopsided expression, the result of Pinocchio's skill.

Pissant wondered what would happen to him if he backed out on Wilson. Would he get off with just a jab in the face?

"You giving me the ten," Bud asked, "or you coming along so you can pay the pumpman in person?"

Pissant tried to forget about the Big Whig and his wooden henchman. He could worry about them in a day or two, when he had to.

"I'm coming," he said. "But I've got to make a few stops here first. Need to go to my apartment for money. Ought to change my clothes. And I've still got business at the department. What time is it?"

"A little after one. Plenty of time. Don't change, though, Doc. You look wracked enough in that suit that you might fit in."

Pissant felt an unusual exhilaration, a surge of the liquid in his chest.

"Perfect," he said.

This was Patton Day. It was time for some wrack & roll.

* * *

Miracle of miracles, Worthing was still in his office. Pissant could see the Physics Department chairman's shadowy bulk through the frosted glass.

Oh thank you, God. I believe in You. I really do.

"You're three hours late, Jackson," Worthing said when Pissant kicked open the door. "I gave you one last chance. I even came in here on a holiday when I should be home with my family. When you didn't show up, though, I found something else to do. I've written a letter to the University Judiciary."

Pissant clapped his hands to the sides of his head, opened his mouth wide, and screamed in mock horror.

"You can leave," Worthing said, pretending to ignore the scream. "There's nothing for us to talk about. You're ill, and you refuse to get treatment. Over the past ten years, you've nearly ruined the reputation of this department."

Pissant clasped his hands in front of his chest, dropped to his knees, and shuffled across the carpet to the chairman's desk.

"Oh, *please*, Massah Wuhthing," he wailed. "Gimme whan moah chanss. Ah'll be *real* good fum now own, honess' an' truly ah wills."

Worthing looked down at him with an expression that was almost pity. "You sorry bastard. I can hardly believe how thrilled we were when you said you'd come to Kansas. We thought we'd died and gone to heaven. At last, we were going to get a Big Name to draw some grant money. And then you showed up, and we found out how much you drank, how fixated you were on that washout of a space program . . ."

Pissant got to his feet and swiped his left arm across Worthing's desk, knocking books, papers, pens, pencils, and calculators to the floor.

"*I'm* a sorry bastard!" he screamed, climbing on top of the desk. "You sheep's abortion, I *did* things before I was flung into this cesspool! What did *you* ever do besides steal your students' ideas and push your tongue up the Chancellor's rosy little tenure-track?"

Worthing's ruddy complexion paled, and he kicked at the floor, pushing his chair away from the desk.

Pissant felt like God. He unsnapped his slacks, pushed them to his knees, and emptied his bladder upon the retreating Philistine.

Then he pulled up his pants, leapt out of the office, and skipped down the hall, his belt buckle jingling like Christmas bells.

Bud was waiting for him outside the main doors, dancing about like a boxer to stay warm.

"Get everything straightened out?" Bud asked, throwing a mock jab at the physicist's head.

Pissant paused on the sidewalk and turned to look back at the soot-speckled limestone of the physical sciences building. It was sufficiently ugly that he felt no sense of loss.

No, that was wrong. The ugliness had nothing to do with it. He'd used up his lifetime quota of sense-of-loss before ever coming to this dump.

"Didn't get anything straightened out," he said, blowing out steam.

His lips drew back from his teeth.

"Got a few things *wracked* out, though."

The numbness in Bud's face must be wearing off, Pissant thought, because the Wracker's smile looked normal. "Rolled right over the Red Army, Doc?"

Pissant began running down the icy sidewalk toward the parking lot.

"You're skaggin' right about that, sputzer," he called back.

Turning his head threw him off balance, and he fell, hitting the sidewalk on his spine.

He didn't mind. Nothing hurt anymore.

He slid down the hill toward the night.

Toward his penance.

Kansas City, Missouri.

He and Bud smoked joints and drank undiluted ethanol on the forty-mile drive to the city, and by the time they reached the outskirts of the Wrack District, Pissant was convinced that Bud's Volkswagen was talking.

"I am a finely crafted example of superior German engineering," the Volkswagen said smugly as it negotiated a corner.

"Skag you," Pissant snarled.

"Same to you, jewbaiter," Bud said. "You didn't have to come along, y'know."

Pissant sucked at the straw in his plastic bottle of booze, waited a few seconds for the burning sensation to die away, and said, "Not you. Your stupid car."

"I was manufactured in St. Louis, Missouri, in 1964," the Volkswagen said. "However, the design of my alcohol-fueled engine is based on plans that were developed by genetically pure Aryans working in Hamburg in 1938."

Pissant made a fist with his free hand and began pounding on the dashboard.

Bud downshifted. "Help me look for a parking space, and stop punching my car."

"I am a nonliving object and thus experience no discomfort from your attack," the Volkswagen said. "You, however, are a weak American like those who put me together. They could never have imagined how to build me had it not been for documents the United States Army stole from the Reich. Similarly, you, Herr Doktor, could never have put so much as a pop bottle into orbit had it not been for the geniuses your nation kidnapped from the Fatherland."

The car radio began playing the majestic strains of Wagner.

"Jesus H. Goebbels Christ!" Pissant shrieked. "Can we shut off that crap, please?"

Bud turned the bug's steering wheel hard to the right, and the car shot up an incline into a drugstore parking lot.

"What're you talkin' about, Doc?"

"The goddamn radio, what else?"

The parking lot was full, but Bud pulled up behind the drugstore's delivery truck and stopped. After shutting off the engine and headlights, he turned toward Pissant and said, "Radio hasn't worked since I bought the skaggin' thing six years ago."

The Wagner cut off. Pissant didn't think he'd imagined the whole thing, but a broken radio was a broken radio.

"Let's go raise Gen'rl George up from his grave," he said, opening his door.

"Die, decadent Americans," the Volkswagen growled.

"Skag you," Bud said. "Sputzing Kraut hunk of scrod."

Pissant paused for a moment, thinking of asking the Wracker whom he was talking to.

But he already knew madness was contagious, so he stepped out into the evening. The sun had gone down during the drive over from Lawrence, and now the multi-colored lights and fires of Kansas City's Wrack District beckoned him as if they were candle flames and he were a large, inebriated moth.

But even more powerful than the lights, more enticing than the smells of reefer and flesh, was the sound of The Music playing nearby.

The tiny sphere of reason inside him said that this wasn't good, that his mind was straddling a rusty blade as it was.

But he had come for his penance, and he couldn't avoid it now. It was too late for reason, so he pushed it down where it wouldn't bother him.

When he had been in his thirties, in the early 1950s when wrack & roll was just beginning to be heard outside the subculture, he hadn't understood the appeal of The Music. It had been violent and frightening, anarchistic and bloody, precisely the opposite of what he'd always thought of as music.

Then 1955 had captured him, and he had understood. He had understood more than he'd ever wanted to.

Twenty-four years later, here he was.

Slumming again.

All right, then. Let's do it.

Pissant took a deep breath to end his reverie and saw that Bud was letting the air out of the delivery truck's tires.

"Should you be doing that?" Pissant asked.

Bud didn't answer until he'd finished with the last tire. Then he stood up, wiped his hands on his jeans, and nodded toward the drugstore. "Ain't open."

Pissant saw that the store's windows were dark and had security bars locked over them.

He sucked on his straw as Bud retrieved the stack of papers from the bug's back seat, and then they both headed for the sidewalk that separated the parking lot from the street.

After swallowing, Pissant coughed and said, "If they aren't open, why disable the truck? It's not going to run over your Nazimobile if there's nobody to drive it."

Bud tucked his papers under his left armpit, then lit a joint as he stepped onto the sidewalk and began walking down the hill toward the source of The Music. "Wracker reasons. If you have to ask, you'll never know."

The physicist looked up at the violet sky and proclaimed, "Bullshit."

Bud grinned, and red, blue, and green lights reflected off his teeth. "This block is Straight. Wrack District doesn't start until the bottom of the hill. That store bills itself as being open twenty-four hours, seven days a week. They *ought* to be open this holiday, because they're open every other holiday. But they're not, and they've put up window bars that they don't use any other night of the year. That's a direct insult. Besides, what if there was an emergency? Some poor old lady might freak for lack of her Valium tonight."

Pissant started to laugh but was cut off as he stumbled over a crack in the sidewalk. Bud caught his arm and kept him from going down, but several sheets of paper, along with the tiny orange glow of the joint, flew out into traffic and were sucked under the wheels of another Volkswagen.

"Take that, genetically inferior creatures," the bug said as it cruised past.

Bud groaned as he stooped to retrieve the bulk of his papers. "I sure hope you aren't gonna jackbugger my night, Doc. I don't wanna have to babysit you."

When the Wracker stood up again, Pissant belched in his face.

Bud belched back. Pissant's eyes stung, and he sucked at his straw to recover.

"I advise you not to continue this battle," Bud said. "The retaliation would be a hideous thing."

Pissant's straw gurgled at him, and he threw the empty bottle into the street. "It'd have to be, coming from you. As for babysitting me, don't worry your pimply head. I intend to find a young lovely to take care of *me*, thank you very much, dicknose."

Bud said something in reply, but Pissant couldn't understand the words. His own joke about a "young lovely" had centered in his brain like a black hole.

He looked up at the sky again, trying to find the Moon. New Moon had been two days ago, so there should be a thin, waxing crescent.

But there was nothing there, nothing but deep violet clouds.

Where are you? Where are you now, my beautiful Moon Lady?

Spinning around, searching, he called out for her. He got no answer but a curse and a crackle of static.

Finally, he found something round and shining. It was featureless except for the drop of blood in its center.

* * *

The band played in a drained concrete fountain in the center of a roped-off intersection that was a mad, multicolored jumble of firelight, jostling bodies, and roasting animals.

The band called themselves Virgin Howitzer because, the leader explained, they had never been blown off.

They weren't as good as they should have been, but Pissant knew they didn't have to be. The Music was a state of mind, and the Wrackers who coursed in and out of the intersection like corpuscles had their brains so finely tuned that the guitars didn't have to be.

Pissant began to think that his own brain must be tuned in the same way, because he felt his body reveling in The Music. He had the feeling that even his heart was beating in time.

He tried to stay close to Bud, but at the sound of a

firecracker he turned away for an instant. By the time he turned back, the pressing bodies had pushed him far from where he'd been. Even if Bud had been pushed as well, the pockmarked young man was now simply one of a multitude of Wrackers, unrecognizable in the variable light.

The crowd, dancing to The Music, eventually carried Pissant around the square to the opposite side of the fountain. Here he had a clear view of Virgin Howitzer's lead singer, a mohawked, middle-aged man wearing strips of torn cloth.

"This is how my daddy looked the night before D-Day," the singer proclaimed between songs, pointing at his own head. "I was eight. Kraut shell cut him in two."

The band crashed into an atonal song:

> *Daddy, Daddy, Daddy, Daddy—*
> *Please don't go to war.*
> *Daddy, Daddy, Daddy, Daddy—*
> *Don't make Mama whore.*
> *She got no job; she got no skills,*
> *What will she do if you get killed?*
> *She'll go downtown, leave me alone,*
> *She'll have the clap when she gets home.*
> *She'll realize your greatest fear—*
> *Your baby boy will be a queer.*
> *So Daddy, don't shoot Germans anymore.*

Most of the Wrackers in the intersection sang along, but they were locals and had doubtless heard the song many times before. Pissant didn't know it, even though he often listened to the radio late at night when he had a good drunk on and felt like punishing himself. The song wasn't bad for a regional band, he decided, but he didn't think the international groups like Blunt Instrument were in any danger of being usurped.

Pissant immediately wished that he hadn't thought of Blunt Instrument. Dizzy and nauseated, he stumbled toward a curb, hoping to find a less crowded spot in which to throw up. But there were too many bodies between him and the gutter, and he tripped and fell.

Clawing for salvation as he went down, the fingers of his right hand closed around a metal ring. As his shoulders hit the pavement, he thought he heard a scream over the chanting of the crowd.

Weird shadows swarmed above him. Faceless heads blocked out the luminous sky.

His tormentors, preparing to nail him to the cross.

An unseen drop of thick liquid impacted on his lips, and his tongue automatically licked it away. The taste was of molten copper.

Two of the faceless beings bent close. He was grasped under the armpits and dragged across the pavement. The dark line of the boundary rope passed over him.

He felt a pressure in his solar plexus.

No. I don't really want to pay my penance. I don't really want to be nailed up—

He twisted and kicked, made contact with something soft, then wrenched free and fell face down—

—onto the charred body of the technician whose skin crumbled into moondust—

—losing all the breath in his lungs as the huge hex nut on top of the fire hydrant hit his chest. He lay draped there, doubled over painfully, until he was grasped under the armpits again and pulled to his feet.

Flickering orange light showed him the faces of two large, shaggy men and a skinny woman with close-cropped magenta hair. All three were half-naked despite the cold, wearing only paratrooper pants and combat boots. Their faces and torsos had been painted with green and brown camouflage sticks. The woman's nipples were black eyes.

The larger of the two men, the one whose facial features looked Oriental, was pressing a hand against his left ear. Pissant saw blood between two of the fingers.

The woman grabbed Pissant's right wrist and brought his hand up before his face.

The middle finger was curled around a large circle of gold that was linked to a smaller, thinner loop of wire. A wetness glistened on the smaller loop.

"This belongs to my friend Magellan here," the woman said. Even through the noise of the band and the crowd, her thin, high voice pierced into Pissant's eardrums. "You took it from him in a violent fashion. You know what we do to Straights who come in here and hurt us for the skaggin' joy of it?"

Pissant opened his mouth, but he couldn't get enough breath to speak.

"We sacrifice them to the great god Patton while asking Dixon's forgiveness," the uninjured man said in a deep, oddly precise voice that Pissant seemed to feel rather than hear. "But first we let them spend a few hours under one of the porta-johns."

The pain in Pissant's abdomen and chest disappeared, and he felt as though he were reentering a state of grace. Perhaps he wouldn't have to be nailed up after all. Perhaps he could be cleansed with excrement.

The Oriental, a big man with a protruding belly, came a few steps closer and peered at the physicist. Then he looked at the other two and gestured with his blood-smeared hand. "Ain't no Straight. Wino, maybe. Or maybe an old-timer."

"Then why doesn't he say so?" the woman demanded.

"Looks like he's hurt worse'n I am," the bleeding man said. "Maybe he can't say so. Now I think about it, he seemed to be fallin'. Probably an accident. I got another earlobe, anyhow."

The other man and the woman looked at each other skeptically, and then the woman shrugged. "Your ear, Maggie. Up to you, peesh?"

The big man nodded, patted Pissant on the cheek with his bloody hand, and plunged back into the seething organism the intersection had become. Pissant braced himself against the fire hydrant and stood there swaying, his senses overloading.

Virgin Howitzer had finished their song about Daddy, and several Wrackers, naked except for bodypaint, had climbed into the fountain with them. Many of the roasted goats were being ripped apart and eaten. Somebody was shouting a prayer to Eddie Dixon, and somebody else was waving a huge poster of Patton urinating into the Rhine.

"Turn on your radios!" someone screamed. "War!"

"The Krauts sucked!" a huge section of the crowd shouted in unison.

The band's lead singer disengaged himself from a tangle of multicolored limbs and grabbed a microphone. "They certainly did!" he yelled. "And all you had to give them for it was a Hershey bar!"

Fireworks went off—Roman candles, firecrackers, Vesuvius fountains, bottle rockets—and the air was filled with spouts of gold, red, and green.

A woman wearing samurai armor beat at the flaming hair of a man in rubber shorts.

A boy wearing nothing but a necklace of human teeth used chopsticks to drum on the stomach of a pregnant woman in a brass bikini.

A man dressed as Omar Bradley was handing out joints.

Two women in war-surplus wetsuits danced together, tossing a goat's head back and forth.

"Turn on your radios!" someone screamed again. "War!"

Pissant felt a hand on his arm. After what seemed like several minutes, he managed to turn his head away from the reveling square and look down at the skinny woman in camouflage paint. The second man, the one whose voice had been like the mechanical rumble of a tank, was gone.

"You OK?" the woman asked. Her voice was a clear note rising above the cacophony.

Pissant couldn't decide what his answer should be, so instead he said, "Where's your friend?"

The woman shook her head. "Can't hear you," she said, tugging on his arm.

He let her pull him down the sidewalk through a crowd of slamming, gyrating Wrackers. Forty or fifty yards from the fire hydrant, she turned into a narrow alley between two brick buildings.

More Wrackers celebrated here, some smoking, some shooting up, some screwing, but the camouflaged woman moved past them as if they weren't there. Pissant stepped on a couple having intercourse and said "Excuse me," but they only moaned and kept on with what they were doing.

The woman took him up a fire escape, and he had to stop twice to rest before she finally got him into the building through an open third-floor window.

Once inside, Pissant was blind. He turned back toward the window for a moment to assure himself that he could still see, and a bottle rocket exploded outside, scorching his eyes with light.

"This way," the woman's voice said, and Pissant felt her tugging on his arm again. "Down the hall. My room's at the end. You need to lie down for a while, peesh?"

He could see nothing except the brilliant green starbursts etched on his retinas, so he let the woman lead him. The soles of his shoes shuffled across gritty linoleum.

"You're my eyes," he said, his voice sounding surprisingly loud to him now that he was no longer in the packed intersection.

The woman's voice came back to him, softer than before. It sounded like a well-played flute.

"If you're one of the old-timers," she said, "I'll be more than that."

Pissant's mouth and throat felt as though he had eaten steel wool, but he didn't want to stop talking now that the woman could understand him. She was his only contact with the world that lay beyond the starbursts.

Maybe she'd have something to drink in her room.

"I'll be fifty-nine in March," he said.

The woman stopped, and Pissant nearly tripped over her feet. There was the sound of a swollen wooden door being pulled free from a doorjamb, and then Pissant was gently pushed.

He moved forward four steps, expecting to drop into an abyss.

The hands that had been guiding him were gone. He couldn't hear or feel the woman anymore.

He stopped and stretched his arms out in front of him. Empty air. Nothing there but the starbursts.

He didn't know where he was or why he had come there.

No doubt about it: he wasn't drunk enough.

"Where are you?" he asked.

The woman's voice came from several feet behind him. "Gotta borrow a light bulb." He heard her footsteps on the linoleum, going away down the hall.

The noises from the intersection filtered up to him as if he were standing on a precipice high above a pit filled with screaming bodies. At a distance, he decided, there was no difference between the sound of a mob having fun and the sound of a mob being burned and pitchforked.

He felt himself swaying again, but now there was no fire hydrant or camouflaged woman to hold him up.

And now, poor soul, must thy good angel leave thee;
The jaws of hell are open to receive thee.

"What's that?" the woman's voice said close beside him.

He hadn't known that he'd recited the quotation aloud.

Yellow light washed up around him, and the green starbursts began to fade. He saw that he was in a small, windowless room with a floor of curled linoleum tiles and walls of crumbling, unpainted plaster. A pile of moldy-looking pillows dominated one corner.

He looked to his left and saw the camouflaged woman standing next to a black card table. A blue ceramic lamp on the table was the source of the yellow light.

"Were those song lyrics?" the woman asked, going to the door and closing it.

"Sort of," Pissant said, shuffling toward the pillows. He noticed that he was still hanging on to the gold earring, so he shoved it into a pants pocket.

"From the early years? Back when Dixon was in prison?"

Pissant collapsed on the pillows, pressing his face into them. They were damp and smelled like old bread.

He turned onto his right side so that his back was against the cold plaster. The woman was pulling a two-liter plastic bottle from a crumpled paper sack.

"It's from an old play," he said, staring at the bottle and praying that it contained something alcoholic. "I don't know if Dixon knew it or not. Think he would've liked it, though. It was about a man who makes a deal with the Devil and winds up going to hell."

The woman sat down on the pillows with him and held out the bottle. "Sounds like he would've, yeah. You like eth with cherry juice?"

Pissant reached for the bottle with shaking hands. "I like eth with damn near anything," he said. He fumbled frantically at the cap, and when he got it off it rolled across the linoleum as if making an escape.

The stuff tasted like thin cough syrup mixed with turpentine, but to Pissant it was ambrosia. He hadn't had a drink since arriving at the celebration.

"Hey, take it easy," the woman said. "It's too fricking potent to guzzle."

He knew that, but he didn't care. He drank down twelve swallows while taking only one breath, and then the woman took the bottle away from him.

"You're gonna kill yourself," she said. "We need you old-timers alive to remind us of our roots. Of who we are."

Pissant felt giddy from the fast drinking, and he laughed at the woman.

She looked ridiculous. Her hair's magenta dye was sickeningly bright in the yellow light, and the camouflage grease on her face and torso was starting to run. She had pimples underneath the makeup. The black spots on her small breasts were exaggerated to make her nipples look twice as large as they really were.

The woman inside all that mess was looking at him as though he were a demigod. She thought he was one of the original Wrackers, one of Dixon's shell-shocked disciples.

It was pitiful.

His laughter stopped for a few seconds. When it resumed, he was laughing at himself.

Who was *he* to judge this woman?

Ah, but if you don't judge her, you might fall in love with her. And we know where that leads, don't we? Shall history repeat itself yet again?

The woman's expression changed slightly. She was

still smiling at him, but her eyes had become piercing. She knew something wasn't as it was supposed to be.

The goddamn Wrackers were like wild animals, every sputzing one of them. They sensed wrongness like a coyote could smell a man with a gun.

He remembered the farm. He imagined his father stalking this woman, hoping to take her ears in for bounty.

But you couldn't get 'em all, Papa. They were too smart for you. You shot at them, chased them with dogs, set traps for them, poisoned them. And still they survived. The original Wrackers.

It was only as he reached out to touch the woman's right ear that he realized why his mind had made the analogy. Just as his bitter, conservative father had waged a private war against coyotes, he, at the bidding of Winton R. Wilson, was being pitted against the Wrackers.

Wilson might not even know that. But ultimately, it must be so.

Didn't Bud's survey put Wilson near the top of the list of those the Wrackers most despised? And hadn't the Wrackers destroyed the Program in the first place, the Program that—

He laughed harder to smother the thought. He didn't want his mind to return to Dallas. He didn't want to have to live through it all over again.

He had told himself that he would come here for penance, but he had lied. Penance required remembrance, and that was too high a price to pay.

Screw you, Mephistopheles.

He was backing out of the deal he'd made with himself.

Well, why do you think she named me Pissant?

"What's so funny?" the camouflaged woman said, drawing back a little as he touched her ear. Her voice had a strange edge to it that hadn't been there before.

"Nothing, really," he said. "It's just that it seems funny to be alone with a woman. I haven't been for a long time."

Her smile broadened, but her eyes were narrowed in

suspicion. "Nothing funny about one Wracker being with another," she said.

Don't tell her.

Tell her what? That I'm not a Wracker, old-timer or otherwise? How do I know I'm not?

No Wracker would lick out of Winton R. Wilson's bowl, skagbrain.

"I guess not," he said.

The woman's suspicion seemed to diminish a little. "You want to exchange names, or keep it casual?"

He started to tell her to call him Pissant, but then he stopped himself. As long as he was letting her believe in his semiholiness, he might as well compound the sin.

"I'm called Yahweh," he said.

A roar outside made him think for a moment that God was sending an earthquake to punish him for his blasphemy.

"I'm Estella," the woman said, unbuttoning the fly of her paratrooper pants. "I'm a stellar sort of person, you see." She leaned close to him and gently bit his left earlobe.

"Maybe you should take it clean off and give it to your friend Magellan," he said.

The dull odor of the camouflage grease mingled with the scent of her skin. To Pissant, the combination smelled astonishingly like a sweet perfume.

"Maybe I should," she whispered as she removed his glasses.

He wished he could want her.

If wishes were horses, I'd be neck-deep in horseshit.

She pushed her pants down over her hips and guided his left hand to her unpainted thigh. The skin felt cool, smooth, and totally alien.

Pissant closed his eyes and saw the scene as if he were a camera in the ceiling.

It was disgusting.

Not because of her. He had come to realize that her hair and bodypaint suited her. But the creature on the pillows with her...

He tried to pull away, but his back was already against

the wall. The spot on his chest where the fire hydrant's hex nut had struck him throbbed.

He opened his eyes and tried to see through the grease to the woman's face. "How old are you?" he asked weakly. It was the only thing he could think of to say.

"Not old enough to know many originals," she murmured. "I want to know you."

She loosened his tie, unbuttoned his shirt, and kissed her way down to his belt buckle.

He wanted to stop her, but he didn't know how.

"Maybe this would help," she said after a few minutes, and pulled a transistor radio out from under one of the pillows. She turned it on and smiled. The Music playing that instant happened to be one of Bitch Alice's few love songs.

Pissant shut his eyes tight and felt his jaw muscles clenching. Poor timing was the story of his life.

Estella murmured to him, kissed and licked him, but he was somewhere else, watching dreams being crushed.

Later, after she had given up and gone back to the celebration, promising to return after he'd rested, he drank the remainder of the cherry-flavored ethanol. Then he vomited into the paper bag from which Estella had taken the bottle.

Afterward, he lay back on the pillows and listened to the radio. The Music paused for a news break, and he learned that the British had invaded some tiny island in the Caribbean.

Maybe this would be the one. Maybe this time they'd all get crazy enough to end it.

Let it be so, he prayed through the white noise of his dizziness. *Dear Yahweh, let it be so.*

He had a vision of a hundred horses defecating on him.

Outside, the coyotes yipped and howled.

8

Happy New Year
From Kathmandu

Everybody here's a good Caucasian,
All Straight descendants of blond Aryans.
No tainted blood can be found in our veins,
No racial flaws to drive our heirs insane.

If we deigned to speak to yellow or to black,
We'd turn around; they'd stab us in the back.
Give those shits an inch; they'd take
        a hundred miles.
They all want to rule the world through
        nasty guiles.

Say, why don't we all just get rid
        of all the rest?
Our grand achievements prove
        our chromosomes are best.
Why did we fight the war
When Hitler could have
        done the job for us?
Let's make color-coded bullets
And maybe this time there won't be a fuss.

—Lieza Galilei,
   "Kansas Kuntry Klub," 1977

Monday, December 31, 1979. San Jorge, Concepcion.

The Journal of Clifton Bonner:

Blunt Instrument is coming!

I'll see Lieza in the flesh, and maybe I'll get to check out that zipper after all!

Yeah, right. Maybe I'll fly to the Moon and have tea with her mother. Maybe Maria will fall at my feet and beg me to save her from Genghis Khan and his Merry Men.

Anyway, Blunt Instrument *is* coming, according to Bill and my radio.

We were all given red plastic radios for Christmas, but the knobs are taped so that they're permanently tuned to Radio Royal Concepcion and are always turned on. Bill says that any evidence of tape tampering will result in the loss of all ten fingers.

Until yesterday, the programming consisted solely of anti-American diatribes by various high muckamucks in Parliament, with a sprinkling of carping from Peking. For that reason, I kept my radio unplugged except when I heard Bill coming down the hall. Friday afternoon, I barely got it plugged in again before he opened the door, and he gave me a look that told me he'd be forced to shoot me if he actually caught me without the Voice of the Empire in my ears.

But I saw something just under that expression. It may be my imagination, but I think Bill sympathizes with us. Or with me, at least. I could swear that he waits before coming in to be sure I have time to get the plug into the socket.

He doesn't have to worry now, of course. There's still an occasional diatribe, but since yesterday morning Radio Royal Concepcion has been devoting most of its 6:00-A.M.-to-1:00-A.M. airtime to The Music, with an emphasis on Blunt Instrument. (An occasional Bitch Alice or Silverbees song is thrown in for variety.)

On the surface, it doesn't make much sense. Wracker culture is no more kindly disposed to Britain or China than it is to any other government, and some of the lyrics I've heard in just the past hour would be enough to throw Prime Minister Carpenter, bless her cast-iron heart, into a slavering fit.

But if the Brits' objective is to brainwash me and the other captive Americans, this sure beats listening to an M.P. from Brighton bitch about unreasonably high tariffs.

Particularly since Blunt Instrument is coming here to play a New Year's concert tomorrow.

The rumor started a week ago, on Christmas Eve, four days after the invasion.

Bill had already told me that some prominent Americans, most notably the (in)famous Winton R. Wilson, were advocating military action to free us students (and, presumably, Concepcion itself) from the iron claw of British imperialism. This allegation turned out to be true, because when I got my radio on Christmas Day, one of the first things I heard was a tape of Wilson describing what a single submarine-launched nuclear missile could do to the Gurkha command post at the airport. (I got the feeling that all of us whom Wilson wants to save would be among the vaporized in such a situation. But what the hell; it'd be a noble, redwhiteandblue death, eh?)

Not much had been said about what course of action President Fitzgerald might be advocating. My guess is that he's thinking about setting up a commission to study the problem in depth, with an emphasis on "constructive dialogue."

If Fitzgerald wins a third term, I should get home sometime after the turn of the century.

Bill also told me that Blunt Instrument, being opposed to both Hobnailism and Dumbassedness, is coming here to play for everyone—natives, invaders, and captives. At first the Brits refused the band's offer because of the security risks involved, but then they apparently decided that the hype value outweighed that concern.

I didn't believe it at first, but I do now. Radio Royal Concepcion has invested too much energy in advertising the concert for it to be a put-on.

Bill never doubted it. He claims Lieza Galilei is a Brit

at heart. He also insists that he read somewhere that she has a drop or two of Nepalese blood in her.

I've tried to convince him otherwise, but he won't listen to reason. I don't mind too much, because it's good to have someone to talk to. He's been spending twenty or thirty minutes with me three or four times a day.

I wonder if this qualifies as consorting with the enemy. I hope not, because Bill, human wolverine that he is, is just a guy making the best of where God and his genes put him. It's not his fault that he has killer instincts and that the Brits took advantage of them. Hell, if the United States had glommed onto them first, the Gurkhas would've been just as happy kicking ass for us as they are kicking ass for the Brits.

Bill's a chip in the Great Cosmic Craps Game. I told him so a few days ago, and he didn't understand. I tried to explain but decided that I didn't understand either.

"All I mean," I said, "is that you'd fight for the President of the United States just as you do for the Queen of England."

He unsheathed his longknife and, smiling, touched its tip to my throat just above my collarbone.

"I dinna hear you too well, bwah," he said. "Say again, pleez?"

I began humming "God Save the Queen," which pacified him. I didn't bother to tell him about the American verses that fit the same tune.

He sheathed his longknife again and patted me on the cheek. "You a pretty good bwah. Too bad y'bird's a tart."

I looked out the window and drank from the bottle of water he'd brought. Bill's good to me, but I wish he wouldn't talk about Maria.

Three days after the invasion, I got up enough courage to ask him to check on her for me. When he reported back several hours later, he told me that he'd found her in bed with an illustrated copy of the *Kama Sutra* and one of the fourth-floor guards.

I don't think I'd be so bothered by the situation if that book hadn't also been *my* introduction to Maria's talents. A couple of days after I met her, I damn near sprained an ankle because of it.

Bill was nice enough not to say so, but I had the impression that Maria had asked him to join her and her guard for a while. And that he, being a gentleman, had accepted.

Oh, well. It's not like we were in love or anything.

Funny how much more she means to me now that I know she's humping a bunch of midgets from the Himalayas.

Not that I'm surprised. I had a premonition of this on Patton's Eve, when she looked so happy as I was being pummeled by Genghis Khan.

If she wants to screw her guard, fine, that's her business. If she wants to screw Bill, that's still her business. But if she gets it on with Genghis, I'll consider it a direct insult. I'll write her parents and tell them the vile uses to which she's been putting her ten-thousand-dollar mouth.

I ought to be ashamed of myself. You're the only one who matters, Lieza. *Wrackweek* says you're not seeing Stigma Sullivan anymore, so why not me?

I've got to do something to get my mind off Maria.

* * *

I have a psychological block against masturbation, so it's been calisthenics for the past hour. It's dark outside now. There hasn't been any machine-gun fire all day.

The radio's playing Lieza's "Kansas Kuntry Klub," and I doubt that the Gurkha who's D.J.'ing tonight has any idea what the song's about.

Doesn't matter. *I* know what it's about. It's about me. My parents. Maria. Her parents.

We're the result of too much inbreeding. It's only a matter of time before we die out and are replaced by those with more vitality in their genetic makeup.

It's a frightening thought, and there's no greater motivator than fear. That's what Hitler was all about. He was scared shitless that the Jews were smarter and therefore better than he was, so he decided to kill them all and thus cut down on the competition.

That's also what the Ku Klux Klan, the Ivory Rebels,

and Winton R. Wilson are all about—the fear that some-one is better than you are. At thinking, at working, at fighting, at sex.

And when someone is better than you are, there's only one way to get back on top: eliminate the opposition.

So if I want Maria back, I'll have to kill Genghis. Probably Bill too. They obviously give her more pleasure than I ever did, which means they're better than me, which means . . .

The hell of it is that I don't even want her. That's the whole history of the human species, particularly us pale types—we don't really want anything; we just want to be able to take it if we decide we *do* want it.

Of course, I'm not going to kill anybody. Unlike most of the blond-haired, blue-eyed jagoffs on the planet, I rec-ognize my own inferiority and am willing to crawl off into an appropriate dark corner while the more vital races claim what's rightfully theirs.

I wonder if Genghis will get Maria pregnant.

Wouldn't that be some kid—the sweet ass of a beauty queen and the blood lust of a Tasmanian devil. Something like Lieza Galilei.

Enough mental meat-whacking. I'm going to have to cut the last several pages before this thing can be pub-lished. I'm writing for money, not catharsis.

The problem is that, except for the news of Blunt In-strument, not much has been happening. At least not from my viewpoint. The Gurkhas invaded on the twentieth, I wrote my first entry in this account on the twenty-first, and since then every day's been more or less the same. If they'd put us into groups instead of keeping us in our indi-vidual rooms, I could at least write about my fellow cap-tives.

I've been taking a few notes, though. I have written proof that the past ten days haven't been completely homo-geneous:

Saturday, December 22: My face is black and blue. Bill confiscates my peanut jar full of piss. Sniffs it once and then pours it over my head. Now I'm black and blue and smell like a toilet.

Sunday, December 23: Breakfast is a piece of toast and a slice of nearly raw bacon fat. Supper is a bowl of vegetable soup. Bill won't let me take a shower. He tells me Maria is having a great time.

Monday, December 24: Christmas Eve. I sleep late because there's nothing else to do. I have a dream in which I am crushed by blue buttocks the size of the Capitol building. In the afternoon Bill takes me down the hall to the showers, saying I smell bad. Lets me shave with my electric razor. He claims Blunt Instrument is coming here for a concert, but he must be full of it. Supper is a slice of canned turkey. I'm getting hungry. I'll bet Maria is eating well.

Tuesday, December 25: Christmas Day. In the morning Bill gives me half a candy cane, a radio, and a basin full of potatoes. He says I am to peel the potatoes, but he won't give me a knife, a peeler, or anything in which to put the discarded peels. I find a microscope slide in my desk drawer and try to use that. It works better than my fingernails. Radio Royal Concepcion plays a short speech of greeting from the queen, and then the prime minister comes on and tells me that if I'm an American, I'm a bloody thieving coward. Some time after noon, Bill comes in, pours milk into the potato basin, and tells me to mash the potatoes. I tell him they're still raw, but he shrugs and goes away. I have to use my bare hands. In the early evening he returns and takes the basin away. A few hours later he brings me a huge plateful of hot (probably microwaved), exceedingly lumpy mashed potatoes, which I can hardly eat despite my hunger. A small pile of potato peels resides in the center of the room.

Wednesday, December 26: My face looks better. The nose is tender, but less discolored. Maria would still get a good laugh out of it, though. Bill checks on me in the mid-morning but brings no breakfast. I eat the pile of potato peels, picking out the eyes and flicking them under my bed. The radio is horrible, so I unplug it and nervously listen for Bill's footsteps outside my door. I consider escape but realize there's nowhere to go. There are hills and wilderness in the center of the island, but I'd never make it that far north before the Gurkhas caught me and played mumblety-peg on my chest. Even if I did reach the hills, what would I do then? I give up the idea and sleep a lot in the afternoon. I dream of murderous white tubers crawling out from under my bed to strangle me.

Thursday, December 27: Same as Christmas Day, except the potatoes are cooked when I get them. Awfully hot, but easier to peel and mash. My hands are pink and hurting when I finish. Bill again tells me that Blunt Instrument is negotiating with the British government to come play here, but that the military is advising against it. I don't wonder why. Tycho, the drummer, could stomp a platoon of Gurkhas into the ground all by himself if he wanted to. He might need a little help if they were armed. But B.I. isn't really coming, anyway. Lieza would hate the political situation around here. She hates all political situations.

Friday, December 28: I get to go outside for five minutes today to help carry in crates and sacks of food. It's cool weather, partly cloudy. Feels like early spring in Kansas City. Genghis Khan supervises. He sees me and smiles. His teeth look better. When I bend over to pick up a sack of corn meal, he kicks me in the butt, knocking me down. I land on the sack, so I'm not hurt much. Nose gets bumped again, though, and bleeds a little. I imagine Maria looking out her fourth-floor window and laughing her cute little blue tush off. Bill touches my shoulder after I get up. A nice gesture, I guess. When I get back to my room, I take a box of unsharpened pencils out of a desk drawer and break them all into little pieces until those pieces won't break any more.

Saturday, December 29: My nose is swollen again. I'm nuts for something to do, so I spend the whole day reading my anatomy textbook. Bet I could pass the exam now. Bill comes in and sees what I'm doing, and he points at the color plates to show me the best places to stick a longknife into someone you want to kill. He gives me a piece of gum. What a guy. More Blunt Instrument rumors. Winton R. Wilson wants to sink the island. President Fitzgerald says nothing. Secretary of State Kirk says a statement will be forthcoming. Jesus is supposed to come back too, I hear.

Sunday, December 30: Breakfast is corn muffins and brown gravy, the best meal so far. By noon, the radio is playing The Music. Lieza's really coming—in only two days. The details were ironed out yesterday. I hope I'll get to see Maria at the concert, although I don't know what I'll say to her. Not "I miss you." Not if I want her to respect me. As if she still could. Or ever did.

Which brings me up to today. More muffins and gravy for breakfast, and an honest-to-Ghod hamburger on a bun for supper. Our captors are starting to take their psychology seriously. I don't think I need to worry about being brainwashed, though. I appreciate the better food and the chance to see Blunt Instrument, and I've even developed a strange kind of friendship with Bill—but my hatred of Genghis Khan counterbalances all that. I could eat better in Kansas City, and I could probably even get into a Blunt Instrument show sometime. As for Bill, he isn't built like Maria, and he'd probably kill me without shedding a tear if Genghis told him to.

There's a Wracker back in the States, whose name I forget, who sings about "living inside my head." That's where I've been ever since the invasion. I don't think I ever spent much time there before, and I've discovered that it's not a pretty place. All sorts of hates, conceits, jealousies, and lusts slog around in there like muskrats in a swamp.

For example, I've been imagining what it would be like to be a Gurkha. The things I've done in my mind while in that fantasy would out-Gurkha anything Bill's ever done, I'll bet. I'm not so sure about Genghis. He, like me, is a real bastard. That's why I hate him. I almost wish Winton R. Wilson's hypothetical submarine would launch its missile just so Genghis would be blasted to gas.

Another thing I've been doing is arranging those pencil bits into obscene words. Last time Bill came in, he walked right over SMEGMA.

And, of course, I've been spending a lot of time fantasizing about Blunt Instrument's visit. I've been trying not to think about it too much, because I'd rather not go crazy before they actually get here, but it's impossible not to have a few daydreams.

The concert's going to be at the airport down at Point Salines, out in the open air. My assumption is that the Gurkhas will be able to keep us under constant observation there since it's the biggest flat, open area on the island. Bill says the stage will be erected at the end of the runway, and we'll all sit on the grass to hear The Music.

Fantasy Number One: I'm in the first row. Lieza is singing "Hungry for a Lover," and her eyes focus on me. Next thing I know, she's jumped off the stage and is raping me. The Gurkhas are too stunned to do anything about it. When she's finished, she drags me up on stage and announces to the crowd that she's taking me back with her, and anyone who tries to stop her will suffer serious injury. After the show, I get into the plane with her, and she rapes me again.

Fantasy Number Two: Same as Fantasy Number One, except Lieza ravishes me with the help of Cherry Angola, whose legs alone are as long as Maria's whole body.

Oh yeah, almost forgot: An integral part of each of the above fantasies is Maria about five rows back, begging me to forgive her.

So I'm a shit. So what else is new?

Tuesday, January 1, 1980.

It's five minutes to 1:00 A.M. on the first day of the Year of the Holy Dead One Who Was Killed for Not Keeping His Mouth Shut Nineteen Hundred and Eighty. Radio Royal Concepcion is playing Bitch Alice's version of "Tomorrow Is the Day," and I am drunk.

See, good old Bill, the Nepalese Killing Machine, came to visit me at a quarter to twelve, laden with six pints of stout and a fifth of something made in Scotland.

I wonder why he chose to share it with me. Doesn't he have friends among his fellow wolverines? Is he an outcast, as I occasionally was as a child? Or is it that he's on duty and has no one else to drink with? I didn't ask him. Didn't want to upset him. It isn't wise to upset a Gurkha.

He, however, has no qualms about upsetting me, because the first thing he started talking about was Maria. It seems she's developing quite a reputation among his regiment.

I'm beginning to suspect her motives. Suppose she's really a spy sent by our government. Suppose they knew all along that the Gurkhas were going to invade. Suppose she's been pumping her abominable snowmen lovers for information while they've been pumping her.

That's it. She's doing it for Ghod and cuntry.

"She has a great deal of stamina," Bill told me, taking the cap off a stout by prying it with his thumb.

"Isn't this a beautiful island?" I asked.

Bill handed me the open bottle and opened another for himself. "How long you her lover, bwah?"

"You follow baseball?" I asked. "Cricket, maybe?"

His eyes glittered at me. "You want subject change, eh, bwah?"

"You're the boss," I answered, and drank down half the bottle of stout without pausing for breath.

"You broody right about that, mate," he said.

The radio announced the New Year by playing the national anthems of both Great Britain and the Democratic Socialist Republic of China. Bill stood and saluted, suggesting that I do the same. I did, of course. Bill wouldn't be above cutting out the heart of a drinking buddy.

We finished our stouts then, and Bill opened two more. A generous man, he is. Also short.

"Plenty other women," he said. "You get 'em by bushels, eh, bwah?"

"Truckloads," I said.

"How many you got waiting back in Kanassassittee?" he asked.

I took a big chance then by drinking the entire pint of stout before answering him. For some reason it tasted more horrible than the first. I'm not used to the stuff, so it took a while to drain the bottle. Bill could easily have gotten mad and done something disgusting to my body, but he didn't. I think the ale had mellowed him a little.

When I emptied the bottle, I looked Bill in the eye. He was still waiting for an answer.

Hell with it, I thought. *I'm a twenty-three-year-old upper-middle-class adolescent pansy mama's boy. It's time to play hardball with the truth. Face up to it, pilgrim.*

Alcohol makes me feel like the John Wayne of self-analysis.

"Maria," I said loudly, "is the only woman with whom I have ever been intimate."

Bill squinted at me as if he didn't understand my vocabulary.

"I lost my virginity a mere four months ago," I said.

Bill cocked his head. He was sitting crosslegged and looked like a skinny, confused Buddha.

"Ain't never been with no other bird," I yelled.

He stood up, went over to the desk, and turned up the radio.

"You gonna talk loud," he shouted, "need louder Music, too."

He didn't mention Maria again. Nice of him.

I mean, hell, even Bill has enough brains to figure out that if Maria's the only woman I've ever managed to sleep with, I must not be too desirable. Maria has demonstrated a lack of pickiness.

I shouldn't criticize her. Never badmouth anyone who's shown you mercy. Ditto for Bill. I'm probably the only captive on the island, besides my lady love, who got to have a New Year's Eve party.

Anyway, it's not that Maria isn't picky. She's just more willing to train the inept than most women are. She's an angel disguised as a spoiled brat from St. Louis.

In the blare of one of Bitch Alice's prophecies of doom, I drank to the health of angels everywhere.

It strikes me now that Bitch Alice went beyond the angelic. She actually deified herself. No other Wracker got as close to heaven as she did.

Heaven *is* somewhere just beyond the Moon, isn't it? Second star on the right, Straight on till morning?

I have just looked out the window to check. God damn if the Moon isn't full and high, like a divine beacon. The night is clear, and the buildings cast shadows like angular holes in the earth.

My wall calendar says the full Moon isn't until day after tomorrow—pardon me, simply tomorrow. Keep forgetting this is the first day of the new year. Understandable since I'm only an hour into it.

Well, the Moon looks completely full to me. Maybe a thin sliver missing from one side. Bill's longknife.

Will it be in the sky when Lieza lands? I wonder if she'll look up at it and pray to her God-Mother before she begins to sing.

Bill left me the bottle of Something Made in Scotland, warning me not to drink it all. I haven't, but I've been taking pulls from it ever since he left at, oh, 12:20 or so.

"Happy New Year to you from the people of my small nation," he said as he left. "Happy New Year from Kathmandu."

The radio just clicked off into fuzz. The last song they played was Lieza's cover of an old Silverbees number, "Waiting for the Walrus." I have no idea what the lyrics mean, but the way she sings them, they must mean something.

If I were a Wracker, I'd understand. If I weren't a lazy, incompetent brat of a Straight, I might have some idea.

I wonder: If I prayed to the Moon Goddess, could she transform me? Could she take my chromosomes and rearrange the genes so I'd be less of an evolutionary misfit? Could she make me acceptable to her daughter?

Quite a change that would be, I think.

But change is the state of the universe, is it not? That's why I and those like me are going to die out. We do not change; we do not adapt. We only scrod things up.

Still, I'm afraid to pray to the Moon Goddess. What would the Baby Jesus of Mom-and-Dad fame think? Would he get divinely pissed and upchuck his Mother's milk all over me, just as Bill dumped my own urine onto my head?

But surely Jesus knows how badly we'd have screwed

the world by now if it weren't for the Wrackers. Perhaps He (or Mohammed, or Buddha, or Vishnu, or Thor, or Jehovah, or Zeus, or Eddie Dixon) sent them to keep us in line.

We're scared of them. That fear keeps us in check.

Which, it occurs to me, is just the opposite of what I wrote earlier.

Which is it? Do they intimidate us? Or do we destroy them? Are the two mutually exclusive?

I should never have continued with this after getting drunk. I'll probably have to throw the whole goddamn mess away. Some account of the Catastrophic Concepcion Invasion. Some wrackwriter. Some jagoff.

No matter, I tell myself. No matter. Tomorrow is another day. (Where have I heard that before?)

Blunt Instrument is coming!

When Lieza sees me in the crowd of captives, I shall be transformed, and the world shall be transformed with me! Filled with the spirit of Life, I shall rise up to become a driving force in the new order that will take humanity to the stars!

And Maria shall enter a convent named after me!

Fantasy Number Three, take one.

9

The Bastard Child Comes to Paradise

The Greeks were sneaky buggers;
They knew just what to do.
Let the people of Troy defeat themselves
With the things they wished were true.
Built a horse with dreams of wood
And a mane of flowing gold—
The city's cynics claimed it hollow;
The rest believed the tale the Greeks told.

If a wooden horse I give you,
It's cut from your own trees.
The things you used to think were strength
Become your dread disease.
I'll play on your loves, play on your fears
With craftsmanship so fine.
But the wooden horse has eyes of glass—
Your box is made of pine.

—Bitch Alice,
"Wooden Horse," 1966

Tuesday, January 1, 1980. Somewhere over the Caribbean.

The Journal of Clifton Bonner:

Bill didn't have time to know he was dying. I didn't know what had happened to him myself, because he fell over backward. It was only when I tried to lift him that I discovered the back half of his head was gone.

I've thrown up into a paper bag. I don't know what to do with it, so it goes under the seat.

My fantasy was warped in the translation. I'm with my idol—she's here beside me, sleeping—but I'm in no condition to make love to her, and she'd kill me if I tried.

Maria is here too. She sought me out, tried to sit with me. I changed seats. I don't want to kill her.

That's not true. I do want to kill her. That's why I changed seats.

Why do I feel so much hate for her? She hasn't done anything wrong, except screw Genghis Khan. But he's paid for that sin.

I brought this notebook to the airport because I wanted to record my impressions. A first-hand account of Blunt Instrument's Concepcion concert, I thought, would surely sell to one of the wire services.

The concert never happened.

It wasn't that the Gurkhas weren't security-conscious. The wooden stage stood on a wide tarmac apron at the end of the runway, and Blunt Instrument was not to visit any other part of the island. They were to get off the plane, be received by the puppet the Brits had set up as Concepcion's prime minister, play the concert, and leave. The whole thing was supposed to run from nine in the morning to no later than three in the afternoon. I had a feeling that Lieza wouldn't like those restrictions, but the Gurkhas, Bill told me this morning, were firm. If Blunt Instrument wanted to play Concepcion, they'd have to play by the rules.

The Gurkhas began hauling Americans down to the airport at seven-thirty this morning. The two buses had to make six trips from campus to Point Salines, a distance of about three miles. I was in the first group.

They made us sit on the ground, twenty yards from the edge of the tarmac. I made it into the second row. I was only three spaces from the end, though, so I was awfully close to one of the blocks of Gurkhas guarding us.

It was cool weather, and beads of dew gleamed on the grass. I couldn't decide whether to keep my jacket on to keep my arms and torso warm, or to sit on it to keep my pants dry. I wound up trying it both ways, finally giving up and keeping it on. So I'd have a wet butt. So would all the other captives.

It was a long wait. I tried to occupy myself by writing a description of the airport, but there wasn't much to describe. Concrete terminal building and hangars, a single mile-and-a-half-long U.S.-financed runway, black tarmac, wet grass. The Point Salines area is the dullest part of the island. I could just see a little of the city of San Jorge to the north, and green hills. The air was hazy, but the sky directly above me was a clear blue with only a few small white clouds.

I doodled. I drew pictures of electric guitars, atom bomb blasts, and ducks with screwdrivers for bills. I had to do something to keep busy, because if I didn't, I'd jump up and start running around to burn off the energy of anticipation. That wouldn't be a good thing, I knew, because I'd be shot.

The audience area was filled almost an hour before the plane arrived. If Lieza had looked out her window as the jet descended, this is what she would have seen just past the tarmac at the northwest end of the runway:

Two blocks of khaki, maybe two hundred armed Gurkhas in each block. Between those two blocks, a rectangular, multicolored patch of over five hundred Americans. Behind that, perhaps four hundred locals. (The Gurkhas must have carefully selected which natives to invite—I couldn't see them from where I was, but someone behind me murmured that the news from the back row was that all of the locals were either too old to cause trouble or too young to know how.) Behind the islanders were more Gurkhas.

I was at the right edge of the block of captives. (My

right.) I could feel the breath of a hundred human wolverines on my face.

One of those closest to me was Bill. I waved to him as soon as I saw him, but he didn't acknowledge me. He was at attention.

Genghis Khan and other noncoms paced back and forth on the grass between us and the tarmac, occasionally gesturing to a soldier to search one of us. I was searched twice, because Genghis didn't like me.

Past tense.

I don't know where Maria was in the audience, but Pete Whoever, the guy who nearly got me killed with his oily face the day of the invasion, was next to me on my left. His complexion was even worse than before. Didn't get enough sun cooped up in his room, no doubt.

A couple of Gurkhas walked among us after a while, distributing little Union Jacks. We were to wave them and cheer, we were told, from the moment the plane landed to the moment it took off again.

I heard whispered curses over this order. One captive, an administrator, whispered too loud and got his chin nicked with a longknife. After that, no one complained. Some of us even started waving our flags before we heard the plane coming. I certainly did. I had run out of doodling ideas, and I needed something to do.

Several times, we began cheering prematurely at the sight of a distant bird or the sound of someone breathing through his nose.

When it finally came, about nine-forty this morning, it took us by surprise. It was as if the great silver jet had materialized out of the stuff of the sky itself.

The humpbacked thing circled five times before losing enough altitude to lower its gear and come roaring down to the runway.

I waved my Union Jack and shouted. I would've ripped off my shirt to wave if I hadn't had the little flag. I would've yelled even if my mouth had been stuffed with rags. I was close to ecstasy despite my wet, uncomfortable pants. The Gurkhas and the other captives might as well not have been there. All I cared about was that Blunt Instrument had arrived. I was going to see Lieza Galilei. To hell with the traitorous Maria.

The jet rumbled down the runway so fast that for a moment my joy faded at the thought that it wouldn't stop in time. But then its speed dropped abruptly, and I began yelling again. It stopped about thirty yards from the end of the apron, only fifty yards away from us. The noise from the engines was incredible at first but soon tapered off. The smell of burning fuel was heavy in the air.

We were allowed—actually, ordered—to stand up and cheer as the engine noise died away and the Gurkha honor guard escorted the puppet ruler to the plane.

I was tired of waiting, and the following seconds seemed like hours. I felt as I had as a kid when I knew I was going to get a present—but not for a while.

At last, the stairway was rolled up against the side of the plane, and the door opened. Simultaneously, the jet's nose tilted up, and men in coveralls emerged and began unloading crates from the cargo bay.

A lot of crates. Big ones. I hadn't known that Blunt Instrument needed so much equipment. . . .

Maybe, I thought, other supplies were being brought in too.

Genghis Khan walked past, blocking my view for a moment. He was scowling as he went over to one of the other noncoms. They gestured at the plane and exchanged words I couldn't hear over the cheering.

Then, at last:

I saw her.

She stood at the top of the stairs, looking out over us like a goddess come down from Olympus to see how the mortals were doing. Her black hair tangled and twirled in the breeze. Until then I hadn't even realized that the wind was blowing. The stink of jet fuel disappeared, and I smelled nutmeg.

Her blouse was blue satin with two rows of gold buttons. The shiny black leather of her jeans reflected silver highlights from the plane's fuselage.

"I love you!" I must have screamed then. "God, Lieza, I love you to death!"

No one, least of all the Bastard Child, could have heard my words. Good thing, because she'd have considered them juvenile and Straight. So they were. So I am.

She came down the steps slowly, disdainfully. She must have been sneering at the puppet ruler awaiting her at the bottom. The Brits intended to use her as propaganda, but she knows how to turn the tables. She must've been planning something outrageous that would humiliate them as much as her visit was supposedly going to humiliate the U.S.

It's her style. She would've done it, somehow.

The big drummer, the Viking Tycho, came down immediately behind her. I hadn't realized just how big he is until I saw him. He's at least six and a half feet tall, maybe a sixty-inch chest, wild blond hair everywhere. Sunlight flashed off his metal nose.

Next came the lead guitarist, the skinhead called Fug. Then the gorgeous Cherry Angola, who looked like she might be even taller than the Viking, although with only half his bulk. Then a short person wearing what looked like a bishop's miter—Rodstein, the one who can play anything.

He just barely got his head outside before the flash. Some of the Gurkhas were probably watching the cargo being unloaded, but if they saw anything coming, they didn't react quickly enough to prevent it.

Heavenly light.

That's what I thought when the white flash blotted out everything. I had just seen a representative of God emerging from the plane, and then the blaze of pure energy, so what else could it be?

Winton R. Wilson's submarine-launched nuke . . .

("Magnesium grenade," a soldier told me as we were being herded onto the plane. "The afterimage'll go away in a couple of hours. You weren't looking right at it, so you'll be okay. Unlike those Limey gooks.")

Screaming, shouting, gunfire. I dropped and landed on top of someone. My left hand clutched a greasy nose. Pete Whatsis. I let go and rubbed my palm on the grass. Someone else landed on me.

More gunfire, more screaming. The white light in my head began to fade, and I was able to see through the green starbursts that floated in front of my eyes.

The equipment crates had exploded. Scraps of wood were scattered all over the tarmac. Men in dark green fatigues crouched there with the men in coveralls, firing rifles and machine guns into the blocks of Gurkhas. Some of them used the stage for cover. More men in fatigues were running out of the jet's cargo bay.

They were good shots. I saw only one captive killed, and she died because she panicked and ran into the midst of the Gurkhas. A couple of others were wounded. I don't know if any of the islanders were hit.

Bullets must have passed within inches of me. I was right next to some of the Gurkhas.

I don't know why I didn't hide my face, why I didn't curl up into a fetal ball against the damp grass and slimy Pete. Maybe I was too stunned to be scared enough to do that.

I remember thinking I was going to die. The thought wasn't frightening, exactly; merely unpleasant.

One other thought pulsed in neon, joining the magnesium starbursts:

I won't get to hear Blunt Instrument after all.

Even as I was thinking that, I looked up and saw Bill. He was surrounded by his comrades, some screaming and bleeding, some shooting and cursing the Bloody Yankees —but he was simply standing there, looking down at me. His assault rifle dangled from his right hand.

"Get down!" I think I shouted.

Slowly, he sank to his knees. Then he leaned backward as if he were going to shift to a sitting position.

But he kept on going. He ended up on his back, his legs bent under him, staring at the puffs of white that drifted across the Caribbean sky.

I put my hand under his head to lift him up, and my fingers sank in.

I don't remember crawling to him. I don't remember saying anything to him when my face was over his. I don't remember wiping my hand on the grass afterward, although I must have. All I remember is that his expression was one of curiosity, as if something had happened that he would like to try to understand.

And I remember the softness that shouldn't have been where it was.

I crawled back into the midst of the captives and lay face down.

A shriek split the air above me. As I began to look up, a longknife buried itself in the ground three inches from my eyes.

Genghis Khan landed on the other side of it. He was bleeding from his mouth and looking at me as if I had raped his mother.

I thought he was still alive. I was sure he was going to reach for his sword and kill me with it.

God of my mother and father forgive me, I kicked him in the crotch as hard as I could.

His eyes closed then, and the blood coming out of his mouth bubbled. Inexplicably, I wondered if his teeth were still bad.

This was the ravisher of my Maria. A skinny, bleeding corpse. I wanted to hate him but couldn't. Maybe that's why I started hating Maria so much.

I spent the rest of the battle on the ground with Genghis Khan, a longknife piercing the earth between us.

The air stank like the Fourth of July.

* * *

As the Rangers hustled me and two or three hundred others into the jet, I looked back through the green starbursts and saw that the Gurkhas were being wiped out. Those that remained fought like demons, taking out American soldiers right and left, but the Rangers were methodical and efficient. They simply machine-gunned anything khaki.

As my group of captives was being herded onto the plane, I saw a smaller group being taken toward the hangars.

"They'll be taken care of," the soldier at the head of the stairs told me. "As soon as our subs cut off the Limeys' carriers, we'll send in another plane."

I asked him what was wrong with my eyes, and he told me. Then I asked him if we were at war, and he shoved me into the plane, saying something about pinhead civilians holding up the mission's progress.

Inside the plane, other soldiers took our names and "escorted" us to our seats.

"All my stuff's at the dorm," I told my escort, who was half-dragging me toward the back of the cabin.

"Tough shit," he said, pushing me into a left-hand window seat three rows from the rear bulkhead.

They filled the plane from back to front. Despite this attempt at order, however, the cabin was like a Victorian insane asylum. People screamed and cried, laughed and cheered, hugged the soldiers and cursed them. Some were in shock over all the killing, and some wanted window seats so they could see more of it. An odor of damp fabric mingled with that of gunpowder.

I saw Maria being put into a seat about eight rows in front of me. She saw me too, and as soon as her escort turned away, she came to me. Slimy Pete had already been put beside me, but Maria told him to go sit where she had been. He obeyed without saying a word. His nose was bleeding.

"You've got a window seat," Maria said as she settled in beside me. "Lucky you."

I didn't say anything. I just looked at her flawless skin and wished I had brought Genghis Khan's longknife with me as a souvenir.

"You're looking better, Cliffie," she said, grinning. "Last time I saw you, your face was a mess."

"Thanks," I said, gripping my seat's armrests tightly, imagining that each was her throat.

She leaned forward and looked out the window. "This is thrilling," she said. "Honestly, I've never had such a terrifying time in my life as I've had the last week and a half. Those Orientals scare me to death. I don't think I've ever been so happy as when I saw American soldiers come out of those boxes."

I stood up. "Excuse me," I said.

Maria frowned. "You have to go to the bathroom?"

I stared down at her. She didn't *look* like a traitoress. She looked like a soft, squeezable, brainless daddy's girl from St. Louis. As lovably American as baseball and the banjo.

The only hard evidence against her was what Bill had told me. How could I trust *him*?

His expression of mild confusion appeared before me again, floating in the dimming green blob at the center of my vision. After a few moments it was replaced by a Cheshire smile that was a replica of what I had seen on Maria's face when I'd gotten the shit beaten out of me.

"Excuse me," I said again, and at that moment something pinged against the fuselage. Everyone but me screamed and ducked toward the floor. I was too full of hate to think of anything else, even my own survival.

"Everybody strap in!" a soldier near the front of the cabin yelled. "We're gettin' the hell out of here!"

The engines began to warm up. The plane rumbled.

"Oh God, Cliffie, I'm so frightened," Maria said, affecting a sob, and clutched my right hand.

She immediately let go of it.

"Eeewwwww!" she squealed.

A gash on the back of my hand was bleeding. I didn't even know I had it until then, and I still don't know how I got it. Maybe Genghis Khan's longknife did it before burying itself in the ground.

I wondered why I didn't feel any pain. Then I turned over my hand and saw that my palm was smeared with dull red stuff. The color was streaked as if I'd tried to rub it off.

My blood on one side, Bill's on the other.

Until today, my only "blood brother" was Tommy Gunther in fifth grade. We pricked our thumbs with a safety pin and rubbed the tiny red drops together. He moved away before the end of that year, and I haven't seen him since.

Bill was the enemy, but now he's my blood brother more surely than Tommy ever was. The only brain cells of his that will ever leave Concepcion are embedded in my palm's lifeline.

I'm the keeper of his thoughts. I have to trust him.

"Eeewwwww!" Maria squealed again when she saw the red smear on my palm. She apparently didn't remember having Sam's blood on her face.

I put my stained hand on top of her head as if I were a priest giving a blessing.

Her eyes widened, and she tried to pull back. I pressed down harder. The guy in the aisle seat looked away.

"The great Genghis Khan is dead," I intoned.

"What are you talking about?" Maria whined, squirming. "Are you crazy? Let *go* of me, Cliffie!"

"Never again shalt thou lie with thine enemy in most foul degradation and sin," I continued.

"Let *go* of me, you *queer*!"

A soldier at the front of the cabin shouted. "Hey! Pretty Boy! Sit *down*, asshole! We're blastin' offa this coconut factory!"

I pushed past Maria, releasing her head, and past the guy on her right. There was an empty aisle seat in the last row. When I was halfway there, I paused and turned around. Maria was staring after me.

"Slut," I said. But by that time the engine noise was loud enough to drown me out.

The soldier at the front of the cabin shouted at me again. I went on to the empty seat, sat down, buckled the lap belt, and closed my eyes.

I kept them closed for a long time, until the plane was no longer climbing. It was during this period, I think, that the green starbursts finally faded away.

* * *

When I felt the plane level out, I opened my eyes. Standing above me was the Great God Thor.

"You're in my seat, Jack," he said in a voice like thunder. "I was in the head."

The god had wild blond hair and a metal nose.

It was only then that I realized I was sitting with Blunt Instrument. Across the aisle from me were Cherry Angola, Fug, and Joel H. Rodstein IV (wearing a top hat, not a miter). Occupying two of the seats just in front of them were a man and woman I didn't recognize but who were obviously Wrackers.

I turned my head to the right and saw two women. The one in the window seat was a stranger, but the woman next to me was Lieza Galilei.

Her expression as she looked at me was blank except for her eyes. The gray irises flashed lightning bolts.

"Move," the Viking god told me.

My muscles began trembling so that I could hardly get my lap belt unbuckled, and I hated myself for being so slow.

Here I was, next to my greatest fantasy, and all I wanted was to get away.

It was too much. After the starburst, and Bill, and the shooting, and Genghis Khan, and Maria, it was much too much.

The two halves of the belt fell away, and I started to push against the armrests to lift myself up.

A soldier appeared and put a rifle muzzle against Tycho's left cheek.

"Anybody tell you to get up, Paul Bunyan?" the soldier asked.

Tycho's face flushed scarlet.

"It's my fault," I said. I was ashamed of the weakness and hoarseness of my voice. "I'm in the wrong seat."

The soldier didn't even glance at me. "I didn't ask you," he said. "This one's a troublemaker. He's already hurt one of my buddies. We want him where we can keep an eye on him. Now, Paul, you come along up front real nice, and ain't nobody going to suffer extreme injury."

Tycho was wearing a vest with no shirt, and I could see the thick muscles of his arms and shoulders starting to contract. I had a vision of both the soldier's and Tycho's brains splattered all over me, joining Bill's.

I pushed myself to a standing position. "Sergeant, or corporal, or whatever," I said, "this really is my fault."

The soldier still didn't look at me. "Shut up and sit down, kid," he said, "or I'll slam your face against the window right after I take care of Paul here."

All the hate I felt for Maria converted for a second and focused on the soldier.

"Look here, skaghead," I began.

A hand grasped my right arm and jerked me down into the seat. Angrily, I looked to my right—and saw that Lieza Galilei had done it.

"Teek, maybe you better go on up with him," she said. "It'll be easier that way."

The Viking's face blazed crimson. "Since when do we take the sputzing easy way?"

"Since we could get a lot of these fricks killed if we messed around with sojerbwahs who have big guns," she answered. "Us too."

Tycho looked indecisive.

"We'll be all right," Lieza said. "If we need you, we'll yell."

Tycho hesitated for a few more moments, then brushed the rifle out of his way and headed up the aisle toward the front of the cabin.

"That's right, Paul," the soldier shouted after him. "Get your freak ass up there, and I'll come keep you company in a minute."

Then the soldier glared down at me and lowered his rifle until the muzzle touched my nose.

"Now then, Pretty Boy," he said, "what was it you called me?"

I was about to tell him, but Lieza squeezed my forearm. I looked at her, and her expression told me not to do it.

"I don't remember," I told the soldier.

He kept the gun on my nose. "You called me a filthy name. I saved your faggoty little carcass from them gooks, and then you go and call me a filthy name. I risk my neck, I get shot at, I get a sword cut on my arm, and one of the guys I did it for calls me names."

He took the gun away then, spat on me, and went back up the aisle.

"I'm sorry," I called after him, and I really was.

"Sputzing Christ," Lieza muttered.

I looked at her as I wiped the soldier's spittle off my forehead.

"I'm a big fan of yours," I said.

"Jagoff," the woman next to the window said. Lieza nodded.

I felt rotten, but I wasn't sure I deserved to. I'd been through a lot.

"I do the best I can," I said, trying to put some defiance into my voice. I also tried to make it clear that I was speaking only to the woman by the window, not to my idol.

"Whoop-te-do," Lieza said.

There wasn't much I could say then. After all, I'm in love with her. When the woman you love despises you, what can you say that'll make any difference?

But although I couldn't say anything, the voice that had sprung from my mouth the day of the Gurkha invasion could.

"Pretty self-righteous," the alien voice said, "for a woman who offered to bring The Music and brought machine guns instead."

The woman next to the window reached for me, but Lieza stopped her.

"Please," the woman said. "Please, babe, just let me get one hand on his neck. It'll be quick and virtually painless, and no one'll hear."

Lieza gently pushed the woman back into her seat. "Not worth it, Bazz," she said. "He's not skaggin' worth it."

"Perhaps not," the alien voice said. "But at least I haven't betrayed anyone recently."

Christ on a crutch why don't I shut up? This isn't me talking, this can't be me, Lieza, I'm sorry, it's someone else, I don't mean it.

That's what I wanted to say. But my vocal cords wouldn't. They were still under the control of the insane alien.

Lieza Galilei, the Bastard Child, the sweet apex of all my desires, looked at me with eyes that would melt tungsten.

"*I* was betrayed," she said. "I chartered this plane to bring us to Concepcion, and that's all. I didn't know the government made a deal with the airline. I didn't know there were soldiers in the cargo bay."

The alien power said oh dear, my mistake, and went away. I was in control of my voice again.

"I'm sorry," I said.

"That's just what you told that Hobnail."

Something buzzed inside my head. I felt as though my bones had melted and drained out of my body.

"I'm sorry for him too," I said, hearing my words but not knowing their meaning. "I'm just..." I tried to think of a better way to express myself and failed. "...sorry."

Lieza made a noise of disgust. "You sure are, Jack," she said, turning her face away from me.

A voice came over the intercom.

"Welcome to Freedom Airways," it said. "I'm your pilot, Captain Jack Dalton, United States Army Airborne. At this moment, more U.S. Army Rangers and U.S. Navy Marines are landing on Concepcion to take advantage of the effects of the surprise attack which freed you folks. The British blockade fell apart once our subs started chasing them. So don't worry about any friends you had to leave behind; they'll be joining you in a few days.

"We're going to stop off at Puerto Rico to refuel, but after that we'll head back to the good ol' U.S. of A. We'll have a stop to make there, too, to switch planes and organize ourselves, before you can be reunited with your families. You know how the bureaucracy is, folks.

"It's an honor and a privilege to be your pilot. Sorry we can't offer you stewardesses in short skirts, but maybe a swift return to freedom will make up for that. Enjoy the flight!"

"Gonna be sick," the woman Lieza had called Bazz muttered as she pulled a paper bag from a slot under the window.

I should have kept my mouth shut, but I wanted to try to make them like me.

"Maybe I can help," I said, stupidly. "I'm a medical student."

Lieza turned toward me, and I wished I were back on

the grass at the airport looking at Genghis Khan's bloody mouth.

"Big scrodding deal," the Bastard Child said.

I haven't tried to talk to her since, and she certainly hasn't talked to me. I sat here for a long time, wishing I could sleep, before realizing that this notebook was folded and stuck into one of my jacket pockets. When I pulled it out, the little Union Jack fell to the floor. It's still there.

Writing's given me something to do. But then, so did throwing up. When that happened, I had to ask Bazz to hand me a bag. She threw it at me without looking to see if I caught it.

I know I'm a Straight, a Jack, a frick, a worthless piece of scrod. They don't have to rub it in so much.

But oh, Lieza.

Can you believe it? I'm sitting next to her right now, this instant.

She's asleep, looking like a child despite her electric-blue blouse and black leather jeans. It's something about her face—the pale skin, the heavy-lidded eyes, the half-open mouth . . .

Joel H. Rodstein IV just leaned across the aisle and touched my arm.

"Don't," he whispered.

I didn't understand. "Don't what?"

"Don't look at her like that. Don't write poems about her, if that's what you're doing."

"Why not?"

He gazed at me for a long moment, maybe a full minute. A strange little man. He looks like a living, breathing Charlie McCarthy.

"Because, dear sir," he said finally, "later you'll wish you hadn't. You'll see things in her features that will trap and hurt you. Look at me if you must look at anyone. I promise to respond favorably, because I sense that you're not too repulsive for a Straight gentleman."

I told him I was sorry, but that I was tired and wanted to sleep. He smiled and turned away.

Looking at Lieza again.

I see so much, too much, in her deceptively peaceful face.

Bill lying dead. Blood on my hand. (I have to stop writing every few minutes and use a jacket sleeve as a compress for the gash. It's smeared blood onto some of the pages.) Genghis Khan humping my faithless Maria like there was no tomorrow, which, for him, there wasn't. Machine gun fire. The poor, chubby woman who wandered into the Gurkhas and was hit by Ranger bullets . . .

Nothing horribly messy. Just three or four neat little holes in her white blouse.

She was in my anatomy class. Toni. Terri. Tracie. Something like that.

I'm sorry you got killed, ToniTerriTracie. I'm sorry I saw it. I'm sorry I never talked to you.

I'm sorry for everything.

Limited Engagement: The Sorriest Human Ever Conceived.

Staring at Lieza.

Rodstein's right. I already wish I hadn't looked. But I can't seem to do anything else.

Hysterical Perspective III

It's been said that without chaos, life would not exist —or if it did, it would be pretty frickin' boring. If true, then the whirlpool of events immediately following the "liberation" of Concepcion was bursting with life—or, at least, wasn't boring.

It would be difficult to discuss this period without attempting to explain how the personalities involved made the events inevitable. It would be even more difficult to actually go ahead and explain, but what the sputz:

Winton R. Wilson was a scrodhead.

So was Annabelle "the Squid" Kirk.

J.D. Fitzgerald had nothing in his head at all.

Clifton "Hack" Bonner, at first only a bystander, was neurotic and perhaps mildly schizophrenic. He was also a Jack who hated his genetic heritage (who can blame him?) and wanted to atone for the sins of his forefathers and foremothers. Yet he had a mortal fear of martyrdom, and thus he could never decide what to do once he got himself into something—which, ultimately, forced him to act randomly. (This condition used to be known as "being an asshole.")

Daniel P. "Pissant" Jackson also suffered from massive guilt trauma, but for more clearly defined reasons. Unlike Bonner, however, Jackson escaped into alcohol. He refused to shape events, preferring to stay numb and let them shape him. No one seems to have liked Jackson much (except for the legendary Theodore "Gator Al" Albert, who apparently didn't have anything better to do), and for good reason. From all accounts, the worst aspect of Jackson's personality was not that he was an alkie, nor that he was sardonic and cynical, nor that he was cruel to children and dogs. Instead, it seems to have been his excessive fondness for nachos and refried beans.

And Lieza Galilei—well, the Bastard Child was who she was, thank Dixon. She was often bitter, sometimes irrational, inevitably abusive, and generally the epitome of

163

what every Wracker should be. It's true, however, that she had a few psychological difficulties, probably due to the fact that she frequently associated with Straights.

Put all these players into the aforementioned whirlpool, add liberal doses of Blunt Instrument, the Secret Service, Whig goons, and geopolitical thud and blunder, and you have the first week of 1980, heading down the drain toward the Apocalypse, hallelujah, chillun.

—Lorna P.N. Chicago-deSade,
A Brief, Biased History,
pp. 284–85. [Secret Service
photo of Annabelle Kirk in
the shower, p. 286.]

10

The Politics of Peace and Other Non Sequiturs

Chalk line on the sidewalk,
Razor in your hand.
If they don't cross, there'll be no loss
Of blood upon the land.

But there's always some damn Jack
Who wants to take a step too far.
He'll cross that line;
You'll know it's time
For you to go to war.

Then the cowards try to sacrifice
A helpless chimpanzee.
Feed him fresh bananas,
Tell him, "Bonzo, rub that line
And maybe if you're good
We'll set you free."

—Lieza Galilei,
"Bonzo's Blood," 1975

Wednesday, January 2, 1980. Kansas City, Missouri.

The soldiers shoved the members of Blunt Instrument out of the airplane ahead of the medical students. The same

165

soldier who had harassed Tycho pushed Ellyn so hard that she tripped. She would have fallen down the steps if Fug hadn't caught her.

Lieza was no fan of soldiers in general, but she particularly disliked those who bullied pregnant women. She promised herself that she wouldn't pass up the chance to injure this one if it presented itself. He had all the redeeming qualities of Secret Service Agent Zackman and Adolf Eichmann.

They were taken across forty yards of ice-slicked tarmac toward a brightly-lit terminal building. The whole place looked like Kansas City's International Airport, but Lieza couldn't be sure. After the jet had left Puerto Rico, the pilot had given no clues as to where they were going.

Lieza could hear the students behind her, their murmurs making them sound like a herd of lowing cattle. She suppressed a shudder.

As Blunt Instrument entered the building, a dozen of the soldiers took them down a corridor and into a conference room. Then Eichmann and two companions pointed their rifles at Lieza and indicated that she was to leave the room with them. Tycho tried to stop them, and Eichmann hit him in the abdomen with a rifle butt. It had no effect, but Lieza's telling the drummer to back off did.

She was taken down a hallway and pushed into a small room containing only a desk with a visiphone. Eichmann's friends went away then, leaving him in the room with her.

He grinned at Lieza, then swirled his tongue over his lips.

She wondered how much trouble she'd get into if she killed him.

The soldier moaned and winked.

"You're supposed to get a call," he said, "but we're fifteen minutes ahead of schedule. We could do a lot in fifteen minutes, hey, sweet stuff?"

Lieza smiled.

Eichmann leaned his rifle in a corner and came toward her.

"You don't wear a bra, do you?" he said, reaching for her blouse.

Three seconds later, he was on the floor in a fetal position, starting to turn blue.

Lieza stepped over him and picked up his rifle.

"You don't wear a crotch cup, do you?" she said.

Eichmann groped for the pistol case on his hip. Lieza mashed his fingers with the rifle butt.

She moved out of his line of sight, removed the rifle's ammunition clip, and put it on the desk. Then she walked back in front of the soldier, squatted, and forced the gun barrel into his mouth.

"Suck," she said.

Eichmann whimpered.

"I didn't crush your trachea, Jack," Lieza said. "It just felt like it. Suck."

Eichmann sucked.

"Continue sucking," Lieza said, "and simultaneously hum 'The Battle Hymn of the Republic.'"

Eichmann choked.

Lieza pushed the gun barrel in a little farther.

"You're not trying," she said.

Eichmann hummed. His face was purplish now, and drops of sweat fell from his forehead onto the brown carpet. The veins on his neck stood out like long blue balloons.

"You were awfully mean to my friend, weren't you?" Lieza asked.

Eichmann, still sucking and humming, managed to nod his head slightly.

"You were rude to me as well, weren't you?" Lieza asked.

Eichmann continued to suck, hum, and nod.

"Give me one good reason why I should let you live," Lieza said.

The soldier tried to speak, and Lieza pushed the barrel in still farther. It had to be scraping his tonsils by now.

Eichmann gagged, and Lieza considered cramming the barrel down past his vocal cords.

Then she remembered what Bazz had said almost two weeks earlier.

She was torturing him, which was chickenshit.

But what other choice did she have? She couldn't kill him, because that would mess up things even worse than they were already messed up. Neither could she bear the thought of letting him go.

The visiphone on the desk buzzed, making up her mind for her.

"Bang," she said, and pulled the rifle's trigger.

There was a hollow click, but Eichmann was already unconscious. An awful smell filled the room.

She opened the door and dragged him out. The other two soldiers were returning down the hall toward her.

"Sleepy boy," she said, pointing at the limp body. "Poor widdew fewwow."

She stepped back into the room and threw out the rifle before closing the door. Then she went to the desk and hit the visiphone's ANSWER button.

President J.D. Fitzgerald's face, set in Pat Expression Number Two, All Is Well Because of Me, appeared on the monitor.

"Mizz Galilei," he said. "I can't possibly tell you how glad I am that Operation Beautiful Music was a success and that you and your colleagues are all right."

"Get off, dink," Lieza said. "Let me talk to the Squid."

Fitzgerald's image blanked out and was replaced by the face of Annabelle Kirk.

"Keep your mouth shut until the President's finished," Kirk said.

The Squid's face disappeared, and Fitzgerald was back again.

"—was necessary, you understand, because surprise was essential," the President was saying. "My administration avoids the use of force whenever possible, but in this case the lives of innocent Americans were in danger. That outweighs even the risk of war, which, I might add, is negligible because of the humiliation the British would have to expose to the world—"

"Kirk wrote you up some nice cue cards, didn't she, Fitzy?" Lieza asked.

"—at large. Our troops were able to get onto the island and free the hostages with incredible ease, and that's something Prime Minister Carpenter would hate to admit. You see, in order to justify a war, she would have to expose the ineptitude of her most elite fighting force. So please don't feel that we used you, Mizz Galilei. We had to keep you in the dark to ensure our success. Our deal is still valid, and—"

"You might jagging think so, Jack," Lieza began, and then she realized that Fitzgerald wasn't receiving a single word she was saying.

The link was set up so that the Squid could hear her, but Fitzgerald couldn't. A technician was probably even altering the image that Fitzgerald saw so that Lieza would look as if she weren't talking. The secretary of state was still running things, and she was making sure that the President wasn't exposed to the Bastard Child's hostility. Kirk wanted Fitzgerald to believe that he was loved, that everything he touched turned to gold.

"—I hope you'll reconsider actively supporting us in our struggle to reclaim outer space. Again, Miss Galilei, I'm sorry for any inconvenience this has caused you, but I'm sure you'll agree that the lives of those students outweighed any hardship that either you or I had to suffer."

The President smiled broadly. "And just think. It's all over for you now, but I've still got to figure out a way to explain all this to the American public!"

Fitzgerald's face faded away, and Annabelle Kirk's faded in.

"I'll bet you douche with kerosene," Lieza said.

The Squid nodded. "Keep it up. As if I needed another reason to send you to Siberia."

"For all I know, that's where I am now. The glory boys wouldn't tell us anything."

Kirk turned her head briefly and whispered to someone off-camera. When she turned back, she said, "You're at the Kansas City airport, which I assume you'd recognize even at four A.M. We've temporarily annexed the building you're in. The rescued students will be put on another plane, which will bring them to Washington. You and your band, of course, won't be making that leg of the trip. You have a farm only a hundred miles from there, correct?"

Lieza sat down in the room's only chair and glared at the smug face in the monitor.

The Squid laughed. "You didn't really think the ownership of that land was untraceable, did you?"

"Not really," Lieza said. "My mother just wanted a place where she could have some privacy once in a while, and I want the same thing. That used to be a citizen's right, or so I've heard."

"You shouldn't have gotten on my bad side," Kirk said.

Lieza picked up the ammunition clip from the desk and began removing the bullets.

"Look, Jackie," she said, "it may make you feel better to lecture me, but it's not getting us anywhere. I want out of here, and I want all of my equipment back. The sojerbwahs wouldn't let us take any of it off the plane. We were shoved in here like prisoners."

Kirk's expression became grimmer. "Your property will be returned, but not until I've finished with you. I didn't call you just so the President could feel better—"

"The invasion was your idea, wasn't it?" Lieza said, throwing a cartridge at the monitor. It ricocheted off the plastiglass without leaving a mark.

"It was a rescue mission," the secretary of state said. "And yes, the President gave the order to commence Operation Beautiful Music at my suggestion. I confess I rather enjoyed the thought of you being hoist with your own petard, Mizz Galilei."

Lieza threw the rest of the bullets, and they rattled against the monitor like hailstones against concrete.

"Perhaps I should state my business before you damage something," the Squid said. "The President wants you to reconsider your position on our Mars project, and I think it would be in your best interest to do so."

"Or what? You'll send your SS boyfriend Zackman after me?"

The Squid smiled thinly. "It's come to our attention that Winton Wilson has hired a scientist from the old NOSS manned space program to serve as a symbol for his campaign. We're afraid that the public will be misled by this man, who is in fact nothing more than an opportunistic alcoholic. As a Wracker, and as the daughter of Alice Pendleton, you should have an interest in exposing the sham."

Lieza leaned back in the chair and rubbed her forehead with her fingertips. "In so doing, of course, I'd be saying that Fitzgerald, not Wilson, was the man for the stars."

"Not directly, if you don't want to. Revealing Wilson's fraudulent schemes for what they are should be enough."

Lieza stood and headed for the door. "I've had enough of you Straights," she said. "You're all scrod. And your little let's-go-to-Mars facade isn't gonna last much longer, because Iron-Panties Carpenter is gonna blow it apart. If you really think the Brits'll let you get away with what you just did, you don't know 'em like I do."

"The name of the so-called scientist Wilson has hired," the Squid's voice said, "is Daniel P. Jackson."

Lieza froze with her fingertips touching the doorknob
. . . and remembered watching television that day in the summer of 1967. She remembered how her mother's bandmates had tried to keep her from seeing it, and how strangely they had acted when the film reports from NOSS headquarters showed the destruction of Mission Control.

Daniel P. Jackson . . .

For a fraction of a second, a man's face had appeared on the screen. A narrow face with a big nose and thick glasses, babbling about somebody whose blood had boiled . . .

She remembered her final, horrible realization of what had happened.

I'll get him for you, mama. Don't worry, I'll get him.

Lieza looked back over her shoulder at the monitor.

"I'll have a look," she said. "If he disgusts me enough, say half as much as you do, maybe I can get worked up enough to do a protest song. No promises. I'll just have to see. This is assuming, of course, that the Brits don't nuke us in the next day or two."

The Squid's smile was like a thin red tattoo. "You have a week to think about it," she said. "And don't worry about the Anglo-Chinese Alliance. One little island doesn't mean that much to them. They were flexing their muscles, and we gave them a minor cramp." The monitor went gray.

Lieza left the room. She felt her lack of sleep as if it were a slab of lead on her back, but she felt her hate even more strongly.

Part of it was hate for the Squid, but as she remembered the pain she had felt when she was ten, she knew that she hated the NOSS man with the big nose and glasses even more.

Daniel P. Jackson . . .

Ultimately, he was responsible. He had been the bigshot in charge of the *Conquistador 18* mission. He had been the one who had killed her mother.

And he was still alive.

The three soldiers were just outside the door. Eichmann was sitting on the floor with his head in his hands. He stank.

"I'll escort you back to the lounge, ma'am," one of the two standing soldiers said.

"Watch her knees," Eichmann said in a shrill voice. "She fights dirty."

Lieza patted him on the head as she passed by. "Life sucks," she told him, "and then you die."

The secret, she thought as she headed back toward her friends, was to make Life pay for it first.

* * *

As Lieza entered the room, she saw that a ring of soldiers armed with assault rifles surrounded her bandmates. Several of the soldiers were tapping their trigger guards with their index fingers.

Tycho was on his back on the floor, muttering. His eyes were closed, and Lieza almost had the impression that he was chanting a mantra. What kept this impression from solidifying was the fact that Cherry, Ellyn, Bazz, and Fug had his legs pinned to the floor, while Joel and Dude held down his arms.

"I'm back," Lieza said. "You can let him up."

"No, they can't," one of the soldiers said. "If he moves a muscle, we'll blow him apart."

Cherry smiled up at Lieza. "One of them poked a rifle at him, and he bent it. Among other things."

"Dreadful sin," Lieza said, sitting down on the floor beside them. "How you doin', Teek?"

The Viking's eyes shot open. "My nose," he said, half-growling. "One of those fricks made a grab for my nose. Said he wanted to hock it."

Joel chuckled. "I say, Teek old boy, how are his fingers digesting, anyway? Might we bring you an antacid?"

Lieza grinned and ruffled the drummer's wild hair. "No wonder the sojerbwahs are ticked," she said. "You're not supposed to *bite*."

A chinless, waxy-faced man wearing a uniform with captain's bars entered the room and pushed his way in between two of the soldiers. He looked down at Lieza and sneered.

"Get out of here, bitch," he said.

"No, no, that was her mother," Joel said, making a cross in the air. "She's the Bastard Child. She speaks for us before the Mother, and before Eddie Dixon, the Great Father Who Has Gone On, Shoo-Wop."

The captain ignored him. "And take your pack of freaks with you. Got one of my men near bleeding to death with no goddamn trigger finger."

Lieza clicked her tongue in mock concern. "Can't shoot anybody, huh? What a jagging shame."

"Don't get smart, bitch. Just leave. And if that big fucker causes any more trouble, I'll say to hell with my orders and give my men permission to turn him into hamburger."

"Where are our things?" Lieza demanded.

"Shut up and move, fishstink."

"Oh my," Joel whispered as they let Tycho up. "I fear there may be retaliation for that, yes?" He looked hopefully at Lieza.

She shrugged.

"Perhaps in the next life, then," Joel said, sighing.

As the soldiers "escorted" them out of the room, Lieza grasped Tycho's right arm around the biceps with both hands. The muscle was knotted, and her fingers couldn't meet.

She looked up at his face, which was twisted into a snarl. His nose was askew.

"Don't do anything," she said. "It isn't worth it."

The Viking growled. "Don't worry. Got to piss too bad to think about anything else."

"Count your blessings," Ellyn said. "At least you don't have a skaggin' baby pressing down on you."

Cherry whistled derisively and said, "Don't try for sympathy yet, sweetmeat. You aren't that far along."

"Maybe not, but this is an active kid. She's doing calisthenics. Slam dancing, gymnastics."

"I feel responsible," Dude said.

"You *are*," Lieza reminded him.

The hallway opened into a circular waiting area at least sixty yards in diameter. The captain and his men were taking Blunt Instrument toward a bank of glass doors directly across the circle.

The students who had been brought from Concepcion were twenty yards to Lieza's left, packed behind a cordon of soldiers who were keeping them well away from the doors. Some of the students shouted and surged forward when they saw Blunt Instrument, but they were held back by the soldiers, and their voices were drowned out by a man in a beige three-piece suit who was giving orders through a bullhorn.

"Please cooperate with the hosts and hostesses who are circulating among you," the man in the suit was shouting. "We must have your correct names, addresses, and Social Security numbers while another plane is prepared for us. Then we can continue to our next stop—Washington, D.C., and a hero's welcome!"

Lieza stopped walking, and the rest of the band stopped too.

"Get moving!" the captain yelled.

"Get stuffed," Lieza said absently. Her attention was focused on the scene going on behind the cordon.

The students had supposedly been rescued and returned to freedom. But the crowding, the "hosts and hostesses" in their look-alike blue jackets, and the taking of names and numbers all seemed to suggest that the "rescued" Americans were being readied for a trip to a concentration camp.

Most of the students looked exhausted, but there were twenty or thirty who were bouncing like excited puppies. Now that the man in the three-piece suit had stopped shouting through his bullhorn, Lieza could hear some happy babbling about "Limey gooks" and "retaliatory strikes."

There were also one or two shouts demanding to know where they were, but the "hosts and hostesses" weren't responding.

Lieza, seeing an opportunity to cause trouble, took a deep breath and yelled, "You're in Kansas City!"

The babble ceased abruptly. The man in the three-piece suit looked across the huge room and made a frantic gesture, indicating that Lieza and her band should be gotten out of there.

"This is the Kansas City International Airport!" Lieza shouted. "Anybody live in the area? Want a ride home?"

The captain started for her, then paused and glared at one of his men. "Shut her up, soldier," he said.

The soldier, with an expression of misery on his face, stepped toward her. Tycho backhanded him so that he collided with the captain, and both went down.

The other soldiers raised their rifles, and Lieza had a sick feeling that she might have gone too far. She started for the glass doors again.

As she did so, the captain, bleeding from his nostrils, scrambled to his feet and screamed, "Fire! Fire!"

The soldiers flicked off their safeties.

"Oh, dear," Joel said at Lieza's elbow.

"Run!" Lieza cried, and at that moment the man in the

beige suit scurried in front of her, forcing her to stop.

"No, no, no," he whisper-shouted at the captain. "Not in front of the hostages, that is, the former hostages. What are you trying to do, ruin the press we're going to get out of this?"

The captain, a trickle of blood curving down past the left corner of his mouth, looked indecisive for a moment. Then, grudgingly, he muttered, "Hold your fire."

The man in the suit leaned toward the captain and whispered, "You can take them somewhere else if you like."

The captain's face seemed to brighten with a heavenly glow.

Lieza started for the doors again, but the captain stepped in front of her.

"You'll get out," he murmured, smiling. "But slowly. Very slowly. You attacked us, and we had no choice but to defend ourselves."

"What a jagoff," Bazz whispered in Lieza's ear.

"Hey!" a high-pitched male voice shouted. "Hey, is this really Kansas City? I thought I recognized this terminal!"

Lieza turned and saw that the voice belonged to one of the medical students behind the cordon of soldiers. He was trying to get through, but the soldiers were stopping him.

"I live here," the student said pleadingly. "I'd prove it, but all my ID's back at school."

Joel touched Lieza's arm. "I say, Leez, that gentleman is the very one who sat beside you on the airliner."

She stared across the circle and saw that the young man from Kansas City had the same perfect brown hair and bruised face as the Jack who had stolen Tycho's seat.

She started across the room toward the cordon. "Didn't recognize him," she said.

"He does look rather the generic Anglo-Saxon American Protestant dink, doesn't he?" Joel said, coming with her. The other members of Blunt Instrument followed.

"Halt or we'll shoot!" the captain yelled behind them.

"Not *here*," the man in the suit said again.

"Grab them, then!" the captain yelled again.

"No, no, no, no violence in front of the hostages!"

Lieza heard the soldiers hurry after them.

"Ah, the pitter-patter of little Hobnailed feet," she said.

Fug grunted.

A few seconds later, Lieza was facing the young man from Kansas City over the shoulder of an armed, helmeted guard.

The student's mouth was opening and closing, but no sound was coming out. He seemed startled to be face-to-face with the Bastard Child again.

"What's your name, Jack?" she asked.

"Uh, I, you—" he said.

"Stupid name," Cherry observed.

This seemed to bring him out of his stupor a little. "Bonner," he said. "Clifton."

"Well, come on, Bonner Clifton," Lieza said. "If you live around here, we'll take you home."

The man in the suit scurried up beside her, waving his finger again. "That won't do," he said breathlessly. "It'll ruin our records. All of the rescued hostages must be processed through Washington for debriefing."

Joel gasped. "You chaps are despicable," he said indignantly. "How dare you claim to rescue a man and then steal his underwear?"

Lieza reached over the guard's shoulder and grasped Clifton Bonner's left ear. "Come on," she said, pulling him.

The guard's rifle knocked Lieza's arm away. Tycho brought his fist down on the guard's helmet, and the man crumpled to the floor.

The crowd of hostages murmured and shifted nervously.

The man in the suit stepped up hurriedly and pulled Bonner out over the crumpled guard.

"Take him, take him," he said, shoving the med student at Lieza. "No more violence, please. This is going to be hard enough to salvage as it is."

Lieza grabbed Bonner's right hand in her left and turned toward the glass doors again.

"Oh, Cliffie!" a woman's voice cried from the crowd.

Lieza looked back and saw a Straight cheerleader-type jumping and waving.

"Get autographs, Cliffie!" the bouncing woman shouted. "We can sell them!"

Lieza felt Bonner's hand tense.

Blunt Instrument and crew, plus Clifton Bonner, walked past the captain and his knot of soldiers. The captain looked furious. Lieza winked at him and ran her tongue over her upper lip. As she expected, he unconsciously mimicked her and got a tongueful of blood.

Bazz nudged in between Lieza and Tycho and whispered in Lieza's ear. "What's with the Straight, babe? He's not worth the spit it'd take to drown him."

Lieza whispered back. "Captain Courageous can't ambush us if we've got Jack with us." She grinned. "Besides, I think I want him."

Bazz looked incredulous and a little nauseated. "That's sick."

Lieza nodded. "Story of my life."

The glass doors opened automatically, and the band stepped into the cold night. Their equipment was piled haphazardly on the broad sidewalk.

"Bert!" Tycho shouted, and charged for the pile. He pulled his ax from its midst and stood looking at it sadly. The handle had been broken in two.

"Jagging jewbaiters," Dude yelled, kicking at a smashed amplifier. "Must be a couple thousand bucks worth of damage."

"We'll worry about it later," Lieza said. "Come on. I think we'd better stick together. I'd hate to leave a guard on this stuff and come back to find him in the same condition as Bert."

She led them away from the terminal to a pay phone at the edge of the parking lot.

"Anybody got a quarter?" she asked.

Only Bonner did. He pulled it from his pants pocket and stared at it as if surprised that such a thing as a quarter existed.

As Lieza took it from him, she foresaw some of what

was going to happen, as if the coin were a psychic transmitter. She felt cheap.

The sensation was not unpleasant.

She looked up at the sky before punching the button for the operator, but the cloud cover blotted out the Moon. She had wanted to ask her mother's forgiveness for what she was about to do, although she was pretty sure that Bitch Alice would have understood.

There was nothing more revolting than a Wracker in bed with a Straight, but that was exactly why it happened so astonishingly often. Sometimes it even produced worthwhile results.

She was living proof.

I wonder who he was, anyway? she thought as she told the operator to call a hotel for her. *You told me he was a Straight, mama, but you never said much else about him.*

She glanced at the shivering Bonner, who looked as if he couldn't decide whether to faint or throw up.

Just as well.

11

Good Morning; Who Are You?

Went to bed last night;
Don't recall what happened next.
Seems to me a witch came in
And fixed me so I'm hexed.

How else to explain the state I'm in?
How else to forgive my mortal sin?
Why else would I lie with one
I'd spit on if I saw him in the street?

At midnight my brain goes away
To some Dreaming Land,
And all that's left is meat.

—Bitch Alice,
"Waking Up with Godzilla," 1962

Thursday, January 3, 1980. King's Crown Hotel, Kansas City.

Bitch Alice was in a moonsuit, bouncing across a gray plain with a burlap sack over her shoulder. The sky was an inverted black bowl, sprinkled with pinholes where white light leaked through.

The Bitch was collecting bright, gemlike stones from

180

the gray dust. She bent down and scooped them up without breaking stride, then tossed them into the burlap sack.

Lieza was running after her, trying to catch up, but with each bounce Bitch Alice drew farther away.

Lieza tried to call "Mama," but her mouth worked soundlessly.

Then she realized that she was naked. She couldn't breathe. Her blood would boil, and she would die, and her mother wouldn't look back because she couldn't hear her.

But if Lieza could pick up one of the bright stones before it was too late, the stone in her hand would shout to the stones in her mother's sack, and her mother would hear and come back for her.

She looked down at the gray dust, but there were no more gems, only tiny craters. Her mother had gotten them all. Every one.

Lieza's lungs sucked frantically, but drew in only the pure essence of cold.

Just as she felt her chest about to burst, she saw her mother pause and turn slowly, slowly around. Bitch Alice's gold-sprayed sun visor was down, making her faceless.

"Lisa," the apparition said, "you got street sense from my genes and brains from your father's, the dink. So why are you out here without a jacket?"

Lieza wondered how she could hear the words when there was no air.

Then the visor slid up, and the face that grinned out was that of Annabelle Kirk. A greenish gray tentacle slithered from the secretary of state's mouth.

Lieza tried to turn and run as the tentacle slithered toward her across the pockmarked powder, but her feet had frozen. She tried to scream, and gouts of slush spewed from her mouth and nose.

* * *

She thrashed and clawed at the sheets, and then Bonner's arms were around her, holding her still.

"Bad dream," he murmured into her ear.

As the pounding in her chest began to subside, Lieza's only thought was that Bonner was capable of saying some incredibly stupid things.

She opened her eyes and saw that the room was filled with cold daylight filtered through blue drapes.

It was one of the loveliest things she had ever seen, but she couldn't enjoy it. She felt as though she were on the floor of a dungeon, held down by rusty iron bands.

"Let go," she said when she could talk.

Bonner's arms were gone so quickly that Lieza felt ashamed, and that in turn made her angry.

He was so worshipful, so awe-filled, so...so... doglike. He was repulsive.

Which was why he attracted her. She had begun wanting him on the plane, almost as soon as he had sat down beside her. It was sputzing awful, and it excited her terribly.

She slid out of bed and walked to the bathroom, feeling him watching her. Her legs felt hot inside her leathers. She closed and locked the door behind her.

After emptying herself, she stood leaning on the counter and staring at the mirrored wall.

"You have screwed the equivalent of the youthful Spiro Agnew," she told herself, and watched her upper lip curl in disgust.

There was no forgiveness in her eyes, but there was some measure of understanding. It didn't make her feel any better.

She turned on the shower, and when the mirrors fogged with the steam, she stripped off her leathers and stepped into the tub. The water was almost scalding hot, but she wouldn't let herself reach down to turn on the cold-water tap. She had read that some types of cancer could be treated with heat therapy, so maybe whatever was wrong with her could be cooked out as well.

Or perhaps only made a bit more tolerable, because she knew she didn't want to get rid of it altogether. Contradictory thoughts and sensations were her way of reminding herself that she was alive.

Her skin felt as if it were being pulped by hot needles, and the air was so thick with steam that she thought this must be what it would be like to try to breathe underwater. The constant loud hissing made her think of giant snakes.

As she soaped up, she closed her eyes against the hot fog and tried to compose a song about living in a superheated ocean with a sea serpent.

She was only two lines into it when a rumbling sound broke her concentration. Her jaw muscles clenched.

It was Bonner, trying to open the bathroom door.

Knotting her hands into fists, Lieza shouted, "Go away!"

There was silence then, so Lieza tried to resume working on her song.

Bonner's tremulous voice called, "Away from the room or just away from the door?"

Lieza stuck her head into the hot stream and yelled, "I don't care what you do, you dinking Straight geek!"

She couldn't tell whether he answered, because all she could hear was the rush of water pouring over her head. In her mind's eye, though, she saw him slinking back to the bed, finding his clothes on the floor, and shakily putting them on. After he had done that, he'd hesitate, start for the door and stop, start for the door and stop again, until he was finally gone. All she had to do was wait.

Instead, she shut off the water, got out of the tub, and put on her leathers without drying herself. Dripping and cursing, she unlocked the bathroom door and stepped into the main room, bringing a cloud of steam with her.

Bonner was lying in bed. He was still nude.

Lieza yelled and leaped on him, shaking her head violently to spray him with water.

"Wait," Bonner protested, and Lieza slapped his mouth with her wet hair.

"My bladder's full," he groaned.

"Too bad, Jack." She hoped the teeth of the zipper would hurt him a little this time.

The room reverberated as someone in the hall pounded on the metal door.

"Go away," Lieza yelled.

"You OK, Leez?" Tycho's voice bellowed.

"I'm fine," she shouted back. "Rupturing a Straight. Go away."

Bonner's face had twisted into a grimace and was beginning to turn red. Lieza couldn't tell if it was from pleasure or pain, and at this point she didn't care.

Great Sputzing Patton, I'm rotten, she thought.

A few moments later, she collapsed, half-smothering Bonner with her hair.

"That'll teach you to stay in your picket-fenced yard," she said.

Groaning, he squirmed out from under her and limped to the bathroom. She laughed at him.

Then she rolled onto her back, put her arms under her head, and looked up at the glitter-speckled ceiling. She felt content for the first time since Patton Day.

She also knew that the feeling wouldn't last long. There was too much trying to insinuate its way into her consciousness, too much trying to distract her from the full-time business of living. There were the Squid and Winton R. Wilson; there was the almost certain approach of nuclear war between the United States and Britain; there were the recurring nightmares about her mother; there was the resurrected specter of the scientist with the big nose and glasses . . .

And there was this scummy little Jack she wanted to simultaneously caress and castrate.

But for now, for this one moment, she smelled the sweet scents of steam, sweat, and sex. She listened to Bonner moaning in the bathroom. Somewhere down the hall, Tycho was breaking something. She could feel her new song re-forming in her mind.

She felt pleasantly cool as the moisture on her skin began to evaporate.

For now, all was right with the world. For now, she was happy.

* * *

When Bonner came out of the bathroom with a towel wrapped around his hips, he looked exactly like the useless, self-conscious Straight he was.

"Whatsamatter?" Lieza said. "Afraid I'll see something?"

Bonner looked morose. "I don't understand," he said weakly.

Lieza sat up, crossed her legs, and gave him what she hoped was a look of contempt. "We just spent the whole jagging night together. What're you covering up?"

Unexpectedly, Bonner's face hardened in a way that almost made him look like a Wracker.

When he spoke, his voice sounded deeper, more dangerous than Lieza would have thought possible. "I'm cold. What's your excuse? Afraid to be naked?"

Lieza remembered a brief moment on the plane, when Bonner had spoken defiantly to the soldier she'd called Eichmann. He sounded like that now. It was as if there were an angrier, stronger being trying to take over his body.

"I've never been afraid of anything, dink-dink," she said, putting especially vicious emphasis on the epithet. "Least of all a little jewbaiter like you, so you can knock off the tough act. That might work on Straight whores like Big Boobs waving bye-bye last night, but not on me."

Bonner's new anger and strength seemed to waver for an instant, and then he dropped the towel and walked toward her.

"You want to keep it attached, you better stop where you are," Lieza said.

Bonner stopped. "You're real good at changing the subject when you don't like it," he said. "Come on—what're you hiding under those jeans? Got ugly legs? Can't be any worse than that purple scar on your stomach."

Lieza turned away from him and crawled across the bed so he wouldn't see her lips and eyelids trembling. "Go home to your scrodding mum and dad, Straight. I've had all of you I want."

She felt the mattress sink slightly as he crawled onto the bed.

"Lieza," he said, and his voice was its normal, quavering self again. "I'm sorry. I don't know what got into me. I didn't mean—"

She turned and kicked him in the chest, knocking him onto the floor.

That's it. Take advantage of his moment of weakness, so he doesn't see yours.

"I wear leathers 'cause I like them," she said. "They gimme a rush. Unlike you. Any other questions?"

Bonner got to his hands and knees, then looked up at Lieza and said, "Do you really want me to go?"

She thought about it.

What do *I want, anyway?*

She decided that right now she didn't care what the pitiful little Jack did, but in a few seconds she might want to either throw him out the window or make love to him until she passed out.

"I don't know," she said honestly, surprised that she could do it. "You decide."

Then the door burst inward, and Tycho, Bazz, Fug, and Cherry tumbled into the room.

Lieza didn't know whether to be furious or grateful.

"We heard noises," Tycho explained, brandishing the half-handled Bert. "Want me to get rid of Jack for you?"

Bonner looked as though he were about to collapse into a mound of pale gelatin.

Cherry squatted beside him, grinned, and pinched his right thigh. "Say, he doesn't look too bad with his clothes off. Mind if I have seconds, Leez?"

Bazz shuddered. "Leftovers. Yecch."

Fug grunted.

Lieza leaned down, grasped Bonner's arm, and pulled him up into bed. He immediately covered himself with the sheet.

"Modest little jagoff, ain't he?" Tycho said.

Lieza pointed toward the open doorway, and the four other Wrackers headed in that direction at a leisurely pace.

"We just don't want you to make a mistake, babe," Bazz said. "Not that you haven't already."

Lieza gave a short laugh. "If I didn't make mistakes, I wouldn't have anything to sing about. Then you'd all be on the streets, trying to make a living in the Straight man's world."

Cherry paused and looked back. "Just don't let that Straight man make a living in you, peesh?"

"Scrod off," Lieza said, angry. She had been trying

not to think about that; she'd run out of pills two months ago and had been too busy to get a refill.

Cherry nodded knowingly and left the room.

Tycho was the last of the four to go. Before stepping into the hall, he said, "Actually, we just came to find out when we oughta get ready to go to the farm."

Lieza shrugged. "Couple hours. Tell Ellyn to rent us a bus, if she hasn't already."

Tycho nodded, then snarled at Bonner and twirled Bert menacingly before going out and closing the door behind him. The latch was broken, but the door stayed shut.

"I don't think they like me," Bonner mumbled into his pillow.

Lieza pressed against him and bit his shoulder just hard enough to leave marks without breaking the skin. "That's OK. I don't like you either."

Bonner made a small noise in his throat, then said, "I know. I can't figure it."

"Don't try. You hungry again yet?"

"I could eat."

Lieza rolled away from him and used the phone on the nightstand to call room service.

"Hope you're not Jewish," she said after sliding up against him again. "I ordered lots of bacon."

"I'm not."

"I know that, scrodbrain. You're about as Jewish as Pat Boone, Dixon rest his whitewashed soul. It was a joke."

"Oh." There were a few minutes of silence, and then Bonner said, "I read in one of the mags that you're half Jewish yourself. Are you?"

"Beats me. Mama never said."

"What about your father?"

Lieza turned away and lay on her back. "Don't be a skagass. You know I'm a bastard."

A long pause. "I thought that might be a gimmick," Bonner said finally. "I thought you might really know who he was."

Lieza felt a rush of fresh disgust. This Jack sure knew

how to put her in a bad mood. She reached over to the nightstand again and touched a button on the television's remote control.

The screen on the far wall flickered to life just in time to reveal a cartoon coyote falling a mile through empty air to impact on a shelf of rock. Lieza changed channels until she found a news station.

"I'm sorry," Bonner said, reaching out to touch her left forearm.

She flinched and said, "Shut up. I wanna find out if we're at war because of you jewbaiters."

He shrank away toward the edge of the bed, and Lieza wondered what would happen to them if the relationship continued past the remainder of the morning. Which one would suicide first?

But the thought didn't stay long. It was inconceivable that they would ever have anything more to do with each other. Besides, the newscast was in the middle of a report on the Concepcion "rescue mission."

Lieza supposed that the medical students really *had* been prisoners, but she had difficulty thinking of Operation Beautiful Music as a "rescue." It hadn't been a raid to free people in mortal danger, but an underhanded betrayal designed primarily to out-propaganda the enemy.

The newscast wildly distorted the facts of the battle as Lieza knew them, and it soon became obvious to her that the students had been "rescued" from one group of oppressors only to be paraded like prize sheep by another group of oppressors. Only one of the hostages in the first planeload had been spared that, and he was lying beside her.

Lieza tried and failed to suppress a chuckle at the thought that even Bonner had only traded one sort of prison for another. She felt him look at her, but she tried to ignore him and focus on the newscast.

Most of the "exclusive, on-the-scene" footage displayed a battlefield absolutely nothing like the Point Salines airstrip. In the first place, the "enemy" soldiers weren't Gurkhas. In the second place, whenever one of them was "shot," he threw his arms up dramatically and fell instantly without a hole visible anywhere in his clothing or body.

Putting a British uniform on an American soldier, Lieza mused, doesn't automatically make him a good actor.

A full minute of the file showed several of the "Limeys" ganging up on a blonde girl in a short skirt, whom they bayoneted repeatedly. Lieza noticed that the camera angle was such that the viewer never actually saw a blade stab into the Jackie's supple flesh. Impossible jets of blood shot up, however, and spattered the camera lens.

If what the "Limeys" were doing was so horrible, Lieza wondered, why didn't the cameraman do something about it?

It was all so obviously false that she wanted to laugh at it, but she couldn't. The commentary that accompanied the film implied that this was actual footage of the hostage rescue on Concepcion, and whatever the commentary said, the Great Straight Public would swallow like juicy gobbets of meat.

In an instant of cold realization, Lieza knew why the administration was doing this. The Squid was deliberately manipulating the Straight public's perceptions of both war in general and war with the Brits in particular, because she meant to slug it out with the Alliance whether the President's other advisors approved or not.

Didn't even Annabelle Kirk have enough sanity to realize that a war with the Anglo-Chinese Alliance would be suicidal?

Perhaps she did, but preferred suicide to letting Winton R. Wilson win the Presidency. Perhaps the Squid was taking the attitude of "if I can't have it, neither can he."

It wasn't necessarily a stupid policy. If Wilson did win in November, he would almost certainly plunge the nation into a nuclear conflict sometime before his term was up. Maybe it would be better to get it over with now and let the cockroaches have a crack at it.

At this thought, Lieza felt even more disgusted with herself than with Bonner. The idea of sitting back and letting the Straights blow her and a few billion others to hell wasn't acceptable thinking.

Eddie Dixon would have disapproved.

Forgive me, first and truest Father, she prayed, *for I have thought like unto a frick.*

Lieza felt Bonner tense as the scene on the TV screen switched to a slow pan of the freed hostages disembarking from a plane in Washington.

The Straight got out of bed and walked around its foot, blocking her view of the screen for a moment.

"Gotta call my folks," he mumbled as he picked up the receiver on the nightstand. "They'll see all this stuff and worry..."

Briefly, Lieza wondered why he hadn't simply crawled over her rather than walking all the way around the king-size bed, but then she realized that there wasn't anything to wonder about. Bonner couldn't know whether to expect a kiss or a bruise from her, so he had taken the safe route and avoided either possibility.

She didn't let herself feel any guilt over that, because she couldn't understand his reasoning. It seemed to her that the risk of pain could only increase the value of whatever pleasure might be gained.

That, she thought, might be the essence of the difference between a typical Wracker and a typical Straight. A Straight took the path of least resistance, settling for half-realized pleasure and suffering only minimal pain, while a Wracker's life swung like a pendulum between torture at one extreme and joy at the other.

That was why Straights kowtowed to their governments, which made their lives only moderately uncomfortable, while Wrackers rolled over the Red Armies and took their lumps.

And that was also why she had to do everything she could to keep both the Squid and Wilson from wasting everything. If she let them continue running the charade as they had been doing so far, the world would be plunged into a conflagration that, this time, wouldn't have any survivors.

If there were no survivors, there were no more Red Armies to roll over.

Still, why should it be up to her? Why should the Bastard Child be the first Wracker to take a stand against the latest round of Straight stupidity?

Because she had been used as a pawn in the opening move of the war.

And because she was Bitch Alice's daughter.

The Squid was already trying to enlist her to fight Wilson, but when Kirk wasn't looking—no, when Kirk *was* looking—she'd hit her too. She didn't know how yet, but she knew she would.

"Mom?" she heard Bonner say nervously. "It's Cliff. I'm fine, Mom, really, don't—No, I'm in the city. King's Crown, you know, near the airport. No, don't come out, because—Well, they stopped here to switch planes, and let me stay. They even—They put me up here for the night. No, don't come; I'll—Mom, cut it out . . ."

Lieza wanted to laugh, but the news show shifted stories and caught her attention again.

Winton R. Wilson's red-cheeked, plastic-looking face filled the screen. Fitzgerald had bungled the rescue operation, he was saying. Because the President had sent in only a small force of commandos, the Brits would get the signal that the United States was afraid to commit to anything really big. They needed to be shown that America wouldn't be pushed around, and they needed to be shown in no uncertain terms.

"Fitzgerald has allowed the Anglo-Chinese alliance to build up an enormous and dangerous advantage in outer space," Wilson said, "and apparently he's willing to let them get away with the same thing down here on earth. All I can say is, if Fitzgerald's afraid to use the weapons for peace that he has at his disposal, he's unfit for the position of Commander in Chief."

Who was, then? the reporter interviewing Wilson wanted to know.

Wilson smiled broadly.

Lieza threw a pillow at the screen. The result was

unsatisfying, so she reached for the phone, but Bonner had picked it up and walked toward the blue-curtained windows. He was talking with his hand cupped around his mouth.

"Hi, Mom," Lieza called, and Bonner cringed.

"The TV's on," she heard his muffled voice say.

Lieza squealed as if having an orgasm, and was rewarded by seeing Bonner cringe again. She would have continued in this vein, but the television picture shifted once more.

It sent her back in time.

She was ten years old, sitting on the floor in the farmhouse's front room with her mother's bass player, Samson Llewellen.

She saw the moonsuited figure on the stark gray landscape and knew it was her mother.

She heard her mother's last words.

And then, soon afterward, there were the scenes of fire and bricks and blood, and the twitching face of the killer, the man with the big nose and glasses.

She hated that face.

Now, sitting cross-legged in bed after having spent the night with a worthless Straight, she saw it again. It was more blotched and veined than it had been in 1967, and the hair was thinner, but it was the same face.

She hated it more than ever.

"Wilson is expected to formally announce his candidacy for the 1980 Whig Presidential nomination this coming Saturday at a rally in his hometown of Kansas City, Missouri," the offscreen newscaster was saying. "At that rally, he is also expected to introduce this man, physicist and space scientist Daniel P. Jackson, one of the driving forces behind America's orbital and lunar manned space programs in the 1950s and '60s. Jackson will explain the importance of manned space exploration to the present security and future prosperity of the United States. . . ."

She heard Bonner hang up the telephone receiver and replace the unit on the nightstand beside her, but she didn't look at him. She wanted to keep her eyes focused on the face on the screen. She wanted to burn it into her brain like a brand. She wanted to be sure she'd know Jackson if she saw him on the street. She wanted to stare into his eyes and ask him why he had let Bitch Alice die.

Why, she wondered, had she waited so many years to do just that? Maybe she had inherited more Straight genes from her nameless father than she wanted to admit.

"Winton R. Wilson's 'Rally for America' is to be held this Saturday, January 5, at seven P.M. in Kansas City's Municipal Arena," the announcer said as the picture blipped away from Jackson and back to Wilson. "Admission to the event is by invitation only, and security is expected to be tight."

The segment was followed by a commercial for KhromeKleen metal polish. The placement of the ad was cleverly calculated, since Winton R. Wilson had served as KhromeKleen's on-air spokesman for nine years before running for the U.S. Senate in 1964.

"Wilson and Jackson," she murmured. "Seven o'clock Saturday. See you then."

"What's that?" Bonner asked.

Lieza turned off the TV and looked up at him. "Nothing that'd matter to you."

She was pleased to see that he looked hurt.

"Cheer up, Jack," she said mockingly. "You've been rescued from the clutches of the blue-and-yellow-blooded peril. You get to go home to mummy and daddy. You should be sputzing ecstatic."

Bonner went to the TV and trailed a finger across the screen. Lieza felt her muscles tighten at the crackling sound of the static discharge.

"You can come back to bed if you want," she said, feeling oddly uneasy at his pensiveness. "Or you can get dressed and go. Doesn't matter to me."

She didn't know whether that was a lie or not.

Bonner was staring at his finger as it tracked through the fine layer of dust on the plastiglass. "When you were watching this," he said, as if talking to himself, "you looked, for a second, like someone... I don't know, innocent. Someone who might've slept with me because she didn't know any better."

Lieza shivered and felt her nipples hardening. The room was too jagging cold.

"Then, after a while," Bonner went on, "you looked like someone who wouldn't have had me in a million years. Like a wounded animal ready to attack."

Lieza pulled a blanket up around her neck and lay back on the remaining pillow. "Very poetic. You oughta write for *Wrackweek*."

"I'd like to."

He was drawing circles in the dust now and seemed unaware of his nudity for the first time.

Lieza wanted him again, and wished she didn't. She turned onto her left side, pressed her cheek into the pillow, and closed her eyes.

"I suppose the first thing you'd write would be a lurid account of your twenty-four hours of passion with the Bastard Child," she said.

A few seconds passed before Bonner answered. "I'd write about you, but I wouldn't say anything about this. I wouldn't know how."

Lieza tasted something bitter and wished she'd rinsed out her mouth when she'd been in the bathroom.

"You'd think of something," she said. "All hacks do. One time one of them wrote that I was pregnant with quadruplets by Prince Charles."

"I wouldn't do that. I wouldn't lie about you."

Lieza pressed harder into the pillow, distorting her lips against the fabric. "Sure you would, Hack," she said, her voice deepened and muffled. "It's the nature of a Straight. You'd have to go Wracker to tell the truth, and the transition would kill you."

A longer silence this time.

"I have to go," Bonner said then. "I don't want to, but . . . you're a goddess, not a woman. You're not somebody real."

Lieza flung off her blanket and sat up. Focusing all her rage at the Straight, she shouted, "So *go*. You don't wanna screw a mirage, do you? No difference between that and jagging off, is there?"

Bonner took a few steps away from the TV and leaned

down to pick up his clothes from the floor. He dressed slowly, and Lieza could see his muscles quivering.

It took a long time for him to finish, and neither of them spoke again until he was almost to the door.

Lieza stopped him with a word.

"Hack," she said.

He stood with his back to her, and his quivering intensified until his body looked as though an electric current were being passed through it.

"Go on home for now," Lieza said, trying to keep her voice gentle and not quite succeeding. "If you want, show up at the Municipal Arena at seven on Saturday."

He didn't move when she'd finished.

Lieza chewed on the inside of her left cheek and stared at the back of a stranger.

"Or don't," she said, lying down and turning away from the door.

She didn't hear his footsteps again. Nor did she hear the door open or close. But when she finally turned back, at the call of "Room service," Hack Bonner was gone.

Ignoring the call, Lieza slid out of bed and went to the bathroom to rinse out her mouth.

Then she said a brief prayer to Eddie Dixon and got ready to leave.

12

Staggering Through the Launch Window

> Gimme one more—
> Gimme one last—
> Yeah, gimme one more—
> Gimme one last blast.
> Tell me—
> Tell me that I'll like it—
> Tell me that I need it—
> Gimme one last blast.
>
> Tell me that it isn't all over yet.
> Tell me that I've still got time
> To wipe out old regrets.
> Sing a song, sing it real pretty—
> Sing it right into my ear.
> Sing about facing the world again—
> Without shaking, without fear.
>
> Gimme one more—
> Give it to me fast—
> Give it to me smooth—
> Gimme one last blast.

—Lieza Galilei,
"Last Blast," 1977

Saturday, January 5, 1980. Kansas City, Missouri.

Pissant was much too aware of the fact that the tiny brick-walled dressing room smelled of urine, and he was also too aware of the fact that the idiot applying his makeup wasn't doing a good job. The mirror clearly revealed that the physicist still looked awful.

He wasn't sure why that bothered him, just as he wasn't sure why he was frightened of going out in front of Wilson's rabidly enthusiastic crowd. He had spent years lecturing to students without giving a damn what they thought of him, so why should giving a short talk give him chills now?

It couldn't be that he was afraid of the crowd itself. Wilson would have them so pumped up by the time Pissant's turn came that the physicist would get a standing ovation even if he did nothing more than stand and slobber for five minutes. There was no challenge to that, and therefore nothing to be afraid of. Wilson was turning him into a symbol, and symbols were cheered no matter how tarnished they might look upon close inspection.

As if Wilson would allow close inspection.

What was wrong, then?

"I need a drink, Pinocchio," he said, shoving the makeup man out of the way so he could see Claghorn's sharp-nosed reflection in the mirror.

"I have already told you," the gnome said in his usual monotone. "I shall see what I can do when we go to the stage. I might be able to find an ounce or two that you can use to calm your nerves before speaking."

An ounce or two. Jesus H. Carry Nation Christ. That was barely enough to taste, let alone "calm his nerves."

Pissant could see what they were doing to him. They were giving him lots of money, but keeping him on such a short tether that he didn't have any opportunity to enjoy it. They were also giving him booze, but only as an animal trainer gives a dog a biscuit.

"Goddamn Hobnails," Pissant muttered.

Pinocchio got down from his stool and came up behind him, resting his fingertips lightly on the physicist's shoulders.

"I'm afraid I didn't hear that very well," the gnome said.

Pissant shuddered and wished even more strongly for a drink. Positive reinforcement wasn't the only tool Wilson employed to keep him in line.

Pinocchio had never done more than slap him, but Pissant was terrified that he would. He had seen what the wooden-faced gnome could do.

Bud had been the first, and mildest, example. Pinocchio had merely stunned him, but he had done it with an effortless jab of his finger.

The second example had been just as effortless, but much more impressive. Pissant had been lying alone in Estella's shabby room on the night of Patton Day, listening to the Wracker-coyotes reveling in the street below, when the door to the apartment had shattered. It hadn't been merely a broken latch; the entire door had *shattered*. And after the splintered pieces had fallen to the grimy floor, Pissant had looked up and seen Pinocchio standing in the hallway.

The gnome had held no weapon or tool. He had simply stood there in his crisp brown suit and said, "Now that you are in the employ of Mister Wilson, spending your free time in such a place is most inappropriate."

The third example had occurred on New Year's Day, at the Rose Bowl. Pissant hadn't wanted to be there, but Wilson had insisted. During halftime, while the Big Whig had been shaking hands and posing for the television cameras, a young man with a scraggly beard had pushed toward him, shouting about nuclear proliferation and the extinction of the human species. He hadn't even gotten within twenty feet of Wilson when he'd simply fallen down. The police had taken him away, and Pissant had heard later that a "spectator" at the game had died of a heart attack.

But Pissant had seen Pinocchio come up behind the bearded man. He hadn't seen just what had happened, but he hadn't had to.

Now, sitting in the makeup chair with Pinocchio standing behind him, touching him, Pissant had a vision of his own "heart attack." The gnome would hit him in a special place behind an ear, or slide a poisoned needle between two of the vertebrae of his neck, and it would be over.

So what would be so bad about that? Wouldn't it be better to kick off rather than continue to let Wilson make his life even more of a sham than it had been for the past thirteen years?

The answers to those questions were easy to think of when he lay in bed each night, too drunk to be coordinated enough to kill himself. But with Pinocchio's fingers on his shoulders, they were nowhere to be found.

"Perhaps you, too, are having trouble hearing," Pinocchio said. "I said that I didn't understand what you just said, and I would like you to repeat it."

Pissant felt his hands starting to quiver, and he clutched the arms of his chair.

"I said," he whispered hoarsely, hating everything in his sight and memory, "that a few ounces before I speak would be nice."

Pinocchio's fingertips slid off the physicist's shoulders, and the gnome stepped back and sat on the stool again. "That is what I thought you said."

The makeup artist, who had been hiding in the corner, stepped forward hesitantly and resumed applying pancake to Pissant's sagging skin.

So this is how it ends, Pissant thought. *Not with a bang, but with a powder puff.*

He remembered the sleek, heavily made-up PR woman he had insulted at the Patton's Eve cocktail party, and he felt like even more of a hypocrite than he had before.

He looked down at his wrists and was amazed to see that there were no eyelets for the strings.

* * *

By the time Pinocchio took him out of the dressing room and down a corridor to the stage, Pissant's limbs were trembling and his face was twitching with a nervous tic. It was as if, he thought, his body were having an allergic reaction to the disgusting thing he was doing.

He tried to argue with himself. What was so disgusting about it? He was going to talk about going to Mars, wasn't he? Wasn't that the topic that had been his obsession for a huge chunk of his life? What difference did it make who was sponsoring him as long as the message got through?

It makes a big difference, a calm voice answered from deep inside his skull. *Wilson has no intention of following through on his promises. He's using you as a symbol of former glory in order to get the masses pumped full of high-frontier patriotism. Once he's elected, he'll forget about conquering the solar system and devote himself to blowing the Brits and Chinks to Kingdom Come.*

Pissant knew it was true, but he didn't know how to get out of the trap he had walked into. He had to have money to survive on, to drink on, and there was no way he could go back to Kansas U. after whizzing on its Physics Department chairman. Furthermore, it was a sure bet that no other university would hire him after Worthing started the story on the professional gossip circuit.

Pissant had to stay with Wilson if he wanted to stay alive.

And he did. Damned if he knew why, but he did.

Winton R. Wilson, surrounded by three bodyguards, two senators, a congressman, the governor of Missouri, and various campaign workers, met Pissant and Pinocchio on the stage's left wing. The crowd was out of sight, but the noise was tremendous. Pissant could feel the cheering and stomping just under his heart: "We want WINT. We want WINT. WIL-SON, WIL-SON, WIL-SON."

The Big Whig, even more heavily made-up than Pissant, grinned a broad politician's grin at the physicist and shook his hand so vigorously that Pissant thought he could feel his shoulder dislocating.

"Damn fine crowd out there, Doctor Jackson," Wilson boomed. "You're gonna knock 'em dead. The time has come, sir, and we are the men who have come for that time!"

Pissant, struggling to control his facial tic, nodded

jerkily. "Yes sir, Mister Wilson. Anything to drink?"

Wilson gestured toward a small table next to the lighting-control panel. It held a stack of clear plastic glasses and several bottles of various liquors. The junior campaign worker manning the lighting panel was looking at the table enviously.

"Onstage we'll just have water," Wilson said, "but a man's got a right to a good, stiff belt before he faces the peasantry, eh, Joe-Fred?" He nudged one of the senators.

As soon as Wilson's attention had shifted, Pissant headed for the table. There was so much there. . . .

Pinocchio beat him to it without seeming to hurry at all. Blocking Pissant from reaching any of the bottles, the gnome carefully poured an inch of amber fluid into one of the plastic glasses.

Pissant grabbed it out of Claghorn's hand and tossed it back in one swallow. It burned nicely going down, warming his throat and chest and making him forget about his facial tic . . . but the effect only lasted a few seconds.

He held the glass out to the gnome. "Refill, barkeep," he said, trying to sound jovial.

Pinocchio shook his head and grasped Pissant's elbow, steering him back toward Wilson and the other politicians.

The shouting from the arena was even louder now: "WIL-son NOW! WIL-son NOW! Dump FitzGERALD! U.-S.-A.! U.-S.-A.!"

Rather than coming from twenty thousand different throats, it seemed to Pissant that the cheers were being shouted by a single great beast with nodulous vocal cords and the brain of a parakeet.

"I don't want to do this," he muttered. "I most definitely do not want to do this."

"I'm having difficulty hearing you again, Professor," Pinocchio said.

Rot, you son of a birch, Pissant thought, strangely amused at his silent pun. *You'll never make a real buoy.*

Wilson, laughing heartily, clapped the governor on the back and then turned toward Pissant and Pinocchio. Instantly, the Big Whig's face switched from joviality to grimness.

"Listen, Dennis," he said in a low voice. "I just got word"—his index finger tapped the button-sized, flesh-colored receiver in his right ear—"that three or four undesirables have made their way into the arena. How they got past the door I don't know, but what I do know is that you'd better get them the fuck out. If they cause any trouble and the networks pick it up, we could be sunk before pulling out of port. Take Gary with you, hook up with some of the temporary men, and search the crowd. When you find whoever shouldn't be there, do whatever you have to as long as you keep it quiet. Earl and Mike'll stay off-stage here to keep an eye on me."

Pinocchio turned and left, followed by one of Wilson's bodyguards.

Wilson raised an eyebrow at Pissant. "One of the trials of public life, Doctor Jackson. Those who love you, love you a lot. Those who hate you, hate you enough to force you to take defensive measures. Sort of like relations between nations, now that I think of it. Ah well, you get used to it." He patted the physicist's shoulder. "Two minutes to showtime, Brains. Got your notes?"

Pissant opened his mouth to answer, but Wilson, jovial again, had already turned away to laugh at a scatological joke told by one of the senators.

Pissant eyed the bodyguards named Earl and Mike, who were peering out at the crowd through a gap in the stage curtains.

If I had a gun, I could kill them all, Pissant thought.

But there was something he wanted to do more.

No one noticed when he went back to the table and put a pint flask of Irish in his right jacket pocket. It was a tight fit, and the bulge of the bottle was clearly visible, but Pissant didn't care. The crowd would only be able to see his left side as he walked out to his chair, and once he was seated, the floor-length tablecloth would serve as cover for filling his water glass.

In the meantime, he'd sample the rest of the booze table's goodies while he had the chance.

Beats knowing what you're doing, he thought as he filled one of the plastic glasses with vodka. *Beats it all to hell*. He took a long drink, then filled the glass again.

Checking his watch, he saw that the gibbous, waning Moon would be rising at just about the time he would probably have to give his speech.

It was marvelously appropriate.

He raised his glass high.

"Here's to you, Ally," he said loudly, not caring if Wilson or the others saw or heard what he was doing. "Here's to you, my beautiful Moon Lady. I invite you again to send down a lightning bolt to strike me dead."

Then he gulped down the vodka and, as always, imagined for an instant that he felt the charge he longed for.

* * *

The brass band seemed to play forever. Then, by the time the governor, the congressman, and one of the senators had finished their speeches praising Winton R. Wilson, Pissant's pint bottle had only a few centimeters of fluid left. Added to that problem was the fact that he had to go to the bathroom. He considered scuttling offstage, but was afraid of what Wilson would do to him if he left in the middle of everything.

As the second senator arose to take the podium and address the cheering throng, Pissant felt the right side of his face tingling uncomfortably. He turned his head and saw the Big Whig, who was sitting two seats away, glaring at him.

The physicist looked away quickly. Why was Wilson giving him the evil eye? Had the politician seen him bring out the bottle?

His eyes focused on the glass in front of him, and then he knew what was wrong. His glass was the only one on the table that contained amber liquid.

Jesus H. Goddamn Holy Christ, why didn't I bring out the vodka instead? It was a fifth but I could have emptied the pint bottle and transferred . . .

He stopped himself in mid-thought. It was too late to think of what he might have or should have done. Wilson had noticed, and although the crowd was oblivious to everything except its political-orgasmic delirium, the TV cameras weren't. Pissant saw one rise out of the crowd on a crane, and he felt the sudden terrible certainty that it was zooming in for a close-up of his booze.

His hands shaking in anticipation of what would be done to him, Pissant snatched up the glass, spilling half of its contents on the tablecloth, and drained it. He imagined that he was drinking the blood that would fill his mouth when Pinocchio removed his molars with pliers.

When he could force himself to do so, he glanced at Wilson again and saw that the Big Whig was watching the senator at the podium. Pissant took the pint bottle from his jacket pocket and tossed it under the table, hoping it didn't slide out past the tablecloth into the full view of the crowd and the cameras.

The governor of Missouri, who was seated to Pissant's immediate right, scooted his chair a few inches closer to Wilson and thus a few inches farther away from Pissant.

Pissant, in addition to his need to head for a rest room, now had an intense craving for hot nacho chips with heavily jalapeñoed chili con queso. His stomach began to churn.

He hadn't been allowed to eat anything since breakfast. Wilson had no doubt intended the fast as a precaution to ensure that the physicist didn't throw up onstage, but Pissant knew he was capable of dry-heaves that would be more revolting than any vomiting the Big Whig had ever witnessed. If that happened, he'd probably lose control of his bladder too, and the result would be a fiasco for Wilson and a painful death for Pissant.

He needed food to calm his stomach, but there was nothing on the table but pitchers of water.

He leaned close to the governor and whispered, "Got anything to eat?"

The governor shuddered and scooted still farther away. Pissant got a whiff of his own breath and realized why.

"Well, then, got any peppermints?" he asked.

Wilson turned toward him and glared again.

What the hell. In for a penny, in for a pound.

He took a deep breath and shouted, "Go sputz, you scrodding dink-dink!"

But the second senator had finished introducing the Big Whig to the crowd, and an earth-shaking roar drowned out Pissant's words.

Wilson, all smiles again, stood and raised both arms, waving to his loving followers.

Pissant sat numbly in the midst of the ocean of sound. He was surprised when he looked down and saw his own hands slapping each other in praise of America's Savior.

You shouldn't be surprised, the voice inside him said. *After all, you timed it perfectly. You cussed him out so you could tell yourself you were a man, but in fact you were listening to Senator Dicknose and knew exactly when the applause would come. Real convenient. No-risk bravery; aluminum-foil-protected balls. No wonder I call you Pissant.*

"Leave me alone," he said aloud, but he couldn't hear himself over the shouts of Wilson's congregation.

He looked out into the smoky air of the arena. Red, white, and blue balloons were falling from nets attached to the faraway ceiling, and myriad spotlight beams played over the mob like living cylinders of white energy.

"Thank you, thank you, thank you," Wilson's voice boomed from a score of amplifiers. Pissant turned to look at the podium and saw that the politician's arms were still upraised, waving like spastic sea serpents. The plaid sport coat flapped open and shut, open and shut, giving Pissant quick glimpses of the shirt underneath.

"You've got pit stains," the physicist yelled. But again, he knew that no one, with the possible exception of the governor of Missouri, could hear him.

He wished he were just a little drunker. Then he could get up from his chair, walk to the podium, pull Wilson's coat open wide, and point to the shirt's armpits so the cameras would get a good shot.

The idea was appealing, and he considered going under the table to retrieve his bottle for a swallow of liquid courage.

Who do you think you're kidding? If you were a little drunker, you'd just lie down and go to sleep. Only this time you wouldn't wake up, because Wilson'd kill you.

Despite the bright lights and the tremendous heat of the place, Pissant felt a chill run up his legs into his chest. He thought he was beginning to recognize the voice.

He smelled something acrid, and fished in his breast pocket for a handkerchief. He couldn't flashback to Dallas now. Not now, while his life depended on being able to get to the podium.

Burning hair.

He found the handkerchief and pressed it to his mouth and nose. The smell of the clean cloth seemed to help for a second, but now he was beginning to hear undertones of breaking glass in the voice of the crowd.

Scorched flesh.

Pissant gagged, sure that he was going to be sick. So much for Wilson's strategy. He closed his eyes and waited for it.

Then he felt a hand on his shoulder and heard a voice in his ear.

"Drink this," the voice said.

Pissant opened his eyes and saw a large black man dressed in a flannel shirt and denim jeans sitting in the chair where the governor of Missouri had been. The man was touching Pissant's shoulder with one hand and holding out a glass of what looked like water in the other.

Pissant lowered the handkerchief and stared.

"What happened to . . ." he began, but could only finish by gesturing at the chair.

The black man chuckled. A copper-colored tooth flashed in the glare of the bright lights.

"Oh, the Gov, he gon' be right back," the man said, and then he nodded at the glass in his hand. "You take this and drink it. Tied one on, ain't you?"

Pissant took the glass. "Damnedest thing," he said, and then drank. The liquid tasted like water with a little sugar in it.

As always, the physicist's eyes closed involuntarily as he swallowed.

"Ain't it, though," the black man's voice said.

How was it, Pissant wondered, that he could hear the apparition's voice over the cheers of the Wilsonites?

He drained the glass and was surprised at how much better he felt. He still didn't feel great, but at least he wasn't going to vomit.

"Thanks," he said, opening his eyes and reaching out to return the glass.

His fingers brushed the polyester sleeve of the governor of Missouri's coat.

The governor flinched away.

"What the hell—" Pissant said, and then saw that the glass was gone, too.

He frequently saw things and people that weren't really there. That in itself didn't surprise him anymore, but he at least expected to recognize them and to feel pain as a result. The big black man with the copper-colored tooth, though, was a stranger—and the drink of sweet water had made him feel better, not worse.

You know him, scodbrain. You're just afraid to let yourself remember his name.

Pissant tried to concentrate, to remember, but Wilson's harangue changed pitch and interrupted him.

"And just what did our so-called President Fitzgerald accomplish on the island of Concepcion?" the Big Whig was shouting, his wattles quivering like gelatin.

"NOTHING!" the crowd roared in answer.

"You bet your boots nothing!" Wilson bellowed. "Twenty-four of the Americans the British were holding captive are still unaccounted for. Why? Because the White House gave the order to pull out all but a handful of our troops before the operation was finished. They'd have us believe otherwise—they'd have us think that the Rangers accomplished their mission and left because there was nothing more to be done. But the fact is that the current administration has once again abandoned a helpless, underdeveloped nation to the Chinese and British. Oh, sure—Secretary of State Kirk assures us that thousands of our troops are standing by in case the Limeys try another invasion. But how can we believe that? Doesn't our experience with this administration teach us that they're afraid to use the muscle necessary to back up their threats?"

While asking this rhetorical question, Wilson knotted his fists and flexed the biceps of each arm as if he were a victorious prize fighter. The implication was obvious: Winton R. Wilson had muscle and wasn't afraid to use it.

The crowd went wild.

Pissant turned away from the podium, starting to feel queasy again at the thought that he was working for this man. Then, since there was nothing else to look at, he scanned the crowd.

Maybe the man who had given him the sweet water was out there.

Not likely. He hadn't looked much like a Whig.

The spotlights were still playing over the crowd. Pissant focused on one of the bright circles and made a game of trying to follow its apparently random motions.

It made him dizzy almost immediately, but he was determined to keep it up as long as he could. Anything to avoid looking back at the podium until he absolutely had to.

He was both amused and disgusted at the discovery that the faces of the crowd might easily have been cloned from the faces of the alumni and deans at the Patton's Eve cocktail party. Once, the circle of brilliance even paused on a face that looked like it belonged to What's-His-Butt Lightman.

Funny. I would've had the little shit pegged as a Dealer.

Pissant was about to dwell on this thought when the spotlight moved on, passing over someone who looked exactly like Bud.

The physicist stiffened. Had it really looked like the Wracker, or had guilt made him *think* he had seen a pock-marked face with a rivet in one ear?

It hadn't been Pissant's fault that Pinocchio had hurt Bud. Nor had it been his fault that the gnome had taken him away from the Wrack District, leaving Bud to wonder what had happened. None of it was his fault. The guilt, though, was his anyway.

He didn't mind. New guilts were useful things, because they took his thoughts away from the old ones.

His eyes followed the spotlight again and saw it touch yet another familiar face.

Pinocchio.

Pissant felt his abdominal muscles contracting in an automatic fear-reaction. If Bud was really out there, and the gnome found him . . .

This time, Claghorn was unlikely to let the Wracker get away with only a jab in the face. The bearded man at the Rose Bowl certainly hadn't. . . .

Pissant wanted to get up from his chair, leap over the table, and jump from the stage into the nearest and most dignified of the invited guests. That would distract Pinocchio and give Bud a chance to get away.

But Pissant knew he would do no such thing. It would be like signing his own death certificate, and he was too great a coward to do that, even for a bartender.

The only thing he could do, then, was pray that Pinocchio didn't find his friend.

The trouble with that was that he had no idea of whom to pray to. He'd been an atheist back when he'd been respectable, and now alcohol served as his God. But booze wouldn't help in this case.

Pray to your Moon Lady, then. Or to the man with the copper tooth, whose name is too holy for you to speak.

He tried, but he couldn't think of any words. He had no Savior to teach him what to say.

His eyes had continued to follow the roving spotlight, and now it swept over what had to be the group of "undesirables" to whom Wilson had referred when sending Pinocchio out on his mission. The three of them were standing far back in the crowd, many rows away from Bud, so maybe Pinocchio would head for them instead.

Sure enough, the spotlight was staying on the "undesirables," and another bright circle was coming to join it. The mob's attention was still focused on the podium where Wilson was raving, so they wouldn't notice. But Pinocchio and the other henchmen would head for the light.

Pissant took a deep breath and let it out in a sigh. Bud

would be all right, then, if it had really been him. It was too bad for the "undesirables," but . . .

They were trying to get away from the lights, and they weren't having any luck. Pissant could see, even at this distance, that they were Wrackers, and that two of them were exceptionally tall. One of the tall ones was slender and chocolate colored, and the other was massive and ruddy, with a flash of silver in the center of his face.

Between them was a shorter one with dark hair and pale skin, a woman—

Then he knew them, and almost wished that the spotlights had focused on Bud after all.

They were members of Blunt Instrument . . . and one of them was the Bastard Child.

"Oh, Jesus H. Christ, what next?" the physicist asked, miserable.

Nobody answered.

* * *

It was only when the governor of Missouri kicked Pissant in the shin that he knew he had been introduced.

Somewhere in the depths of his brain, he could remember Wilson criticizing President Fitzgerald's inability to "put America back on top in space." He also had a vague memory of Wilson referring to "an American who was there at the Space Age's birth and who will be there at its rebirth."

Pissant forced his eyes away from the spotlighted Wrackers and saw that the crowd was watching him. They weren't on their feet, but they were applauding and cheering. The governor's heel struck his shin again.

Pissant kicked back and hit the governor's ankle.

Winton R. Wilson had stepped away from the podium and was applauding vigorously. His face was smiling, but Pissant saw something in the Big Whig's eyes that threatened death if the physicist didn't get up there and start talking.

Pissant scooted his chair back, nearly tipping it over, and somehow got to his feet. He made it to the podium only because he was leaning in that direction.

Wilson threw an arm around him in a gesture that

would look like a manly hug to the audience. In fact, though, the politician lifted Pissant up onto the eight-inch platform and steered him to the microphone.

"Make it good, Brains," Wilson whispered fiercely.

Pissant braced himself against the podium with his left hand and fumbled in his breast pocket for his note cards with his right. He couldn't find them.

The applause was dying down. In a few seconds, he would be standing there mute and open-mouthed, looking like what he was—a useless souse—in front of Wilson's minions.

He looked out over them and saw the Bastard Child again.

He also saw Pinocchio enter the periphery of one of the two spotlights and move toward her.

There was a roar in his ears that was not the roar of the crowd. It felt as if his head were a glass sphere being sucked into a tremendous whirlpool.

"I—" he began, and stopped when he heard a weird, metallic rasp reverberate back to him from the distant walls.

The crowd murmured restlessly, and Pissant saw frowns on some of the closest faces.

At the rear of the crowd, the ruddy blond giant swung something at the tiny figure of Pinocchio. The gnome dodged easily.

Pissant felt a surge of panic like hot lead bubbling up in his lungs.

"I wonder if we could have all the lights out for a few moments," he blurted.

His peripheral vision told him that Wilson was stiffening in his seat.

"I'm quite serious," Pissant said, trying to keep from watching the faraway struggle. "Would someone backstage please shut off the lights? I'd like to make a point."

Miraculously, all of the lights, including the spotlights, winked out. The arena was immersed in complete darkness. The crowd's murmuring became almost fearful.

Pissant felt completely disoriented, unsure even of which way was up. But that had been what he'd hoped for.

Men were not friends with the dark.

But coyotes were.

Now's your chance. Run off into the night, where Papa and his guns and greyhounds can't find you. Burrow into the cool earth and cover yourselves until he's gone past and it's safe to come out.

Pinocchio was deadly, but it was the deadliness of men and puppets. It couldn't stand up to the survival instincts of coyotes, not when they had the night on their side.

At least, Pissant hoped it couldn't.

Whatever happened now, though, he had done all he could for the Wrackers. He hoped Blunt Instrument—and Bud, too—would have enough sense to get the hell out of there. If they didn't, it wasn't because he hadn't tried.

I did try, Ally. That was all I could do. Now I've got to look after my own pitiful ass.

"Utter darkness," he said as dramatically as his raspy voice would let him. "Imagine yourselves in a complete void, suspended in black emptiness, cut off from everything you know of the world, everything you know of your friends and families, everything that makes you who you are."

Pissant smiled an invisible smile. It sounded like he was describing himself on a particularly good drunk.

"Now imagine that there are only a few people with you," he continued. "Perhaps the two on either side of you, the one in front, and the one behind—and they are in the same situation as you are. They are cut off from everything except the black space you occupy. No blue sky, no trees, no pets, no sunshine. Imagine further that you must live like this for eight to ten months, and you will have some idea of what life will be like for the first Americans to undertake a voyage to the planet Mars."

It was a pretty weak justification for turning out all the lights, but Pissant was hoping that Wilson's penchant for grandstanding would convince the politician that the ploy had theatrical value.

For Pissant, the most amazing thing about the situation was that he was still standing. His grip on the podium was even relatively steady now that he had begun talking. If the lights were to stay off, he thought, he might be able to continue for hours if for no other reason than that he would be unaware of the passage of those hours. Not being able to see the crowd would help, too.

But he knew Wilson wouldn't allow that.

"You may bring the lights back up," the physicist said.

The crowd clapped hesitantly as the lights came on again.

Pissant blinked and tried to see whether his ruse had helped Blunt Instrument. He wasn't sure, but he thought they were gone.

He couldn't see Bud anywhere, either.

Hot damn, he thought, and cleared his throat.

"Sacrifice is nothing new to us Americans, however," he said, trying to give the words the same intonation that Wilson would have. "Though the risks and hardships for the first voyagers to Mars will be considerable, I have no doubt that we shall have thousands upon thousands of brave volunteers from which to choose. It would not surprise me in the slightest if most of you here would gladly undertake such an endeavor for the profit of your country."

The applause and cheers that followed this statement told Pissant that he had hit the mob's resonant frequency. Glancing over at Winton R. Wilson, he saw that the Big Whig was smiling.

Pissant began to breathe a little easier. Maybe he'd be able to get through the night without having his thumbs broken after all.

Even as he had that thought, though, he realized that the crowd's applause was dying and that he had absolutely no idea of what to say next. He felt for his note cards again, but they still weren't where he was sure he'd put them.

"Uh, I . . ." he began, and felt the familiar sweat that normally preceded delirium tremens break out on his face and neck.

The applause was gone now, and another glance at

Wilson revealed that although the politician was still smiling, his eyes had become dangerous.

Pissant looked down at imaginary notes on the slope of the podium and tried to remember at least part of the text Wilson had given him. It had been a rousing, rallying, red-white - and - blue let's - beat - the - Chinks - and - Brits - to - another-world speech, short on technical details and long on circumlocutory hyperbole.

Pissant couldn't remember a word of it.

"Shit," he whispered, and was horrified to hear the sibilant come hissing back to him from the distant walls.

His panic forced words up from his chest, and he found himself talking about delta-V, hyperbolic excess velocity, and launch windows. It was as if a tape recorder inside his body had been turned on by an unseen hand and was now replaying random bits of every lecture on space flight that he had ever given.

"The cheapest way to the red world is the synodic, or conjunction-class mission," he heard his voice saying. "The earliest conjunction-class launch window for which we could hope to have a spacecraft ready will be just before New Year's of 1984. However, although such a mission is cheapest in terms of delta-V, it requires a mission time of nine hundred and eighty dyas—two hundred and sixty days to get there, four hundred and sixty days on Mars before the next window back, and two hundred and sixty days to get home. This may be too long for a first mission, so we might want to consider a more expensive but shorter trajectory, an opposition-class mission, for which the earliest launch window we could make would be in, um, March or April of 1984. The difficulties with this approach . . ."

His lips, tongue, and vocal cords were working without his will, so Pissant let them talk while he looked at Wilson again.

The smile of Kansas City's Native Son was faltering.

Jagging hypocrite, Pissant thought. *What's he expect, anyway? Did I ever claim to be an apple-pie munching, flag-waving, drooling idiot? Did I ever claim to be anything but what I am?*

What is that, anyway?

A scientist, goddamn it. A goddamn sputzing scientist. Maybe not a respectable or a coherent scientist, but a scientist nevertheless. And if the Honorable Winton R. Wilson wanted something else, he should have hired a skagging actor. He damn sure knows enough of them.

Pissant looked out over the crowd again and was glad that he could no longer identify any individual faces.

"A third possibility," his voice was saying, "would be to use the gravity of the planet Venus to shorten the return path and thus hasten the spacecraft's return to Earth."

Venus had a way of doing that.

* * *

Pinocchio dragged Pissant out of the elevator and down the hallway toward his room in the King's Crown Hotel, twisting the physicist's right arm behind his back. It hurt so much that Pissant could hardly breathe.

"Please slow down," he gasped. "This is painful."

"I am aware of that," Pinocchio said matter-of-factly. "Unfortunately, you caused Mister Wilson some difficulty tonight. Not only did your order to turn off the lights prevent me from apprehending our intruders, but your speech was, shall we say, rather different from the one you led Mister Wilson to believe you would present."

Pissant tried to twist his body to relieve some of the pressure, but that only threw him off balance so that he fell to the floor. A red rush of agony told him that something in his right shoulder had torn.

Pinocchio stood above him. "Stand," the gnome said.

Pissant made it up to his knees and clenched his teeth against the raging fire in his arm. "Give me a second," he said, groaning.

Then he heard one of the three sets of elevator doors open behind him and a high-pitched voice ask, "Pardon me, but is this the fifty-first floor?"

The voice sound strangely familiar.

"There is no fifty-first floor in this building," Pinocchio said. "Kindly leave."

"My goodness gracious me," the voice said. "Is that man hurt?"

"It is none of your affair," Pinocchio said, stepping toward the elevator. "Kindly leave, or I shall be forced to hasten your departure."

Despite the pain, Pissant managed to look back over his shoulder and see that the person with the high-pitched voice was a gray-haired, humpbacked woman in a long black skirt. Pinocchio was approaching her and raising his arm to jab her in the face.

"Oh, all right, all right," she said, reentering the elevator.

Pinocchio turned back toward Pissant, and as he did so, the woman leaped out swinging a baseball bat. The sound as the weapon connected with the back of Claghorn's head was that of wood on wood.

The gnome fell to the floor and rolled, aiming a kick that would have shattered a kneecap had it connected. But the woman, no longer humpbacked, had dodged to the side. The bat came down on Pinocchio's ear. This time, the gnome's body shuddered.

"And one for good measure," the woman said in a voice that was no longer high-pitched.

The bat slammed into Pinocchio's head again, and there was a cracking sound.

"Piece of scrod," the woman said, throwing the halves of the broken bat down the hall.

The gray hair fell to the floor, and Pissant realized that the woman was no woman at all.

"How's it going, Bud?" he asked.

Bud stripped off the long skirt, revealing cutoff jeans underneath. "Can't complain, Pissant," he said. "Straight man's world, but I get by, peesh?"

The Wracker pulled the skirt over Pinocchio's limp body, then dragged the gnome into the center elevator. He jumped out as the doors started to close.

"Is he dead?" Pissant asked.

Bud shrugged. "I don't skagging know or care. All I'm sure of is that he's going to the basement."

The Wracker helped the physicist to his feet, causing only minimal pain to the injured shoulder.

The two stood awkwardly, facing each other.

"Now what?" Pissant asked.

Bud shrugged. "Up to you, Doc. When I couldn't find you the morning after P-Day, I asked around. Somebody saw you being dragged away in an arm lock, and the description of the Jack doing it sounded like the sputzer who whacked me. I figured you might be in trouble, but I didn't know what to do until I heard about this gig tonight. Had a dinking hard time getting in, and then I had to leave your speech early because I'd found out where you were being kept and wanted to get here first."

Pissant frowned and kneaded his throbbing right shoulder with his left hand. "Why'd you bother?"

"To see if you wanted out, jagoff. Once I agreed to take you to the District with me, you became my brother. I'm not crazy about the arrangement, but that's the way it is. Besides, I owed Croquet-Ball Head one. Now, are we cutting out, or are you sticking with Winton R. I'd-Sell-My-Mother's-Vital Organs-for-A-Vote Wilson?"

Pissant felt as though his bones were made of putty. He didn't think he was capable of doing anything but falling unconscious.

Standing there swaying, he stared at Bud and mentally drew connecting lines between the Wracker's facial pockmarks.

"Come on, Doc," Bud said, a note of urgency entering his voice.

Pissant shook his head, and the motion caused a fresh twinge of pain in his shoulder. "I don't know, Bud . . . I don't want to stay, but I've got nowhere else to go."

"You've got a whole community of Wrackers, Doc. If I accept you, they'll accept you. I guarantee it. Ain't no Wracker from here to either coast that hasn't read at least one Gator Al 'zine."

"Gator Al?" Pissant croaked.

"You don't think everybody calls me Bud, do you? Now make up your mind—Wrackers or Wilson?"

The choice, Pissant realized, should have been easy. For a sane human being, life as a denizen of Kansas City's

Wrack District would have been infinitely preferable to pseudolife as an appendage of Winton R. Wilson's political body.

But Pissant wasn't wholly sane, and there were things in the world of the Wrack District that frightened him even more than Wilson did. At least with the Big Whig, he had the opportunity to stay numb. That was impossible for someone trying to live as a Wracker—especially for someone who would have to live among people who by all rights should hate him.

A single night of revelry was one thing. A lifetime of being forced to actually *feel* his guilt every minute of every day would be something else.

On the other hand, if he stayed, what would Wilson do to punish him for all that had happened? Would the politician blame Pissant for what had happened to Pinocchio?

A bell chimed, announcing the arrival of one of the elevators.

Bud grabbed Pissant's left arm and began pulling him down the hall. "Now or never, Doc. We gotta head for the stairs."

Making his decision on the basis of necessity, Pissant began turning to run with Bud. But his legs were weak, and he knew that he wouldn't be able to move fast enough if the occupant of the elevator was one of Wilson's security men.

He hadn't yet fully turned away when the center set of doors opened and Pinocchio stepped out.

His muscles went limp.

"Doc, come *on*, let's—" Bud began, but stopped when he saw the gnome.

The Wracker's grip on Pissant's arm relaxed, and the physicist crumpled to the floor.

Pinocchio walked toward them. The trickle of blood on his right temple looked as if it had been painted there.

Bud stepped between Pissant and Pinocchio.

Pissant tugged on the ragged edge of Bud's shorts. "Don't be stupid," he said hoarsely. "They can't kill me now that they've gone public with me. Get out of here while you can."

Bud hesitated, then turned and jumped over the physicist.

Pissant could hear the sound of sneakered feet running away down the carpeted hall, and then the clang of the stairwell door slamming against a wall.

Pinocchio stood above him.

"Hi, there," Pissant said.

The gnome yanked him up by his right arm, and the jolt that went through his shoulder almost made him pass out. He saw the black and red checkerboard pattern in the air.

Then, without knowing how he had gotten there, he was facing the door to his room. Pinocchio unlocked it and shoved him inside.

"You will not leave," the gnome said flatly. "I have business with your friend, so I must find him before he leaves the area. I also have business with you, however, and I expect you to be waiting here when I return. If you are not, your life will only become more unpleasant."

Then the door slammed shut, and Pissant was left in darkness, standing on legs that felt unaccustomed to gravity.

He began to fall, and the lights blazed on. He was caught by a bearded blond giant with a silver nose.

"Greetings, sputzer," the giant said.

Pissant, feeling sick, turned his head and saw who had switched on the lights.

Lieza Galilei.

"My child," Pissant said, and closed his eyes.

13

Union Jacking

Guess I'll live in London.
The U.S. got nothing left for me.
Unless I'm very much mistaken,
Things ain't right in the home of the free.
Got me a Japanese camera,
Take me a picture of Big Ben.
Have tea and scones in the Circus,
Think about my lost American friends.
Yeah, I've gone Union Jacking.
Left Uncle Sammy 'cross the sea.
Didn't want to leave my family,
But the CIA wouldn't let me be.

They call it Domestic Surveillance
To catch subversives wherever they play.
They've bottled up the Constitution—
Didn't like Texas, anyway.
They ran me out; they'd run me in
If I gave 'em a cross-eyed look.
Do I make love with my eyes shut?
They've got it in their book.

—Bitch Alice,
"Domestic Surveillance," 1964

Saturday, January 5, 1980. Kansas City, Missouri.

The giant, Tycho, put Pissant on the bed, and the physicist collapsed back against the headboard. He wanted to die, or at least keep his eyes closed, but he couldn't stop staring at the dark-haired, leather-jeaned apparition who was looking at him as if he were a slab of maggot-infested meat.

Lieza Galilei. The Bastard Child.

It had always bothered him to see her image on TV, but he'd usually been able to get rid of the unpleasant feelings with a good drunk. Now, though, with her standing at the foot of the bed like the Angel of Death, he felt a steel spike in his chest that no amount of alcohol could dissolve.

"What did you call me?" she asked sharply.

Pissant tried to shake his head, but he couldn't make his neck and shoulder muscles work.

"I'm hurt," he said.

"You called me 'my child,'" Lieza Galilei said, mocking his voice. "Who do you think you are, some skagging priest?"

Pissant saw the Beautiful Moon Lady in her eyes.

"No," he said, whispering. "I've been unfrocked and excommunicated."

The Bastard Child's expression became an odd combination of defiance and puzzlement.

Tycho had crossed back to the door and was standing with his ear pressed against the metal. He held a short-handled ax, apparently ready to attack anyone he heard.

"Better make it fast, Leez," he said. "We got people waiting on us."

The Bastard Child nodded, then came closer to Pissant until she was leaning over his face.

"I heard your speech," she said. Her voice was full of venom.

Pissant swallowed. Did she know who he was?

"I saw you," he said. "I shut off the lights for you."

The puzzlement in the Bastard Child's face grew stronger. "Why would you do that?"

"Wilson's men were about to get to you. I wanted to give you a chance to get away."

Lieza Galilei's eyelids half-closed. "Why would you do that?" she said again.

Should he tell her? he wondered. Or would the answer only make her hate him more?

"I don't know," he said. "I suppose I didn't want to see anyone harmed."

The woman's eyes opened fully again, and her upper lip pulled back from her teeth. "Yeah, you're a real humanitarian. Why weren't you worried about people being harmed in '67?"

The steel spike in Pissant's chest began radiating cold into his limbs.

Don't make me go back again. Not now, with you here.

"I didn't have anything to do with the hardware," he said. "I wasn't in on the design of that valve. It wasn't my fault."

Lieza Galilei raised her chin and looked down at Pissant with an air of mock superiority. "Ach, zo," she said. "Eye vass honley vollowink horders, mein herr. Eye pullt ze lever, aber I vas nicht rezponzible fur ze Chews Eye killt."

But it's true! Pissant wanted to scream. *I calculated launch windows, fuel requirements, delta-V's. I monitored tracking stations and transmissions. I would've done anything to help her, but I couldn't! I couldn't!*

What he said was, "Believe what you want, then."

The Bastard Child leaned closer to him. "No good, dink-dink. I've waited thirteen years to ask you why you let my mother die, and I skagging well want a better answer than that."

"I don't have one."

She gripped his right shoulder, and red pain washed over him like a wave of blood. He whimpered.

"I didn't know you were hurt," she said, releasing him.

Pissant felt tears on his cheeks and was ashamed. "I

told you I was," he said, half-sobbing, and was even more ashamed. "What do you want from me, anyway?"

Lieza Galilei pushed her hands into the front pockets of her black leather jeans and looked away from him. Her eyes seemed to focus on some point beyond the wall.

"I want to know," she said, "if you or anyone else deliberately had Bitch Alice killed. She had enemies, and some of them would have done it if they could."

The words drove a second stake into Pissant's heart.

The idea had never occurred to him before. But there had been plenty of Straights in NOSS who had objected to Bitch Alice being the celebrity passenger on *Conquistador 18*, and they might have even—

No; it was inconceivable. No NOSS employee would have sabotaged the lander just to get rid of a Wracker.

But Winton R. Wilson was the junior senator from Missouri then. He was on the NOSS subcommittee . . .

Pissant forced the thought away. "No one would have done that," he said, his voice a thin rasp. "Least of all me. I . . . had a great deal of respect for her."

"Big sputzing deal," the Bastard Child said, glaring down at him again. "Your respect didn't do her a scrodding bit of good when she was stuck on the Moon with those other poor jagoffs, did it?"

Pissant said nothing. The answer was obvious.

Tycho spoke again. "Somebody's coming, Leez. Let's crank it out of here."

The Bastard Child turned abruptly and went to join her companion.

Pissant began to breathe easier, but as the giant opened the door, Lieza Galilei looked back at the bed with dark fire in her eyes.

"I'm not satisfied," she said. "You've got something dirty inside you're trying to keep covered up."

Pissant brought up his left hand to rub the moisture from his cheeks. His fingers twitched at the sudden prickle of stubble.

"I know," he said. Then, before he realized what he was doing, he blurted, "That's why she called me Pissant."

He saw an expression of horror on the Bastard Child's face as Tycho pulled her out of the room, and then the door slammed shut.

An incoherent bellow and the sounds of running followed.

A few seconds later, the door opened again. Pinocchio looked in.

"Did they injure you?" the gnome asked, with no concern in his voice.

Pissant found that he could shake his head now. It was painful, but he could do it.

"Good," Pinocchio said. "I must pursue them to ensure that they do not return. I myself shall return shortly."

"I can hardly wait," Pissant said, trying to sound defiant. It was wasted effort; the gnome was already gone.

Pinocchio was going to work him over soon, but the physicist no longer cared. Something else had taken center stage in his mind:

Why did she have that look on her face when she left? Did I give away too much? Should I have said anything? Or should I have come right out and told her?

As usual, Pissant didn't know what he should have done or what he wanted to do now. Beyond urinating and getting tanked again, anyway.

Maybe Pinocchio would bring back a bottle and let him drink from it after beating him up.

* * *

Pissant had wet his bed many times in the past, but right now he wasn't crocked enough to do that. He almost wished he were, because his shoulder was killing him.

And that wasn't the only problem. The instant his feet touched the floor, he was so dizzy that he knew standing was out of the question. He would have to crawl to the bathroom and back like a three-legged dog.

He half-slid, half-fell out of bed, ending up in his lambda position. In this posture, he could see under the bed.

Greenish eyes glinted out at him.

"I thought they'd never leave," a woman's voice said. "How about you?"

Pissant fell onto his right side. He wished the pain would simply knock him out so he wouldn't feel it anymore.

A thin, pale woman with short magenta hair crawled out from under the bed. She was wearing a blue denim jumpsuit.

A burly, hirsute man wearing the same type of clothing came after her. He had a rash on the left side of his face.

Pissant felt like giving up everything—holding his bladder, breathing, life.

"I don't have any money," he said. "You can search if you like."

The magenta-haired woman sat cross-legged on the floor beside him and smiled. "You don't remember me, do you, Yahweh? Or do you want to be called Pissant now?"

Pissant looked at her through watery eyes. The hair was familiar, but—

"No messing around," the burly man said in a voice like cannon fire. He stood up and scratched his face. "Let's get out of here."

The woman waggled an index finger. "Now, now, Bentley, we mustn't rush things. Professor Jackson has been through an ordeal. We must give him the opportunity to clear his head and make up his own mind."

"Bentley" snorted. "Yeah, and then grab him anyhow if he doesn't decide our way. Let's not waste time."

"Please, dear heart. A minute."

A grumble reverberated in the burly man's barrellike chest, and he sat on the edge of the bed, scratching his face and looking unhappy.

The magenta-haired woman looked at Pissant again, transfixing him with her green eyes. "Don't you remember me, love? You cut our date short. I told you I'd be back, but you left. No way to treat a lady." She giggled. "Or me either, for that matter."

Something in the tone of her laugh triggered Pissant's memory, and he recalled yet another in his long string of humiliations.

"Estella?" he said tentatively.

She clapped her hands. "Oh, you remember after all. Here, let me help you up."

Bentley snorted again. "You're playin' fookin' Florence Nightingale when we oughta be halfway to Whitehall by now."

Estella got to her knees and grasped Pissant's left arm. She pulled him up to a sitting position and then licked his neck.

The sensation intensified Pissant's misery. He was used to his impotence, but he disliked being reminded of it.

"Oh, that's bloody disgustin'," Bentley said. It seemed to Pissant that every time the burly man spoke, he sounded more and more Cockney, as if anxiety were eroding a carefully crafted American accent.

"Shut up," Estella said, snuggling against Pissant. "I'm convincing him to go with us of his own free will."

"Fookin' 'hoor."

"Um-hmmm," she said, and bit Pissant's earlobe.

"S'posin' he prefers 'em wi' tits, eh? What we gonner do then?"

Pissant still felt dizzy, but nothing else. He cleared his throat, hoping to make Estella stop.

She didn't. She talked and nibbled simultaneously, which made her voice sound oddly distant and muffled.

"You want to say something, love?" she asked. At least, that was what Pissant thought she asked.

"I, uh, didn't—" he began. Then he gasped as Estella worked her fingers inside his shirt and dug her nails into his skin. "Uh, didn't recognize you without your makeup."

"Um-hmmm," she said, unfastening his belt. Pissant had an unpleasant sensation of déjà vu.

"Great bloody Jesus," Bentley said irritably. "How much bloody time d'yer think we got, anyhow?"

Pissant cleared his throat again, directly in Estella's ear. She didn't seem to notice.

"You smell different," the physicist said. "Like pine-scented soap. Before you smelled like—like—"

"Bloody goddamn crankcase grease," Bentley suggested, scratching his face more vigorously. "Wouldn't ha' put the bloody stuff on if I'd ha' known it'd gimme these bloody two-weeks-and-counting bloody hives."

Estella unzipped Pissant's pants and leaned down farther. "Bentley says 'bloody' an awful lot," she said.

Pissant felt as though he were being pulled down a drain. His emotional state was one of misery, but he reminded himself that he was used to it. Far worse than the emotion was the physical remembrance that he still had to urinate.

At that moment, the doorknob turned with a metallic click. Bentley leaped up from the bed and reached inside his jumpsuit.

"Roight!" he shouted. "That's it, Steller!" He pulled out an automatic pistol and fired four quick rounds into the door.

The explosions pounded at Pissant's head like hammers as Estella grabbed his arms and yanked him to his feet.

Nobody, he realized, cared that his shoulder was giving him intense pain.

Bentley leaped over the bed, tore the drapes away from the large window, and broke out the glass with a chair. A frigid wind blasted in, making Pissant's eyes sting.

"Give 'im to me quick, an' I'll get 'im out first!" Bentley yelled, throwing out the chair after the last of the glass.

Estella dragged Pissant to her companion, who picked up the physicist as if he were a hollow plastic doll.

"Wait," Pissant said, half-choking on his own saliva.

"No bloody time!" Bentley cried, turning toward the night.

A second gust of icy air hit Pissant hard, and he felt his bladder about to go.

"We're on the twelfth floor," he managed to say.

Bentley paused, and his forehead creased. Then he turned back toward Estella, apparently oblivious to the fact that he still held Pissant in his arms.

"Bloody fookin' hell," he said.

* * *

No one came into the room, so Estella took Pissant to the bathroom while Bentley put a few more rounds through the cratered metal door "justa make bloody sure."

Estella had to help the physicist stand, but that didn't bother him as much as the fact that his muscles spasmed at the crash of each shot. By the time he finished, he'd decided that he might as well have wet his pants in the first place.

"Let's bloody go!" he heard Bentley shout, and then came the sound of the door opening.

Estella steered Pissant out of the bathroom and on into the hall.

"You do want to come with me, don't you, love?" she asked sweetly.

He was about to answer when he saw Bentley crouching beside the supine Pinocchio. Blood soaked the front of the gnome's shirt, and a raw wound the diameter of a baseball showed through one of the holes in the fabric.

"Think I bloody got 'im," Bentley said.

Pissant's abdomen contracted, and he began dry heaving.

"There, there," Estella said, patting him on the back. "It's all right. He can't hurt you now."

Her companion stood and gestured toward the elevators. "Let's go, eh? This bugger's likely to have friends."

Holding his pistol high, Bentley moved cautiously toward the elevator doors. Estella followed, leading Pissant past Pinocchio.

The gnome's hand closed around Pissant's ankle.

"Come on, love," Estella said, tugging on his arm without looking back.

Pissant looked down and saw that Pinocchio's eyes were open, and that his lips moved silently:

"We still have business to discuss, you and I."

Pissant choked.

Estella turned to pound him on the back again. "Now, now, now, now, now," she said, repeating the word in time with her pounding.

"He, he, he, he, he," Pissant said in the same rhythm, unable to get any other words out.

"He what?" Estella said, stopping the back-pounding.

A bell chimed, announcing the arrival of an elevator.

"Come bloody fookin' *on*, God-bloody-dammit," Bentley said impatiently.

Pissant stared down at Pinocchio. The gnome's eyes were closed again, and his hand had released the physicist's ankle.

"He grabbed me," Pissant said.

Estella took a quick step and kicked Pinocchio in the head so hard that the body flopped over onto its stomach.

"He's meat," Estella said. "Now, love, no more fooling around. You're coming of your own free will, aren't you?"

Pissant couldn't take his eyes off Pinocchio.

"What if I don't?" he asked.

Estella grabbed his hair and dragged him backwards into the elevator.

"Should ha' done 'at in the first place," Bentley said as the doors shut.

Estella released Pissant's hair, and he slumped to the floor. As the elevator began to move downward, he imagined its cables breaking and how it would feel to be in free-fall for a few seconds.

The thought made him happier than he had been in a long time.

* * *

Pissant knew he was in a private jet or turboprop airplane with a tastefully upholstered gray interior, but he didn't know how he had gotten there. He couldn't even remember leaving the elevator, much less getting from the hotel to the airport from which the plane had taken off.

That it had taken off was certain. A low, steady whine hummed through the cabin, and within seconds of awakening, Pissant felt a soft bump of turbulence. The oval window on his left revealed nothing but blackness and an occasional hint of stars. There was no way of knowing how much time had passed since the plane had left Kansas City.

Pissant was glad of the memory loss, actually; take-offs always made him sick.

Estella was in a seat facing him. She smiled.

"I'm glad you're awake," she said. "I had to hold a bag over your mouth for a while, and I was afraid you'd drown in your own upchuck."

That explained why his tongue tasted like spoiled liver.

He shifted in his seat and was surprised to discover that his shoulder didn't hurt. In fact, he couldn't feel it at all.

"I gave you a shot for the pain," Estella said. "Hope you don't mind."

"What was it?" Pissant felt as if he were talking through a mouthful of cotton.

"Oh, nothing dangerous."

Pissant looked at Estella's ingenuous face and knew that he could never trust anyone who looked as innocent as she did. Besides, she had nearly ripped his scalp off.

"'Nothing dangerous,'" he repeated, bringing up the left corner of his upper lip in a sneer. "Some nice, safe heroin, maybe? Get me addicted and I'll follow you anywhere, is that it?"

Estella didn't stop smiling. "You're already addicted to one drug, aren't you, Yahweh? A second would probably kill you."

Pissant shuddered. "Don't call me that."

"What? Yahweh? But that's what you told me to call you, love, and I like it. It rather excites me to think of God as a dirty, disreputable drunk."

A voice crackled from a speaker set into the ceiling. "Buttered muffins excite you, y'hoorin' tart."

Estella giggled. "True, sweet Bentley. You must be awfully jealous to eavesdrop like this."

There was no reply, and Estella laughed.

"Bentley's flying this?" Pissant asked.

Estella nodded, grinning broadly. "Um-hmmm, and he hates it. He doesn't want to admit that he has an incredible case of lust for me, but it's driving him crazy that I'm back here alone with you."

Pissant felt slightly nauseated. "He doesn't have to worry. I don't even remember my last woman."

Estella leaned forward and rested her hand on his left thigh. "Let's hope I make more of an impression."

Pissant pushed her hand away. "Sex no longer has any attraction for me," he said bitterly. "At least Wilson knew which buttons to push."

Estella stuck out her lower lip. "You think I'm a whore for hire."

"Is there any other kind?"

The pout disappeared and was replaced by the grin again. "Good point, Herr Doktor. The fact is that I'm not under contract to get you to screw me. I just like a challenge."

Pissant looked out the window even though there was nothing to see. Estella's grin and hair were starting to bother him.

"A challenge," he said. "I'll tell you what a challenge is. A challenge is getting my mouth to stop reminding me of dead animals."

In his peripheral vision, he saw Estella stand and go forward in the cabin. When she returned, she held a small glass in her hand.

"Peppermint schnapps," she said. "Satisfactory, sweet Yahweh?"

He turned away from the window but avoided looking at Estella's face. "It's the most vile stuff known to man," he said, taking the glass. "And stop calling me that."

"Apologies, dear Jehovah."

Pissant tried to ignore her as he rinsed and gargled with the schnapps. It truly was horrible, but it made him feel better.

When he had drained the glass, he held it out and tapped it with a fingernail, signalling for more.

"In a little while," Estella said. "We really ought to talk first."

Pissant groaned and dropped the glass onto the floor. At that moment the plane lurched slightly, and the glass rolled in crazy arcs across the gray carpeting. Pissant tried to think of it as a metaphor for his life, then decided that was too maudlin even for him.

"Are you listening, Yahweh?" Estella's voice rang in his ears like the song of the Sirens. "I said we need to talk, love."

Pissant kept his eyes on the back-and-forth motions of the rolling glass. *If you don't look at her, she can't pull you to her with the magnetic rays from her irises.*

"'Talk,'" he said. "That's what Pinocchio said he wanted to do whenever he really meant to slap me around a little."

"I won't do that," Estella said. "Unless you ask me to. The fact is, though, that I expected you to be full of questions when you woke up, and I had all my answers ready. But so far you haven't asked anything."

The glass had stopped rolling.

"Let me guess," Pissant said, pushing his fingers behind his thick lenses to rub his eyes. "If I ask the right questions, I'll get more schnapps."

"You'll get the schnapps anyway, love. Or rum or bourbon or whatever you choose to ravage your body with. Personally, I'd like you to ravage it with me, but that's not a choice I'll force on you. No, you don't have to ask me a thing if you don't like. I just thought you might be curious about who we are and where we're taking you."

Pissant's eyes were getting sore, so he rubbed them harder. "Hell, no," he said. "Questions used to be my whole life, but even then only when the answers mattered. In my current situation, the answers are the same as they were yesterday, and the day before, and the day before that, so they're no longer important. Change has stopped for me, so the questions must stop too."

Estella grasped his wrists and pulled his hands away from his eyes, knocking his glasses askew.

"That's not true," she said. "Change is an essential quality of life, and you still live."

Pissant shook his head. "Don't confuse walking, talking rigor mortis with life. I'm dead, and I have been for a long time. I'm a puppet more surely than Pinocchio ever was. A few hours ago Winton R. Wilson pulled my strings; now you do. You and Bentley might be Dealers sent to kidnap me away from the Whigs, or you might be Brits sent to throw a monkey wrench into American politics. All I know for sure is that you aren't Wrackers, although you did a couple of pretty good imitations on Patton Day. But whatever you truly are doesn't matter from my point of view, because I'm only an object, a thing to be used."

He reached into his pocket, took out the gold earring he had carried for two weeks, and threw it at Estella. "There. Payment in advance. Now may I have more of that putrid schnapps?"

Estella's smile had faded. "Boy," she said after a long pause, "are you cynical."

"Cynicism involves derisiveness and contempt," Pissant said, adjusting his glasses. "I don't care enough about anything to indulge in either of those."

"You're lying. You care too much."

"Don't tell me what I think. Do I get the booze or not?"

Estella sighed. "Soon, dear Yahweh, but first I shall attempt to combine the answers to all the questions you really want to ask into a few brief statements. I must do this, you see, because my boss will be upset if I don't."

"I don't care," Pissant said, putting emphasis on each word. "I'm dead. Or, more precisely, not living."

"Shut up for a bit, will you? Now, then: I used to be a Wracker, although not a devout one. I didn't follow in Dixon's civilly-disobedient footsteps, but went to live in Kansas City's Wrack District because my socioeconomic status forced me into it and because I got off on The Music. Then, a couple of years ago, I met Bentley, who hired me to work for the Crown as an intelligence gatherer."

"The usual term is 'spy,'" Pissant said.

Estella shrugged her thin shoulders. "Whatever. Now, where was I? Oh, yes... Prime Minister Carpenter feels that the United States' invasion of Conception—that's what *we* call the island, you know—was the result of President Fitzgerald's desire to rob Winton Wilson of some of his thunder by proving that *he* could be tough, too. But Wilson isn't going down. Instead, he's gearing up for a big propaganda push, and he's decided to couple a big-stick policy with a colonize-Mars-for-America campaign. You're a big part of that, Yahweh, mainly to symbolize Former Greatness That Can Be Reattained."

"You're boring," Pissant said as he began to stand up. He could probably find the liquor on his own . . .

"If you stand before I'm finished," Estella said, "I'll kick you in the balls."

"Vicious bitch," the ceiling speaker crackled.

Pissant relaxed his muscles.

"Given the current situation," Estella continued, ignoring Bentley, "one of two things is likely to happen. The first is that Fitzgerald, smelling the stench of his impending defeat, will become desperate and start a nuclear war with the Anglo-Chinese Alliance, figuring that he's got nothing to lose. The second is that Wilson will win the election and do the same thing within a few short months of his inauguration. He's already saying the U.S. should use nuclear weapons to retaliate for the misunderstanding on Conception.

"Clearly, the only way to avoid those two alternatives is to discredit Wilson. Losing you will make him look foolish, and looking foolish is death in politics. Thus, the threat of nuclear war is averted due to Wilson's downfall. So we're taking you to Cuba, and from there to London, where you'll be put on Her Majesty's payroll for your trouble until, oh, sometime after the election. You'll rate five pounds a day, I believe."

Estella took a deep breath and let it out explosively to signal that she was finished.

Pissant felt a headache coming on. Either she thought he was awfully stupid, or she herself was awfully stupid.

" 'Losing' me won't ruin Wilson," he said. "He can probably hire an actor who looks just like me, or close enough, and who can do a better job of reading cue cards than I can."

Estella waggled her finger at Pissant as she had done at Bentley. "Ah, but then he won't have a real scientist. Do you mean to imply that he doesn't really intend to put America back into space and usurp the Anglo-Chinese ascendancy there?"

"Of course not. He'd much rather nuke somebody else's space station than make his own. Did you really think—"

Pissant cut himself short and stared at Estella, whose smile looked decidedly more artificial than it had before.

"Oh, Jesus H. Wilhelmina Christ," Pissant breathed. "What the prime minister's really worried about is a resurrected U.S. space program, isn't she? All the rest of that was bullshit. Since the Brits have Churchill-Chiang, they aren't the least bit worried about the U.S. starting a nuclear war, are they?"

Estella looked indignant. "We simply want to cover all possibilities . . ."

"Real bloody tactful, Steller," Bentley's voice buzzed over the speaker.

"Doesn't matter," Pissant said. "I know Wilson has no intention of following through on the Mars business, and I'd be willing to bet that the same's true of Fitzgerald."

Estella giggled softly. "You don't quite get the picture, love. All I've told you is true, and yet . . . we didn't snatch you just to let you sit around and get fat on crumpets. True, we've got the Moon, and Churchill-Chiang, but the technology we needed for those was . . . well, borrowed, you might say. Our own space scientists are still mucking about like prep schoolers when it comes to planning for a voyage to Mars."

Pissant's headache hit him in full force, rivaling the best of his hangovers.

"You want me to work for the Limeys," he murmured. "You want me to work on getting them to Mars. You want me to be a traitor."

Estella rolled her eyes and made a clicking noise with her tongue. "Really, Herr Doktor Yahweh. Treason is such an obsolete concept. Look at me, a Kansas City girl super-snooping for the United Kingdom. The work is what matters, not who's signing the paychecks. You said yourself that neither Wilson nor Fitzgerald really plans on taking America to Mars, which means that your talents are wasted in the United States. Working for the Crown, you'll actually participate in sending human beings to another planet.

What does their nationality matter? It's the species that counts, isn't it?"

Pissant wanted to laugh long and loud, but his head hurt too much.

"Do you have any idea," he said, his teeth throbbing with each word, "how long it's been since I've worked on the kinds of problems you're talking about?"

"Oh, come now. Riding a bicycle and all that. Get back on and pedal. I'll be there to encourage you."

Pissant gave up and gestured toward the whiskey glass on the floor. "Now, please?" he asked.

Estella retrieved the glass, went forward again, and returned with a larger glass and a bottle of Scotch.

Pissant's headache began to subside with the first swallow.

"A toast, Estella," he said, raising his glass.

"Sorry, dear Yahweh. Can't drink on the job."

The physicist chuckled. "You will before all this is over. You see, my toast is to Chaos. Which is exactly where the great Alliance space program will wind up if you plug me into the system."

Estella tilted her head and looked at him in mock suspicion. "Sabotage will be impossible, Herr Doktor. You'll be working with numbers only, your computer will be separate from the Euro-Asian Space Agency's mainframes, and your work will be checked."

Pissant gulped three large mouthfuls of Scotch. "Check away. Even in the early seventies, when I was still making half-assed attempts at doing real work, I was discovering new and better ways to jackbug everything. Now I've got my method perfected, and it's impossible to tell when I'm doing it because I don't know myself."

The speaker in the ceiling crackled. "I don't think this is gonner bloody work out, Steller. He's a stinkin' Yank drunk who ain't gonner do Her Majesty no bloody good. Not to mention that we're all gonner bloody fry in a bloody nooklur war anyhow. On top of everythin' else, we're about to run into a bloody thunderstorm."

Pissant threw his head back into the gray seat cushion and cried, "And I don't even care!"

"Yes, you do," Estella said.

"I don't. I don't care about you or Bentley or Mars or crumpets or apple pie or the slightest goddamn thing."

Even as he drank down more booze, though, he knew that he hadn't told the truth. There were in fact a few things he cared about:

He cared that Bud would once again have no idea what had happened to him.

He cared that Lieza Galilei hated him even though she didn't know the whole truth.

He cared that Pinocchio—who was *not* dead—still had "business" to do with him.

He cared that he couldn't even begin to respond to Estella, who was rubbing his thigh again.

Most of all, though, he realized as the plane began bucking wildly, he cared that he was about to get airsick and waste some of the best Scotch he'd ever had.

14
Bucolic Bopping

Get on out to the country,
Get a rippin' down the highway,
Gonna leave the city limits behind.
Get a funny little feelin',
Get a-wrackin' and a-reelin',
Maybe think you're gonna lose-a your mind.

Got some pure ethanol,
Gonna have us a ball,
Got a blower and a four-on-the floor.
Don't you take no pity
On the people in the city,
Every one-a them is some kinda whore.

Now don't you ever ask-a me to cry
For them-a lovers we're-a leavin' to die.
Now don't you ever ask-a me to explain
Why that-a radio makes me feel insane.
Gotta go unwind, gotta save my behind
Before the flash in the sky a-gonna
Make my eyes go blind.

—Bitch Alice,
"Pure-Eth-Chevy-Nuclear-Blast-
Over-Kansas-City Blues," 1966

Sunday, January 6, 1980. Near Osawatomie, Kansas.

The Journal of Clifton Bonner:

"Hack."

So Lieza has dubbed me. The name fits, because it implies lack of direction and control. Much more appropriate than the refinement of "Clifton," and light-years beyond the cutesy-juicy lick-and-giggle of "Cliffie."

"Sputzing frick."

Those were the first words out of Lieza's mouth this morning.

Yet now she seems to want me to go where she's going, to take the risk with her. She won't say so, but the way she squeezes my arm when the others can't see . . .

I have the feeling that the hell they used to tell me about in Sunday School is a much more pleasant place than where I'll have to go to stay with the Bastard Child.

* * *

I woke up first this morning, half-suffocating, and poked my head out from under the patchwork quilts into the bedroom's cold air. Frost framed the window on my left, but the center of the glass was clear enough for me to see snow falling. There were already at least five inches on the ground two stories below.

I shivered, and Lieza shifted in her sleep. The top of her head was all that showed beyond the edge of the quilt, and I found myself imagining her as a sleepy child. As the little girl she must have been years ago.

The fantasy didn't last long. It's easier to believe that she sprang fully grown from Bitch Alice's forehead—already sneering at Straights, already with her left-handed black guitar slung over her shoulder, already in her crotch-zippered leather jeans, already a Wracker.

I kissed the top of her head, which immediately went under the covers. The leather sheathing her hips rubbed my thighs, then flinched away.

Even in her sleep, she keeps changing her mind about me.

So if I go with her, I may be doomed to reliving our first day over and over again:

In the early morning of January 2, she took me away from the other Concepcion hostages and brought me to her hotel room, where we fell into bed. I hadn't even washed Bill's blood off my hands yet.

Later, after the first insane lust flamed out, I took a shower. When I came to bed again, she was waiting to tell me that I had the personality of something found beneath a damp rock.

But after she finished haranguing me, she went under the covers and did things even Maria hasn't heard of.

Then she ordered room service, and we had breakfast in bed, eating enough for five.

She laughed at the way I wiped my hands on my napkin after every bite. "What's the matter, dink-dink?" she said. "Afraid of getting blood on your food?" She touched the cut on the back of my right hand with her left index finger, pushing hard enough to break it open again.

Somehow, that struck me as being even more cruel than some of the things I had seen on Concepcion. I started to leave.

She raised her blood-smeared finger and touched it to her tongue.

I wonder what a psychologist would say about my reaction to that. I finally wore out in the early morning of January 3 and collapsed on top of her.

"Get off," she said.

Several hours later, after we'd slept, made love yet again, and watched a fabricated report on the Concepcion battle (where'd they get that stuff, anyway?), she told me to go home.

I was sure that was the end; she'd had a Straight, just to see what it was like, and was done. And I'd had my goddess, if only for a day.

Then she told me to show up at the Municipal Arena on Saturday night if I wanted to continue. She had been in control of everything up to that point, but now she was putting the responsibility for what happened next onto me.

I don't handle responsibility well.

I rode home in a taxi. Then, through all of Mom's hugs and Dad's shoulder claps, all I could think of was

Lieza.

Fantasies aren't supposed to take on flesh and wrestle you to the floor.

Mom and Dad had a special-guests-only welcome-home dinner for me that night. No one asked how med school was going. All they wanted to hear about was my ordeal as a hostage of the Evil Empire.

I told them about the machine-gunnings, the helicopters, and the Gurkhas. I even told them a little about Genghis Khan, although I didn't call him that.

I tried to tell them about Bill, too, but the words wouldn't come, and Mom there-there'd me. She must have thought that Bill had tortured me. She was right, in a way. . . . Bill's *still* torturing me. So is ToniTerriTracie, and I never even knew her.

Along about Friday afternoon, though, I began to feel better as I settled back into my family's Straight routine. Great food . . . expensive trinkets on the mantel . . . one hundred and six TV channels.

There was a full-blown party for me Friday night, and one of Dad's clients, a real estate developer, offered me a job. He said I could start the first of February.

"With what you've been through," he said, "folks'll fall all over themselves to buy from you. You're a goddamn gold mine, son."

It sounded good. I wouldn't have to worry about bringing my aborted medical studies back to life, and I'd be involved in something that was safe and Straight. My affair with the Bastard Child would be filed away as a mere psycho-sexual hallucination. Leather and zippers, after all, are the stuff of dreams; the only thing that's real is the bottom line.

I slept well Friday night.

* * *

Then, early yesterday evening, Saturday, Maria called from St. Louis.

"Ohh, Cliffie!" she squealed, and I cringed. "You actually got taken away by Blunt Instrument! I was sooooo jealous—but you missed the reception in Washington! I actually got to meet the President, and the secretary of state, and senators, and just all kinds of important people. I only got home an hour ago, and I just *had* to call and see how you were. Did you get the autographs I asked for?"

I mumbled something. It didn't matter what, because Maria hardly paused for breath.

"But anyway, I'm going to their show next week!" she said. "I told Daddy how disappointed I was that I didn't hear Blunt Instrument on the island, and he's getting me a visa to go to Paris, and from there I can get to London, if Daddy pays the right people. Blunt Instrument's going to be there on Friday, and I told Daddy I just *had* to go! I'm going to party here tonight, then fly to Europe tomorrow!"

"Don't go to Britain," I said. "Things between America and the Alliance are bad. There might even be a war."

Maria giggled. "Not over a silly little fight with some Orientals! The President has more sense than that. Anyway, the reason I called is, I wondered if you'd like to go with me. I'm taking a few other friends too, but I thought that since you'd met the band, you might be able to get us backstage."

I felt as if my head were encased in a solid block of air that had begun to crack. Maria was rattling on about Blunt Instrument as though they were a grade-school sock-hop band.

Didn't she realize that The Music was beyond the grasp of people like her? The Bastard Child played *wrack & roll*, for Dixon's sake, not Straight bubblegum scrod.

And then I asked myself, who the hell am I?

The answer came back: the male version of Maria, that's who.

It was as if a sledgehammer had hit the block of air around my head and shattered it.

I am not. I am NOT.

I hung up the phone, then went to my room to pack a suitcase.

* * *

Mom and Dad didn't want me to go after being home for so short a time, but I told them that I'd planned a trip months before and had forgotten to tell them. I said I was going camping with some old college buddies.

"In January?" Mom asked.

"Venezuela," I said.

Dad gave me two thousand in traveler's checks and said I deserved a vacation after what I'd been through.

So I made my getaway, but as I got into the taxi and told the driver to take me to the Municipal Arena, I knew that even that triumph had been a failure. The only real way to win would've been to tell Mom and Dad—and Maria—where I was going and why.

Instead I'd taken the Straight way out, and lied.

They'd be proud of me if they knew.

* * *

I waited at the curb outside the Arena's main entrance, walking around and around my suitcase to keep warm. The two uniformed guards at the doors stared at me as if they thought the suitcase might contain a bomb.

"I'm expecting some friends," I called to them, but they looked even more suspicious. You'd think they'd know a loyal, mild-mannered Straight when they saw one.

As I paced, I imagined several versions of what my reunion with Lieza would be like.

One, she would laugh at me for thinking that she'd been serious.

Two, she would throw her arms around me and thank Dixon that I'd cared enough to come back to her.

Three, she'd walk past without recognizing me.

What actually happened was that I was still pacing, with my arms crossed and my hands jammed into my armpits, when three of the main entrance's eight doors swung open and three-fifths of Blunt Instrument charged out. One of the guards was knocked down, and the other reached for his gun.

"Sputzing Hobnails!" Cherry Angola yelled as she smacked the standing guard with her open hand. He spun and tripped over his partner.

As I was watching him fall, I heard an engine roar behind me and smelled burning ethanol.

Lieza rushed past me. "Grab him, Teek!" she shouted.

The Viking grasped my elbows and tossed me about seven feet.

I landed on my side on a hard, carpeted surface, then heard tires squealing and felt myself starting to roll. My suitcase dropped onto my ribs.

"I say, Mister Bonner," Joel H. Rodstein IV's voice said above me, "you might be more comfortable in the seat here beside me."

We went around a corner at about fifty miles per hour, and I was slammed against a metal wall. My suitcase hit me in the face.

"Clumsy scrodhead," I heard Tycho mutter.

Rodstein pulled the suitcase away and helped me into the seat. I saw then that I was in a minibus and that the lead guitarist, Fug, was driving. He was ignoring traffic lights, stop signs, crosswalks, and other vehicles.

Lieza was sitting in a bucket seat beside him. "King's Crown, where we stayed Tuesday and Wednesday," she said. "Heard one of the Hobnails say that's where Wilson and company are spending the night."

"What're we going to do when we get there?" a voice behind me asked. I turned and saw Cherry Angola and Tycho.

"I've got business," Lieza said. "Teek and I'll go in, but the rest of you'd better wait."

"Oh, good," Rodstein said, patting my knee. "That'll give us a chance to get better acquainted."

Fug looked at me in the rearview mirror and grunted. The minibus's right wheels hopped the curb, and we sideswiped a phone booth.

The bus shuddered to a stop under a streetlight half a block from the King's Crown, and Lieza and Tycho got out. I watched them walk away, puffs of steam rising above them like warnings from volcanoes, and wondered why I hadn't stayed in Prairie Village where I belonged. I had just done the most difficult thing in my whole life for Lieza, and so far she hadn't even said hello.

Fug turned and glared at me, growling. Cherry laughed.

"Pay no attention to them," Rodstein said. "They're simply jealous that our dear Lieza likes you so much."

I touched my sore nose, which had been reinjured

when the suitcase hit me. "She likes me, huh? I wouldn't've known if you hadn't told me."

"That's why I did so."

I stared at Rodstein's pale face, which was even paler in the violet-tinged glow of the streetlight.

"You have to understand, Mister Bonner," Rodstein said. "Intellectually, Leez despises the world that created you, and therefore despises you as well. However, the Bastard Child's emotions are, well, circular, like those of most other Wrackers. Starting at the top of the circle, if you will, *love* is to the right and *hate* to the left. But if you go far enough in either direction, you come round to the other. Does that make it easier to understand?"

"Not really," I said.

Cherry chuckled. "Look at it this way, shugahplum. I'm crazy for chocolate, but the scrod makes my skin explode."

Rodstein sighed. "Cherry, dear heart, you're only going to confuse the poor man."

"Poor man my skaggin' ass. I just found two thousand bucks in his coat pocket."

Fug growled.

"I suppose you're going to tell me *he* likes me, too," I said.

Rodstein leaned forward and scratched Fug's head. "He's the most brilliant actor among us, Mister Bonner. Intelligence quotient of a hundred and seventy, and musicianship Mozart would have killed for. Yet he chooses to present himself as an inarticulate lout. Quite true to Wracker philosophy, actually: to outwardly deny one's best qualities is to inwardly strengthen them. I, for example, am in fact a teetotaling Quaker opposed to loud music and dancing." He produced a flask from inside his coat. "Care for a drink?"

"No thanks," I said, looking out one of the rapidly fogging windows.

I heard the gurgle of the flask being tipped back, and then Rodstein said, "I fear I've offended you, Mister Bonner."

"Gee, that'd be a jagging shame, wouldn't it?" Cherry said.

I shook my head. "No. I just want to know what's going on. Why's Lieza going to the hotel?"

"None of your concern, Straight," Cherry said.

Rodstein sighed again. "Now, now, that isn't quite true. Leez is indeed going to see a gentleman on a personal matter, but she also has all of our welfares in mind. In case you weren't aware, Mister Bonner, we may be on the brink of a nuclear holocaust. Awfully exciting, isn't it?"

I still didn't see what that had to do with Lieza's going to the King's Crown. Was she going to see Wilson? If so, how could that help?

I voiced those questions, and Rodstein sighed a third time. "I'm not sure," he said. "However, the Bastard Child has never led me astray. I cannot help but think that what we do here tonight may have a tremendous impact on the future of our species. Perhaps we shall all grow tails."

"You gonna share your eth or what, dink-dink?" Cherry asked.

Rodstein handed the flask back to her.

No one spoke for a long time then, although Fug still growled at me occasionally.

"Where's everybody else?" I said to break the silence.

"If you're referring to our colleagues Dude, Ellyn, and the delectable Bazz," Rodstein said, "they're at the farm."

"What farm?" I asked.

"You'll find out, jewbaiter," Cherry said, slurring the words. She sounded as though she'd drunk the equivalent of three of Rodstein's flasks.

"Indeed you will," Rodstein said, patting my knee again. "As soon as Lieza and Tycho return, we'll be going there. It's a lovely place."

I pulled my coat tighter. "Is 'lovely' on that circular scale too?"

Rodstein raised one eyebrow and regarded me with an expression of mock pride.

"By George and Eddie," he said, "I think you've got it."

* * *

I fell asleep, and when I awoke, the minibus was roaring down a dark gravel road. I could see Lieza's head silhouetted in front of me and sensed the presence of Tycho's bulk behind me.

"Hey," I said, yawning. "Where—"

Rodstein cut me off by elbowing me in the ribs. "I'm afraid she's not in the proper mood to hear your voice now," he whispered.

I took his word for it. Lieza would probably throw me out at full speed if I irritated her.

God Almighty, what am I doing here? I wondered, but God Almighty didn't answer. I considered asking Eddie Dixon or Bitch Alice instead, but they might've thrown me out too. Asking Patton would have made it a certainty.

We reached "the farm" about two o'clock this morning, and I was able to see most of the place at a glance because the clouds coming in from the west hadn't yet covered the Moon. The two-story white-frame house shone like an iceberg.

It sits near the northern edge of a rectangular ten-acre plot. Tree-lined dirt roads form the northern and eastern boundaries, and sloping meadowland stretches away to the south and west. The first few flakes of snow were just beginning to fall as I stepped out of the bus, and I thought that even the bare trees must be shivering.

"Where are we?" I whispered to Rodstein as he led me toward a back door. I felt ridiculous carrying my suitcase.

"Geographically or spiritually?" he asked.

Lieza came up behind me and grabbed my arm, jerking me around to face her. My suitcase swung and hit her in the knees, but she didn't seem to notice.

"Why did you come?" she demanded, her breath like steam in my eyes.

I felt the alien voice trying to speak through my mouth again, but I fought it down and said, "You asked me to."

"Skagging hell if I did," she said.

Fug walked past us and grunted, then went up the concrete steps and into the house after Rodstein. Cherry came next, winking at me and staggering a little.

It made me feel braver, somehow.

"All right, then," I said, without knowing whether it was me or the alien speaking, "I came because I'm a Wrack-lusting Straight Jack, and I wanna get a little dirty."

Tycho appeared beside us, looming like a mountain, and hefted his short-handled ax. "You want Bert should cave in his head, Leez?" he asked.

Lieza squeezed my arm harder and steered me toward the steps. "No thanks, Teek. Those are the first honest words I've heard out of this jagoff."

She half-dragged me through a large kitchen and down a hallway to a staircase. We went upstairs, then down another hallway and into a bedroom furnished with only a plain wooden bureau and an iron-frame bed piled high with quilts.

She wouldn't answer my questions about what had happened at the King's Crown. She wouldn't talk to me at all.

And she still wouldn't take off her leather jeans.

* * *

"Sputzing frick," she said this morning, as she got out of bed. She was talking again, at least, but she sounded strangely preoccupied, as if my presence only reinforced something already preying on her mind.

I sat up and shivered as the cold air hit my bare chest. "What happened in the city last night?" I asked for the fourth or fifth time.

She opened the door and left the room.

I sat there for a little while, wondering how I'd get home if she threw me out again, and then I got up and put on fresh clothes from my suitcase. I didn't know where the bathrooms were, so I wanted to be prepared to explore.

As it turned out, I didn't have to go far. The sound of a shower came from behind a white door just a few yards down the hall from the bedroom.

I put my hand on the doorknob and hesitated. I knew it was Lieza in there; what I didn't know was whether she'd want to share the bathroom with me.

If I'd taken a half-second to think, I would have

known the answer. Instead, I turned the knob and went in.

The room was like a steam bath. The air was so thick and damp that I could hardly breathe, and I could just barely see the outline of Lieza's body behind the foggy plastic shower door. I planned to use the toilet and leave before she knew I was there.

She slapped off the shower and opened the door.

For the first time, I saw my goddess naked. Her torso was so pinkened from the hot water that her appendectomy scar looked faded, and her hair was molded to her head like a glistening black helmet.

Her legs were perfect.

Incredible, smooth, muscled, ivory—all of these words are right, and none is enough. Droplets, like dew, clung to the invisible hairs on her thighs.

"Skagging *Straight*!" she screamed, and then I was on the floor beside the toilet, my head humming.

Out of my left eye, I could see her above me, struggling to put on her leathers. My first thought was that she was crying, but then I realized that it must only be water from her hair.

"Jewbaiting piece of scrod!" she shouted, and tried to kick me. But her leathers weren't pulled up yet, and she fell on top of me.

Automatically, I put my arms around her. She pulled away and hit me in the face with the heel of her left hand.

The pain brought the alien to the surface.

"What the hell's your problem?" my voice yelled. "I only wanted to take a piss. I'm tired of getting beaten up, all right? I'm *sick* of it!"

I tried to grab her arm, but she avoided me easily and scrambled across the room to the sink. Then she stood, her leathers around her ankles.

"What a hideous crime I've committed," my voice said bitterly. "To see you without your pants after we spent half the night humping. I should be executed."

She opened the mirrored cabinet over the sink and began flinging its contents onto the floor. Medicine bottles, plastic bandages, a roll of gauze, some dental floss—

Razor blades.

My first thought was that she was going to kill me, and I started to crawl for the door.

She took a blade in her left hand and pressed its edge into her thigh.

I stopped crawling and dove for her, grasping her wrist with both hands. As I tried to pull her hand away from her leg, we stumbled backward and fell again. My shoulder hit the edge of the tub, but I didn't let go.

I managed to get the blade away from her skin, and blood welled from the cut.

Lieza was looking at her thighs as if she hated them more than anything in the universe.

The alien inside me had disappeared during the struggle, and I could control my voice again. "You can't do this," I said. "Your legs are *perfect*."

She relaxed, and the razor blade fell to the tile floor, *snikt*.

"Let go," Lieza said, her voice calm.

I started to release her wrist, then changed my mind and held it even tighter.

"Not until you promise not to hurt yourself," I said.

She drove her right elbow into my gut, and I let go.

"I promise," she said sarcastically, and stood up.

I coughed and repeated, "Your legs are perfect," like a scratched record.

"I know," Lieza said, pulling her pants up to her knees.

She glanced down at her left thigh. A single drop of blood slid down from the cut, leaving a red trail.

"It's an improvement," the Bastard Child said.

* * *

By the time I made it down to the kitchen, everyone except Rodstein was outside having a snowball fight. I watched them through the windows.

They were tumbling and laughing, and they didn't look much like my Blunt Instrument poster.

"Is your bedroom upstairs?" I asked Rodstein as he handed me a fork and a glass of some kind of multi-vegetable juice.

"Why, yes," he said, going to the stove to turn three pancakes. "So is Cherry's. Everyone else has rooms downstairs."

I sat down at the rough-hewn wooden table and sipped the juice. It was so cold that it made my teeth hurt.

"So why didn't you or Cherry come help me keep Lieza from slicing open her leg?" I asked.

Rodstein gave me a wry look. "I assumed you were engaged in mutual rapture. Besides, I was already down for breakfast, as was Cherry. You and Leez were the last ones up. I'm afraid Tycho and Bazz are especially upset with you; they fear that you're leading our dear Lieza astray into a life of Straight softness."

"If 'Straight softness' means I'm opposed to self-mutilation, then I'm guilty as charged."

A voice in my skull laughed at me. Big, tough Cliffie. As if a Hack could ever change the Bastard Child.

Rodstein flipped the pancakes onto a plate and brought them to me. "Based on the limited information you've given me, Mister Bonner," he said, "I infer that you made the mistake of seeing Leez without her leathers. If so, then I should inform you that you are the first to do so in well over a decade. She keeps her legs covered, and none of us would think of invading that privacy. Neither should you."

"But—"

"'But I'm her lover.' Is that what you're thinking of saying, Mister Bonner? Please don't, lest I blow my chow. The fact that Lieza has seen fit to allow a portion of your body into a portion of hers has no bearing upon any other aspect of her life or yours, so I suggest that you invade only those portions of her body and life that she specifically invites you to invade. Otherwise, she may do you serious injury, or allow Tycho's friend Bert to do the same. Peesh? Now, kindly eat our pancakes before they grow cold. I enjoy cooking, but it infuriates me when those I serve dawdle until the results of my skill have spoiled. Maple syrup may be found in the small silver pitcher in front of you. That pitcher's made from the same ingot as Tycho's nose, by the way."

I poured syrup over the pancakes, then cut into them with the fork. "How'd he lose his real nose, anyway? Some of the mags say it was bitten off in a fight, and others say he was born without it."

Rodstein sat down across from me, put his elbows on the table, and rested his chin on his fists. "You really must learn to mind your own business, Mister Bonner," he said.

Then he whispered, "Something to do with a lady with a chainsaw fetish."

I grinned, and started eating. The pancakes were terrific.

* * *

After I finished, Rodstein and I both put on coats and gloves and went outside. He plunged into the fray, whomping Fug in the face with a snow-boulder, but I stayed close to the house, watching.

How could I join? I was an outsider, a stranger, a Straight, a frick.

Cherry Angola ducked a white missile thrown by the roadie named Dude and ran toward me.

I wanted to go back inside, but was afraid to move.

"Hey, Jack," Cherry said when she reached me. "You ever done it in the snow?"

I swallowed. "Uh, done what?"

Her huge white teeth gleamed at me.

"The backstroke," she said, and then she grabbed my right arm and threw me. I skittered on my back like a hockey puck and plowed into a drift.

I exploded out of it and went after Cherry with a pitifully small snowball. She ducked it and threw me into the drift again.

This time I came up more slowly, and when I got to my feet the woman named Bazz was standing in front of me. She was wearing a miniskirt, and I found myself staring at the goosepimples on her thighs.

"When are you leaving?" she said in a low voice.

I looked up at her reddened face. Her eyes were slitted, angry.

"When Lieza tells me to skag off," the insane alien said with my voice. "Not before. Peesh?"

Bazz wrestled me down and pushed my face into the snow, then put her mouth close to my ear and whispered, "Maybe Leez knows what she's doing with you, and maybe she doesn't. But I'll tell you this—if you ever betray her, or any of us, I'll wear your balls for earrings."

Then she left to rejoin the main fight, and I struggled up to a sitting position and wiped my face with my gloves. My nose and ears were numb.

The roadie named Ellyn trudged up to me and smiled. "Looks like you're making lots of friends," she said.

I tried to smile back, but it probably came out looking like a grimace.

"I'd get better acquainted with you myself," Ellyn said, "but Buick here says he's getting cold." She patted her belly.

"Buick?" I asked.

"If it's a boy. Chevrolet if it's a girl."

She went on to the house while I wondered who the baby's father was, and whether it mattered.

* * *

I was mainly an observer for the rest of the snowball fight, except for a few moments when I became a designated target. I watched Lieza, mostly. She wasn't wearing a coat, but the cold didn't seem to bother her. She played like a child.

They all did. Even Tycho, who used Bert as a bat in a brief game of snow baseball. Fug cavorted, Joel tumbled, Bazz and Dude raced, Cherry ran and slid.

It was all completely un-Wrackerlike.

Don't apply your dinking Straight prejudices to people you can't even begin to understand, skagbrain.

Good advice, even if it did come from my own brain. I can't even understand myself, let alone anyone as complex as Lieza. Or Joel. Or Tycho. Or Bazz.

None of them seem to be able to make up their minds about *me*, either. Lieza seems to love me one moment, despise me the next; Joel is kind, but disapproving; Bazz is out-and-out hostile, but at the same time oddly chummy; Tycho is suspicious, but good-natured; Cherry is seductive, but wary.

So what have I become now, or what am I becoming? The Hack of January 6 isn't the same man as the Clifton Bonner of December 20 ... but I don't think I like either one.

Such were my thoughts as my feet and face froze. I was just about to try to enter the thick of the fight, if only to get my circulation moving again, when Ellyn stuck her head out an open window and called to Lieza.

"Better come quick," she said. "You were right. The scrod's hitting the slinger."

Lieza dropped the snowball she was working on and ran into the house. The rest of us followed, with me bringing up the rear.

We stopped in the big downstairs living room. The TV screen set into the north wall was on, and a panicky-looking newscaster was in the middle of reporting something that didn't quite register at first:

"... so-called U.S. 'spy' satellite within twenty-four hours to prove that they are serious. The destruction of this satellite, the Alliance spokesman said, is nonnegotiable. It is guaranteed that Churchill-Chiang Station will dispatch a nuclear device to the satellite before 11:00 P.M. Eastern time tomorrow. Then, unless all American troops have left Concepcion within another seventy-two hours, the space station will launch a second nuclear weapon, this one at Fort Eisenhower in Central Siberia. If the U.S. then refuses to remove its troops from Concepcion within another day, Moscow will suffer a nuclear attack."

"Sputzing hell," Tycho said. Fug grunted in response.

"Quiet," Lieza said, and everyone was.

"... promises that any American retaliation at any time will result in the destruction of ten major continental-U.S. cities. The Alliance spokesman pointed out that since the weapons will be launched from space, U.S. defenses will be powerless to stop them. Fitzgerald administration spokespersons deny this, but—"

I couldn't watch the screen anymore. The Straight announcer's face looked too much like mine. Instead, I turned toward the Bastard Child.

Slush dripped from her hair and from the end of her nose. Her skin was flushed bright pink, but her gray eyes looked like two small stones—hard, unfeeling. Her face was empty of emotion.

I could still hear the announcer. He was saying that the Fitzgerald administration was promising a "policy statement" soon, and that Big Whig Winton R. Wilson was urging a first strike. We don't have a space station, Wilson thundered, but by God we've got submarines. It's our duty to punish the Lemon-Limeys. Not only have they threatened us with war, but they've kidnapped our most eminent space scientist to boot.

A muscle in Lieza's cheek twitched, but otherwise her expression remained the same.

After a while, the announcer began repeating himself, and Ellyn turned him off.

"Let's see, now," Cherry said. "This is Sunday. The satellite buys it tomorrow, then Fort Eisenhower three days after that, on Thursday. Then seven million Russians and one million Americans bite the big one in Moscow—while we're giving our London concert on Friday."

"Only if our troops don't leave Concepcion," I said, desperate to believe things were better than they were.

Bazz looked at me with an expression of utter disgust. "Get real. Fitzgerald couldn't make up his mind in time even if Kirk'd let him, and the Alliance would probably waste at least the Army base anyway."

"They do sound rather upset, don't they?" Joel said.

"They don't know the meaning of the word yet," Lieza said softly. "Ell, when are we leaving for Paris?"

"Wednesday night, supposedly."

Lieza went to the black divan against the east wall and sat down. "Not soon enough," she said, staring at the floor. "Get us a flight tonight. Tomorrow at the latest."

Ellyn shook her head. "I dunno, Leez. The Squid'll cut off travel to Europe, and—"

"Get us a flight," Lieza repeated. "Tonight if possible, tomorrow if not. Make sure we leave from somewhere besides KCI, because they'll be waiting there for us. Our best bet's probably to fly to Toronto and catch a trans-Atlantic there, providing SAC isn't shooting down everything that crosses the Lakes."

Ellyn sighed and patted her abdomen. "C'mon, Buick. First thing we'd better do is let Stig Sullivan know we want to show up early, and see if he can help us do it." She left the room.

Dude followed her. "Better get our scrod together," he said. "Y'wanna help, Fug?"

Fug grunted and went with him.

The rest of us stood in the living room, looking at Lieza.

"Uh, Leez, none 'a my business maybe," Bazz said, "but what've you got in mind?"

Lieza smiled thinly.

"Only thing I know, babe," she said. "Wrack 'n' roll."

"Rammin'," Bazz said, raising a fist, and she and Tycho went into the hallway together.

Lieza stood. "Once we're all packed, we'd better try to catch some extra sleep. I doubt that we'll get much for the next week."

"Jolly good," Joel said, and he and Cherry headed for the stairs.

The Bastard Child and I were alone. She was looking toward me, but her eyes seemed focused on a point behind and above my head.

Then, as if at a sudden signal, she walked quickly past, squeezing my arm as she went by.

"Up to you," she said.

Then she went to help get Blunt Instrument ready to go.

* * *

I'm sitting alone in the living room with my notebook. Within twenty-four hours, my country—well, my country's spy satellite—will suffer a nuclear attack. Even as that's happening, Lieza will be on her zigzagging way toward London.

So what should I do? Leaving Prairie Village to come out here, I now realize, was easy—because I could always go back. Now, though, the situation has changed.

The Bastard Child is going to the Enemy.

But she's going to fight them. I don't know how, or whether she has a chance of winning, or what will happen to her if she loses, but I know she's going to try.

If I go with her, her fate will be mine.

My choice, then, is a clear and simple one:

I can stay in the United States, Straight and probably safe (for the President won't *really* let the Alliance kill us, will he?), letting those who run the world continue to run it as they see fit.

Or I can go with Lieza, and probably die with her.

Even if I were to survive, the odds would be high that I'd never see Mom and Dad or Prairie Village again.

When I think of that, I want to go home to the land of certificates of deposit and of fickle, sweet-assed, easy-to-understand Marias.

But when I think of this morning, of the Bastard Child pressing a razor blade into her flesh, I experience a revelation:

She needs me.

Under that layer of leather, she's a victim of self-hate; so I, experienced in that art, can provide her a service that none of the others can. Whether she knows it or not, that's why she wants me around.

I'm a bottomless receptacle for her loathing. I can take the psychic bruises she would otherwise give herself, thus leaving her soul free for the great task at hand.

Or, on a more basic level, I can try to keep her from carving up her legs.

Whatever.

I'm going to London with Blunt Instrument.

15

The Good, the Bad, and the Jackbugged

Daddy's got a little army,
Mama's just a little sore.
Sister got a little knocked-up,
Brother wants a little war.
Grandma's just a little frightened,
'Cause Uncle's just a little boy.
Give him a little pistol,
He'll think it's a little toy.

How long will you hurt them?
How long can you fight?
Will you cross the ocean?
Do you have the right?
How much is it worth now?
How much can you bleed?
I'll call up the vampires,
And you can let them feed.

> —Lieza Galilei,
> "Vampire Picnic," 1979

Monday, January 7, 1980. Somewhere over the Atlantic.

The Journal of Clifton Bonner:

Lieza and I awoke this morning at 1:00 A.M., less than an hour before we were to leave, and the moonlight shining in through the open window revealed that there was a bald man in bed with us.

By the time I sat up, Lieza had him on the floor and was doing something that made a crunching noise.

I scrambled out of bed, stumbled across them, and hit the light switch. The yellow glare hurt my eyes.

"Dodsie!" Lieza said, in a tone of surprise rather than anger. "What the skag are you doing here?"

As my vision cleared, I saw that she was standing, letting the stranger—although he was no stranger to her— get up from the floor. He was wearing a long coat and black pants, and my immediate impression was that he looked like an assassin.

He moved slowly, and I could tell that he was hurting. Lieza had probably cracked a few of his ribs.

"Dodsie" glanced at me as he got to his feet, and his grimace of pain was briefly replaced by an amused smile.

I remembered that I was nude.

I went to the bed and yanked off the top quilt, a red and blue patchwork, which I wrapped around my waist.

The intruder looked at Lieza. "I—" he began, and grimaced again. "I came to give you a message."

Lieza crossed her arms under her bare breasts—I wished she'd cover herself—and said, "Too bad spy school didn't teach you about phone calls, telegrams, or smoke signals. I hear some people even send letters. For that matter, why didn't you just knock on the front door?"

"Dodsie" tried to laugh and ended up coughing. I began to feel sorry for him. Either Lieza had hurt him even worse than I'd thought, or she'd aggravated earlier damage.

"Your Viking wouldn't have let me near you," he said hoarsely. "As for a phone call, Mizz Galilei, you've demonstrated a dislike for the medium. Besides, your line's tapped. Annabelle knows you're about to leave the country."

Lieza sat on the edge of the bed. "You here to keep me home, Dodson?" Her voice was hard-edged, and I had the sick feeling that she would kill him if he didn't give her the answer she wanted.

What would I do then? Would I stand by and watch as she took out a razor and sliced open a man who, for all I knew, had done nothing wrong beyond breaking and entering?

Or would I try to stop her?

It's a dilemma I may have to face before my relationship with the Bastard Child is over. She is, after all, perfectly capable of killing. She did it five years ago when a drunk made the mistake of trying to rape her. Her action then was justifiable . . . but slitting his throat didn't bother her at all, according to *Wrackweek* and the other mags. She tossed the body out of a ten-story window and went back to sleep. The subsequent investigation proved that she acted in self-defense, and yet—

Who am I to judge what she did or how she did it? Nobody's ever tried to rape *me*.

"Personally, I'd *like* you to leave so you'll be one less problem for me," Dodson said, "but you'll only make it if you leave immediately and avoid major terminals. I suggest going through Canada, but how you do it is your business. I just came to warn you that Zackman—remember him?"

"Like a bad case of the piles," the Bastard Child said.

Dodson half-smiled, half-grimaced. "That's the man. Kirk's put him in charge of her own little commando unit, which is illegal as hell, and they're on their way here. My info says their job's to sit on you until you give them what they want, whether you've got it or not."

Lieza frowned and cocked her head slightly. "You turned traitor to the service, Dodsie?"

He looked angry. "Kirk's acting without the President's knowledge, and I can't tell him without putting him at risk—she's bugged the whole damn White House. But as soon as I and my partners find out how many agents she's bought, we'll purge them and put things right again."

Lieza laughed. "Dodsie," she said, "things ain't ever been 'right.' You Straights keep exchanging one brand of scrod for another, figuring that a slight difference in stink means you've got a whole new product. But Angus or Holstein, cow flop is cow flop. And you seem to be forgetting that a few Alliance space toys may 'purge' all of us while you sputzers are busy playing cat-and-mouse."

"Yeah," I said, and they both looked at me as if I'd eaten my own foot.

Dodson moved toward the door. "Your opinion's of no interest to me," he said to Lieza. "I did what I came for, and now I'm getting out. Hope you don't mind if I take the stairs instead of sliding back down my rope. My shoulder is killing me."

He opened the door, and Tycho was there, brandishing Bert.

The drummer roared and swiped the ax toward Dodson's neck. The bald man ducked, and the ax head buried itself in the door.

"Knock it off, Teek," Lieza said. "He came to warn us that his buddy's heading this way with a pack of Cub Scouts."

Tycho clamped his massive left hand around Dodson's neck and tugged at the ax with his right. "All right, jagoff," he growled. "How many Cub Scouts?"

Lieza walked across the room to the bureau and opened the top drawer. "Let him go," she said. "He's got an urgent appointment elsewhere."

Tycho nodded toward me. "Y'don't suppose he could take Jack there with him, do you?"

Without warning, the insane alien voice surged up in me and said, "Go hock your nose."

Tycho released Dodson and yanked his ax free of the door. "If you were half the skagger you just tried to sound like," he said, glaring at me, "I might even like you a little."

He looked as if he were about to throw Bert, so I let go of the quilt around my waist and went into a crouch, ready to dodge.

Dodson, coughing and rubbing his neck, was trying to get out through the doorway again, but Tycho was still in the way.

In my peripheral vision, I saw Lieza take a white tee-shirt from the bureau and slip it on.

"Teek, put Bert down," she said. "And Hack, stop making like a sumo wrestler. You haven't got the body for it."

Tycho lowered his ax and squinted. "He ain't got much of a body for *anything*, does he?"

It was at precisely that moment that I heard a sound just like the thumpa-thumpa-thumpa I heard the day of the Concepcion invasion.

Dodson hit the door with his fist. "Try to do a good deed," he said. "Just go ahead and try." He glared up at Tycho. "I'll be leaving the way I got in, thanks."

Then he rushed past me, bounced across the bed, and went out the open window. A rope was dangling outside. I found out later that it was attached to a grappling hook caught on the chimney.

"So what's wrong with the door?" Tycho asked as Dodson disappeared.

The thumpa-thumpa-thumpa was getting louder by the second.

Lieza came back across the room and patted Tycho's bare shoulder. "Remember the Hobnail named Zackman we played with in D.C.?"

The drummer's scowl intensified. "I'll wake up the others."

The helicopter-noise became more than sound. Now it was as if small bombs were detonating over the roof, shoving down shock waves of compressed air that rocked the house. A brilliant white beam of light stabbed into the yard.

"Don't bother," Lieza yelled to Tycho, who was heading down the hall. "I have a feeling that everybody's already awake. Insomnia, maybe."

She turned toward me and gave me a smile that was almost a smirk.

"Put on some pants," she shouted. "Don't want to get anything frostbitten, now, do we?"

Then she went after Tycho, leaving me alone in the rumbling bedroom.

* * *

The helicopter landed on the meadowlike lawn south of the house. Two spotlights mounted above its landing skids cut through the night, making the chopper itself almost impossible to see.

Then the spotlights flickered, and I saw the silhouettes of armed figures. They flattened themselves against the snow about ten yards north of the helicopter, and I knew that at least one of them was aiming at me.

I had yanked on a pair of jeans and dashed out of the house after everyone else, figuring that we'd jump into the prepacked minibus and get out of there—but I should've known better.

Wrackers don't run away.

In the glare of the spotlights, my feet freezing in the snow, I couldn't help thinking that the Bastard Child and her companions were idiots, and that I was an idiot for staying with them.

I was standing next to Bazz, who nudged me with her shoulder.

"The keys are in the bus," she said quietly.

She knew what I was thinking. She knew me for the Straight I am.

The creature inside me was pissed that she could read me so easily. I looked at her spotlight-illuminated face and saw that her eyes were full of contempt.

"I'm not going anywhere, skagbreath," my voice said. The steam from my mouth roiled into her face, making her blink.

It was ludicrous. There I was, barefoot and shirtless in the subzero night, about to be blown away by commandos, and I was arguing about my right to be there. Hadn't I seen, touched, and tasted enough blood on Concepcion to last me an eternity? Did I really want more?

"Talk's easy," Bazz said. "My money says you're

gonna squirm off. Ain't no cock gonna have to crow three times, either. You'd kiss her on the cheek and hand her over if you thought it'd save your pitiful ass."

I turned away to face the lights again. My experience with Maria had made me feel that every Straight should've been named Judas, but I didn't want to think about whether that applied to me, too.

I also didn't want my balls made into earrings.

Lieza and Tycho were standing ten feet closer to the helicopter than the rest of us were, and their dark shapes were outlined against the light. Without willing it, I took one step, and then another, and another, until I was standing beside the Bastard Child.

She glanced at me. "Shoulda put on a shirt," she said.

It was only then that I realized I was shivering violently. I still don't know how much of it was due to the cold and how much was due to terror. No wonder Bazz thought I was about to run.

Who am I kidding? She'd have thought that anyway, and if I were capable of making decisions, she might've been right. As it was, I wound up trying to look brave.

I don't think I fooled anyone.

The chopper was winding down, its blades making only a slow whuff-whuff-whuff sound.

"LISA PENDLETON," a voice boomed through a loudspeaker.

"These dinks are *not* getting on my good side," Lieza muttered.

"How many of 'em are there?" Tycho asked. He sounded as if he were planning to take on any number up to a hundred thousand.

"I counted ten," Lieza said.

"Eight of us," Tycho said. "Eight and an eighth if you count your boyfriend."

"YOU WILL STEP FORWARD, LISA PENDLE-TON, OR WE WILL BE FORCED TO OPEN FIRE."

"They've got guns," I blurted.

Joel's voice rang out behind me, singing, "We got guuns, they got guuns, alluh God's chillun got guuunnns!"

I was confused. "You've got guns?" I asked Lieza.

"Of course not, frick," she said. "He's doing a number from *Duck Soup*."

Then she was walking toward the helicopter.

Tycho started to go with her, and the loudspeaker boomed, "PENDLETON MUST COME FORWARD ALONE, OR WE WILL OPEN FIRE."

"'Must?'" Tycho bellowed. "We don't know the *meaning* of 'must,' you jagging jewbaiters!"

Lieza looked back over her shoulder. "Just stay there, Teek. Plan D."

The Bastard Child continued toward the helicopter.

"What's Plan D?" I asked Tycho.

"I got no sputzing idea," he said, scratching his head with his ax.

Joel appeared between us. "'D' stands for dance," he said as he pirouetted in the snow.

"Is that supposed to distract them?" I asked. My throat was beginning to feel scratchy and sore.

Joel gave me a puzzled look. "My dear Mister Bonner," he said, "it's supposed to be *fun*."

He did another pirouette.

Strangely, insanely, my numb feet began to shuffle and hop, and I found myself doing a jig while the Bastard Child walked toward the muzzles of machine guns.

Above us, the gibbous, waning Moon shone faintly through a thin layer of clouds. I wondered if Bitch Alice was watching, and whether she might be dancing too.

* * *

Lieza came trudging back in less than a minute, a sardonic smile on her face.

"The Squid thinks we've got Daniel Jackson," she said, "and Zackman's here for him. Somebody must've been watching when you and I went into the hotel Saturday night, Teek."

Cherry, Bazz, Fug, Dude, and Ellyn came to stand with the rest of us. "Don't they watch TV?" Cherry asked angrily. "They oughta know as well as we do that the Brits took Jackson."

Lieza shrugged. "That's according to Wilson, who's also saying that the administration knew about the kidnapping plot a week ago and did nothing. I get the idea that the Squid was planning a snatch of her own and was beaten to it, so she's taking it out on us as the nearest available scapegoats. Then, on the off chance that we actually did it, she can make Wilson out to be a liar."

"What happens when we don't produce Mister Wizard?" Ellyn asked. She was the only one of us wearing a coat.

"Whattaya think?" Tycho said. "They're gonna blast us apart."

Lieza nodded. "The Squid's upset with me anyway, and if I don't produce what she wants this time, she's given Zackman the OK to disembowel me, which would please him immensely."

"So what do we do?" I asked, weakly.

Bazz looked at me with hatred in her eyes. "I say 'we' give them *you*, then crank out of here before they figure out they've got the wrong Jack."

"Now, now, Bazz," Joel said soothingly. "Mister Bonner is our guest. Besides, Straights don't really all look alike." He peered at me. "Pity he isn't thirty years older, isn't it?"

"YOU'VE GOT TWENTY SECONDS," the loudspeaker roared.

"Anyone for a quickie?" Cherry asked.

Tycho twirled his ax in his right hand. "Take the time to do it right, Cherry-mash. They've got bullets, but I've got Bert and Fug's got teeth. Right, Fug?"

Fug growled and charged toward the helicopter with Tycho close behind.

Lieza grinned at me. "Beats freezing to death," she said as she followed Tycho and Fug. The others, even Ellyn, went with her.

They were running toward Death. They were *laughing* about it.

I couldn't do it. No matter how much I loved Lieza, I couldn't run into a wall of bullets.

Then Bazz glanced back at me. I didn't see her expression, but I didn't have to.

The creature inside me took over my legs, and I was screaming and running after the Wrackers.

"HALT IMMEDIATELY OR WE WILL SHOOT YOU DOWN IN YOUR TRACKS," God told me.

The alien used my mouth to tell God to go stuff Himself.

I had passed Bazz and was about to catch up to Lieza, who was only fifteen yards from the first of the gunmen, when both of the spotlights on the helicopter went dark. I heard two loud popping noises and the oddly dull sound of shattering plastiglass.

"Drop!" I heard Lieza yell, and my body dropped. My skin was so cold by now that I didn't even feel the snow.

Without knowing why I was doing it, I began to crawl toward the helicopter. Maybe the alien wanted to sneak up on our attackers and kill them one by one, or maybe it just wanted to keep moving.

I heard a *thunk* and a groan, and I knew that Tycho had introduced one of the attackers to the flat side of Bert the Ax. I began to think that we might get out of this mess alive after all. The only question I had was about how Lieza had managed to knock out the spotlights.

I should have known better. Lieza doesn't plan ahead for things like that. She had been acting as a Wracker, on instinct—prepared to die, but ready to react to whatever happened next.

Someone else had taken care of the lights, and for his own reasons.

"Everyone will please stop moving," a monotonous voice called from the trees along the road fifty yards to my left. "Those who are armed may keep your weapons, but all motion must cease. Anyone who continues to move, or who attempts to use a weapon, will be killed. My companions and I are equipped with infrared rifle sights."

I stopped moving.

"This is beginning to feel like a rerun," I heard Cherry mutter just ahead of me.

"Very good," the monotonal voice called. "My name is Dennis Claghorn. I represent Mister Winton R. Wilson, and have been sent by him to discuss certain matters with those persons occupying this residence. I will now approach alone, but my companions are keeping weapons trained on each of you. Please do not attempt to harm me."

The helicopter's loudspeaker crackled to life. "WHY DON'T YOU GO STRAIGHT TO—"

A barrage of shots exploded from the trees and peppered the helicopter. At least one of them hit the loudspeaker dead center, reducing the voice of "God" to a series of squeaks and buzzes. Zackman's men fired back, but from what I could see with one eye above the snow, they were aiming too high, hitting the trees' upper branches when they hit anything at all.

The shots stopped, and the monotonal voice called again: "There are three groups here, each in opposition to the other two. I suggest that one representative from each group walk into the open yard approximately twenty yards northeast of the helicopter. There, each of us will be equally vulnerable to attack—and thus equally protected."

A flashlight came on just outside of the trees, and it bobbed closer.

Lieza stood up.

"For Christ's sake, get down!" I whispered at her. "They're going to kill you!"

She nudged my left armpit with her foot. "Didn't know you cared," she said. "Cherry, Joel, everybody—go wait beside the house. Zackman's Dumbasses won't shoot as long as the Hobnails have them pinned down." She walked toward the flashlight.

Tycho appeared out of the night and pulled me to my feet. I could see a dark smear on one side of his ax.

"Just when things were gettin' interesting," he said, giving me a push toward the house.

* * *

By the time the Bastard Child returned from her second "meeting," I was beginning to have some feeling in my fingers and toes again. Ellyn had sneaked into the house and brought me a sweatshirt, gloves, and socks.

"Here's the situation," Lieza said, rubbing her bare

arms as she came close to us. "The Dumbasses *and* the Hobnails think we snatched Jackson. Publicly, Wilson says the Brits kidnapped him, but privately, he thinks we're responsible. If you ask me, Wilson wants Jackson back so he can kill him and blame *that* on the Brits too."

I noticed that Lieza hesitated every time she said "Jackson." It was as if the name made a bad taste in her mouth.

"Great Dixon," Bazz said in disgust. "The scrodding world's a day away from nuclear war, and these dinks are tiddly-winking over a waste-case. I say we tell 'em to skag off. We're likely to be radioactive powder before the week's out, anyway, so we might as well go down swinging instead of sizzling."

"Bravo, hear hear, yessirreebob, and other assorted noises of agreement and support," Joel said.

Lieza shook her head. "The Hobnails've got something of ours. They want to make a trade, and Zackman claims to be willing to hang back until the swap's completed. Says he wants to see Jackson before he decides whether to blow us all away. Sweet of him."

Joel cleared his throat. "Leez, dear," he said, "you're talking rather large circles around those of us who have destroyed most of our cerebrums with chemicals. To what sort of 'trade' are you referring?"

Lieza cupped her hands and blew into them. Even the Bastard Child is made of mere flesh.

"They've got Gator Al," she said. "I know it's true, 'cause I could see him in the trees. The Hobnails holding him slapped his face a few times to make their point."

"Sputzing Patton," Dude said through clenched teeth. "How're we gonna get him out when we've got no Jackson to give them?"

Tycho lifted Bert the Ax over his head and shook it. Fug growled.

"Who's Gator Al?" I asked. I have no idea what difference my knowing could've made.

"Midwest Wracker grapevine junction," Cherry said. "Met him a couple of years ago. Nice guy, great lay."

Joel laughed. "Cherry, m'love, your definition of a 'great lay' is anyone who manages to see you naked without fainting."

"Hardy-har, jagoff."

A burst of machine-gun fire shattered the kitchen windows above our heads.

"Will we make an exchange, or will we not?" the monotonal voice called.

Lieza's body tightened visibly, as if she were a cornered animal ready to leap. The moonlight made her features look sharp and deadly.

"Teek, Fug," she said in a low voice, "when I say so, go through the house and out to the north road. Double back through the east road's ditch and see if you can get to Gator Al. The rest of us'll hit Zackman's Cub Scouts while they're watching whatever you're doing to the Hobnails."

Tycho hefted Bert again. "Let's kick some Straight butt," he said, and then he looked at me. "No offense."

Fug grunted.

Lieza turned to face the trees and cupped her hands around her mouth. "It's a deal," she yelled. "Jackson's inside. I'll have two of my people bring him out, and we'll make the trade in the open. Then you and Zackman can work out your other problems without us."

"Three of my colleagues must accompany your two representatives," the monotonal voice called. "My three will be armed; your two will not. I must also remind Agent Zackman that any shots fired by his group will result in the destruction of all."

Lieza glanced at Fug, who grunted again, and then at Tycho, who licked his lips and dropped Bert.

Three figures dressed in white hooded snowsuits scuttled out from the trees. They would have blended in perfectly with the white ground if it hadn't been for their black assault rifles. They came to us without saying a word, then followed Tycho and Fug into the house, guns at the ready.

Almost immediately, I heard three soft thumps.

"Ein, zwei, drei," Dude murmured.

None of the Wrackers had felt even the slightest doubt

that Fug and Tycho could disable three armed Hobnails once they were in close quarters.

What is it that gives them such confidence? What is it that makes them willing to run toward Death, gambling that Death will turn tail?

"Wonder how long we've got before they realize we aren't going to deliver," Cherry said quietly, and as she finished the sentence, a high-pitched electronic trill cut through the night. It took me several seconds to realize that it was coming from the helicopter.

I looked at Lieza and saw that she was gazing up at the Moon. I couldn't read her expression.

The sound cut off after about twenty seconds, and then I heard someone—Zackman, I think—yelling and cursing.

"Goddamn lemon-lime–bellied bastards!" he shouted. "They said they'd wait until 11:00 P.M.!"

"Looks like we've got ourselves a diversion," Bazz said. She didn't sound happy about it.

Zackman's shouts could mean only one thing: Churchill-Chiang Station had nuked the spy satellite.

The war had begun.

I felt a chill that had nothing to do with the snow.

Lieza lowered her eyes and frowned. "You always go too far, Mama," she whispered. I think I was the only one who heard her.

The helicopter engine revved up again, and a figure waving a white handkerchief came toward us and stopped about twenty yards away. He had short-cropped blond hair and was wearing a belted trench coat similar to Dodson's. He looked like a Nazi, and I knew immediately that this was Zackman.

"I've got another assignment," he shouted. "National emergency. You have thirty seconds to hand over Professor Jackson. If you don't, we're going to hit the house with an air-to-ground missile as soon as we've got enough altitude."

"And risk killing the man you're supposed to be rescuing?" Lieza yelled. "Don't give me that scrod. Besides, aren't you forgetting your friends in the trees?"

"They've been bluffing," Zackman yelled. "They wouldn't dare launch an attack on representatives of the U.S. Government. The retaliation would wipe them out."

Immediately, blue-white flashes of fire danced among the trees, and a series of staccato explosions provided a counterpoint to the noise of the helicopter engine.

Zackman whirled and ran.

The Wrackers and I dropped to the snow again, and I watched Zackman running in a zigzag pattern back to the chopper. He looked ridiculous. If the Hobnails in the trees had wanted to, they could've pumped a hundred rounds into him without even aiming. Instead, though, I could tell that their shots were meant to form a barrier over the helicopter to prevent it from taking off. They took the threat of a missile seriously even if Lieza didn't.

Then, all at once, the flashes of blue flame in the trees began pointing inward, leaving the chopper free to go. Claghorn and company had unwelcome visitors.

The Wrackers beside me got to their feet and ran for the trees. I had a feeling of déjà vu and a premonition of doom.

But I followed. Stumbling and numb, with my head being buffeted by the frigid windstorm from the helicopter blades, I followed. I caught a glimpse of my right hand and was surprised to see that I was carrying Bert the Ax.

As we ran, some of the gunfire shifted. Even in the midst of the helicopter noise, I heard slugs whizzing over my head.

Over my head?

I stopped just before reaching the trees and looked back at the house.

There, on the roof, a moonlit figure wearing a patchwork cloak waved to me.

The figure's face was hidden by the cloak, but I had the overpowering feeling that it had to be a god—Eddie Dixon, perhaps, come down from heaven to chastise us. Or Bitch Alice, beamed down with the moonlight.

The helicopter roared louder than ever, and I involuntarily turned to look. It rose from the ground, pivoted when it reached a height of about fifty feet, and headed for the house.

I had been standing still too long and was hit from behind. As I fell, one of Winton R. Wilson's white-clad mercenaries rushed past me, wildly firing his rifle at either the chopper or the figure on the roof.

I realized that both Zackman and Claghorn must think that the cloaked god was Daniel P. Jackson.

My body lunged forward, scrambling on all fours through the snow, and tackled the mercenary from behind. He fell on his face, and I jumped knees-first onto his lower back. Something crunched in his spine, and he shuddered and became still.

The insane creature inside me laughed. I tossed Bert away and snatched up the mercenary's assault rifle.

As I stood, I saw a cable and harness being lowered from the helicopter's open doorway. Apparently, Zackman hoped "Jackson" would choose an uncertain fate in the aircraft rather than face Wilson's hired guns.

I pointed the rifle at the chopper, but the insane alien didn't know how to operate such a weapon any better than I did.

As the helicopter paused over the house, the figure on the roof threw off its patchwork cloak. Moonlight gleamed off a bald head.

Dodson.

He raised a pistol and fired five quick rounds at the chopper, which tilted crazily and lost altitude.

One of the landing skids hit the agent in the head, and he fell onto his belly and slid down the snow-covered shingles feetfirst. His left foot caught in the rain gutter, but his momentum pulled his body over and slammed his back against the side of the house.

His foot stayed in the gutter, and he hung upside-down, his ankle and leg impossibly twisted. He reached for something to grab hold of but found nothing.

The helicopter, looking as if it would crash at any second, wobbled off to the north. It wouldn't be firing any missiles.

I had a choice. Should I go help Dodson down from

where he was dangling in obvious agony, or should I turn to fight alongside my Wracker friends?

There was still gunfire in the trees behind me, so I chose Lieza. But as always, I didn't choose soon enough.

When I turned, the mercenary I thought I'd killed hit my face with a fist like a chunk of ice.

I floated down like a snowflake.

The rifle disappeared from my hands.

As I lay there, the noises of battle seeming a hundred miles away, I saw a white ghost flip a switch on his weapon, raise it to his shoulder, and fire three bullets into the chest of the man hanging from the roof.

Tycho leaped into my field of vision, scooped up Bert, and swatted the mercenary to the ground.

I lay unmoving for a long time. The thick, warm taste of failure filled my mouth.

* * *

Counting the three men that Fug and Tycho disabled in the house, the Wrackers fought and defeated eleven armed Hobnail goons, killing only one of them—the one who shot Dodson. Tycho and Bert caved in his head as if it were an empty shell of papier-mâché.

On our side, only Bazz was hurt badly enough to require a bandage. Her right biceps was bleeding from an oval wound. I asked her whether it was from a bullet or a knife, but she only glared at me.

Ellyn examined my battered face, which is never going to heal, and clicked her tongue in what might have been genuine sympathy.

"Pretty ugly?" I asked.

She half-smiled and shook her head. "Just a little jackbugged," she said, and then went to help take care of the Wracker called Gator Al.

He was in worse shape than any of us. Wilson's men had beaten him repeatedly, and Joel and Cherry had to carry him inside. He's about my age, I think, with greasy black hair and a rash of facial pimples.

Tycho and Fug, on Lieza's order, unpacked Blunt Instrument's equipment from the minibus and replaced it with all of the Hobnails except Claghorn. Then they dumped the captured automatic weapons beside the bus and proceeded to turn each rifle into scattered junk.

Twice, I saw mercenaries open a bus door slightly, and in both cases the potential escapees were rewarded with rifle parts caroming off their faces.

The ultimate focus of the battle's aftermath, though, was Claghorn, who turned out to be a small man with a sharp, protruding nose.

Dude and Lieza pinned his arms to his sides and took him to face the upside-down body of Dodson. I followed numbly, not knowing what else to do, and picked up Dodson's "cloak" from where it lay in the snow several yards from the house. It was the quilt I had used to cover my nakedness less than a half hour before.

The body swayed slightly. One of the slugs must have hit the aorta, because blood had sprayed nearly all of the snow in a five-yard semicircle.

Why aren't I sick? I wondered. *Did Concepcion make the sight of a man's butchered body seem commonplace to me?*

I shuffled to Dodson, staining my socks, and wrapped his torso in the quilt. Then I pulled him down, almost certainly breaking his ankle if it wasn't broken already.

It was hard not to tell him I was sorry.

"See this?" the Bastard Child asked Claghorn. "When you get back to Wilson, you can tell him that we don't have Jackson and that the man you killed was a Secret Service agent. That makes you a Federal fugitive—and Wilson too, I imagine, since he hired you."

Claghorn looked down at Dodson's purplish face. "Regrettable," he said, his lips barely moving.

" 'Regrettable?' " Lieza said, her eyes flashing with concentrated moonlight. "Regrettable that you killed the wrong man? Regrettable that you Straights have started a nuclear war and can't find anything better to do about it than shoot popguns at each other?"

"No, Mizz Galilei," Claghorn said. "Regrettable that I was wounded two and a half days ago and am not at my best. If that had not happened, Mister Wilson would not have burdened me with fools he was led to believe were trained in my skills. I would have come alone, and I would have gotten what I had come for. I will not allow myself to be so burdened in the future. I shall come for Professor Jackson again, alone, and I shall accomplish my objective."

Lieza rolled her eyes. "Yeah, yeah, yeah. Save it for that fateful day, Jack. Right now all I want from you is some untraceable transportation. I only heard the one helicopter, so how many cars did you dinks come in, and where are they?"

"We arrived in two sedans and a van. They are parked one mile south of here, in a field just off your miserable, unplowed excuse for a road."

Lieza looked surprised. "That was easy. I thought I might have to beat it out of you."

"This mission is a failure," Claghorn said. "There is no point in prolonging it."

The Bastard Child shoved him toward the bus. "So go, then, and tell Wilson to make whoopee with a fence post. The keys are in the ignition. By the way, it's a rental, due back in Kansas City a week from this coming Friday. The address is on the sticker on the dashboard. Happy Trails."

Claghorn walked around Tycho and Fug's pile of junk, got into the minibus, and started the engine.

I stared at Lieza. "You're just going to let them go?"

Lieza eyed me dubiously. "Why not?"

I pointed at Dodson's body. "They—they *killed* him. Shouldn't you at least call the county sheriff?"

The minibus backed out of the driveway.

Lieza walked toward the kitchen door. "Hack, you've got the brains of a vole. If you don't know by now that I don't follow Straight law, you haven't been paying attention."

The minibus roared off down the dark, snowy road.

"But, Lieza," I said, frustrated and furious, "they *killed*—"

Lieza went into the house without looking at me again.

I stood staring at the closed door, clenching and un-clenching my fists.

Dude moved into my line of sight and looked at me steadily. "Teek wiped the one who wasted this Jack," he said. "He didn't mean to, but he did. Whether it was chance or whether Patton reached down and did it, that's the way it happened. You want better justice than that, you better spend the rest of your life watching TV."

Then Dude went inside too, and I was left to watch Tycho and Fug finish tearing apart the last of the rifles. My feet were on the verge of frostbite when the Viking finally pulled me into the house behind him.

* * *

Death sleeps next to me.

Wouldn't I, after all, be better off with Maria? She's traitorous and hedonistic—but she's also bouncy, supple, laughing, *Life*. She's *Life*, goddamn it.

Or what I've been trained to think Life is.

Maybe the truth is that this woman, Death, beside me has more of Life in her than a thousand women like Maria will ever have.

I don't know. How could I, when I came from the womb of a Maria, grew up with Marias, spent my whole life expecting still more Marias? How could I know any-thing about Death, this Bastard Child of God?

After Tycho dragged me into the house, Ellyn exam-ined my feet and hands and pronounced me free of frostbite, but barely. I then managed to change out of my wet-and-bloody clothes into dry, clean ones. While I was doing that, Bazz yelled at me to zip up my suitcase and do it fast if I wanted to go. She hoped I wouldn't.

What does one take on a journey across the river Styx? Five pairs of briefs, same of socks. No holes, now; it wouldn't do to face Death in ratty underwear.

We took the mercenaries' vehicles and drove to Em-poria. I rode in the second car in the back seat next to Joel. The van, crammed with instruments and equipment, brought up the rear.

My lover, Death, was in the first car, leading the way.

At Emporia we boarded a twin-engine Piper, and Fug flew us without lights to a pasture outside Neopit, Wisconsin. There, a shaggy, bearlike Wracker provided us with a faster, quieter Beechcraft turboprop. The takeoff was rough, but we made it into the air and flew across Lake Michigan.

I expected to be shot down as we crossed the border over Lake Huron. For one awful minute I was sure I saw another plane pacing us, but then I realized that it was only a flashing light atop a distant radio tower.

When we landed in Toronto, I had only one more chance to escape. Once the chartered jet left to cross the ocean, there would be no more choices.

As if I ever made one on my own.

We boarded the jet and took off. As we reached international airspace, the captain told us he had just received word that an American aerial blockade was forming to prevent flights to Europe. Ours was the last plane to make it out.

Again, the flow of events chooses for me. The world chooses for me. Death chooses for me.

My parents, my home, my Straight life—all gone.

What is left is the Bastard Child.

She dozes beside me now. When we reach our destination, will she awaken as a sweet lover, or as something deadly?

Is there a difference?

Did I mention that we left Dodson's body in the snow?

Hysterical Perspective IV

So Blunt Instrument, plus Hack Bonner the shmendrick and Gator Al the gadfly, went on a hippity-hoppity course into Canada, from there to Paris, and from there to London, where they became largely responsible for the weirdest four days in history. Records indicate that agents of both the Dealers and Whigs attempted to stop them at several points along the way, but we can assume that the Bastard Child and company either evaded them or pounded them silly.

Once they made it to London, forty hours after the Battle of Osawatomie, what did they find?

Well, they found Wrackers, of course—but not the same variety as those Stateside, because British wrack & roll had gone into a decline at about the same time that the Alliance had begun ascending to power. "Power corrupts, and absolute power corrupts so that you don't notice until it's too late."

Suffice it to say that by the late 1970s, British Wrackers still felt the beat, but didn't hear The Music. In retrospect, we can infer that they were only waiting for someone who could sing loud enough to reach them... or that they needed a good swift kick in the tender regions.

Sadly, that kick was not to come from Stigma Sullivan, who in January 1980 had just turned forty years old. One of the original Silverbees, Sullivan had begun his career as the Brits' equivalent to Bitch Alice (who was his lover in the mid-1960s), but by 1978 had quit The Music to live a quasi-Straight life in a penthouse. He still kept his Wracker connections by handling concert arrangements and record deals for others—but in so doing he became nothing more than a moneychanger on the steps of the temple.

In Sullivan's defense, we can conjecture that he was demoralized first by the death of Bitch Alice and then by the deaths of his bandmates. But neither the Bitch nor the other Silverbees would have accepted that excuse, so perhaps we shouldn't either.

On the other hand, Sullivan was just the sort of person for whom Eddie Dixon would have had sympathy.

"Don't you tell anyone it's easy to buck the boss," Dixon said in his speech in Montgomery the day before the wreck. "Don't you say it's easy to be right, that 'right' stands out strong as a cast-iron anvil. Not a day goes by that I don't question what I've done. Not a day goes by that I don't question whether all this wrack an' roll ain't crazy. So when you see a brother or sister slippin', don't knock 'em down. Hold 'em up, 'cause, man, they need it."

Is it any wonder that many of those who said that Dixon did not die also said that he went to London, where he was needed most?

If so, why did he hide? Why didn't he come out and become an inspiration to British Wrackers, thus preventing their fall? Was he that sick of publicity? Was he that afraid of the thousands of Straights who wanted his blood?

Maybe, a Believer would answer, he was just waiting for the right moment to reveal himself.

And the right people for whom to do it.

—Lorna P.N. Chicago-deSade,
A Brief, Biased History,
pp. 312–13.

16

Boogie in the Bunker

There's nothing left . . .
Nowhere to go.
I asked my mother . . .
She said it's so.
So I'll just take a walk
Down to the sea.
Lie down on the gray sand . . .
Diamond-spray in the breeze.

Yeah, I'll be waiting . . .
Waiting for the walrus
To rise from the foam
And take me away.
Yeah, I'll be singing . . .
"Goodbye, sweet Mary,
"I cannot tarry,
"For my friend the walrus
"Is coming today."

—Stigma Sullivan and the
Silverbees, "Waiting for
the Walrus," 1966

Tuesday, January 8, 1980. London, England.

Sullivan's penthouse was atop a hotel in George Street, a half mile north of Hyde Park and the edge of London's Wrack District. The curtains of the living room's picture window were pulled back, revealing a bird's-eye view of the fires and lights to the south.

But, Lieza thought, it was nothing more than a view. The fires were separated from the apartment by distance and a thick pane of plastiglass. Out there was darkness, sweat, and danger; in here was an elegant room furnished in grays and whites, with a sunken "conversation pit" in the center. A faint scent of lilacs tinged the air.

Lieza shifted in the plush armchair and smiled bitterly as she realized how perfect the place was for what Sullivan had become. Like his home, he clung to the outer fringes of wrack & roll, but was no longer truly a part of it. Even his voice was evidence of the borderland he'd created—in one sentence he sounded like ol' Stiggie from Liverpool, and in the next like a bored aristocrat.

As soon as Lieza, Tycho, Cherry, and Hack had arrived, the Bastard Child had asked Sullivan to move up Blunt Instrument's concert from Friday to Wednesday, because she wanted to perform *before* the Alliance tossed its next bombs. She had started writing a new song during the flight over the Atlantic, and she felt the overwhelming need to finish and sing it while there were still people left to hear.

But Sullivan, apparently unconcerned with the shortness of the time left to them, had ignored her request. All he wanted to talk about was his art. Dressed in a paint-spattered smock and blue jeans, he stood beside a teacart in the center of the pit and held his latest canvas in front of his chest.

"Come on now, Leezer," he said, tapping the frame with his right forefinger. "Is it good or isn't it?"

Lieza couldn't look at it; instead, she found herself scrutinizing Sullivan's face—the thinning, swept-back brown hair, the crinkly lines at the corners of his mouth, the round wire-rimmed glasses. He looked old, and she knew the painting was hiding a paunch that was ludicrous on his skinny frame.

Yet there was still something of the old Stig in his blue irises and in the set of his shoulders. It almost made her remember why she had wanted him in '77, as her mother had wanted him fifteen years before that.

"It looks like a chunk of liver rotting on a sidewalk," Cherry said. The bassist was stretched out on one of the pit's two enormous cream-colored divans, her head in Tycho's lap and her feet in Hack's.

Sullivan looked down at his work. "Then I've succeeded," he said. "Pity I've no place to hang it."

Lieza glanced around at the walls, which were covered with canvases. Sullivan had stopped making The Music after the other four Silverbees had been killed in a plane crash, and his creative energy had needed to go somewhere.

"What a waste," Lieza said.

Sullivan blinked. "What's that, love?"

"All this grease you've been smearing the last few years. Maybe it's got value and maybe it hasn't, but nobody's going to know one way or the other because you keep it shut up in this miniature fortress."

Sullivan sighed. "Ah, sweet Leezer. Just like yer mum. Always got a thistle up yer arse." He propped the painting against the teacart and lay down on the second divan.

Lieza stood up. "We've been here fifteen minutes, and you haven't heard a word I've said. Don't you know what's happening, Stig? We'll be dead by the end of the week if we don't do something."

Sullivan let his head loll and looked across the pit at Cherry, Tycho, and Hack. "Where's the rest of the band, love? Didjer trade 'em for that Yank?"

Lieza glanced at Hack and saw that the Straight was biting his lower lip. He looked jealous. The thought pleased her for a second, but then she forced it away and looked back at Sullivan.

"Everyone else is in the Park, spreading the word around Rotten Row that we're here early," she said.

"Oh, there's no need for that," Sullivan said. "Send the Yank down to find 'em, why don'tcher, and you can all stay here tonight. I'll find you proper lodgings tomorrow."

Lieza stepped closer to him. "You rented a two-story house for us just off Kensington Road near the New Royal Albert, remember?"

"Not I. Jesse must've done that. He's my secretary now. Have I ever mentioned him? Probably not; we don't keep in touch these days, do we?"

The Bastard Child reached down and grasped the front of Sullivan's smock with both hands, then pulled him up to a sitting position. "I'm trying to get in touch now," she said, "but you've turned into a TV cartoon character."

Sullivan's lips pulled back from clenched teeth, revealing something of his old anger—a good sign, as far as Lieza was concerned.

"Getcher bleedin' hands off me, y'scroddin' hoor," he said, half-snarling, and grabbed her wrists.

Tycho leaped from the opposite divan, nearly banging Cherry's head against the teacart, and stopped with Bert's edge only inches away from Sullivan's face.

"It's all right, Teek," Lieza said. "He's had his hands on more than my arms, you know." She wanted to look over her shoulder to see how Hack reacted to that, but kept her eyes focused on Sullivan instead.

Tycho stepped back but stood ready.

The anger faded from Sullivan's face, and his grip relaxed.

"Sorry, Leezer," he said slowly. "Guess I've got some of the ol' demon in me after all. Thought I'd purged him."

Lieza shook her head. "Don't think that. When he's gone, you're dead. You're too far down that road as it is."

Sullivan released her wrists and rubbed his eyes, his fingers edging in behind the lenses of his glasses. "You don't understand, love," he said. "That road leads where I want to go, whether you approve or not. But if it'll make you happy, I'll listen, although I've heard enough already to know that there's not a dinkin' thing I can do for you."

Lieza turned away from him and walked to the window, where she pressed her palms against the plastiglass and looked out at the streetlight halos in the mist that was starting to fall. The scene reminded her of Patton's Eve in Washington, so it wasn't a pleasant sight—but it was better than the face of a Wracker who was willing to give up without fighting.

"It's like this, Stig," she said, her breath forming a translucent oval on the window. "Churchill-Chiang nuked a U.S. satellite yesterday, and there's a rumor that American troops from the Central Trust Territory are heading for the Eastern, although I'm damned if I know what they'll do once they get there. It won't matter, because Churchill-Chiang is going to hit either them or Fort Eisenhower by Thursday at the latest, because the U.S. won't withdraw from Concepcion. Fitzgerald would give in if Secretary Kirk would let him, but at this point I'm not sure it'd make a difference. The Brits and Chinks have wanted to punish the States for a long time, and now they've got an excuse."

She thought she heard Sullivan yawn behind her.

Her hands clenched into fists. "The Alliance is also threatening to wipe Moscow on Friday or Saturday," she continued, emphasizing each word, "but I wouldn't bet my life on your Prime Minister Carpenter waiting that long. American cities'll be next, so as soon as Moscow goes, or maybe before, the States will counterattack. It'll be suicide, but Fitzgerald won't have any choice. The Squid— Kirk—will see to that. She wants a war as bad as the Whigs do, and maybe worse than the Alliance bigshots. She isn't sane. None of them are."

Lieza paused. When Sullivan didn't speak, she said, "You know what all that means, don't you, Stig?"

"Certainly," he answered. "It means it's a good thing we've already got Christmas out of the way."

The Bastard Child spun away from the window and glared across the room at her former lover, who regarded her with a faint smile.

Hack Bonner rose from the divan, looking first at Sullivan, then at Lieza. "Good Christ, look at his face," he said. "He *wants* to die."

Sullivan made a tsk-tsking sound and shook his head in mock sadness. "Poor little Yank mummy's boy. Him all upset his Unca Sammy can't cover his lily-white arse anymore."

Tycho made a metallic snorting noise. "Ain't nobody covering yours either, Stiggie. London'll be wasted too."

Sullivan folded his hands behind his head and reclined on the divan again. "As you can see, I'm dreadfully upset."

Lieza took a few steps toward him, then stopped. She didn't want to strangle him just yet.

"You're pissed at the world," she said, straining to keep her voice from breaking into a scream, "and since you're part of it, you think you deserve to die too. But peesh this, jagoff—I *don't* identify with the world and would prefer to change it or leave it instead of croak with it. And since I can't leave, I've got to take a shot at the 'change it' option before the Straights scorch me."

Sullivan chuckled. It was a hollow, hopeless sound. "Oh, come off it, Leezer," he said. "You just said yourself that we'll be vapor by the end of the week. Whatta you propose to do between now and then? Appoint yourself God Almighty and appear between the opposing armies of Armageddon, saying, 'Knock it off, skagheads, thou hast incurred my sputzing wrath'?"

Cherry rose to a sitting position and looked at Lieza. "Sounds like we'd better go after it on our own, sugar. Stigma here's ready to chow down at his own wake."

Sullivan chuckled again, and this time it evolved into a full laugh. He brought his hands out from behind his head and clapped. "Colorfully put, Cherry, love," he said when he could speak again.

Cherry glared at him. "You think I talk funny, Chubs?"

Sullivan shook his head. "No, no, sweet. It isn't how you speak; it's what you and Leezer are *saying* that's got me giggling. You actually seem to believe that there's something to be done about the whole bleedin' mess."

"There's The Music," Lieza said. "You do remember what that is, don't you, Stig?"

Sullivan's laughter died away, and in seconds his face became an emotionless mask.

Moving like a machine, he stood and walked past Lieza to the window.

"Yeah," he said in a low, changed voice. "I remember Eddie Dixon, and Tyler Sharkfin, and the Painful Bite, and your mum, and me four mates. They all kicked off, and fer what? Fer bangin' on guitars and jaggin' around like spastic monkeys. And 'ere you are sayin' it can fend off a thermonuclear burst over Buckingham Palace. Right, Leezer. It couldn't even protect Dixon from a few redneck Straights, or Tyler from eatin' too many magic mushrooms, or your mum from runnin' out of oxygen . . . or me mates from havin' the flesh burned off their bones. So don't be givin' me any 'wrack and roll can save us' scrod. It's time to join the lucky buggers who went on before, and ain't nothin' we can do to change it."

He was silent then, staring out at the mist and the lights.

Lieza didn't try to hold in her rage anymore, but strode across the pit, snatched up Sullivan's new painting, and smashed it down onto the teacart. A teapot spout ripped through the canvas, and cups and saucers went flying.

Then the Bastard Child flung the painting like a discus, and the frame smacked into the window beside the ex-Silverbee.

"Missed," Tycho said.

Sullivan sank to his knees and reached out to touch his ruined work.

"Bitch," he said, running his fingers across the canvas.

"That was her mother," Cherry said.

Lieza kicked over the teacart, which hit the floor with a loud bang and clatter. "What's the difference, Stig?" she asked. "Your art's gonna flame too, so what does it matter whether it gets skagged now or in a couple of days?"

Sullivan looked up at her. His eyes were wet, and for an instant Lieza felt a twinge of guilt.

But then she was angrier than ever at the thought that these bits of colored cloth were more important to him than The Music, than other Wrackers, than Life.

"It matters to *me*," Sullivan said. "It matters more to me than you ever did."

"No wonder I always felt two-dimensional when we screwed," Lieza said. "Look, man—if you love your paintings, then help me for that reason if you can't think of anything better. Truth is, I don't know that The Music can make a difference; but I know that I at least want to do it one last time, to go down rammin'. So please help me, OK?"

Sullivan stood and wiped his hands on his jeans. His facial muscles were twisted in a combination of a pout and a sneer.

"'Help me, help me,'" he said mockingly. "That's all I ever bloody hear. 'Help me, Stig, can you get me band a gig?' 'Help me Stig, I got me bird stuffed fulla seed, y' know where we can get it removed?' 'Help me, Stig, I ain't got a ticket for the concert.' 'Help me, Stig, I need me a gall bladder operation.' Help me, help me, help me. Stinking sick of it, I am."

"This is different," Hack shouted. "This is the world we're talking about."

The Straight sounded like a whining child, so Lieza gave him a shut-up-jagoff look.

Shouldn't have brought the dinking Jack here in the first place, she thought, and wondered why she had.

"Oh, well, let's hear it for the bleedin' world, why don't we?" Sullivan said. "Let's hear it for rape and murder and taxes and graft. Let's hear it for cheating and stealing and blackmail and dogshit."

"Whoopee," Tycho said. "Now, you gonna give us a hand, or should me and Bert do things to your furniture?"

Sullivan gritted his teeth and ran his hands back through his hair. "You say you want to do the show tomorrow. Bloody hell, do you know what time it is? Almost midnight. London's six hours ahead of you Midwestern-U.S. people. I couldn't get hold of any equipment or logistics people before nine ayem tomorrow, and then we couldn't open the Hall or get the power allocation we'd need. Thursday's impossible for the same reasons. We've got the New Royal Albert Hall from eight to midnight on

Friday, and that's that. Even if we *could* do it early, where would your stinkin' audience be? Waiting for Friday, that's where."

"We could use the grapevine," Lieza said. "Gator Al's with us. By noon tomorrow we could fill the Albert ten times with the Wrackers that'll show up."

Sullivan rubbed his eyes again. "Oh, Leezer, Leezer, Leezer. You think you're in Kansas City? Even supposin' you could do that, what good d'you think would come of it? You think the power of your voice would throw up a field of pure force that'd keep the bombs from droppin'?"

"I already told you, I don't know," Lieza said. "But in the beginning, wrack 'n' roll was more than just The Music. It was a movement, and sooner or later it would've pushed the Straight world into the sea—"

"So what happened to all that glory, pray tell?" Sullivan asked sardonically.

The Bastard Child took a deep breath. "It died with my mother, who was its leader after Dixon. If it hadn't, we wouldn't be in the scrod we're in now. But—but it didn't actually *die*; it became dormant. This is our last chance to bring it back to life, and if we wait past tomorrow, there may not be a day after that. Even if there is, Friday will be cutting it too close. If Moscow goes, millions will burn even if that's the last bomb." She paused. "And it won't be."

Sullivan's expression changed to one that was close to pity. "Oh, dear child," he said. "You think a three- or four-hour concert to a mere twenty thousand Wrackers can change a million years of decline?"

Lieza's legs began to feel weak, and she walked across the pit to sit in the armchair again. "For the last time, I *don't know*," she said as the cushion compressed beneath her.

But for your sake, Mama, she thought, looking toward the window and wishing that the Moon wasn't hidden by the mist, *I've got to try.*

"But it's not going to be just twenty thousand, Stiggie," Cherry said. "You're going to arrange for world broadcast. I don't know just what Leez is planning to sing, but even if we're going up like a can of eth, we've got to give her the chance. Don't you owe her that much? Don't you owe The Music that much?"

Sullivan's shoulders slumped, and to Lieza he looked like a man thirty years older than he was. "Perhaps," he said. "But whether I owe it or not, it can't be done. I couldn't get a satellite-bounce arranged by Friday, let alone tomorrow—even assuming that Her Majesty's government would allow us access, and that Uncle Sammy wouldn't jam the transmission, both of which assumptions are lunatic fantasy. Even granting that the concert were broadcast across the Atlantic, everyone on this side would still see to it that we go up in smoke. Or radioactive ash, as the case may be."

"Why's that?" Tycho asked, patting Bert in his palm.

Sullivan looked at him. "Because, oh great Silver-Nosed One of the Nasty Ax, your beloved leader has never spent more than a few weeks in Britain. Even our brief but fondly remembered affair took place in the States."

"What's that got to do with anything?" Hack asked angrily.

"What it has to do with," Sullivan said, "is the fact that British and European Wrackers—and, I assume, Chinese Wrackers, if they exist—have only two things in common with their American counterparts: They dress wretchedly and listen to the radio a lot."

"You know better," Cherry said. "It hasn't been that long since you were more than just a booking agent."

Sullivan's lips pursed for an instant. Then he looked at the floor and said, "It hasn't been that long since Alice died, either, or since Dixon disappeared in a ball of burning alcohol. But go on down to Rotten Row and ask 'em what Bitch Alice means to them. Then ask 'em what Napoleon means to them, or Jack the Ripper, or Alexander the Great. The Ripper'll be the only one to draw any enthusiasm. I'm tellin' yer—why do you think there's never been any real stab at a Wracker Revolution? Because the huge majority of Wrackers here, maybe everywhere, just don't give a bloody shit. Put 'em in suits an' ties, and you've got Straights."

Without looking up, he waved a hand at the picture

window. "The world's goin' to hell this week, but out there it's business as usual. The Straights don't believe there's *really* goin' to be a nuclear war—and surprise, surprise, neither do most Wrackers. And those who do, don't care."

"Like you," Lieza said.

Sullivan didn't look up, didn't speak.

"Yes, like him," a deep voice said behind the Bastard Child.

Lieza's spine stiffened. The voice didn't sound threatening, exactly . . . but there was something ominous about it. Something that made her think of darkness, of rotting vegetation, of swamps.

Tycho brandished Bert. "Who the rutting skag are you?" he said, baring his teeth. "And where'd you come from?"

"My name is Jesse," the voice said. "I'm Stigma's secretary. I'm from America originally, but just now I came from my bedroom, down the hall."

Lieza could actually *feel* Jesse coming up behind her, then walking around the armchair to stand in front of her. He was over six feet tall and weighed at least three hundred pounds.

It wasn't his bulk that Lieza found intimidating, though.

It was his eyes.

Dark, cavernous eyes, with such heavy lids that only thin rims of white showed around the irises.

And in the centers of the pupils were dull gleams of something pale, like bleached bones.

It was only after several long seconds that Lieza realized she was seeing reflections of her own face.

Despite the room's humid warmth, she felt cold.

"Jesus," Hack whispered, and Lieza knew that he was feeling it too.

"I couldn't help hearing a portion of your conversation with Stigma," Jesse said. "I should tell you that his attitude is due to things I've shown him."

Lieza thought of turning her head to look at Sullivan, but she found herself unwilling or unable to break her gaze away from Jesse's.

"So we've got you to blame," she said, unsure of whether she was asking a question or making a statement.

Jesse's head moved almost imperceptibly, and Lieza realized that he was shaking his head *no*.

"Blame for the truth cannot be assigned to one who observes it," he said. "Nor to one like Stigma, who has no choice but to accept it."

Lieza felt short of breath. The smell of lilacs had become overpowering.

"Whom *do* we blame, then?" she asked. "And how do we know it's too late to stop them?"

Jesse's eyelids almost closed, leaving only the pale reflections showing. "I am a twin. My brother died as we were being born, but he still speaks to me. He can see what has passed and what will come to pass. He can see those who have died and those who will die."

"Does he know Dixon?" Cherry asked.

Jesse bowed his head slightly. "The man of whom you speak has not yet passed on to that plane. But he soon will, as will we all. My brother has revealed this to me: In three days' time, the world will be consumed in fire."

Sullivan moved away from the picture window and into Lieza's field of vision. His eyes were still downcast.

"You see?" he said, almost mumbling. "You see now? It's our destiny."

Lieza felt as though her throat were constricting, as though the strength had left her arms and legs and had concentrated behind her tongue to choke her.

"Jesus," Hack whispered again.

It wasn't the word itself that broke the spell for the Bastard Child. It was the fact that Hack Bonner had been able to speak and she hadn't.

She forced the tightness out of her throat and into her limbs. Then, as her muscles knotted, she exploded from the chair and shoved Jesse away with a strength that astonished her.

She felt her nostrils flaring and her lips pulling back from her teeth.

"Skagging jewbaiters!" she screamed. "Sputzing *cowards*!"

She ran out of the pit to the nearest wall, where Sullivan's paintings hung in multihued splendor.

The first one she reached was a surrealistic study of the Hyde Park statue of Wellington. She yanked it from the wall and stomped a hole through it with her left boot.

As she was doing that, she tore down another and flung it at Jesse. It struck him in the chest and fell to the floor. He didn't even flinch.

Lieza's rage intensified until she saw everything as if she were looking through pale red lenses. She continued yanking paintings from the wall, ripping at them with her fingernails and teeth.

"Please," she heard Sullivan plead behind her. "Please don't. They and Jesse are all I have . . ."

She felt his hand on her left arm, and she turned and threw him over her shoulder.

Whimpering frick. How could we have done it with him, Mama? How could we have ever done it with someone willing to roll over and die once he's had it?

Sullivan landed on the nearer divan and rolled off onto the floor. His glasses flew across the pit.

Jesse moved toward Lieza, and instantly Tycho was in front of him, pressing Bert's edge to his throat.

Lieza was a little surprised to see that Hack had started toward Jesse too. Cherry hadn't bothered, knowing that Tycho was all that was needed.

"Don't," Sullivan cried, scrambling up to his knees. "I'm all right."

Jesse moved back a step, and Tycho lowered the ax.

Looking up at the Bastard Child as if in prayer, Sullivan said, "Why are you trying to hurt me? Why are you trying to take away the last bits of comfort and pleasure I'll have before . . . it happens?"

"Because I'm a Wracker, that's why," Lieza said, breathing hard. "Like my mother. Like Eddie Dixon. Because I'm trying to make you remember what that means. It means that you don't take what they're giving. Visions from the dead or no visions from the dead, a Wracker doesn't cave in to *anything* without spitting in its face first. So peesh this: If you're not a Wracker, you're one of the enemy. And I'm gonna spit in your face."

"You cannot change the future," Jesse said. "It is what it is."

"So's a clam," Cherry said. "Crack it open, you got meat."

"Whatever the sputz that means," Tycho grumbled.

Sullivan crawled to retrieve his glasses and then pulled himself up onto the divan. He moved like a man half-paralyzed.

"I can't reschedule the concert," he said, the words rasping from his throat. "Whether I'm a Wracker or not, that much is out of my hands. If you want to save the world, it'll have to keep itself alive until Friday. But I promise that one way or another, even if I have to kill every BBC bureaucrat and barricade myself with the equipment, I'll get you planetwide broadcast. Assuming there's still a planet by then."

"It will not exist as it does now," Jesse intoned.

Sullivan rubbed his eyes. "I know," he said. "But I've promised." He took his hands away from his face and looked up at Lieza again. "I'm doing this one last thing for you. Then, whatever happens, we're even. Dead people generally are."

Lieza managed a short laugh. "You're filling me with confidence." She gestured to Tycho, Cherry, and Hack. "Come on. We didn't get what we came for, but we got all that's here to get. Stig has work to do now."

"But what if . . . something . . . happens before Friday?" Hack said tremulously.

The Bastard Child looked at him and smiled wryly. "Then we'll die, Jack. I know not what course others may take, but as for me, I intend to kick and scream."

The four of them left the penthouse. Before closing the door, Lieza glanced back into the living room and saw that Sullivan was rubbing his eyes again.

Jesse didn't look as though he had any eyes at all.

17

The Ghost of Piccadilly

> *Who are the dead*
> *That we should honor them with*
> *Granite monuments of*
> *Bleating sheep and bleeding men?*
> *Do they climb up*
> *From the dirt in darkest night*
> *To run their senseless fingers*
> *Over the smooth and dew-wet stone?*
>
> *Honor the living,*
> *For only the living can*
> *Pull us from the pit.*
> *Can you tell them from shadows,*
> *Would you give them a home?*
> *Will you take what they're giving,*
> *Or lie beneath your monument,*
> *All alone?*

> —Bitch Alice,
> "Under the Monument," 1965

Wednesday, January 9, 1980. London, England.

Big Ben struck midnight as Lieza, Hack, Tycho, and Cherry walked south through mist-shrouded Hyde Park. The Bastard Child paused and listened.

"How far away is that?" she asked. "It never sounds as if it's in the same place twice."

"Noise twists and turns around these schizo streets," Cherry said. "Whitehall's two miles southeast of here, if you could fly. A little farther on the pavement."

Big Ben . . . Whitehall . . . Downing Street. Beyond Lieza's vision, they hulked on the bank of the stinking Thames, the spires of Parliament waiting like dark spikes while the thirteen-ton bell counted the planet's last hours.

And no one seemed to care. As Lieza looked around in the mercury-vapor lamplight at the few Wrackers filtering through the park, she wondered: Why had Speaker's Corner been empty when she'd passed? Why weren't London's Wrackers protesting what their Straight government was doing? Where were the hordes that had jammed the park in the Fifties, demonstrating simultaneously with their friends in America for Dixon's release from prison?

As if in answer, a tall, stubble-headed youth in a fake-leopardskin bodysuit approached from an intersecting sidewalk. Two short, chubby girls trailed after him, wearing metal-studded leather outfits that made Lieza feel vaguely uncomfortable with her own leathers.

"'Ay there, coves," the leopard-skinned kid said, nodding at Tycho and Hack. "Tradjer my two fer yours." He tilted his head to one side and let his mouth hang open.

"I beg your pardon?" the Bastard Child said.

The kid frowned. "Wasn't talkin' to you, was I, Mizz Crumpet?" The chubby girls giggled.

Every muscle in Lieza's body became a hard knot.

"Uh-oh," Cherry said.

Tycho took a step toward the Leopard Boy, but Lieza gestured for him to stop.

The kid's face brightened with enthusiasm. "Now, that's cranked," he said, pointing at Tycho's face. "Where'd y'lose the meat?"

Bert swung slowly in Tycho's right hand. "Do you know who we are, sputzer?" the Viking growled.

"Sure," the Leopard Boy said, scratching his crotch. "Big jagger with an ax and a rammin' nose, a wormy-

lookin' Straight, and their chicks—one vanilla, one chocolate."

"Uh-oh," Cherry said again.

Lieza was on the kid before he drew another breath, and threw him to the dead grass beside the sidewalk. Even as she did it, she regretted not slamming him to the cement.

He landed on his back and stared up incredulously. The chubby girls gaped, mirroring his expression.

Lieza waited for him to get up so she could throw him down again. He represented everything that was *wrong*, and she wanted to hurt him.

Hack Bonner walked over to the Leopard Boy, who was starting to struggle up to a sitting position, and said, "Stay down."

"Like fricking—" the kid said, slurring the words.

"Skag off, Hack," Lieza said.

Bonner squatted and put a hand on the kid's chest.

"Stay down," he said again. "She's the Bastard Child."

"No scrod?" the Leopard Boy said. He raised himself on his elbows and looked at Lieza. "The silver nose—I thought that was a dress-me-up. But he's really Tycho, and she's Cherry Angola, and you're...Man, this is great! I've been beat up by Blunt Instrument!"

The chubby girls made reverential noises.

Lieza's anger faded a little as she remembered what Bazz had said the day she'd cut Dodson's shoulder and ear. Here she'd been wanting to rip the Leopard Boy limb from limb—and he was just a kid playing at masquerade.

"All right, Hack," she said, trying to make her muscles relax. "I won't disembowel him. Not right away, anyhow."

Bonner looked dubious, but took his hand off the kid's chest and stepped away.

The Leopard Boy sat up and grinned. "Look, Mizz Galilei," he said. "I wonder if I could run over home—I live up north a bit, off Marylebone—and pop back with a few albums for you to bite. If it wouldn't be any trouble, of course—"

"A minute ago you were talking like I was a piece of chicken meat," Lieza said.

The kid stood. "Well, I thought you were just another Wracker."

"I am. If you were too, you'd be doing something besides showing off your harem."

The Leopard Boy looked puzzled. "What's that?"

Lieza stepped closer, then clenched her left fist and raised it until it was only inches from the kid's face. "You'd be fighting, because the world wants to kill you before the week's out. But instead you're strutting like a TV cock of the walk, getting in some chest-puffing before Uncle Sam's subs flame you and your chippies into plasma."

The Leopard Boy's expression changed back to a grin. "Oh, I see what you're on about. Y'needn't worry, Mizz Galilei. Ain't nobody here in danger—the Station'll see to that. In fact, it's a bloody good thing you came over. Once Johnny Bull gets through wi' Rusher and the States, there won't be nobody there to play for."

Lieza stared into the kid's eyes and saw that he believed everything the BBC had told him.

"Churchill-Chiang can't save you," she said.

"Sure it can," the Leopard Boy said. "It can shoot down missiles before they get near us."

The Bastard Child shook her head. "That wouldn't even be true if the Alliance had a *hundred* defensive satellites. Besides, your precious Station's not in geosynchronous orbit, so—"

"Huh?" the kid said.

"It isn't sitting still over either Britain or China," Lieza said, "so what's it going to do for you if it's on the other side of the world when a sub sneaks around Ireland?"

The Leopard Boy grinned and smacked his right fist into his left palm. "It's gonner wipe Los Angeles, Detroit, and Lubbock off the frickin' map, that's what."

Lieza nodded slowly. "That'll be a great comfort to the cockroaches who move into your chest cavity."

She turned and walked away, leaving the Leopard Boy and his girls calling after her for an autograph.

Hack, Cherry, and Tycho fell into step beside her.

"Jeez," Cherry said. "What a dink."

Normally, Lieza would have made a similar comment. Now, though, name-calling seemed pointless. The Leopard Boy was going to die, and die dressed as a Wracker.

It was too hideous and depressing for words.

The walk past Rotten Row was just as bad. After the Second World War, the stables had closed and the sand track had become a Wracker haunt because it was a good spot for fires—but now the few people who gathered there seemed spiritless and complacent, as if they were all Leopard Boys.

Maybe, Lieza thought hopefully, the phenomenon was confined to Hyde Park. Maybe farther east, in the heart of the Wrack District, things were different. Maybe the people who had known her mother, and Dixon before her, were still in the Circus and still remembered. Maybe there was still a chance of turning things around.

Oh, sure. Find a couple of old-timers, and you can remake the world in two days. No sweat.

When they reached the rented house in Trevor Street, Lieza kicked open the front door, went inside, and flopped onto her back on the living room couch. She felt drained.

Dude and Ellyn came down the staircase at the far end of the room. "The others are upstairs getting some sleep for a change," Dude said, "so keep it down."

"Concert going to be tomorrow?" Ellyn asked.

"No," Cherry said, closing the door.

Ellyn frowned and patted her belly. "Well, Buick, at least Armageddon's coming before you'll have to see it. Too bad you won't get to hear the Instrument one last time."

"Don't think this city's gonna be much of a loss," Tycho said. "You oughta see the sputzers in the park who call themselves Wrackers. Even Hack's got more blood in his balls."

"Thanks," Hack said weakly.

"Don't mention it."

Lieza wished she didn't have to hear them. She wished she didn't even have to think.

The red digits of the wall clock across the room said that it was 1:00 A.M.

The Bastard Child turned over, pressed her face into the rough weave of the couch, and let herself drift into a deep sleep for the first time in over thirty hours.

* * *

Bitch Alice, in a helmetless moonsuit, looked down at Lieza with disappointment in her eyes. Flecks of silver gleamed in the blackness behind her.

"You let it go out of tune, Lisa," she said, reaching down. "Give it back."

Lieza clutched her guitar to her chest. "You said it was mine. You promised."

Bitch Alice shook her head. "I promised it would be yours if you used it to play the one song that matters. But you've never finished that song, Lisa. You've started it several times, but that isn't enough."

Lieza backed away, shuffling in the gray dust.

"I'll finish it," she said desperately. "I swear I will. Just give me one more chance."

Bitch Alice folded her arms across the moonsuit's blue nipples. "All right," she said. "Let's hear it, then."

Lieza stopped moving and looked down at the black left-handed electric. Tentatively, she put her right hand on the neck and brought her left hand down to strum.

The strings sliced through the flesh and bone of her thumb and cut up through the wrist. Bright globules of blood sprayed out and floated down to the lifeless dust.

Lieza screamed.

"That's more like it," Bitch Alice said. "Now let's hear the second verse."

* * *

The Bastard Child awoke to find herself sitting up, with her left wrist clamped in her right hand. Her chest felt constricted, and for several seconds she could hardly breathe.

As her eyes focused, she saw that the room was lit by gray light filtering through the curtains over the room's single window. The wall clock read 12:23 P.M.

The only other person in the room was Hack Bonner.

He was sitting in a chair under the clock, a spiral notebook and a pen in his lap.

"Nightmare?" he asked.

Lieza ignored him and took a folded piece of paper from her left rear jeans pocket.

Scrod, she thought as she opened the sheet and read the two and a half verses written there.

She crumpled the paper, then stood and walked unsteadily across the room. When she reached Bonner, she picked up his notebook and tore out three blank sheets.

"Borrow your pen?" she asked.

He handed it to her, and she went into the kitchen, where she found Dude making cold sandwiches.

"Afternoon," he said, handing her a tomato-and-cheese on whole wheat.

Lieza sat down at the table with the empty pages before her and tried to think of a better title than the one she'd come up with on the plane.

Come on, Mama. If you're going to torture me in my sleep, you can at least give me a hand when I'm awake.

She waited a few minutes, hoping for a response, then gave up and began to write.

* * *

"Leez, you tranced?" Cherry asked.

The Bastard Child's head jerked up, and the first thing she saw was the watch on Cherry's wrist. Except for several bathroom breaks and a ten-minute shower, she had been sitting at the table for over nine hours.

She had written six lines.

"We've been wondering what we ought to be doing," Cherry said. "I mean, we've been here a whole day, and so far all we've done is strike out with Sullivan."

Lieza stood and tore up the piece of paper she'd been using, then went into the living room with her bass player.

Tycho, Dude, Ellyn, and Hack were there, and they all looked at her strangely as she entered.

She wanted to shout, *So I've wasted a day and brought us that much closer to Death. So who do I look like—God?*

She sat down beside Dude and Ellyn on the couch. "Where's everybody else?" she asked.

"Couple hours ago, Gator Al came limpin' downstairs and said he wanted to get into the District," Dude said. "Ell didn't think he ought to, since he's still jackbugged from having the Hobnails dance on him, but he said he was headin' out whether we liked it or not. Had to respect that, so Fug, Bazz, and Joel went with him. The shape he's in, it might take all of 'em just to hold him up."

Lieza bit her lower lip. "Skag it," she muttered. "We need to get to work."

"Get to work on what?" Hack asked. "I still can't figure out what good you thought it'd do to move up the concert, much less what we can do now that there's no chance of it happening before Friday."

Lieza looked at the Straight and said, "What's the prettiest spot in Kenya?"

He frowned. "I don't know."

"That's because you've never been there," Lieza said. "Same applies here—you've never been a Wracker, and you never will be. I can't explain myself to you."

"In other words," Ellyn said, "she doesn't know what she's going to do either, but she's tired of waiting to be blown up. Buick here has the luxury of not knowing what's going on, but none of the rest of us do."

"He does," Tycho said, jerking a thumb in Bonner's direction. "Straight boys swallow what the boss men feed 'em, then chirp for more."

Hack's expression became darker, angrier. "Yeah, I was raised Straight," he said. "But if I were locked into it, I wouldn't have this swollen nose or these bruises, would I? I wouldn't have come over here with you, would I?"

"Sure you would've, as long as it meant getting into Leez's pants," Tycho said. "And that's good enough for her."

Bonner looked at the Bastard Child. "Are you going to let him say that about you?"

The exchange had made Lieza feel a little better, and she smiled. "What I think of you or want from you has

nothing to do with what Teek or anybody else thinks of or
wants from you. Peesh?"

Hack's anger crumbled, as it always did, and Lieza
felt a twinge of disappointment.

"I'm sorry," the Straight said.

"Don't be sorry for what you are," Ellyn said gently.

"Instead," the Bastard Child said, "be sorry for not
trying harder to be what you should."

Good advice, she thought.

As soon as the others returned, it would be time to
start trying harder to be what *she* should, too.

Whatever that was.

* * *

Gator Al, Joel, Bazz, and Fug returned shortly after
eleven o'clock. The bruises on Gator Al's face were worse
than those on Bonner's, but it was his expression rather
than his wounds that bothered Lieza.

"Things are bad," he said, taking off his denim jacket.

Fug grunted.

"How so?" Lieza asked, without wanting to know.

"Well, Leez dear," Joel said, pushing his top hat back
and perching on an arm of the couch, "You may safely
assume that our good friend Mister Al is not referring to
the weather, which, by the way, is also abominable."

Bazz, who was leaning over to massage her goose-
pimpled legs, said, "The District is full of Jacks. It's as if
the plane landed us in Peoria and the pilot told everybody
there to talk as if they had cotton up their noses."

"Still, the Circus looks as I remember it," Joel said
thoughtfully. "The drug-and-comic-book shops, the art-
work painted onto the streets, the sadomasochistic-
religious clothing, the general air of anarchy—all seem
unchanged. However, when one speaks to the residents,
one finds—"

"Jewbaiting scrod-suckers," Bazz said.

Joel raised an eyebrow. "Bazz my sweet, you're positively psychic."

Lieza rubbed her left wrist. Sullivan, the Leopard
Boy, and Rotten Row had been omens of things to come.

Gator Al sat down on the couch beside Lieza and crossed his arms. He smelled of sweat and herbs.

"Even the grapevine seems to be deteriorating," he said. "I could almost believe that Carpenter hired kids to move in around Piccadilly and subvert the subversives."

"So what would you say the odds would be of using the vine to set up a street concert between now and sunrise?" Lieza asked. "We've got our instruments, but we need amps, speakers, cables, a soundboard—"

"What'd be the point of a street show?" Gator Al asked.

Lieza, irritated, stood and walked a few steps away from the couch. The question had sounded like something Hack might have asked.

"The point," she said, "is that I don't think we've got until Friday before the Straights start throwing things, and I want to play. I *need* to play."

Gator Al frowned and then winced as he reached up to touch his bruises. "I can peesh that, but the logistics are impossible. Besides, Parliament's announced that war powers are in effect, which means Carpenter can order blackouts. If you tried a street gig, you'd strum a note and have your juice cut off. The New Royal Albert, on the other hand, has generators, because the basement's supposed to be a shelter in the event of the Big One. Say, is Sullivan gonna get you world broadcast Friday?"

"He says he'll try," Lieza said.

Gator Al nodded. "OK, then. That's your only chance, concert-wise. The Sermon on the Mount, or whatever you're gonna do, will have to wait until then."

Tycho, who had been standing silently against a wall, stomped across the room and kicked over a potted fern.

Lieza felt the same way. She had to do something *now*.

But you don't even have the song written . . .

"So that's it?" she yelled at Gator Al. "We just let them kill us?"

"Give him a break," Hack whispered.

Lieza glared at the Straight. "I'll give *you* a break. I'll break your scrodding femur."

"I've got an idea, if you're interested," Gator Al said. "Wilson thinks we took Doc Jackson from him, but his public claim is that the Brits did it, right? And Carpenter's been denying it, right? Well, surprise—what few sources there are out there say that Jackson's in central London, probably in a covert-operations house so that nobody at Whitehall can be bought off for him. If we could go out and squeeze some specifics on where he is, we might be able to use him as a lever."

Lieza had a queasy sensation in her abdomen. Why was it that every time that alkie's name came up, she felt as though she were about to be sick?

"That's why she called me Pissant."

"How—" she began, and found that she had to swallow a mouthful of saliva before she could continue. "How do you figure that?"

Gator Al shrugged. "It's a gamble. Plan A assumes that they need him for some zip-zap space project, which means we'll only have power if we snatch him. That's power as in, 'Fry that city, and the egghead gets it.' Plan B doesn't assume he's that valuable; we just find out where he is and threaten to expose Carpenter to her Chinese allies as a liar, since the word is that they weren't in on the kidnapping. Trouble is, that might be as likely to make her *want* to start throwing bombs as it would be to make her hold off."

Joel cleared his throat. "I'm afraid that my feeling is that each plan sucks large blocks of limestone."

Fug, who was picking at the wall plaster, grunted in agreement.

Lieza was about to add another negative vote, because by now the Brits surely knew that Jackson wasn't worth having—but she stopped herself.

Finding the physicist would be useless . . . and she wanted to do it anyway. She wanted to face him one more time and finally get the truth out of him.

Why did my mother have to die?
Why didn't you do anything about it?
Why did you call me—

"All right," she said. "Anybody who'd rather stay

here is welcome to. I don't think this is going to be productive enough to require all of us."

Ellyn got up from the couch. "In that case, Buick and I are gonna snooze," she said, heading for the stairs. "Y'all have a cranking good time, peesh?"

Gator Al stood and looked at the wall clock. "Eleven-thirty. Unless *everybody* in London has gone Straight, my bet is that we'll have something by dawn."

Lieza stepped back and let Gator Al lead the way out of the house. She hoped he was right.

And, somewhere inside where a nameless fear lived, she hoped he was wrong.

* * *

Lieza, Hack, Tycho, and Joel walked northeast along Piccadilly Street toward the Circus, and Gator Al took the others into Hyde Park. The reasoning behind the split was that the Bastard Child might be able to coax information from anyone in the Circus who had been reluctant to talk to Gator Al, while the grapevine master made new contacts along Rotten Row.

Like everything else about the project, that logic seemed like so much scrod to the Bastard Child; but her own reasons for the search would be enough to keep her at it until it was time to rehearse for the concert, or until the world ended. Whichever came first.

Look at the bright side. Maybe we'll waste so many hours that I won't have time to face that song again.

Yesterday's mist had been replaced by cold fog, and the lights along Piccadilly—those that weren't broken— were surrounded by bluish halos. Beneath most of the halos, groups of Wrackers drank ethanol and listened to boom boxes.

In one of these spots, ten or twelve youths dressed in denim and chains were cooking meat on a hibachi. Joel jumped into their midst, grabbed a hot dog, and spun around a light pole crooning "Singin' in the Rain," using the wiener as a microphone.

Lieza laughed. Joel could always make her feel better, even when there was nothing to feel better about. She began to look around her with renewed interest.

The buildings were splashed with bright paint that seemed to battle the fog, and The Music roared from windows and boom boxes in a constant cacophony of Silverbees, Sharkfin, Bitch Alice, and Blunt Instrument. As Lieza climbed over one of the wooden barricades at the end of Piccadilly Street and entered the body-packed maelstrom of the Circus, someone was playing "House on the Hill" especially loud.

She had the feeling, though, that no one in the crowd could understand what she'd said in that song, or would care if they could. The colorful, noisy facade of the Circus, presided over by the painted statue of Eros and his fountains, made the place look like the site of an eternal Patton Day celebration—but the undertones were of something less pure.

Lieza stopped beside a broken streetlight and stared through the haze at various Wrackers, trying to determine what it was about them that seemed so wrong.

It didn't take long to realize what it was.

There were the denims-and-chains. There were the leathers-and-metal-studs. There were the purple-stockings-and miniskirts. There were the body-paints-and-camouflage-suits.

Everyone inside the Circus could be identified as belonging to one of several groups. Everyone was a conformist. They had taken the phenomenon of wrack & roll and turned it into a collection of grotesque mirror-images of Straight classes and cliques.

Three young women belonging to the purple-stockings-and-miniskirts club approached Lieza, looking at her as if not quite believing that she was alive.

"Ain't you the Bastard Child?" the middle one asked.

"That's right," Lieza answered, appalled by the stench of the girl's perfume. She didn't want to talk to any of these cardboard cutouts, but she had to start somewhere.

"Oh, terriff," the girl said. "We got tickets f'you."

"Hope they're still good," Lieza said.

The girl on the right frowned. "Why wouldn't 'ay be?"

"Tickets that crisp to ash are invalid."

The three purple-stockings-and-miniskirts exchanged puzzled glances.

Lieza took a deep breath through her mouth and let it out explosively. "Never mind. Any of you hear anything about a Yank being kept locked up somewhere in London?"

"Straight brainy-scientist type," Tycho added. "Nose stenciled with drinker's tattoos."

The girl on the left nodded. "Rocket man, right?"

Lieza felt as if something cold were being injected into her spine.

Behind her, Joel said, "Would you ladies have any notion as to where we might locate him?"

The middle girl shook her head. "Naw. Old Mose might, though. He knows everythin'." She pointed north. "He's usually on that side this time o' night, by the pipe an' weed shop."

"And what, pray tell, are Mister Mose's distinguishing features?" Joel asked.

Before the girls could answer, Hack Bonner said, "Oh, Jesus God."

"Shoulda gone before we left," Tycho growled.

"You don't understand. It's—"

Lieza turned and saw what Bonner saw.

A man in a long coat leaned against the brick wall of a bake shop. He was half-hidden by the crowd, but Lieza saw the reflection of a streetlight in mirrored glasses and caught a glimpse of a blond crewcut.

Zackman.

How and why had he come here? Did the Squid still want Blunt Instrument that badly, or was he after something else? Was he alone, or did he have his playmates with him?

None of the answers mattered at the moment. All that mattered was that the Squid's agent had been following her, and it was time to see how he liked being on the other end.

The Bastard Child sprinted toward Zackman, shoving pseudo-Wrackers out of her way as she ran. She heard Tycho bellow behind her.

Zackman darted away, cutting north across the Circus.

Lieza followed, but she knew that if she didn't catch him quickly, she'd lose sight of him in the crowd. She tried to put on a burst of speed, but a fat leather-and-metal-studs stepped into her path.

She pushed away from him and began running again, but could no longer see her quarry. Taking the chance that he hadn't changed direction, she continued north until she reached the other side of the Circus.

As she stepped up onto the sidewalk, though, she knew that he had escaped her. There were fewer people here, and the Squid's agent wasn't among them.

The loss didn't bother her much. Now that she knew Zackman was in London, she could keep her guard up. The fact that he'd run probably meant that he was working alone.

Her companions were nowhere in sight, so Lieza walked to a bench beneath a shop window with a flaking decal that said WELLER'S SMOKES. Maybe, she thought as she sat down, Tycho had seen where Zackman had gone and had kept after him. In any case, the Viking, Joel, and Hack would no doubt come looking for her before long.

Both of the closest streetlights were broken, and all of the nearby shops were dark. The fog seemed to be dissipating, and some of the crowd with it.

Big Ben struck midnight. It sounded as if the bell were right behind her.

Thursday, January 10.

"You lost, Mizz?" a deep voice asked.

Lieza's head snapped up, and she saw a large, shadowed figure standing in the doorway of the pipe-and-weed shop.

How long have I been here? she wondered. *Who's—*

She remembered what the miniskirted girl had told her.

"You Mose?" she asked.

A tiny red glow burned briefly in the doorway, and Lieza smelled sweet cigar tobacco.

"Maybe," the voice said. "What's in a name?"

The Bastard Child stood and moved toward the doorway until she could see that the man was dark skinned and wore a plaid flannel shirt and blue jeans. Smoke hid his face.

"There's a lot in a name," she said. "That's why Wrackers choose their own."

The big man chuckled. It was a deep, rumbling sound that Lieza felt as much as heard.

"So they say," the man said. "More often than not, though, I 'spec they only fool themselves into thinking they choose. Take you—you let your mama pick your name."

Lieza felt her anger stirring. "I took my name after my mother died."

The man's broad head moved from side to side in its cloud of smoke. "She called you Lisa, and you just changed a few letters to make it sound meaner, like you thought she wanted you to be. Your second name you took from a book you found beside her bed: *The Starry Messenger and Other Works of Galileo Galilei*."

Lieza's anger became transmuted to something closer to fear.

How could he know that? Could someone in Mama's band have seen it, and . . .

"Don't be surprised," the shadowy man said. "I know lots of things."

The Bastard Child tried to regain her usual boldness. "Where can I find Daniel Jackson?"

"Pissant," the man said.

Lieza began to shiver. She wished she'd worn something heavier than a thin cloth jacket over her T-shirt.

"That's him," she said, her voice cracking.

The red glow appeared again for a moment.

"Why you want him?" the man asked after exhaling the smoke. "For revenge, or because you want him to stop what's comin'? You're likely to draw a blank on either one."

"My reasons are my own," Lieza said, forcing some defiance into her voice. "You going to help me or not?"

There was a moment of silence before the man spoke

again. "Now, I s'pose I could try to, just like I could've tried to help others since I been on this island. But help tends to backfire unless the help-ee is ready for it. Nobody here's been ready. And you're gonna find that when *you* get ready, you're gonna have to be the help-er. I could maybe encourage you then, but as for these other souls— they're your responsibility. Welcome to it."

Lieza tried to step closer, but found that her legs wouldn't move.

"Who are you?" she whispered.

The cigar tip glowed a third time.

"Somebody cursed with the gift of prophecy, like your friend's man Jesse," the deep voice said. "'Cept I see more than one path. The one Jesse sees, that's the most likely. There's also one where nobody gets hurt, but its entrance is choked off with weeds. Then there's a third path where you, Mizz Galilei, decide to do somethin'. People still get hurt, but . . . shoot, that path splits into so many different directions that there's no tellin' whether we're goin' to hell or heaven or any place in between."

Lieza strained again to step closer, and failed again. "What is it," she began, stumbling over the words. "What is it that I . . . should decide to do?"

The cigar glowed a fourth time, and before its fire died completely, the big man grinned.

The red glow was reflected in a coppery tooth.

"Now, how would I know?" the apparition asked. "Ain't you the one who says you do what you do? Tell you what, though—don't be too hard on these kids here. They just ain't had the right one to set 'em on a better path. I've been waitin' for a long time to say that, and now anything else I do is gonna be piddly. The job's yours, and ain't nobody but you can decide just what it's gonna be."

There was another rumbling chuckle. "Just like nobody but you can decide whether you stick with that Straight boy. But don't be too hard on him either, or on yourself. You've got a good heart, with a few bad spots for flavor. And that song that's givin' you trouble—stop tryin' to make it perfect, hear? *Perfect* don't exist, and you know it. You've got to settle for *close-enough*."

The door swung open behind the man, and he disappeared into the pipe-and-weed shop.

"Wait!" Lieza cried, and found that she could walk again. She stepped into the doorway.

"'Bye, now," the deep voice said, and the door closed.

Lieza grabbed the doorknob, but it wouldn't turn.

Beyond the door's single pane of glass, the shop was utterly dark.

"Teek!" she shouted. "Teek, I need you!"

Even as she said it, though, she knew it was a lie. The pane in the door was real glass, and she could have broken it and climbed inside.

But the truth was that she didn't want to catch the copper-toothed man.

Lieza stepped out of the doorway and saw Tycho dragging Hack up onto the sidewalk. She marveled for a few moments at the pale light that allowed her to see them so clearly, and then realized that the fog was gone.

She found the Moon just above the rooftops to the east. It was entering its last quarter.

Just when I need you, you start to leave. But tell me first: Just what is it I'm supposed to do, Mama?

But she already knew the answer, she realized. It was the same answer she had given Stig Sullivan.

The Music.

Even if that answer was wrong, it was the only one she'd ever know. There were no gods to hear her prayers, and Bitch Alice was a frozen, dehydrated corpse.

No one ever got an answer from one of those.

The Bastard Child, as always, was on her own.

18

Satis House

> Ooooh baby, you want
> Breakfast in bed?
> Ooooh baby, you got
> Rocks in your head.
> I came over here
> Just to have me some fun.
> You want a wife,
> Go out and buy yourself one.
>
> 'Cause I got better things to do
> Than remember where you put
> Your dinking shoes.
> Maybe if I were short of cash today—
> I'd do what you wanted,
> If I got paid.
>
>   —Bitch Alice,
>   "Get Your Own Damn Tomato
>   Juice," 1965

Thursday, January 10, 1980. Bastwick Street, London.

Pissant awoke at 2:00 A.M. wanting a drink, but when he took a pull from the bottle on the nightstand, it was no good. He wondered whether he was finally losing all sensation in his taste buds, or whether Scotch simply didn't have any flavor before dawn.

He recapped the bottle and shifted in bed to lie on his left side. Estella, who had been snoring softly, mumbled in her sleep and turned to settle her rump against his abdomen. Her shoulders smelled like baby powder.

Pissant hoped she wouldn't wake up and try to seduce him again, since there was no way in hell he'd be able to respond, but he was glad she was with him. With the lights off, the windowless room was as dark as if it were underground, and he needed protection from the fanged visions that swarmed from the black air. Without Estella to cling to, he knew he would run from the room in terror, which would trigger an electric shock down the hall that would awaken Bentley. The burly guard had promised that such an event would put him in a rotten mood.

Pissant wasn't sure that Estella's companionship was adequate compensation for his confinement, though. She and Bentley gave him almost everything he asked for, but that didn't change the fact that the place he had come to call Satis House was a prison.

He had been blindfolded when they'd brought him here, so he didn't know what the building looked like or how large it was. For that matter, he didn't even know *where* Satis House was, although he was sure it was in England. He was allowed in only three rooms: the bedroom, the "workroom" with its computer and software, and the adjoining bathroom.

The confinement itself wasn't a hardship, because over the last decade he had actually come to prefer spending most of his time in small, enclosed spaces. What bothered him now was that he didn't have any choice. Bentley and Estella were in charge, and the only power he had over them was to dictate his choices for breakfast, lunch, dinner, booze, and videotapes. Any other requests—such as for a newspaper, or real-time TV—were turned down. He was here to do a job, they said, and news of the outside would only ruin his concentration.

Pissant wasn't sure he bought it, particularly since Estella's explanations on the plane had been so contradictory and confusing. Since they'd arrived here, Estella had stuck to the story that Pissant's "job" was to evaluate the Euro-Asian Space Agency's proposed Marscraft project; and, to be sure, the software in the workroom contained specifications for a seven-man ship and a tentative mission schedule—but every time he tried to pore over all the deltas and sigmas and integrals, he felt as if he were trying to relearn a language he had lost at the age of four . . . and it didn't seem reasonable for the Brits to have expected anything else, no matter what they said.

So perhaps his kidnapping had been mainly a political ploy after all, although not in the way that Estella had described. He knew that his disappearance couldn't *reduce* the danger of war; if anything, it would increase it.

Just what had happened, he wondered, when Wilson had found him gone? Whom had the Big Whig suspected, and whom had he accused?

Pissant hoped none of Wilson's people had seen Lieza Galilei enter or leave the hotel. No matter how much pain he felt whenever he thought of war, it would multiply a thousand times if he knew that anything had happened to her because of him.

Don't worry about that one, the voice in his head said. *She's inherited her mother's toughness and intelligence, despite the fact that the other half of her genes are those of a useless Jack. She's coyote, not toy poodle.*

Pissant uncapped the bottle and took another drink, trying to keep his mind free of thoughts of the Bastard Child. It was only a short step from her to Dallas, and he couldn't face going back there. Not now, in the dark, with his demons poised and waiting . . .

He wasn't strong enough to hold them off on his own, so he turned on the nightstand lamp and grasped Estella's shoulder. If she would only talk to him for a while, he'd be all right.

The day before, she had said that she'd done a tour of duty on Churchill-Chiang Station as part of her training. The physicist had been drunk at the time of the comment and hadn't thought to ask her to describe the experience, but now it seemed like the perfect thing to do.

"Wake up," he said, shaking her. There was no point in being gentle; after all, she was his jailor, and he had no reason to care whether she liked him or not. Besides, she was being well paid to serve him. "Estella, I can't sleep."

Estella finally groaned and turned onto her back, wincing at the lamplight.

"Whassa matter, love?" she said, slurring the words. "'Nother nightmare?"

"No. I just feel like talking."

Estella yawned. "Y'wanta sleep, I'll get you a pill. What time is it, anyway?"

"A little after two. I want you to talk to me."

Frowning, Estella sat up and shoved her pillow against the headboard to form a backrest. "The pill is faster and won't get me grumpy."

Pissant started to shake his head, then stopped because it hurt. "A pill can't tell me what it's like to be in space. You can."

The thin, magenta-haired woman rubbed her eyes and yawned again. "To make a brief story even briefer, it was a lot like what we're doing now—staying cooped up. The whole thing was a short and minor disappointment before I went on to better things."

"There's a place to start," Pissant said, scooting up to sit beside her. "Exactly why was it disappointing?"

"Because I barfed every time I went from the hub to the rim. It was inconvenient for my co-workers, who said I should return to where flush toilets were available in abundance." She sniffed and wrinkled her nose. "Yahweh, have you been hitting the juice already this morning? You're worse off than I thought."

Pissant gave a short, sardonic chuckle. "I'm worse off than *anybody's* thought," he said, "but I'm not the current topic. What did you do besides throw up?"

Estella rolled her eyes and set her mouth in an expression of exasperation. "Really, didn't your all-American flyboys fill you in? What could I possibly say that you don't already know?"

Pissant took another swig from his bottle, and the

stuff tasted a little better this time. Maybe his tongue just needed time to wake up.

"We never had people living in space for extended periods," he said. "So, tell me—what's the housing up there like? How was the food? How many times did you EVA? What were the duty hours? What sorts of recreational facilities are there? Did you have zero-G sex? Did—"

The physicist cut himself off, immediately regretting his last question.

Estella grinned lewdly. "What do you think, Yahweh?"

She reached for him, but he flinched away.

Her grin faded to a pout. "There was a bay in the hub that was lined with foam pads, and people signed up for times. But after my first week, nobody'd ask me. I kept barfing."

Pissant gave her what he hoped would look like a kindly smile. "You'd have the same experience with me, kid, so count your blessings."

Estella's pout became a little less pronounced. "I could change your attitude if you'd let me. I could've gotten used to the Foam Room, too, if they'd given me a few more chances. A couple of the Wrackers were willing to, I think, but they dropped me when they found out I was there to monitor snoop satellites. Wrackers are pretty snobby to spies." She sniffed. "*Everybody* was prejudiced against me for one reason or another."

Pissant was surprised. Not at the fact that Estella had made few friends on the Station, because he knew how irritating she could be, but at the fact that the Alliance actually allowed non-Straights into space.

"How many Wrackers are up there?" he asked.

Estella shrugged. "I dunno. Maybe thirty out of the hundred and fifty. Most of those aren't *really* Wrackers, though; they just play The Music and wear the clothes. The quarters are so cramped that everybody develops a few odd habits to keep things interesting."

The physicist scratched at the stubble on his throat.

"Did you meet anyone there you'd consider a real Wracker?"

"Oh, sure, a dozen or so. Contemptuous of authority, bad manners, snobby to spies, the whole bit."

Pissant felt an alarm going off in his head. There were demons living nearby.

But he wasn't able to stop himself from trying to find out more.

"Why does the Alliance let them up there?" he asked. "For that matter, why do they want to be there in the first place? I'd think that after..."

No. Stop here.

He felt a sensation in his right palm like glass cutting across his lifeline. He dropped the Scotch bottle, and amber fluid gurgled onto the blue bedspread.

Estella grabbed the bottle. "Yahweh, love, you're still half asleep. No wonder you're onto all this rot. You've been dreaming about when you were training to go up, and about what happened to keep you from it, haven't you? Poor dear."

I would have been on Conquistador 21, *he thought. I would have walked on the Moon...*

Pissant smelled something burning, and he knew he needed more booze fast.

"Give it back," he pleaded. "Please, give it back, and keep talking. About anything."

Estella handed the bottle back to him. He took a long drink from it, then held it under his nose so that he couldn't smell anything but Scotch fumes.

"Well, um," Estella said uncertainly, "the, uh, Wrackers on the Station were good at what they did, so I suppose that's why they were allowed up. Couple of engineers, couple of mechanics. None of them in the military contingent, of course, but they must've had security clearance, or they wouldn't't've been there. Most Brit Wrackers don't get radical. Those on the Station did have one topic they were adamant on, though—they hated Yanks for what happened to Bitch Alice."

Pissant felt himself slipping into an abyss. He had

hoped that Estella could keep him from it, but instead she was pushing him down.

"Come to think of it," Estella went on, "that must be why they got clearance. I heard one of 'em say that we'd have people livin' on Jupiter's moons by now if it weren't for Uncle Sam killin' the Bitch, and . . . Oh, Yahweh, don't take it like that. You know *I* don't feel that way about you. I think you're wonderful."

Pissant clutched the bottle. He could hear screams in the distance, getting nearer and nearer; he could see the moonsuited figure becoming sharper in the monitor . . .

"There, there," Estella said, putting her arms around his shoulders and rocking him back and forth. "We'll talk about something else. Baby ducks, hmmm? Or sausage and omelets. Would you like an early breakfast, Yahweh? I'm not like the woman in that old song; I'll bring you juice."

Pissant wanted to scream at her, but his jaw muscles were clenched.

You're doing this on purpose. I don't want to hear any more, no more, no more—

A bellow of rage cut into his brain, and his right arm jerked convulsively, smashing the Scotch bottle against a corner of the nightstand.

Estella let go of him and leaped out of bed. "Bentley!" she shouted. "What is it?"

Pissant stared at the broken glass on the floor and the nightstand, and at the booze running off the smooth wood and dribbling to the carpet. It was so pretty that he began to think that maybe everything was all right.

Then he saw the fresh cut on the palm of his right hand, and he knew it was happening again.

"Bloody miserable fookin' bloody bastards!" Bentley's voice roared.

Something else smashed, and there were shouts and curses.

Coming closer, and closer . . .

"You lied to her!" the ragged man screamed. *"You sent her there to die!"*

"And you're gonna pay!"

Estella yanked open the nightstand drawer and removed a syringe, then bit off the plastic cap and jabbed the needle into Pissant's right deltoid. He cried out in surprise and pain.

"Just to keep you calm, love," Estella said as she pushed in the plunger.

She threw the empty syringe across the room, then reached into the drawer again and pulled out a pistol.

"You're naked," the physicist said, hearing his voice as a faint buzz in the midst of an intensifying roar.

Estella gestured with her free hand. "Up, Yahweh," she said in a low, hurried voice. "Bentley's holding them off for now, but I've got to help. Do just what I say: Crawl under the bed and hit the power socket, and a section of the wall will pop in. Get inside, and it'll pop back. You'll be safe there and have a nice sleep until I get you out."

Why was this technician naked, Pissant wondered, and where had she gotten a gun? How had she come up with the insane idea that Mission Control had secret compartments?

The woman grabbed his wrist and dragged him from the bed.

Broken glass jabbed into Pissant's feet.

"Why am I in my shorts?" he asked. "Why are people screaming?"

The woman slapped him, and he remembered that her name was Estella. This wasn't Mission Control, but he had no idea of just where it was.

Estella grasped the back of his neck and shoved his head toward the floor. He went down to his knees.

The bedroom door burst open and slammed against the wall.

Estella released Pissant and whirled, bringing up the pistol.

A young man with a bruised, pockmarked face and greasy black hair appeared in the doorway.

"Hey, Pissant!" he yelled.

The pistol's hammer clicked back.

"Here's another punk gonna get what he deserves,"
the security man said, cocking the .357.

Pissant wrapped his arms around Estella's legs, trying
to tackle her. An explosion ripped the air, and then a large
woman wearing hot pants and a bicycle-chain garter belt
appeared and snapped her elbow into Estella's neck.

Estella fell onto the bed, and the other woman
wrenched the pistol away from her.

Pissant, still on his knees, looked at the greasy-haired
young man, who was examining a fist-sized hole at eye
level in the door.

"Hello, Bud," Pissant said hoarsely, amazed that he
remembered the name.

Bud ran a finger around the jagged hole. "Sputzing
Patton," he said, and then he looked at the physicist.
"Would that have cured my acne, or what?"

"Or what," the woman in the bicycle-chain garters
said, unloading the pistol and tossing it into a corner.
"Now, what do we do with this cookie?"

Estella was rubbing her neck and groaning, but Pissant noticed that she wasn't rubbing the side that the other
woman had hit.

Bud came across the room and helped Pissant to his
feet. "Beats me, Bazz. The Doc here's the one she's kept
locked up. He ought to say."

Pissant looked down at Estella, and she looked back
at him with watery eyes.

She can put on quite an act when she wants to, can't
she? the voice in his head asked.

"I'm not even sure I want to leave," he said.

Bazz clenched her fists and closed her eyes. "Great,
Gator. Mister Universe tries to cut me in two, Bathsheba
here nearly exposes your sinuses, and Professor Jagoff
isn't sure he wants to go. So far I *hate* England."

"I'm sorry," Pissant said, feeling dizzier by the second. "It's just that they haven't treated me badly. I don't
want them hurt."

"So we'll leave them locked in the bathroom," Bud
said. "By the time they get out, we'll be so many twisty-
turny streets away that they'll never find us."

"They're with the British government," Pissant said, stumbling toward the closet to get his clothing. "You'll get into big trouble."

Bud laughed. "So what else is new?"

* * *

In the workroom, Pissant saw that Bud and Bazz had three companions, two of whom he recognized as Cherry Angola and Fug of Blunt Instrument. Cherry and a slender man in a blue bodysuit were sitting on Bentley, who was prone on the floor. The wild-eyed, stubble-headed Fug was chewing on Bentley's ankle, and the pair of socks stuffed into the Brit's mouth did little to muffle his bellowing.

"Well, I'll be skagged and jagged," Cherry said when she saw Pissant, and then she nudged the man in the body-suit. "Gator's grapevine bore fruit, Dude. It's Jackson."

"Wasn't a doubt," Bud said. "Triangulation of sources never fails. Now, let's get Tarzan and Jane wrapped in some wet sheets and put 'em in the bathroom. We've gotta crank it outta here in case their fellow spies have been monitoring any bugs. Unless they're as lax as Tarzan here, they're probably already on their way."

"I'll miss you, Yahweh," Estella said wistfully just before Bazz dragged her into the bathroom and crammed a washcloth into her mouth.

Pissant turned away and leaned against a wall.

Typical. This is how you treat everyone who's been nice to you, isn't it?

Once Bentley and Estella were taken care of, Bazz and Cherry grasped Pissant under his armpits and lifted him. He was wearing the suit he'd worn at the Rally for America, but Bentley had taken his shoes away on Sunday, so he was barefoot. The cuts on his soles were bleeding, but he was aware of the pain as only a distant tickle. Whatever Estella had injected him with was making him go numb.

With Fug and Dude leading and Bud bringing up the rear, the Wrackers carried Pissant down a hallway into a room with a broken window. A streetlight gleamed through a remaining shard of glass like a nearby star.

Fug butted the shard out of the frame, and he, Dude,

and Bud vaulted outside. Bazz and Cherry handed Pissant through as if he were a rolled-up rug, then jumped out themselves.

Within seconds, the coyotes were running down a cobblestone walk, carrying Pissant as before.

The physicist looked back and saw that Satis House was an ordinary building of gray stone, exactly like every other house on this side of the street. Each one was lit by the bluish glow of streetlights, and each one looked as though it would be unbearably chilly and damp.

But Satis House had been warm and dry. It was the outside that was cold and wet.

There was also a smell like an open sewer.

Pissant faced forward and saw Dude glance at a wrist-watch. "Three minutes and forty-two seconds from entry to exit," the Wracker said. "Too dinking slow."

"No such thing as 'too slow' unless we get caught," Cherry said, panting, "and that ain't happened yet."

"Day's young," Bazz muttered.

Fug grunted. To Pissant, the noise sounded as if it couldn't have come from a human throat.

He opened his mouth to ask where they were taking him, but found that he couldn't speak. His lips and tongue felt anesthetized.

It didn't matter. As always, he was letting others make his decisions for him. If he was willing to relinquish that responsibility, he might as well relinquish the right to know what the decisions were, too.

He looked toward the small, dark shops on the other side of the street, amazed at the clarity with which he could see them. This was definitely Britain; probably London. The area didn't look much different from certain sections he had visited in 1953, in happier times, before—

His thoughts shattered like paper-thin china.

In a doorway across the street stood a small man with a sharp nose. His face shone in a streetlight's glare like polished wood.

The Wrackers weren't looking. They didn't see him, they didn't know—

That Pinocchio was here.

Pissant tried to tell them, but all that came out was a wheeze.

"It's OK," Bud said, his voice seeming to echo inside the physicist's skull. "Everything's gonna be all right."

As the Wracker spoke, Pissant saw another figure standing in the mouth of an alley several shops away from Pinocchio. This man was large and dark and wore a plaid shirt.

Pissant remembered his hallucination at Wilson's rally and wondered if he might be having it again.

Then both Pinocchio and the dark man were out of sight.

"Doc, snap out of it," Bud said breathlessly. "You gotta stay alert. The Alliance has hit a satellite with a nuke, and you can bet cities are next. You might be able to help, though; I'll explain after we stop. We've got big things to do, man, if we want to stay alive."

Pissant wasn't surprised to hear what the Alliance was doing. Nuclear war had been in the cards for a long time, and he had known it, and he hadn't cared.

He still didn't. He wanted to, but it was pointless. If anything could prevent what was coming, it would have to be done without any aid from him.

The reason was simple:

Only the living were capable of action, of doing what Bud called "big things."

And hadn't Pissant proven himself to be less than living? Didn't the gnome's presence confirm what he had known all along?

Pinocchio had been killed, but had refused to be still. Now he was one of the Walking Dead, come to claim his brother.

Come to take Daniel P. Jackson to hell.

19

Brighter Than a Thousand Butane Lighters

The gods looked down
At clumsy Man
And said, "We must do
"What we can
"To keep our children safe
"From what will hurt them."
But man was such a clever boy,
He soon devised his own new toy
And lit the night with the glare
Of his creation.

Burn, baby, burn,
Brighter than a thousand suns.
Scream, children, scream—
You know he meant it all in fun.

How could he scorch the earth
Before he'd even reached the sky?
Well, he's nothing but a little boy...
Don't even try to ask him why.

—Lieza Galilei,
"Prometheus Plays with Matches,"
1978

Thursday, January 10, 1980. London.

They took Pissant into the Underground, and there he saw dozens of people whom he at first thought must be Wrackers.

Then he noticed something different about them, and they began to melt and change, to become monsters . . .

"You're dreaming, of course, the voice inside said. *The Underground train is nothing more than a psychosexual symbol, and the "Wrackers" are in fact your own fears and failures. That's why there are so many of them.*

See the woman with steel-tipped nipples? Mizz Impotence the Pure.

The child with the scabs over his eye sockets? Master Hideaway the Gouger.

And that one, the hideous male with the fangs and the bug eyes—oh, excuse me; that's your reflection in the window, isn't it?

Stop trying to speak, to scream. It isn't worth the effort. When have you ever had anything interesting to say?

Ah, here's a good one. A charred corpse walking toward you, it's skin sloughing off in great black slabs. It's reaching for you, I see.

I wonder. What could it possibly represent?

I really have no idea.

Have you?

* * *

Trevor Street.

Bazz and Cherry lowered him to a tan couch that he was sure must be real. He could feel the pebbled texture of upholstery against his hands, just as he could feel cool fingertips against his forehead.

"He's feverish," Bud said.

"I'll get Ellyn," Cherry said, and ran up a staircase at the far end of the room.

If this wasn't a dream, Pissant knew, he had to tell Bud what he had seen. He had to warn him.

"Pih—pih—pih—" he stuttered, closing his eyes tight with the effort.

"That's right," Bud said. "You're Pissant, and you're

all right now. We aren't going to let anyone hurt you."

"Fug and I are going to find Lieza," Bazz's voice said, and there was the sound of a door opening and closing.

A rush of cold hit Pissant's bare feet and shot up into his chest.

*   *   *

Ally splashes you with ice water for the third time, so you charge out of the shower, dripping and bellowing, finally catching her in the bedroom.

The sheets are thoroughly wet by the time you both roll off onto the floor, laughing.

"I'm divorcing Susanne," you say after a long time.

Ally grins. "Don't you mean she's divorcing you?"

"Well, yes. But all that matters is that in less than a year, by mid-'56, maybe, you and I—"

She touches the fingers of her left hand to your mouth.

"Won't be able to change," she says.

"But we could get married, and—"

"Kill each other." She shakes her head. "No, Pissant. I'm going to change my name, but I won't marry anybody to do it."

Feeling the anger beginning to surge up, you stand and leave the room, water still dripping from your hair.

"You're a loveless bitch," you shout.

Downstairs, you take a pint of Kentucky sipping whiskey from your coat pocket and drain it.

Then you break every record album she owns.

When you finish, you turn and see her leaning against a doorjamb at the foot of the stairs.

"The last ritual," she says. "We're separate now. We may meet again, but we'll never again be as we've been these past five months."

Her eyes burn at you, and you wish there were someplace to hide.

"Ally," you say as you take a stumbling step toward her.

"Bitch Alice," she says, and goes back upstairs.

Three years later, you hear that she had a baby in June 1956.

You call her a whore for sleeping around on you.

* * *

He opened his eyes and saw a ball of fuzzy light with Bud's distorted face in its center.

"Hey, Pissant," the Wracker said, shaking him. "Ell, he's sick. I found a hypo in the room where they had him, probably a tranquilizer—but they must not have considered how his body chemistry's been screwed up."

Bud's face moved out of Pissant's vision, to be replaced by that of a woman he had never seen before.

"He's a little warm," she said, "but the pulse isn't bad, and he's breathing fine."

Her voice seemed to reach him after traveling through a thick blanket of cotton.

"So our first priority is to dress the cuts. . . ."

* * *

You watch as a single dark drop falls from the base of your thumb and splatters on the cheek of the dead man at your feet. A broken bottle, its jagged end smeared with red, rolls from the Wracker's limp fingers.

The security guard named Jim pushes you aside, and then he cocks his pistol again and fires into the side of the Wracker's head. Blood and bits of bone spray your clothes.

A second wave bursts into Mission Control, igniting ethanol bombs with cigarette lighters. One of the bottles bursts nearby and splashes alcohol onto your terminal, and blue flames dance madly on the buttons and keys. The plastiglass of your monitor begins to bubble.

But the big screen on the wall across the room is still displaying the live transmission from the Moon. The four NOSS astronauts are off-camera, pretending to do something about the lander. They'll keep on pretending, you know, until their oxygen is gone.

Bitch Alice isn't pretending.

The picture is no longer being broadcast to the networks; it's been reserved for the hell that Mission Control has become. All around you, guards and technicians fight an enraged horde, and above them all, sitting on a gray boulder, is the Bitch.

You can't see her eyes behind the gold-sprayed helmet

visor, but you feel an overpowering certainty that she's looking out of the screen—

At you.

Jim fires again and again, but you hardly hear the shouts as you listen to the voice in your earphones, as you hear the static-riddled words that no one else ever will.

"They're after you by now," she says. "But you've also cut me off by now, so I can't send them away, can I? Just in case, though— Stop, my friends, my family. I was wrong to ask you to punish them. Instead I should have asked you to find out who is responsible, and—

"But no one down there's even listening, are you? Pissant, if you're there . . . but of course you aren't. You've run by now, and I'm glad. I don't want you hurt. I don't want anyone hurt. I was just angry. Dixon would be ashamed of me. . . ."

You reach for the button on your console that would let you answer, but the fire drives you back.

"Gus, Rance, Neil, and Lucy are lying to themselves," the voice from the earphones says. "The valve has burst wide open, as if a bomb had been inside. And it probably was, wasn't it? The fuel is gone. No more songs. Hey, that rhymes."

A pause. Then: "That's all I ever wanted to do, you know. Make it rhyme."

The figure on the screen reaches for the latches that seal the helmet to her suit. You scream, but the roar of the fire swallows your voice.

A female Wracker leaps over your console, kicking at you, and the guard shoots her in the face.

On the screen, thick-fingered gloves fumble with the first latch, and then the second. You stand as if frozen, wanting to scream at her again, knowing that she can't hear.

Knowing that it wouldn't make any difference if she could.

The third latch. The fourth. The fifth. The sixth.

The gloved hands grasp the helmet on either side and turn it counterclockwise.

Then push up.

For a brief, timeless instant, the woman with the dark hair and fiery eyes glares out of the screen, defiant and beautiful.

"Ally," you breathe.

And then the face isn't Ally, isn't anything human.

A firebomb bursts against it.

And she's gone.

* * *

A sharp sting in his nose made him choke, and then the black and red checkerboard dissolved as he sucked in a huge lungful of air.

Bud grinned above him and tossed away a damp cloth. "Lucky for us Dude found some KhromeKleen polish under the sink. I thought you were gonna swallow your tongue. Now, how about we see if you can sit up? They gave you something back there, and we ought to make you walk it off. Dopers who O.D. gotta keep moving, Pissant, or they die."

Cherry Angola's face appeared next to Bud's.

"'Pissant?'" she asked. "Is that what you keep calling him?"

"It's his nickname for himself," Bud said, reaching under the physicist's shoulders and raising him to a sitting position.

As Pissant sat up, something seemed to come loose in his throat. "It's—" he said, half-croaking. "It's—"

Bud picked up a ceramic mug of hot coffee form the floor and held it to the physicist's lips. The stuff smelled awful and tasted worse, but Pissant's only choices were to drink it or drown in it. As he drank, he looked down and saw that his right hand and both of his feet were bandaged.

He drained the mug and dropped it. "It's not . . . my nickname for myself," he said. "I already told you . . . it's what *she* called me."

"Who's 'she'?" Bud asked.

Pissant reached out with his left hand and touched Bud's arm. "I told you," he said, his voice growing stronger. "The beautiful . . . Moon Lady."

Bud frowned. "You were drunk when you said that,

and now you're stoned on whatever was in that hypo."

Cherry picked up the mug from the floor and looked at it thoughtfully. "I met Samson Llewellen a couple of times," she said slowly. "He was in Bitch Alice's band. Once he told me that 'Pissant' was what Alice called the sputzer who got her pregnant."

The bass player looked directly at the physicist. "No wonder Lieza's been acting so jackbugged since seeing you. That's the only name for her father she's ever known."

She spoke in a tone of accusation, but Pissant welcomed it. At last, he had the chance to unload some of the dirt he'd been carrying around; at last, his soul might be on the verge of being cleansed.

"That's right," he said, his voice barely quavering. "The Bastard Child is mine."

He had denied it so strongly twenty-three years earlier that he hadn't allowed himself to think of it consciously since. But now, the saying of the words made him feel that they must be true.

Bud looked from Pissant to Cherry, then back at Pissant. "Sure, Doc," he said gently. "If you wanna think so, why not?"

Pissant surprised himself by being able to smile. "For almost a quarter century, ever since Ally left me, my life's been going from bad to worse. I tried to fight back by helping to start humankind on the path to other worlds, and I even came close to kicking booze. But then Ally came back into my life because of *Conquistador 18*, and . . .

"You know what I've been like since. But it just occurred to me that if I had something to do with the creation of Lieza Galilei, then I'm *not* worthless. There's something I've done that I can be proud of."

Cherry gave a derisive half-laugh. "You ain't gonna be proud much longer, on account of we're all gonna burn if somebody doesn't figure a way out of it. Since Gator here thinks you're a major piece in this game, I'll ask you plain and simple: How do we keep Johnny and Sammy from blowing the scrod out of each other?"

Pissant's feeling of well-being began to fade. What

were they expecting of him? What was he supposed to do?

"Look, Doc," Bud said. "I didn't tell the others, but I wanted to find you mainly because you're my brother. The fact is, though, that you might have to volunteer to be a bargaining chip. Both sides want you for some reason that makes sense only to them, and right now the one chance I can see for us to avoid dancing the mushroom-cloud mambo depends on how *bad* they want you. But you're beat, so that's something you can think about after you recuperate for a few hours."

"'A few hours,' like jagging hell," Cherry said. "Fort Whatsis is gonna fry sometime today, and then we're next. Death, the Big D, is heading this way."

The Big . . .

Pissant's last bit of happiness was engulfed by fear as he remembered that there was an even more immediate danger than the one Bud and Cherry were worried about. All this time he'd been talking and letting them talk, while coming closer and closer by the second—

"Pinocchio," he blurted. "As you were taking me out of Satis—out of where they were keeping me, I saw Pinocchio across the street."

Bud looked at Pissant skeptically. "Doc, that chick gave you something. You've been hallucinating off and on ever since, and a couple of times you thrashed around like you were being stabbed with hot needles. Don't worry; Pinocchio's umpteen thousand miles away from here."

Pissant pressed his hands to the sides of his head and tried to think coherently.

He was sure. He was *sure*.

"I'm telling the truth!" he shouted. "Pinocchio was across the street from Satis House!"

Dude and the woman called Ellyn appeared on the staircase. "What's all the yelling about?" Ellyn asked.

"Fartbrain's been seeing puppets," Cherry said. "Next thing you know, he'll say Howdy Doody's comin' to get him."

Bud glared at her. "'Pinocchio' is what the Doc calls Claghorn. Remember him? He nearly killed me, and he took a few good shots at you, too."

Cherry's expression instantly changed from contempt to concern. "Why didn't you say so? If that skagger's in London, we've got serious trouble."

"As opposed to the unserious trouble of being vaporized?" Dude asked.

Bud sat down beside the physicist and put an arm around his shoulders. "Look, Pissant, I know you're not lying. But when we found you, you could barely stand, and a few minutes ago you almost had a full-blown seizure. Since then you've been jabbering like a coke addict, and now you're acting paranoid. I don't know what Jane pumped into you, but I do know that we can't trust anything you remember until we have other evidence, peesh?"

Pissant shook his head and tried to stand, but his leg muscles were still numb.

"We're talking about Wilson's killing machine, a thing that isn't human," he said desperately. "Just because I've been hallucinating doesn't mean that I was when—"

The front door opened, and Pinocchio Claghorn came in.

"I regret that I do not have time to ensure that you all die," he said, pointing a red plastic object at Bud.

More than anything else, Pissant wanted to believe that the gnome *was* a hallucination, but both Bud and Cherry saw him too and ran at him.

There was a clicking sound, and they convulsed and fell to the floor, writhing.

Pissant tried again to stand and failed again.

He was forced to sit and watch what happened next.

Dude threw a chair, but Pinocchio dodged it and pointed the red plastic thing. Dude went down.

Ellyn dashed in while Pinocchio's attention was still on Dude, and managed to hit him in the throat. The gnome stumbled, then spun and kicked her in the abdomen.

Ellyn doubled over, but she didn't fall until Pinocchio used the plastic object a third time.

By now, Bud and Cherry's spasms were beginning to subside, but the gnome didn't give them a chance to recover. One by one, he kicked each of the four Wrackers in the head.

When they all lay still, Pinocchio smiled and came to Pissant.

"Hello again, Professor Jackson," the gnome said. "You will recall that I said we still had business between us."

Dear God, dear Dixon, dear Moon Lady, Pissant prayed. *Dear Whoever's listening, please, please just give me enough strength to break his Tinkertoy neck.*

But he still couldn't even make himself stand.

He looked into Pinocchio's dead eyes. "Wipe off that stinking smile and get it over with," he said.

Pinocchio's smile broadened. "Why, whatever can you mean, Professor?"

Pissant nodded at the object in the gnome's hand. "Do whatever it is you do with that thing."

Pinocchio raised the red oblong and looked at it fondly. "A new and effective tool that Mister Wilson was able to acquire for me. It delivers an electric shock sufficient to stun, but leaves the question of life or death up to the skills of its user. Ordinarily, I eschew weapons, but I am in a weakened state as a result of the wounds I received Saturday, and this device is elegant enough to suit my sense of aesthetics. Now, you will come with me."

Pissant was sick of being a pawn, of being at the mercy of forces outside himself. But he still couldn't move; still couldn't fight. Estella's drug was keeping him weak.

Do you suppose you'd be able to do anything anyway? Whatever real strength you may have is buried under too many layers of guilt and alcohol.

So Pissant performed the only act of defiance he could, and spat in the gnome's face.

"You'll have to kill me," he said. "I can't imagine what value I could have to Wilson now, but it doesn't matter. I'll die before I'll let him use me again."

Pinocchio's smile broke into a grin. He seemed unaware of the spittle on his face.

"You shall indeed," he said, "but this is not the proper place. We must return to where the British are keeping you captive. There, alas, the Alliance curs will murder you. But do not despair, for the world will learn of their treachery and will know that if President Fitzgerald had listened to Winton Wilson, you would not have suffered such a fate. As it is, however, the British will have killed you in order to slap America in the face—and the Whig call for a patriotic first strike will at last be heeded, in your honor."

Pissant stared at Pinocchio, barely able to comprehend what the gnome was saying. It sounded too ridiculous to be true.

It also sounded like exactly the sort of thing Winton R. Wilson would come up with.

Pinocchio put the electric weapon into his coat pocket, and when he withdrew his hand, it held a hypodermic needle.

Jesus H. Christ on a Crutch, not again.

"This won't hurt a bit," Pinocchio said, removing the plastic sheath from the needle. "After all, you are numb, are you not, Professor?"

"And what's going to happen to you once Wilson gets his heart's desire?" Pissant asked, wincing as Claghorn pushed the needle into his shoulder. "You're going to burn too, because London's high on his list."

Pinocchio finished the shot and replaced the syringe in his pocket. "Just as I found a way into this country," he said, "I shall find a way out. If by some chance I do not, then I will die knowing that I performed my duties well."

Pissant felt as though his head were filling with styrofoam. Whatever Pinocchio had injected him with was taking effect more rapidly than the stuff Estella had used.

"Jus' in case I don't get another chance," he said, struggling to stay awake, "I want you to know that you're a jagoff and that your mother hated you."

Pinocchio, with surprising strength, lifted the limp physicist from the couch and slung him over his shoulders in a dead man's carry.

How appropriate, Pissant thought.

He saw Ellyn move slightly as they passed her.

No. Stay still. Don't let him know—

She tried to grab for Pinocchio's ankles.

The gnome kicked Ellyn in the head again, then in the side. She shuddered and was still.

Then Pinocchio took Pissant back into the freezing night, and the shock of the cold held off the physicist's unconsciousness for another few seconds.

In his mind's eye, all he could see was the pain in Ellyn's face and the slight swelling in her abdomen that meant pregnancy.

Winton R. Wilson and his minions wanted power so badly that they didn't care whom they hurt. They didn't even care if they started a war that killed *them*.

Given that, Pissant realized just before he was no longer able to think, it wasn't surprising that the Big Whig had no qualms about killing a useless old alcoholic.

20

Hyde and Seek

> *We went to different schools together,*
> *Though the classrooms we sat in*
> *Were the same.*
> *I do not mean to speak in riddles;*
> *Two people cannot*
> *Share a single brain.*
>
> *What you remember*
> *Is not what I know.*
> *The crop you harvest*
> *Is not what I sowed.*
> *For your tomorrow*
> *Will be my future yesterday—*
> *My final heartbreak*
> *Will be your first hurray.*

> —Stigma Sullivan and the
> Silverbees, "Different Schools,"
> 1964

Thursday, January 10, 1980. Charing Cross Hospital.

The Journal of Clifton Bonner:
    It is evening, and it's raining outside. I'm sitting in
the hospital cafeteria, which is nearly deserted.

The room is as cold as a meat locker.

On the table is the three-hour-old fish dinner I haven't been able to eat. I only ordered it so I'd have an excuse for staying. Lieza told me to go with the others, but I can't. Not yet.

Not until I make sense out of what's happened. The past three days feel as distant from me as my numb feet do.

Horrible simile. Maybe I'd be better off in med school after all.

Not bloody likely.

Bloody.

Why couldn't I have had it in me to save just one life? Just one?

Gray, gray, gray. No wonder I can't feel what I should.

* * *

Begin with Sullivan, then.

I've heard his songs since I was a kid. Some were true wrack & roll, and some were bubblegum, but all were unforgettable. Even when he wrote crap, the Silverbees made it sound like the most important crap in the world.

And when he wrote of beauty or pain, the Silverbees made you see the glory, feel that ache. Bitch Alice was the best songwriter of her generation, but the Silverbees were the best band. And Stigma Sullivan was their leader.

So on Tuesday night I went with Lieza, Tycho, and Cherry expecting to meet a legend.

What I found was a paunchy, middle-aged cynic; a self-indulgent Nero fiddling while the world burns.

His walls are covered with canvas after canvas of paint blobs, a great grand cacophony of visual noise, signifying nothing. Even when his songs were at their most opaque, there was *something* real there, but now he's given up meaning entirely, preferring instead to stroke himself.

Look at this. The cesspool calling the sewer filthy.

Is Sullivan really that slimy, or am I reacting out of jealousy, out of fear that Lieza is still attracted to him?

She tried to hide it behind her rage, but I could see the flame in her eyes, those same eyes that waver between lust and nausea when she looks at me. There's a part of her that still worships him, still wants him—maybe only because of what he used to be.

After all, now he's only a pasty-faced fat man with thinning hair and a psychic boyfriend.

The boyfriend is a big, black-haired, deep-voiced man called Jesse. The instant he walked into Sullivan's living room, I wanted to run. He carries a piece of hell wrapped around him like a cloak.

What poetry. What jack-scrod.

The truth is that he spoke a prophecy of doom that only confirmed what I've been feeling ever since my hand sank into the back of Bill's head. I hate him for that.

But look out these windows. Rain.

This miserable city is too cold and wet to burn.

Please.

* * *

We had taken a taxi to Sullivan's, but when we left we headed back to Blunt Instrument's rented house by walking through Hyde Park. There, I discovered that some British Wrackers actually *want* the Alliance to vaporize the U.S.

Lieza would have killed one of them, I think, if I hadn't gotten in the way. Now I wonder if I should've let her do it. That kid in the leopard skins is going to die anyway, and he would've had a better death from the Bastard Child than the one he's going to get.

The one we're all going to get. Me, Mom and Dad, President Fitzgerald, Maria—

That reminds me: I wonder if Maria made it over before the blockade was set up? She and the kid in leopard skins would get along well, I think.

But there's someone else here she'd get along with even better.

How much of this cold I feel is due to fear?

Can fear make your feet numb?

* * *

Late yesterday, a full day after the confrontation with Sullivan, Gator Al said that he'd learned Daniel P. Jackson was in London, and that finding the scientist might help postpone the war. I didn't understand his reasoning, and I don't think Lieza did either.

She agreed to the plan anyway.

I've noted before that her voice changes when she says Jackson's name, and in the house last night, I saw something in her face change too.

Daniel P. Jackson means a great deal to her, and after this morning I think I know why.

But I don't want to pursue it. I don't want to know.

I don't want to see myself in him.

* * *

Lieza, Joel, Tycho, and I walked to the Circus along Piccadilly Street, where Wrackers in leather, denim, and metal warmed the pavement with their body heat as they drank, danced, smoked, and screwed. Fires burned in metal boxes, and The Music blasted from dozens of portable stereos. It was exactly like what I've always imagined a Patton Day celebration might be in a District back home.

The Hyde Park kids, I thought, had been nothing compared to this. Throughout the walk to the Circus, I felt that I was seeing *Wrackers*, not watered-down imitations; and I couldn't understand why Joel, Bazz, and Gator Al had said so many derogatory things about them.

I leaned down toward Joel, who was skipping beside me, and whispered, "I don't get it. What's wrong?"

"Why, whatever do you mean, Mister Bonner?" he asked, tossing up his top hat with one hand and catching it behind his back with the other. "Absolutely nothing's wrong. Oh, well, of course, the weather's horrid, the superpowers are preparing to kill us all, and we're spending our last hours on earth engaged in a futile search for a drunken physicist, but other than those trifles, everything's positively wonderful. Positively *dancingly* wonderful!"

He leaped and spun, landing in a split.

"Oh, dear," he said. "I do believe I've ruptured something."

I started to help him up, but he bounded away and snatched a wiener from a grill. Then he whirled around a streetlight, sang a few bars of "Singin' in the Rain," and dashed back to my side again.

He was still in the mood to sing. "I get no thrill from

squid brains," he crooned. "Mere ethanol makes it impossible to ball, but—"

He did a handspring and a back flip, losing the wiener in the process.

"—I'm always sick, 'cause of yoooooou," he concluded, and bowed. Some of the surrounding Wrackers applauded, but others grumbled about the wasted meat.

Lieza and Tycho were several yards ahead of us by now, and we hurried after them.

"What I meant to ask," I said as we jostled through the crowd, "was why were you talking about London Wrackers as if they were scum?"

"Why, because they are," Joel said. "In contrast, you, although a Straight, don't really pretend to be anything else, which puts you far ahead of them."

We caught up to Lieza and Tycho, and I looked around at the crowd again. I still couldn't see that they were "pretending" anything, but I took Joel's word for it.

He was the only one who liked me.

* * *

Piccadilly, Regent, Coventry, and Shaftesbury Streets are blocked with wooden barricades as they feed into the Circus, so there's no vehicular traffic inside. I had expected that, but otherwise the place didn't correspond to the mental picture I'd had. The statue of Eros was too small, and his bow and arrow had been broken off. He was wearing spray-painted purple shorts. The fountains were operating despite the cold, but the water spewing from them was so rusty that it looked like orange juice.

The Wrackers were like those along Piccadilly Street, except that there were more of them.

Three girls in incredibly short skirts told Lieza about someone called Mose who might know where Jackson could be found.

"And what are Mister Mose's distinguishing features?" Joel asked.

The sound of his voice made me turn toward him involuntarily, and as I did so, I saw the crew-cut man who had come to Lieza's farm in the helicopter.

The man called Zackman.

He was standing against a wall several yards behind us, watching and waiting . . .

I think I yelled. All I'm certain of is that Lieza and Tycho ran after him, and that he started across the Circus, shoving people out of his way as he went.

Joel and I followed the Bastard Child and the Viking. I had no idea what they intended to do with the agent if they caught him, but they probably didn't either.

I lost sight of Zackman almost immediately, and had only gone about fifteen steps before I lost Lieza and Tycho as well. Joel was hopping up and down as he ran, trying to see over the heads of the crowd, but he didn't have any success until he stopped me and climbed onto my shoulders.

"Oh, dear, he's turned west," Joel cried, "But Leez is still going north, and Teek is splitting the difference!"

He leaped away, and before I knew what had happened, I was alone in Piccadilly Circus.

I tried to follow, but a hundred more people spilled into the Circus every second, and it became impossible to run without ramming somebody. When a beefy man wearing chains and a jockstrap offered to "smear yer face on the kerb," I decided to slow down and get to a sidewalk.

I would look for the shop where the girls had said Mose hung out. Whether she caught Zackman or not, Lieza would go there eventually.

I hoped.

* * *

As I worked my way across the Circus, I realized for the first time how much the crowd stank.

They were filthy even by Wracker standards. I saw a woman whose neck was encrusted with dirt; a man whose beard looked as if it had been dipped into garbage and soft wax; a boy defecating in the gutter; a man with teeth that were yellowish-gray and rotten.

I felt as if a spear of ice had skewered me.

Yellowish-gray and rotten . . .

I had to look again. I had to convince myself that it wasn't true, that people who were dead stayed dead, that ghosts didn't return to revenge themselves upon the living.

Instead, I saw the teeth again, and the leathery, leering face.

Genghis Khan.

He was in civilian clothes but was grinning the same grin that he'd had on Concepcion, the grin that said there was nothing that would give him as much pleasure as hurting me would.

People flowed aside as he came toward me. I wanted to run, but the ice spear held me still.

Genghis stopped with his feet nearly touching mine and his head tilted up. His breath smelled of spoiled meat.

Even through the noise of the crowd, I heard his whisper:

"Ah, Mister Number Fifty-two. So good to see that you survived what so many of my comrades did not."

His right hand shot to my throat and clamped onto my trachea.

No one around us seemed to notice.

"Tell me, Mister Number Fifty-two," Genghis Khan said, his breath becoming almost unbearable, "is it fair that so many died? Is it fair that they were slaughtered when we had no intention of harming you and your fellow students? Is it fair that your nation is now threatening to attack Her Majesty simply because she chose to defend that which is rightfully hers?"

I tried to shake my head, but the pressure of his fingers increased until I was afraid even to breathe.

I saw bright flecks of light, like white sparks, swirling before my eyes.

"Is it fair," the Gurkha continued, "that you struck me a vicious blow when I was in no condition to defend myself?"

The pressure increased again, and I knew he was going to kill me. I could feel the cartilage about to cave in like a cardboard tube.

All this way, I thought. *All this way, and I could've gotten it over with weeks ago.*

"No," Genghis said. "No, that was not fair, but now that I can once again defend myself, I shall do so."

The insane alien took over my body and flailed at him with both fists.

Don't bother, I thought. *You'll only make him mad.*

And then, like a cry from heaven:

"TEEK!"

The shout sounded surprisingly close. I was only a few yards from where Lieza must be, I realized, and if I could get her attention—

Genghis felt me strain toward the sound, and he snapped his head in that direction.

"TEEK!" the cry came again. "TEEK, I NEED YOU!"

Miraculously, the thumb of my windmilling left hand caught Genghis in his right eye. The pressure on my trachea disappeared as his hand went to his face; then, realizing his mistake, he reached for me again—

And I was gone, swept up by a massive arm.

"Jagging Straight," Tycho roared in my ear. "Are you deaf?"

I didn't answer, but I don't think he expected me to.

* * *

We burst up out of the crowd onto a dark patch of sidewalk that was strangely empty of people. It was as if this one spot were a place where partying was taboo.

Tycho dumped me onto a bench, and I saw Lieza standing in front of a nearby doorway. She was looking toward me, but her expression was the one that meant she was staring at something far beyond.

The Viking pointed at me. "Leez, we gotta get rid of this Jack. He was maybe thirty feet away and didn't do nothin' when he heard you yell."

"I couldn't;" I croaked, and then coughed. It felt as if a piece of broken cartilage was suspended below my Adam's apple. "Genghis Khan had me." I looked out into the Circus, but the Gurkha was nowhere in sight.

Tycho seemed even more disgusted with me than usual. "Genghis *who*?" he said, and then I remembered that I'm the only one who knows who that is.

The Bastard Child's trance broke.

"Tonight's a night for ghosts," she said. "I saw Dixon."

The Viking scowled. "In the sky, like a comet?"

Lieza gestured at the doorway. "Here. He went inside."

Tycho unhooked Bert from his belt, strode forward, and shattered the door with three quick blows.

"I didn't mean for you to do that," Lieza said.

Tycho shrugged. "Shoulda said so." He went into the shop, and Lieza and I followed.

The place was dark, and full of odors that made me dizzy. I bumped into a glass counter and nearly fell.

"Watch it, klutz," Lieza's voice said from the darkness ahead of me.

"Ain't nobody here but us," Tycho said.

"Is there a back way out?" the Bastard Child asked.

"Not unless it's behind these jars of skunkweed. You want I should knock 'em down to see?"

"No. Let's get out of here."

I turned around and saw a short figure in the doorway, backlit by the glow from the Circus.

I thought it was Genghis Khan, and I screamed.

"Sputzing hell," Tycho barked.

The figure in the doorway put on a top hat.

"I say," Joel said. "I haven't gotten a response like that since I infiltrated a Mormon choir and removed my pants halfway through the service."

* * *

I made it outside and sat down hard on the bench. I felt miserable, ashamed, and terrified.

Genghis Khan *was* here. He *is* here. I could still feel his fingers on my throat as I sat outside that shop, and I can still feel them in this freezing cafeteria.

If there's still time, he won't waste it. He'll come for me.

But no matter what he does, I won't humiliate myself again.

I won't scream.

I swear I won't.

* * *

Joel went into the shop and came out with an ivory pipe, a silver lighter, and a small block of hashish.

"Gonna scorch your throat," Tycho said.

Joel took two crumpled five-pound notes from his jacket and tossed them through the doorway.

"Then I shall be warmer than anyone else in this rottenly chilly city," he said, crumbling a corner of the block into the pipe bowl. "Besides, one might as well prepare oneself for what's coming, eh?"

Lieza sat beside me. "Lose Zackman?" she asked Tycho.

He nodded. "Right after I lost you."

Joel paused while trying to light his pipe and said, "I followed the scoundrel into Regent Street. At that point, he entered a vehicle and, to employ a cliché, sped into the night. Not very sporting, but at least he didn't use that nasty machine pistol of his this time."

Tycho snorted. "Sputzer probably thought he was surrounded by Wrackers and was afraid he'd get his lungs ripped out before he could get off a shot."

"That may not stop him again," Joel said. "I've been wondering what reason he could have for being here and have reached two possible conclusions: one, Madame Squid still wants Doctor Jackson—highly probable, given her tenacity and limited imagination—and two, Madame Squid wants to have us killed for failing to behave as she wished. I would add that these possibilities are not mutually exclusive. Once Zackman has Jackson, or discovers that he cannot obtain Jackson, possible conclusion number two will become definite probability number one. Wouldn't you agree, Leez?"

Lieza didn't answer. She was looking at the sidewalk, preoccupied again.

I thought I knew why. "Did Dixon talk to you?" I asked.

Tycho stuck Bert back into his belt. "Dixon's dead," he said.

Then Lieza spoke, as if in a dream. "He said that what

happens next is my choice, that he's been waiting for me, that I'm . . ."

Her voice trailed off.

She didn't sound like the Bastard Child, and it scared me. I wanted her to be defiant and angry again, even if it meant that her anger would be directed at me.

"That you're the next God?" I said, trying to sound sarcastic.

She looked at me, and her eyes flashed.

"Yes," she said.

Joel, having succeeded in lighting his pipe, took a long drag and exhaled pungent smoke.

"You've got my vote," he said.

Tycho shifted his weight from one foot to the other. He looked uncomfortable.

"Mine too," he said.

Lieza gave a short laugh. "So what do I do once I'm in office?"

There was a long stretch of silence, and then I said, "Whatever you have to."

Silently, I added, *Amen.*

It seemed like a good time to get religious. Not in the sense that Mom and Dad always meant, but in the I'll-pray-to-anyone-who'll-cover-my-ass sense.

Perhaps Eddie Dixon really *had* been transformed into a deity and had come back to earth to find the right prophet to revive his gospel.

After all, Jesus knew nothing of nuclear bombs, so how could He—or Muhammad, or Buddha, or Krishna, or Apollo—possibly save us from them?

In a nuclear war, the only effective prayer would be to a nuclear-age god. To Eddie Dixon. Or to Bitch Alice.

Or perhaps to the Bastard Child.

* * *

We spent the next several hours in a fruitless search. It was almost daybreak when Bazz and Fug found us.

"We've got him," Bazz said.

The six of us ran to Piccadilly Street and piled into a taxi. Fug pushed the operator aside so he could drive.

We were fast, but not fast enough. When we got to the house, the door was open, and I knew something was wrong.

The others rushed in, but I hung back and asked the taxi operator to wait.

Then I walked to the house slowly, putting off what I would see inside as long as I could.

The front room smelled of urine.

Cherry, Gator Al, and Dude were lying near the door, unconscious. Cherry had a lump the size of a golf ball behind her left ear.

Ellyn had crawled to the foot of the stairs. Blood soaked the thighs of her bodysuit.

Lieza knelt beside her and cradled her head.

"He's gone," Ellyn said dully.

Daniel P. Jackson was nowhere in sight, but she wasn't talking about him.

Joel snatched up the telephone from the table beside the couch and punched buttons rapidly.

Tycho lifted Cherry in his enormous arms. His face was flushed, and I saw in his eyes what he wanted to do to whoever had hurt his friends.

"Tell me who did it," Lieza said to Ellyn.

Ellyn put her face against the Bastard Child's shoulder.

"Gator called him Pinocchio," she said, her voice muffled. "It was Wilson's man, Claghorn. He said he was taking Jackson back to where the Brits were keeping him."

Zackman . . . then Genghis Khan . . . now Claghorn.

The only men I've encountered who truly personify evil, and all three had followed us.

Correction: Two had followed Lieza, and one, intentionally or not, had followed me.

* * *

What a strange word I've used: *evil*.

After all, Zackman doesn't see himself that way, because he's acting out of patriotism, isn't he? And Claghorn is motivated by loyalty to Wilson, isn't he? And Genghis Khan feels that I and my country have wronged him, doesn't he?

If you believe your cause is just, can you be called *evil*?

Well, what is "evil," anyway, but another way of saying "stupid"?

In which case I'm more evil than any of them.

Maybe definitions and intentions are meaningless. Maybe end results are all that matter.

Where Zackman, Claghorn, and Genghis Khan are concerned, the end results are pain and death.

With more on the way.

* * *

Joel called for an ambulance, but Lieza didn't wait once I said that the taxi was still outside. We carried the injured Wrackers to the cab, and then Lieza and Fug drove off with them while the rest of us—including the taxi operator—set out for Charing Cross Hospital on foot.

"This is robbery," the taxi man said shrilly. "I won't stand for it. Yer all goin' to the stinkin'—"

Tycho took Bert from his belt.

"Not one more skagging word," he said.

The taxi man stopped walking, and we left him behind.

None of us spoke during the rest of the trek to the hospital. The dawn came as a slight change in the sky's shade of gray.

Joel didn't dance.

* * *

At seven-thirty this morning, Tycho, Joel, Bazz, Fug, and I were in a waiting room on the fourth floor when Lieza returned and told us what the doctors had said.

Ellyn had lost her baby. It would have been a boy.

Dude, Cherry, and Gator Al had regained consciousness, but they and Ellyn all had concussions and suffered from occasional muscle spasms. They had received electric shocks in addition to their other injuries.

"There's nothing more to be done for them now," Lieza said. "They just need time to recover. Lots of time."

"Lots of time" was the one thing none of us had.

The Bastard Child looked at Bazz and said, "Where did you find Jackson?" Her voice was low, and what radiated from her metal-gray eyes was so deadly that I was afraid to look at them.

"Fug and I'll take you there," Bazz said.

Lieza shook her head. "No. Blunt Instrument has a war to fight, but someone should stay here for the others. Someone who can make sure nothing else happens to them." She glanced at me, then back at Bazz. "You're elected."

Bazz opened her mouth as if to protest, then closed it and nodded.

I felt miserable, but Lieza's judgment on me was nothing less than I deserved.

Fug went to the Bastard Child and put a hand on her shoulder.

"Follow me," he said in a voice like rusted hinges opening. They were the first words I'd heard him speak.

Fug, Lieza, Tycho, and Joel left the waiting room.

I hesitated.

I was afraid, even more so than I'd been when Genghis Khan had grabbed my throat. I could hear the last seconds of my life ticking away with those of the world, and I didn't want to spend them wading through more death.

I had seen and felt enough. If I was to die, I at least wanted to go somewhere comfortable to do it.

But no matter where I went, I would hear the screams of the others and feel the same fire that they felt.

The only way to survive, I thought again, *will be if Dixon answers my prayers.*

And the only way he'll answer my prayers will be if I follow his prophet.

As if I'd ever really had a choice.

I stood and put my notebook, which I'd grabbed at the house, onto my chair.

Bazz was regarding me with a cold stare.

"Tell the nurses to save me a mattress," I said, and then ran after Blunt Instrument.

Look out, Reaper, here I come.

Tag.

You're It.

21

The London Blitz

Man kill man in the name of God,
Lay the heathen in the cold, hard sod.
Read your Bibles, pray your prayers,
Take the land for the chosen heirs.

Tell the children, "Don't have sex,
"Lest Pastor break your pretty necks;
"Instead fulfill our hearts' desire—
"Set the sacred Cross on fire.
"We shall make of it a sword,
"And wreak the vengeance of the Lord."

When I hear your talk of heaven,
And the things that I must do
If I have hope to get there,
Then I must say to you:

If that's your heaven . . .
If that's your heaven . . .
If that's your heaven . . .
If that's your heaven—

Then I'll race you to hell.

> —Bitch Alice,
>   "Race You to Hell," 1967

Thursday, January 10, 1980. Charing Cross Hospital.

The Journal of Clifton Bonner:

When I awaken, my cheek against the cold tabletop, I wonder for a moment whether it's all been nothing more than a nightmare.

Then I see what I've written and where I am. My watch says it's almost Friday. Bleary-eyed doctors and nurses are staggering in for coffee. They look dazed, shell-shocked.

I want to go back up to the fourth floor to see if Lieza is still there, but I know she is, and that I won't be welcome. She's sitting next to Cherry's bed, writing her last song, so interrupting her would be a sin worse than all those I've committed before.

And there's not much time left for penance.

The English are a sporting people. Perhaps I should ask one of the doctors if he'd like to make a wager on the number of hours.

But what will we bet?

* * *

This morning, again:

The taxi was gone when we left the hospital, so Fug took us to the nearest Underground station. When we left the train two stops later, the Wrackers began running. They moved so fast that I lost sight of them twice, and both times I thought I would end up wandering around London alone until the flash came.

I finally caught up with them as Fug entered a narrow yard beside a stone house.

"Try not to breathe so loudly," Joel whispered to me.

I did my best, but felt as though I were being stifled by a cold, wet pillow.

Fug led us to a broken-out window, and Lieza raised a hand for silence.

From far back in the house came the sound of two men talking. I could hear only brief snatches of what they were saying, but I remembered the voices from the confrontation at Lieza's farm.

They belonged to Claghorn and Zackman.

". . . must abandon my usual methods and use this crude British weapon to execute . . . only found two shells, but I shall not hesitate to use one of them upon . . ." Claghorn said.

". . . God's will, you little shit . . ." Zackman responded.

Fug growled.

"Can we get in without them knowing it?" Lieza whispered to him.

Fug growled again. It sounded affirmative.

". . . both want him dead, do we not?" Claghorn's voice said, louder than before.

"Not unless I can nail you for doing it, Shorty," Zackman answered.

The Bastard Child nodded to Tycho, who grasped the sill and pulled himself inside. Lieza followed, then reached out to help Fug and Joel.

When I stepped up, she looked at me skeptically.

Then she shrugged and took my wrists.

Once she'd pulled me into the bare room, she held on longer than she had to and squeezed.

Joel was standing beside me. "I'm rather fond of you too, Mister Bonner," he murmured, and winked.

". . . a standoff?" Zackman was saying. "How about a compromise—"

His voice shifted in mid-sentence, and he yelled, "Watch that son of a—"

A blast rattled the walls.

Fug charged into the mouth of a darkened hallway with Tycho and Lieza close behind. Lieza reached down as she ran and pulled a razor from her left calf pocket.

"Pip-pip, cheerio," Joel shouted as he sprinted after them. "Yea, verily, the time for kicking ass is nigh!"

As usual, I went last. But I went.

* * *

It was a windowless bedroom about fifteen feet square. On the floor to the right of the doorway lay a big man wearing pajama bottoms that were bloody from the knees down. He was gritting his teeth and groaning.

A nude, unconscious woman lay near the left wall. Claghorn stood over her, cocking a sawed-off pump shotgun.

Across the room from him was Zackman, who was holding a submachine gun.

Between them, on the bed against the far wall, lay the still form of Daniel P. Jackson.

Lieza, Tycho, Fug, Joel, and I stopped just inside the doorway—Tycho and Fug on the right; Lieza and Joel on the left; me slightly behind. I was standing over the man Claghorn had just shot in the legs.

It was the strangest moment. We simply *stopped* and stared at the Whig and the Dealer, who stared back at us.

For two seconds, the room was a tableau.

In my memory, what followed that is a tangle of limbs and a spray of red.

But my mind keeps going over and over it, trying against my will to piece together what happened:

Tycho threw Bert to the right. The ax hit Zackman's wrist, and the submachine gun went flying. Before it hit the floor, Fug had leaped and buried his teeth in the Dealer's neck, and Tycho was diving to retrieve Bert.

A click to the left. Claghorn had cocked his shotgun and was turning toward the bed. The arc that the gun muzzle was tracing in the air was going to end at Jackson's head.

Lieza started for Claghorn then, and he spun so that the shotgun muzzle was no longer moving toward Jackson, but toward her.

He would pull the trigger before she could touch him.

I jumped for Lieza, and it wasn't the insane thing doing it this time.

Dear God, I prayed, *I don't care what happens, just please, please don't let her die.*

I was going to grab her around the waist, shove her to the wall, and shield her with my body.

I swear I was.

But Joel was faster. He simply darted in front of her and took the blast.

Red droplets spattered Lieza's jacket as I hit her.

I had failed again.

We slammed into the wall and fell onto the naked woman, but Lieza was up again in an instant.

My head was ringing, and I couldn't feel my legs, but somehow I got to my feet.

Joel was on his knees. His white shirt had turned dark, and his top hat was crushed under his right leg.

Lieza was going for Claghorn again.

The Whig dropped the shotgun and produced what looked like a red toy pistol.

Then a roar ripped through the ringing in my head. It was Tycho, wild-eyed, raising Bert to cut Claghorn in two.

The ax swooped down, but Claghorn somersaulted out of its path. The blade knocked the plastic gun from his grasp, though, and drove it to the floor, shattering it.

The Whig disappeared into the hall.

Tycho yanked Bert from the floor and whirled to follow.

"Teek!" Lieza yelled. "Joel's down!"

The drummer's eyes changed, and he made a low moaning sound.

Across the room, Fug was beating Zackman's face on the floor, but he stopped when Lieza shouted. Then he grabbed the submachine gun and hurried over to us.

Joel was staring at Jackson.

"That . . . looks rather nice," he said as Lieza grasped his left arm. "I think I should like to lie down also."

He sagged to the right, and Lieza lowered him to the floor.

Zackman, like Claghorn before him, fled.

The man with the bloody legs had stopped groaning, and was looking at Joel as if glad he wasn't him.

"Find a phone," Lieza told Tycho. "Get an ambulance. Get a doctor. Get *anything*."

Tycho was gone in an instant, and then the Bastard Child was looking at me.

"You were in medical school," she said.

I knew what she wanted, and I also knew that I couldn't give it to her.

I went through the motions.

I didn't pray, though. The Wracker gods couldn't change what had already happened, and I had asked my last favor of the God of Mom and Dad.

He always requires a sacrifice, remember?

* * *

I unbuttoned and pulled apart what was left of Joel's shirt.

First-year med students don't see shotgun-blast wounds. Even if they did, the holes would be in the chests of anonymous cadavers. . . .

I couldn't identify what I saw as anything having to do with human anatomy. All I could see was Life, pumping out, filling and overflowing my hands.

Again.

I took a pillow from the bed and tried to use it as a compress. It was soaked in seconds.

And Joel was Bill, and Bill was Joel. My palms, stained with the blood of one, were washed in the blood of the other.

The only Bible passage I ever memorized reverberated in my skull:

Eloi, Eloi, lama sabachthani?

Then the smell took me back to the swimming pool once more, to the day the money thieves got me for snitching on them. My mouth had bled, and I had tasted the stuff, really tasted it, for the first time. It was like chewing on green copper that shredded my tongue and cheeks.

The smell of the air in that room, where Joel lay like a limp puppet, was like that taste. After a little while, a stink of excrement joined it.

A rustling sound came from the bed. Jackson was moving weakly, like a sick animal.

"Ally," he murmured. "Please . . ."

I glanced up at Lieza. She was watching Jackson, and in that moment her expression was that of a child who is about to cry.

* * *

"Mister Bonner," Joel whispered.

The sound was so faint that I had to put my ear against his lips to hear the rest.

"She will never say the word," he breathed, and my ear ached with warmth. "So I will."

Then, I felt more than heard:

"Love."

The warmth faded, and I lifted my head.

He winked, and I felt his heart stop. I tried to push Life back inside, but too much had spilled out.

There was a rush of air from the doorway. "The ambulance is on its—" Tycho began, but didn't finish.

When I stopped, long after there was any point, I looked first at Tycho . . . than at Fug . . . and finally at Lieza.

Their faces had become like stone.

And the hardest of all was that of the Bastard Child.

"Ally," Jackson murmured again. "Please . . . don't call me Pissant . . ."

* * *

At one o'clock this afternoon, a doctor came into the waiting room and said, "The short one is dead, I'm afraid."

None of us acknowledged him, because he was telling us what we already knew. Joel H. Rodstein IV, the Charlie McCarthy look-alike, the greatest keyboardist and reed man in the world, was gone and wouldn't be coming back.

I kept my eyes fixed on the TV screen on the wall, which was flickering with the mindless scenes of a comedy-variety show. The sound was turned down, but occasionally the laugh track became audible. It sounded like dogs barking in the distance.

"As for your other friends," the doctor continued, referring to the clipboard in his left hand, "Mizzes Angola and Flacke and Misters Reineman and Albert are doing as well as can be expected. They'll be stiff and headachey for a few weeks after they're up and about, which won't be for three days, I'd wager. Mister, ah, von Braun—" He raised an eyebrow; Lieza had registered Jackson under a false name. "—needs a bit of detox and nourishment, but should also pull through."

Lieza's face still looked as though it had been carved from solid rock. "What about the other two?" she asked.

The doctor frowned. "Other two?"

"Thin woman with reddish hair. Big Jack with his knees shot off."

"Oh, them," the doctor said, and coughed. "Well, I really shouldn't say..."

"Do it anyway," Tycho said.

The doctor coughed again. "Well, a couple of army fellows took them off in a military ambulance. The chaps seemed to think we had someone else of theirs too, but they wouldn't say who and apparently didn't see the name on our rosters." He hesitated. "They were in too great a rush to search for him, they said, and for some reason they told the bobbies to bugger off, too. Odd, isn't it?"

There was silence for several long seconds. The doctor seemed to think that someone should ask another question or perhaps thank him. No one did, so he finally coughed a third time and left.

Lieza stood. "I'm going to sit with Cherry," she said, starting for the doorway.

She passed between me and the TV, and when I could see the screen again, the comedy show had been replaced by the face of an announcer. The words SPECIAL BULLETIN appeared under her chin.

"Wait," I said, and Lieza stopped. When she saw what I was looking at, she went to the control box and turned up the sound.

"...wanton aggression against the Royal Crown Colony of Conception has forced the Alliance of Occidental and Oriental States to retaliate. At 12:22 P.M. Greenwich Mean Time today, January the tenth, nineteen hundred and eighty, the military command of the Churchill–Chiang Orbital Platform delivered a five-megaton warhead to the Siberian region of the so-called U.S. Central Trust Territory. The warhead was airburst over Fort Eisenhower. American casualties are not known but are expected to be low, in the five to eight thousand range, because of the cowardly flight of most personnel.

"This means that the number of U.S. casualties in this retaliatory strike is less than one tenth of the number of British and Chinese civilians murdered by American forces since the end of the Second World War, and it should come as no surprise that the commandant of Fort Eisenhower refused to evacuate the surrounding community of Siberian peasants. As a result of this callous treachery, an unknown number of civilians died today, victims of U.S. militarism.

"Her Majesty's government and the Alliance still desire a peaceful settlement. However, Prime Minister Carpenter has informed the President of the United States that war is inevitable if his government does not take appropriate measures before 12:01 A.M. Greenwich Mean Time January the twelfth. Because of the belligerence of the American military machine, it will no longer be enough for all U.S. troops to leave the invaded Crown Colony; instead, removal of all U.S. military personnel from all nations with ties to China or the United Kingdom will be required.

"All patriotic Britons are asked to support the Alliance and Her Majesty's government in this just cause with their good wishes and prayers.

"We now return you to 'Denny Dillard's Stuff and Nonsense.'"

Bazz took Bert from Tycho's belt and threw the ax at the TV, but the screen was plastiglass and wasn't even scratched. Denny Dillard, oblivious, put his head into a bucket of water.

"What the jagging hell does that mean?" Bazz yelled. "'Removal from all nations with 'ties' to the Alliance'—what are 'ties,' anyway?"

Lieza shut off the set. "It means the Station's going to nuke cities next, starting with Moscow. The good news is that unless the U.S. starts throwing stuff in the meantime, the Alliance'll probably wait until their deadline. British punctuality, you know."

She headed for the doorway again.

"What are you going to do about it?" I asked, and was surprised at the demanding tone of my voice.

Things had gotten to the point that I didn't even know whether it was me or the insane alien talking.

The Bastard Child paused.

"I'm going to tell Dude, Ellyn, and Cherry about Joel," she said.

Then she touched her left hip pocket, and I heard paper crackle. "After I've done that, I'll stay with Cherry and finish this song."

I felt frustrated and angry. Lieza seemed as cold as the streets outside.

"And that's it?" I said. "That's all the newly-elected God of the Wrackers can do?"

A faint, bitter smile broke out through the stone of Lieza's face, and I saw a hint of the self-hatred that I'd seen when she'd cut her thigh.

"That's all there is," she said, and turned toward Tycho, Fug, and Bazz. "Get to the house and grab our scrod, but don't stop if you see Straights hanging around. When you're done, go to Stig's and get some sleep. If he won't let you in, break down the door." She hesitated. "Bazz, I'd like you to come back here to stay with the others after you've slept a few hours. Tycho, Fug, and I have to start rehearsing as soon as we can get into the Hall."

Tycho snorted, and his nose rang. "Assuming that a sub doesn't waste London first."

Lieza nodded.

"What about Jackson?" I asked, but it was much too late to try Gator Al's idea, and I knew it.

Lieza's gaze shifted to the blank TV screen.

"I need a couple of seconds with Hack," she said.

Tycho retrieved Bert from the floor, and then he, Bazz, and Fug left the room. As Bazz passed me, she muttered, "Jagoff."

I waited until I realized that I didn't know what I was waiting for, and then asked, "What do you want me to do?"

The Bastard Child spoke to the TV. "I want you to stay away from me until the band and I are done rehearsing tomorrow. In case it's too late by then, I'll tell you now that I'm sorry."

"For what?"

Slowly, she turned toward me. But when she stopped, her eyes were focused on the floor.

"Better get to the house if you want your clothes moved to Sullivan's," she said. "Otherwise, Bazz might throw them into the street. Once you're at Stig's, go to a back room and keep clear of the others."

I took a deep breath and said, "I want to stay here with you."

She shook her head. "I've told you how it has to be, and I'm being as nice as I know how. For Joel, because he liked you."

I almost went to her then, but she wouldn't have felt my touch.

"No matter what he thought of you, though, you're a Straight," she continued, "and until I have Blunt Instrument ready for tomorrow night, I don't want you around."

She left the room then, her eyes still downcast. Her leathers made a soft, oily sound as she walked.

After a while, I stopped waiting for her to come back. I took my notebook and went down the hall to the elevators. When I got downstairs, though, I came into the cafeteria instead of leaving for Sullivan's.

I didn't care if Bazz threw my clothes into the street. The hell with her.

The hell with me, too.

* * *

Stigma Sullivan entered the cafeteria as I finished the previous sentence. He started toward the food counter, but then he saw me and came over to my table. He didn't sit down.

"You gonner eat that, Yank?" he asked, pointing at the cold fish dinner, but didn't wait for an answer before grabbing a fillet and stuffing its end into his mouth.

Without thinking, I said, "What are you doing here?"

Sullivan eyed me condescendingly as he chewed. "Not that it's any of yer business, but I was drumming up somethin' on the Row when the grapevine said someone in Blunt Instrument was killed. For all I knew, it was Leezer, Tycho, Cherry—all of 'em." He swallowed the mouthful. "Too bad about Joel."

I gripped my pen so hard that I thought it would break.

Sullivan took another bite of fish and looked thoughtful. "I don't suppose Cherry'll be able to play. I went up and found her mumbling about somebody called 'Pissant' bein' the Child's father—but then Leez came in and threw me out before I could figure out what Cherry meant. You know anythin' about it?"

I did, but didn't want to.

"No," I lied.

Sullivan picked at his front teeth with a fingernail. "It was a funny thing about the Bitch. She called *all* her lovers Pissant—she called *me* that in the Sixties—and she must've had six or seven 'Pissants' on the string in the year before the Bastard Child was born. I'm just curious to know which one Cherry was referrin' to."

He examined his fingernail. "I suppose it doesn't matter, though. Whoever it was is either already dead, or will be soon . . . along with the rest of us."

"Suppose so," I said weakly.

He tossed the rest of the fillet back onto the plate. "Thanks for the bite, Yank. I'd eat it all, but I've got to get back to the Row. Oh, by the way—as she threw me out, Leezer told me to put you in a room by yourself. I'll call Jesse, and he'll have it ready when you get there."

He gave me an odd smile. "I'll bet Leezer's calling a little wog like you 'Pissant' too, ain't she?" he said as he turned away.

I wanted to tell him that she's not doing any such thing, but then I realized that "Hack" is close enough.

* * *

After Sullivan left, I put my head on the table and fell asleep again. This time I dreamed, and knew it.

It was a soothing dream at first, set in a huge building with a doomed ceiling and brightly colored banners on the walls. The place was deserted except for me and a bouncy, sweet blonde girl in blue shorts and a frilly white blouse. She was exactly like the girls in high school my friends and I all claimed we had fondled but never had.

She danced across the floor toward me and laughed, teasing me.

Then her bare thighs started bleeding and wouldn't stop. I took off my shirt and tried to use it as a tourniquet, but she screamed that I was killing her.

The blood pooled up to my knees, my waist, my throat. The walls of the building shook, and frothy whirlpools spun around me.

The heads of Bill and Joel floated past, bobbing like corks in the red current.

The girl wouldn't stop screaming.

We both went under.

I woke up choking on saliva.

Friday, January 11.

Bong, bong, bong...twelve times. It's a new day. Exactly twenty-four hours to the arrival of the Gehenna Express.

Unless it shows up early, which wouldn't be surprising, considering how efficiently it's been slouching this way.

Time has quadrupled its pace. Soon Bazz will return and Lieza will leave, so I have no choice but to go now if I'm to get to Sullivan's before she does. She won't want to see me...but somehow I have the feeling that she'll want to know I'm there.

I dread the journey. Not because I'm afraid of encountering Sullivan again, or even Jesse, although they're bad enough...but because it's still raining.

Tiny drops, like a baby's tears.

When they hit my skin, my brain will say *fallout*. It'll feel as though they're burning through to the bone.

Maybe I can do penance after all.

But first I've got to go to the restroom and try once more to scrub the blood from my hands.

Out, out.

Gotta have them clean for applauding. After all, tonight will be my last chance to see Blunt Instrument in concert. No repeats, no rainchecks.

No refunds.

In case of annihilation, the show will not—repeat, will not—be rescheduled.

Hysterical Perspective V

The death toll in the Fort Eisenhower blast of January 10, 1980, was 9,707 Americans and 6,452 Siberians.

And you think: Hey, that's *nothing* compared to what happened to Berlin and Tokyo in 1945.

True; but in terms of sheer meanness and stupidity, it was as big as any slaughter in human history.

Did the Alliance (specifically the British) really think that such an attack would go unpunished?

Probably. The hell of it is, they might have been right, too, if events had been solely in the hands of the Fitzgerald administration.

Immediately after Churchill-Chiang delivered the warhead, President Fitzgerald disappeared from public view, and we now know that he took an extended trip to the Nut Farm. The result was that the Squid became *de facto* President, which was what she'd been anyway. (Vice President Edward Appleyard had been vacationing in the Virgin Islands since 1977. Nobody seemed to mind.)

Kirk, attempting a show of strength, sent ten subs steaming toward the U.K. but ordered them not to attack unless they received a "direct Presidential (sic) order."

The submarines moved slowly.

Within five hours of the blast, Winton Wilson was on TV, screaming for immediate vengeance.

Interestingly, though, the Squid had already attempted a token nuclear retaliation. A mere three hours after the attack, a U.S. sub sneaked up on New Zealand and launched a three-megaton missile...which promptly nose-dived into the ocean and sank without so much as a "bang."

We can't suppose, though, that Kirk gave a rat's ass about avenging the Siberia deaths—because after Wilson began demanding All-Out Holy Nuclear Revenge, she became determined to do *anything* but what the Big Whig wanted.

So, on Friday morning, the White House released a list of economic sanctions against the Alliance, and Congress began a heated debate. The Whigs claimed that the sanctions would be "calamitous to American business interests."

Really.

Needless to say, none of this decreased the likelihood that the planet would faw down and go boom—and although Kirk had postponed a military response (with the exception of the ill-fated New Zealand missile), she was also sticking to her refusal to remove the American force from Concepcion.

Thus, on January 11, few right-thinking persons (of which there were few to begin with) doubted that a global holocaust would commence within twenty-four hours.

No one expected, though, that the first counterattack would come from Blunt Instrument. . . .

> —Lorna P.N. Chicago-deSade,
> *A Brief, Biased History,*
> pp. 322–23.

22

Crucifixion

Friday, January 11, 1980. New Royal Albert Hall, South of Hyde Park.

> "Mama?" *Lieza tried to call, but there was no sound.*
> *There was nothing at all but a gray plain and black sky.*
> *Her mother was gone.*
> *The Bastard Child began walking, with no destination in sight.*
> *The gray plain stretched on forever.*

* * *

She awoke to chanting:

"Give us The MU-SIC . . . MU-SIC . . . MU-SIC . . . Give us The MU-SIC . . . MU-SIC . . ."

Lieza shifted on the metal chair and raised her head. Her neck felt as if nails had been driven between the vertebrae.

The first thing she saw was the mouth of the twenty-yard tunnel that led to the stage. The crowd wasn't visible from here, but it sounded as if there were a million of them.

She realized that it must be almost 8:00 P.M. and looked across the Green Room at Tycho and Fug, who were sitting next to the three doors that opened onto the loading dock. They were watching her expectantly.

She gave them as strong a smile as she could manage, but she doubted that it encouraged them.

Rehearsal hadn't gone well. Without Joel or Cherry, the band simply wasn't Blunt Instrument. Lieza had written her new song at Cherry's bedside, hoping that would make a difference, but—

The chanting became louder.

Sullivan had estimated that thirty thousand people would pack inside the auditorium—more than half on the main floor where the seats had been removed, and the rest in the three semicircular tiers that rose above it. The stage would jut into the midst of the crowd, so standing out there would be like being suspended inside a giant funnel of metal, leather, and flesh. The red and gold banners hanging from the ceiling would wave as if saying goodbye.

Lieza could smell scorched meat, which meant that the crowd had brought metal boxes inside and started fires. It would be a miracle if the place didn't burn down before a Yank missile had a chance to do the job.

Dude, Hack, and Sullivan emerged from the tunnel.

Dude was leaning on Bonner, who had brought him to the Hall that afternoon. The roadie said he was in better shape than the other injured Wrackers, but he couldn't even walk on his own. He should still be in the hospital with Ellyn, Lieza knew, but she was glad he was here instead.

As for Hack . . .

He was staying clear of her, which was what she wanted.

At least, she thought that was what she wanted.

Dude sat down on a stool at the sound-and-light board to the right of the tunnel's mouth, then gave Lieza a faint grin. "Fifteen minutes to showtime," he said. "If anything jackbugs, I insist on being absolved of all blame."

Lieza made a cross in the air with her left hand. "I hereby absolve thee, skaghead."

Sullivan, scratching his belly, approached her and said, "All right, Sleepin' Beauty, here's what you've got. I talked some coves at the BBC into a satellite feed, and we've hooked their scrod into the board. All of the little blue lights are on, so I assume the mess is working."

Lieza stood and stretched. "You did your bit, Stig."

Sullivan grimaced. "You always did know how to make me feel like a Jack."

"One of the many charms I inherited from dear old Mum."

Sullivan rolled his eyes. "You ain't kiddin'. But gettin' back to what I was sayin', I want you to know that Her Majesty's censors are gonner cut off your transmission if you say anything as subversive as 'bugger,' so—"

"You want me to keep the show nice and sweet," Lieza said, starting to feel contempt for him all over again.

The ex-Silverbee gave her a pained look. "Let me finish, will yer? I got hold of a friend on the Row while you and Fug were plinkin' on your miniamps, and he's gonna transmit you on shortwave. I gave the relay boxes to Dude, and he did whatever needed to be done. The Music'll sound like chain saws by the time it gets across the pond, but it'll get there. Word's been goin' out since noon, so some of your Yank radio stations'll be set to patch in on that if the BBC craps out."

Lieza was impressed. "Maybe you've still got it."

Sullivan rolled his eyes again. "Whatever the skag 'it' is," he said, heading toward the triple doors.

Before he reached them, the center door opened and Jesse entered carrying a long black case. A blast of frigid air came in with him.

Even from across the room, Lieza thought she could see tiny white skulls in the pupils of his eyes.

She shuddered. The place felt too much like death as it was.

The chanting from the auditorium became louder still.

"They in place?" Sullivan asked Jesse, almost shouting.

Jesse set the case on the floor. "I got good people."

Lieza took a few steps toward them. "Got good people for *what*?"

Sullivan gave her a sidelong glance. "This isn't Rosie-Pat Island, where all the natives are friendly. I put in an order for security."

"Not that it matters," Jesse's voice rumbled. "Nothing will fend off the holocaust."

"Sputzing Christ," Tycho said angrily, then stood and went to the sound-and-light board.

Fug snarled at Jesse and followed the Viking.

"Stig," Lieza said, "you know how I feel about—"

Sullivan waved a hand at her. "Yes, yes, I know. You hate 'security' because it's far too sensible. Well, love, I had Jesse get them because *I* want them. They'll watch the stage and the doors, but you won't even notice them."

Lieza smiled wryly. "What's the point of hiring protection if you're sure you're going to die anyway?"

Sullivan shrugged. "I'm resigned to burning to a crisp, but I want to stay healthy for whatever time's left."

Great attitude, Lieza thought, but didn't want to waste any more energy arguing with him.

It was almost time to play.

She returned to her chair. As she sat down, her eyes focused on the black case Jesse had brought in.

"What's that?" she asked, pointing.

Sullivan pushed his fingers behind his glasses to rub his eyes.

"Nothing important," he said. "Just something I thought we might need, maybe . . ."

The Bastard Child didn't press for a better answer. She thought she already knew what it was, and it saddened her to see how ashamed Sullivan was to admit it.

She shifted her gaze to a point above the triple doors and tried to concentrate on The Music. If she could enter a trance tonight, everything might still go well.

But time was closing on her like a vise, and she knew she wouldn't be ready soon enough.

The chanting blasted from the tunnel like a hot wind.

* * *

At 8:15, Lieza walked to the mouth of the tunnel, taped a mike to her throat, and slung her black left-handed guitar over her shoulder. Fug stood to her right, tuning his red Stratocaster, and Tycho was on her left, smacking Bert's blade with a drumstick.

Hack, Stig, and Dude were at the sound-and-light board. In her peripheral vision, Lieza saw that four of the 7-inch video monitors at the top of the console were displaying various views of the stomping, swaying crowd. The fifth displayed the backstage view from the auxiliary sound board at the other end of the tunnel.

All of the pictures were wavering, and the walls of the Green Room vibrated.

Even more strongly than that vibration, though, Lieza felt the cold presence of Jesse, who was standing beside the triple doors like a guardian of the Underworld.

Tycho leaned down. The tip of his silver nose brushed Lieza's cheek and made her shiver.

"Let's do it," he said.

It was past time.

The Bastard Child took one step into the tunnel, then turned and reentered the Green Room, unstrapping her guitar.

It wasn't right. It wasn't *right*.

She wanted to run outside, find the Moon in the sky, and scream at Bitch Alice for leaving her in this impossible place.

But the Moon wouldn't rise until after midnight.

Lieza swung her instrument like an ax and sent a chair flying into the door beside Jesse.

Feedback screeched from the tunnel, and Dude, wincing, flipped several switches on the console to cut off power to the stage amplifiers. Sullivan pretended to watch him.

But Hack, Lieza saw, was staring at her.

For an instant, she felt the same awful desire that she'd felt when she'd first met him eleven days before.

Then she recognized the look in his eyes.

He thought she was afraid. He was ashamed of her.

"I can't go out there like this," she shouted. "Not with only three of us, not for those jewbaiters. They aren't worth it. The whole scrodding *world* isn't worth it!"

The crowd noise had taken on a demanding tone. The young Brits out there lived for entertainment, and Blunt Instrument wasn't doing its handstands on schedule.

Let them burn, Lieza thought. *I'm not a clown who lives to make little boys and girls happy.*

I'm a Wracker.

But would a Wracker refuse to play The Music?

She felt that every contradiction that had made her the Bastard Child was manifesting itself, pulling her first in one direction and then in another:

Her mother was Bitch Alice . . .

. . . and her father was the lowest of Straights.

She felt pride in her band, in The Music . . .

. . . and she loathed her own body.

She had loved first a Wracker and now a Straight . . .

. . . and she hated them both.

She had worshipped Dixon as a god . . .

. . . and now he had come to her as a chuckling old man who said the world's fate was *her* responsibility . . .

The thought of Dixon conjured up an image of Patton.

They were yin and yang. Without the conflict between them, there would be no wrack & roll.

She had always known that, but it was only now that she realized what it forced upon her.

Dilemmas can't be resolved. They can only be lived through. . . .

"They can only be *survived*," she said aloud.

"What's that?" Dude asked, frowning.

Lieza began to retune her guitar.

"Anything that matters," she said, looking across the room at Jesse. "That goes for you too, Sunshine."

Jesse stood like a slab of marble.

"We going out or not?" Tycho bellowed.

"In a minute," Lieza answered. "We won't be Blunt Instrument, but damn the torpedos, *ad astra per aspera*, etcetera." She wished she felt as cocky as she sounded.

Sullivan walked past her toward the triple doors. "Well, Leezer," he said, squatting to unlatch the case Jesse had brought in, "if you aren't gonner be Blunt Instrument anyway, there's no sense in there being only three of you."

When he stood again, he had a silver electric bass slung over his right shoulder and a coil of black wire in his hand.

"It ain't a radio job," he said self-consciously. "But I imagine there's a jack I can plug into, eh?"

Dude toggled a switch on the console. "There is now."

Sullivan looked at the Bastard Child. "You mind?"

"Not as long as you can keep up," Lieza said. "We're starting off with two of Mother's—'Tomorrow Is the Day' and 'Race You to Hell.'"

The ex-Silverbee seemed to gain two inches in height. "I was playing those while you were in diapers."

It wasn't true, but that didn't matter.

Lieza turned toward the tunnel again. "The third song is new, but if you follow Fug's lead you'll pick it up."

That wasn't necessarily true either, but, again, it didn't matter.

"Let's roll over that Red Army," she said as she and Sullivan joined Tycho and Fug.

"Break a leg," Dude called, putting on a headset.

Fug grunted.

I don't know what the skag I'm doing, Lieza thought. *Any ideas, Eddie?*

There was no answer.

Didn't think so.

The Bastard Child entered the tunnel and ran toward the roar, toward the future she would create.

* * *

The tunnel opened onto the stage behind the auxiliary sound board and the drum platform. The board's status lights and the diffuse glow from the metal-box fires in the crowd provided the only illumination.

There was no way for the audience to see the musicians as they came out, but Lieza could tell from the mass-scream that the Brits knew she was there.

Sullivan jacked his cable into the auxiliary board, then leaned close to Lieza and shouted, "Now what?"

"We wait until we can see."

After what felt like several minutes, a bank of lights over the drums began glowing softly. Tycho tucked Bert into his belt and mounted the platform.

The roar became incredible.

Something brushed Lieza's right arm then, and when she turned she saw Cherry beside her. Farther back, just inside the tunnel, stood Gator Al and Pissant Jackson.

The Bastard Child's joy at seeing Cherry was almost

overwhelmed by the sinking feeling she got from seeing the man she was now sure was her father. He stared at his feet as if afraid to meet her eyes.

Gator Al gave her a thumbs-up sign, and then he and Pissant limped back toward the Green Room.

Lieza's sinking feeling stayed.

"Are you well enough to play?" she said into Cherry's ear.

"I'm standing, aren't I?" Cherry's voice was ragged but strong. "We all decided we'd rather die here than at Charing Cross, 'cause it smells better. Bazz stole a wheelchair for Ellyn." Her long fingers struggled to tune her red bass. "My only problem is getting this jagging thing to sound like it should."

Sullivan unslung his own instrument. "Try this one, love. She can shake down the walls if you pluck 'er right."

Cherry took it, and the ex-Silverbee left the stage without looking back.

Lieza wanted to thank him, but there wasn't time.

Tycho began pounding a tom-tom, and the stage lights blazed on full force.

"Joel liked it loud," Cherry shouted. "Let's do it so he can hear."

The fingers of Lieza's right hand closed over her guitar's neck.

Now it starts, she thought.

Or ends.

Fug leaped over the auxiliary board and ran to the front of the stage, his Stratocaster screaming the opening notes of "Tomorrow Is the Day."

Cherry hunched over the silver bass and walked out unsteadily, but the throb from her amplifier was driving and solid.

Lieza waited, trying to let The Music take her, but there were too many things in the way.

Joel's death . . . Cherry's obvious pain . . . Pissant Jackson . . . Hack . . . the Squid . . . the coming firestorm . . .

At least she'd burn while singing.

She flicked on her mike, then strode into the glare and let thirty thousand voices wash over her like a tidal wave.

"I AM THE BASTARD CHILD," she cried, "AND WE ARE BLUNT INSTRUMENT!"

A large section of the crowd chanted, "SO WHAT?"

"To-mor-row," Lieza sang, "is-the-day!"

But she was afraid that the estimate was far too optimistic.

* * *

Thousands of the Brits danced and slammed throughout "Tomorrow Is the Day," and still more joined in when the Bastard Child, sweating and shouting, led Blunt Instrument directly into "Race You to Hell."

Lieza looked out at their faces, singing, "Man kill man in the name of God,/Lay the heathen in the cold, hard sod./Read your Bibles, pray your prayers,/Take the land for the chosen heirs—"

And they looked *happy.*

All they wanted was something they could dance to. They didn't care whether The Music said anything or not.

It's my fault, she thought. *I've pretended that my songs meant something the way yours did, Mama, but I've always cared more about the muscle-jump and crowd-worship. I only played dress-me-up, because I was afraid of the pure stuff, of real wrack & roll. . . .*

On the final chorus, she stopped playing her guitar and thrust her fists into the air, trying desperately to get the mob to listen:

> *If that's your heaven—*
> *If that's your heaven—*
> *Yeah, if this is your heaven—*
> *Then I'll race you to hell.*

Fug and Cherry ended the song with a series of chords like bomb blasts.

The crowd cheered.

The Bastard Child stared at the seething ocean of flesh and let her arms go limp. She felt empty.

They couldn't listen, and there wasn't time for them to learn how. She could do nothing here, and the ghost of Dixon had been wrong to tell her otherwise.

The house lights brightened, and Lieza saw grease and raw red holes.

"Shut your ugly mouths," she said. Her voice echoed from the distant ceiling.

The roar dissolved into a confused murmur. Some of the faces out there looked displeased now, but most were blank, uncomprehending.

Lieza's gaze stopped at the grim features of twenty or thirty Straights who formed a line around the stage, and she realized that these must be the "security" people.

The one directly in front of her was a crew-cut man wearing mirrored glasses and a long, belted coat.

It was Zackman, and he was applauding.

The Bastard Child's emptiness became filled with fury as she saw that the Secret Service agent thought he had her right where he wanted her.

We'll see, dink-dink. We'll see.

She looked out over the mass of young Brits again.

"You know why I'm sick of you?" she asked.

Jumbled shouts and hoots came in answer.

Lieza jabbed a finger at them. "Because you're animated corpses, that's why. You're bouncing around, rubbing your pimply bodies together—but you're dead, because you let the Straights dictate the rules. You're zombies, going through the motions of being alive, but you don't know what it means to *live*."

A rim shot cracked behind her, and she looked back at Tycho.

"You tell the little scrod-suckers, Leez!" the Viking bellowed, brandishing Bert.

Behind and below him, standing beside the auxiliary board, was Hack Bonner.

His expression was unreadable.

Which was he, Lieza wondered—Straight or Wracker? Zombie or human?

She licked her lips and turned back toward the crowd.

"We just played two of the angriest songs ever written," she shouted, "and you didn't know what they meant. You weren't here to be touched by the flames of the last war, and you're so jagging lazy that you don't care about the flames that are coming *now*."

"Who the skag d'you think you are?" a voice cried.

Lieza struck a jarring chord, and the feedback shrieked like a banshee.

"I've already told you," she said. "I'm the Bastard Child. So are you, but you're too stupid to know it."

The murmur became louder and angrier.

Lieza looked at Zackman again.

He was laughing at her.

She wanted to leap off the stage and cave in his skull with her guitar. She wanted to make him pay for what he and his kind had done, for what they were still doing—

Something coppery glinted behind him.

Lieza looked past Zackman then, and saw the broad, smiling face of Eddie Dixon.

"You're out of your mind," she said.

The crowd hissed.

Go on, Dixon's mouth said silently.

"They aren't worth it."

Go on anyway.

Lieza took a deep, shuddering breath, and struck the chord again. "The Straights killed Joel Rodstein yesterday," she said, "but because of who he chose to be, he's still more alive than any of you. We've got a new song we're going to do for *him*."

The Bastard Child glanced at Zackman and saw that he was no longer laughing.

"It's called *Take Back the Garden*," she cried, and then began strumming and singing:

> *Our parents ate of knowledge*
> *And angered Him who was Lord,*
> *So He sent down an angel*
> *Who carried a burning sword.*
> *The angel said, "Go from this place*
> *"And never come again."*
> *Our parents left there crying,*
> *Ashamed that they had sinned.*

And when they looked back sadly,
Afraid of the life in store,
They saw the sword at Eden's gate,
Shutting them out forevermore.

Miraculously, as she finished the verse, Lieza felt herself entering a trance.

But it wasn't a trance like any she had ever felt before. Rage, love, defiance, and joy blended inside her to form a new emotion, a new strength, and shot from her fingertips as a swirl of golden sparks.

Her bandmates began playing with more energy than ever before.

It was as if Joel had heard her song and had returned to become part of Blunt Instrument one last time.

She hoped Hack felt it. Joel would have wanted him to.

The Music filled her.

She looked down through a shower of gold and saw that Dixon was gone.

That was all right. She didn't need him anymore.

But Zackman was still there. He reached inside his coat and pulled out a chrome handgun.

Wonder if he misses his machine pistol? she thought, and sang the next verse:

Then came from hell a demon
Who stole away the sword.
He put a fence around Eden,
And walls of concrete poured.
He rode a dragon to the sun
And cooked his mind insane.
When he came back he swung the sword
And gave us all the mark of Cain.

Zackman raised his weapon.

Lieza turned and waved to Tycho to quicken the tempo.

Hack was no longer by the auxiliary board, but she could feel that he was still close by.

Listen, Clifton Bonner. Listen to me now.
Whirling back to face the crowd, she flung her arms
wide and cried:

> *Now the demon, drunk and crazy,*
> *Wants us to fight his war.*
> *He tells us to lie in his bed of pain*
> *And love the fusion bomb, his whore.*

Zackman tore off his glasses, and his eyes were like
glowing coals.
Blue flame spat from the chrome muzzle.
The Bastard Child felt nothing, but knew that she had
stumbled backward.
There was a red hole in her left wrist.
Her congregation's scream spiked around her like
lightning.
Zackman took aim again, and The Music stumbled.
Your choice, Child, a deep, warm voice said.
And Lieza knew that it was.
She flung golden sparks at her bandmates and sang:

> *Is it right that we should burn*
> *For finding evil, trying to learn?*
> *Is it right that we should pay*
> *For knowledge that's been warped this way?*

The blue flame spat again, and the Bastard Child's
right palm burst.
She didn't care, because The Music was soaring
again.
A woman in the audience clamped an arm around
Zackman's throat, but the agent whipped the gun back and
hit her in the face.
Lieza felt dizzy with her strength, and let herself sink
to her knees as she neared the end of the song:

> *We must storm the walls—*
> *Rush the fence—*

> *The demon thrives*
> *At our expense.*

Zackman flung off his attacker.

But Lieza saw how weak he'd become, and she exhorted her flock, singing:

> *Take it back—*
> *Take it back—*
> *Take it back—*
> *Take it back—*
> *Take back the Garden!*

The blue flame spat a third time, and the body of the black guitar shattered, driving splinters into the Bastard Child's arms and side.

A concussion shook the Hall, and a red and gold banner fell from the ceiling like an angel from heaven.

Before the reverberation had died away, Zackman was buried under a hundred Wrackers. Some of the security people tried to rescue him, and they too disappeared.

Lieza saw thousands of faces wet with tears.

Why now? she wondered. *Why now, but not before?*

Then a coppery light floated before her, washing out all else.

Righteous wrack an' roll, the deep voice said.

She felt a joy so intense that it became pain, and knew what to do.

"Go to Downing Street and Pennsylvania Avenue," she shouted. "Go to your leaders, your generals. Tell them it's enough. Tell them no more. If they won't listen—"

A whirlpool began to pull her down, and she cried:

"TRASH THEM!"

Then came the watery roar of a billion voices, and above her she saw Tycho, Cherry, Fug . . .

Hack.

"Pretty good, huh, Straight boy?" she said.

"Better than that," Bonner answered, his words like bubbles.

He wavered and became her father.

"Better than anything," he murmured.

Lieza closed her eyes. The show was over, and she could rest.

For now, Child, the deep voice told her.

Only for now.

23

Resurrection

Friday, January 11, 1980. New Royal Albert Hall.

The wind made Pissant feel as if his blood were freezing, and he tried to hug himself tighter inside his suit coat. It didn't help. He stared at the huge domed building before him and thought that it was the largest tomb he had ever seen.

His soles throbbed with yesterday's wounds, but his bandaged palm was numb.

He hadn't wanted to come here. He had been relatively safe and warm in his hospital bed, and the drugs had worn off enough for him to be thinking about how to get a drink—but then Cherry Angola, Bud, and Bazz had come into his room, pushing a wheelchair carrying the woman named Ellyn.

"It's seven-thirty," Bud had said. "Let's go."

"Why should I want to do that?" Pissant had asked.

Bazz had found his clothes and had thrown them to him. Automatically, he had gotten dressed.

"Because Pinocchio probably knows you're here," Bud had said. "Also because Blunt Instrument's doing what may be their final show in a half hour, and if you're Lieza's father, this may be your last chance to act like it."

Bud is an idiot, Pissant thought as he stood outside the Hall. *He ought to know she's better off without me.*

The physicist hadn't tried to use that argument at the hospital, though. The Wrackers had wanted him to go with them, and as usual, he had let himself be manipulated by those who were stronger.

"I'll get the d.t.'s if I don't have something to drink," he'd told Bud as they'd entered a taxi.

So, when they'd arrived at the Hall's rear parking lot, Bud had run off to get some booze. Bazz and Cherry hadn't waited, but had wheeled Ellyn up a ramp into the building.

Now Pissant stood alone, shivering, watching a few milling British Wrackers jeer at the two Straights guarding the three doors at the top of the ramp.

A Wracker with spiked hair approached Pissant and said, "Hey, you a relative of somebody, maybe get me backstage?"

The question struck the physicist as cruelly funny. He cackled and coughed, then said, "Why go inside when the real entertainment's going to be out here?"

Spike-Hair looked confused. "How's that?"

Pissant pointed a quivering finger at the sky. "A big light show's coming, courtesy of the United States Navy."

Spike-Hair's confused look was replaced by a sneer. "If you weren't gonner help, y'old fart, y'coulda told me," he said, and walked off across the parking lot.

That's what I should've told them all, Pissant thought. *Sorry, folks, this old fart's not gonner help.*

A small, shining disk appeared before him, and he saw his own distorted reflection. It was hideous.

After a few seconds, he realized that the disk was the rivet in Bud's ear. The Wracker handed him a plastic flask, then grabbed his arm and pulled him up the ramp.

One of the guards opened the center door. A large, pale man with black hair looked out and nodded, and the guard waved Bud and Pissant inside.

Once the door closed behind him, Pissant found himself surrounded by a steady roaring noise. It was like standing under a waterfall.

"My name is Jesse," the dark-haired man said. "Welcome to the last night of the world."

Bud released the physicist's arm and hurried across the room to Bazz and Ellyn.

Pissant looked up at Jesse's cavernous eyes and said, "Thank you. It's a pleasure to be here."

* * *

The man named Dude sat at a console covered with switches and video monitors. Standing beside him was a young man who looked hauntingly familiar.

He looked like the Daniel Jackson of thirty years ago.

Pissant put his flask into a coat pocket and shuffled toward the console. The roaring became louder as he went.

Dude's concentration didn't shift from the lights and monitors, but the proto-Jackson stared at the approaching physicist with what could only be recognition.

Jesus H. Christ, it is *me*, Pissant thought. *My younger self has come to take over the life I've sputzed up.*

He reached out to touch the face of his youth, but it flinched away in revulsion.

"Sorry," Pissant croaked, hoping that he could be heard over the roaring. "I couldn't tell whether you were real."

"My name is Bonner," the young man said loudly.

"We call him Hack," Cherry Angola's voice called.

Pissant looked over Bonner's shoulder and saw Cherry standing in a dark doorway. She was trying to untwist the shoulder strap of a red electric bass, and after a moment Bud came over and helped. They both looked as if they were about to be overcome with dizziness.

The waterfall noise rushed from the doorway and pounded at Pissant's head.

"Better hurry," Dude shouted. "The natives aren't going to wait."

Cherry went through the doorway.

Bud came to Pissant and put an arm around his shoulders. "Come on, old Icarus," he said. "Let's see how high your own Child is flying."

Without wanting to, Pissant stumbled through the doorway and found himself inside an unlit tunnel.

Something was glowing at the far end, but as it grew brighter it became even more frightening than the darkness.

* * *

They stopped where the tunnel opened onto the stage, and Pissant's senses were bombarded to the point of overload.

Blue, green, and red lights winked at him . . .

The waterfall noise became the bellow of an enormous beast . . .

Orange flames flickered in the midst of a dark, undulating sea . . .

A smell of seared flesh cut into his nostrils . . .

The vibrating floor tried to pull him down and shatter his bones . . .

And the Bastard Child glared at him with eyes of bright, merciless steel.

It had been less than a week since he'd seen her in Kansas City, but he had forgotten how tall she was, how much raw anger radiated from her.

The muscles under her black leather jeans were taut.

Cherry and a male stranger were standing close to the Bastard Child, but Lieza didn't seem to be aware of anyone but Pissant. He felt the message her eyes shot at him:

Die old killer of women jewbaiter die go from here die old swimmer in filth die old liar die old failure die old user die die die.

It burned along his optic nerve like acid.

He looked down to end the pain and saw that he was still wearing the blue paper slippers from the hospital. The left one had torn open at the toes, so he tried to count the loose fibers.

Finally, Bud took his arm and steered him back the way they had come.

The tunnel seemed to have stretched to infinity.

Somewhere on the journey, the roar became The Music, and Pissant heard the piercing clarity of his daughter's voice. She was singing of holy fire.

He wished he could bathe in it and purify himself.

* * *

When at last they came out beside the console, the physicist put his mouth close to Bud's riveted ear and said, "Why did you do that to me? I thought you were my brother."

Bud's forehead creased. "I *am*," he said. Pissant could barely hear him over The Music pulsing from the tunnel. "I thought you'd want to see her. I thought you *should* see her. Sorry to mess up your tender head, Doc."

The Wracker turned away and joined Dude, Bazz, Ellyn, and "Hack," who were watching the console's video monitors.

Pissant caught a glimpse of Lieza singing Bitch Alice's song, and he looked away quickly, back toward the tunnel.

His eyes met those of the stranger he had seen on the stage.

"Incredible, ain't she?" the man said in a Liverpool accent, rubbing his eyes behind wire-rimmed glasses. "I soddin' wish there were some point to it."

Pissant adjusted his own glasses and mumbled something, then limped across the room toward the triple doors.

Jesse stood there, his arms folded.

"It will be the same wherever you go," he said.

Pissant didn't respond. In another second he was outside, the frigid wind slashing into his lungs like a razor.

Even here, though, he could hear the crash of the guitars and the cry of the Bastard Child.

He stumbled down the ramp into the parking lot, intending to run until he couldn't hear her anymore.

Then the flask in his coat pocket bumped against his hip, reminding him that there was an easier way to escape.

* * *

Pissant sat on the asphalt, his back against a concrete planter filled with dead twigs. The wind seemed to be losing strength with each mouthful of cherried ethanol he swallowed.

The cough-syrupy flavor made him think of Estella.

He hoped she wasn't dead. Even if she was alive, though, he wouldn't see her again.

Too bad she didn't take to life in space, he thought. *If she'd stayed up there, she'd've had a chance to survive.*

A jangling chord came to him from the hulking building across the parking lot. He shuddered and pulled his coat collar over his ears.

In Dallas, he had watched Ally die two hundred and forty thousand miles away. Tonight, people he cared for would die much closer to where he sat.

How the goddamn hell had he let himself care for anybody again?

He held his breath and drained the flask, hoping it would put him out. Instead, it only made him feel sick.

The distant sound of The Music increased in volume, and he recognized the beat of "Race You to Hell."

It was the song Bitch Alice had been about to sing when the valve had exploded.

"I wonder who'll finally win that race?" he mumbled, tossing the flask away.

"As always, Professor Jackson, the strongest shall win," a monotonal voice said above him. "A man of science should know that."

The ethanol in Pissant's veins seemed to turn to ice.

He couldn't bring himself to look up, but he didn't have to. There was no mistaking that voice, or the faint smell of polished wood that accompanied it.

Pinocchio Claghorn climbed down from the planter and stepped in front of the physicist, then stood there looking at him with eyes like glass beads.

Pissant's first thought was to get up, to run—but he wasn't surprised to discover that once again his body wouldn't do as he wished. It was as if the booze had reactivated the other drugs, paralyzing him.

"My work was interrupted yesterday," Pinocchio said, "but things will soon happen that will make that failure irrelevant. Nevertheless, I am a man of honor and always fulfill my obligations. You will stand, please."

"Why?" Pissant asked. "Can't you kill me while I'm sitting down?"

The suggestion of a smile flickered across Pinocchio's lips. "We can be seen here, and I would not appreciate any interference. Now, please do not dawdle. To insure that Mister Wilson's vision for the future comes to pass, I must also perform a task within the concert hall. Thus I cannot spend as much time with you as I would like."

The gnome leaned down, grasped the collar of the physicist's coat, and pulled him upright. Pissant kicked out weakly with his left foot but only brushed Pinocchio's slacks.

The torn paper slipper fell, and Claghorn stepped forward, crushing it. Then he bent down and drove his right shoulder into Pissant's abdomen, lifting him in a dead man's carry as he had the day before.

"If you would be so kind as to relax," Pinocchio said, "I can promise you little discomfort. Alas, I do not possess a second dose of the narcotic you enjoyed yesterday, so you will have to use your imagination."

Several Wrackers lounging against automobiles stared at Pissant as he was carried across the parking lot.

"Help me," he called weakly, but the only response he received was laughter.

They think I'm just a drunk who's made a nuisance of himself, he thought.

It was, after all, the truth.

* * *

Pinocchio stopped at the edge of the lot behind a brown van, raised the vehicle's hatchlike rear door, and threw the physicist inside.

Pissant landed on his left shoulder, and his cheek pressed against the cold, corrugated metal.

He could see the lights of Kensington Road just a few yards past a low brick wall. But there were no people in sight, and what little traffic there was shot by rapidly. There was no one to help him.

The noise from the Hall was only a distant hum now. He couldn't even tell what song was being played.

Pinocchio reached into a coat pocket and withdrew a small black pistol.

"I despise these nasty little British things," the gnome said. "However, Alliance agents must be blamed for your fate. It is due to them that you are here in the first place, is it not?"

Pissant forced some strength into his arms and tried to grab the gun away, but he knew even before he did it that the attempt would be futile. His hand closed on empty air.

Pinocchio's faint smile returned. "Will that be all? Are you content now that you have made the 'heroic' effort our culture seems to require?" He reached into his coat pocket again and withdrew a short black tube.

Even with his sideways view of the world, Pissant knew that the tube was a silencer.

"Don't bother, Pin-head," he croaked. His throat felt as though it must be bleeding. "Nobody's going to hear such a little bang when such a big one's coming."

Pinocchio began to attach the tube to the muzzle of the pistol. "Perhaps not, but I loathe noise and all other forms of inelegance. I felt quite ashamed yesterday, being forced to use a weapon as crude as a shotgun—almost as ashamed as I felt when I had to resort to planting a bomb on a spacecraft to eliminate one of Mister Wilson's enemies."

Pissant's abdomen knotted.

The gnome's smile broadened. "That is my farewell gift to you, Professor. The deaths of those brave astronauts and of the despicable Bitch Alice were no fault of yours. I sincerely hope you feel better about the matter."

But Pissant didn't feel anything but fury at Winton R. Wilson and his puppet.

God, Ally, if I'd only taken the time to think, I would've realized even then what Wilson was, and what he was willing to do . . .

"I suggest that you close your eyes," Pinocchio said.

Then Pissant's thoughts dissolved, leaving him with only the knowledge that the van was his casket. The last thing he would feel would be cold metal on his cheek.

He closed his eyes.

And heard the reproachful voice he had heard at the Rally for America:

Nothing like taking the easy way out, is there? Especially when what the Bastard Child has to go through will be so much worse . . .

The words stung, making him feel that he had to try to fight the gnome one last time. Maybe a kick with *both* feet, aimed at the crotch . . .

He opened his eyes and saw that Pinocchio was having difficulty attaching the silencer.

He also saw a black man in a plaid shirt sitting on the brick wall.

Pissant had seen him before; but this time, he knew who he was.

"Now, that ain't nice," a low, resonant voice said, and a copper tooth gleamed.

Pinocchio's eyes widened, and he whirled, bringing up the pistol.

The silencer swept past a streetlight that looked like a bluish sun—

—and then there was a glare as bright as a nova.

A thunderclap struck Pissant like a fist. His muscles contracted, and his body jerked up to a sitting position.

Pinocchio turned back toward him . . .

. . . and then, with the slowness of a tree, fell over backward.

The gnome's right hand was a mass of pulp, and a metal shard protruded from his forehead. A dark trickle ran down the right cheek.

It isn't wood after all, Pissant thought, amazed.

He raised his eyes to meet Eddie Dixon's.

"What did you do?" he asked, his voice a hoarse whisper.

Dixon jumped down from the wall. "Exactly nothin'," he said, his breath rolling out in crystalline clouds. "I don't know much 'bout these things, but I 'spec he didn't have that extender on right. He got so anxious to do you harm that he forgot the harm he could do to himself."

Pissant felt as though he must be dreaming—or as though Pinocchio had shot him, and this was his last hallucination before death.

"Where did you come from?" he asked.

Dixon grinned, and the tooth gleamed again. "Same place we all came from," he said, sweeping his left arm through the air in a gesture that seemed to encompass the world. "From my mother's womb."

Pissant tried to smile. "I always had a feeling I must've been hatched."

Dixon chuckled, and Pissant felt the sound in his chest. "Ain't got no scales or feathers, do you?"

Pissant looked down at his hands. There was a bandage, but that was all. "I guess not."

"Tell you one thing, though," the resonant voice continued. "You shouldn't drink so damn much. That shit could kill you."

Pissant raised his eyes again, but Dixon was gone. For a moment, a wisp of breath marked where he had been, and then that was gone too.

* * *

Bud appeared in its place, and Pissant saw himself in the rivet.

He was smiling.

"Sputzin' Patton, Doc, what'd you do to Pinocchio?" Bud asked.

The physicist looked past his brother and saw five British Wrackers standing over Claghorn.

"I came out to find you," Bud said. "Then I heard somethin' go *blam*, and—"

Something tickled Pissant's eardrum, and he raised a finger to his lips. Bud fell silent.

Faintly at first, then growing in volume and strength, The Music came to Daniel P. Jackson:

> *We must storm the walls—*
> *Rush the fence—*
> *The demon thrives*
> *At our expense.*

And as he heard his daughter's song, Pissant felt strength returning to his arms and legs. He pushed himself out of the van and stood looking down at Pinocchio Claghorn.

A finger on the gnome's left hand moved.

Old horrors never die, Pissant thought.

But sometimes they have to be forgotten.

He turned to Bud. "We've got to get inside. These boys can take care of him, can't they?"

Bud glanced at the other Wrackers. "I'm sure he's in good hands."

Pissant forced his body into a hobbling run. His remaining slipper shredded after only a few steps, and the wounds on his feet reopened, but he knew he would make it. Bud was beside him, holding his arm, helping him.

The Hall seemed a hundred miles away, like a mountain ridge glimpsed from a plain.

Pissant tried to run faster as The Music grew louder and louder:

> *Take it back—*
> *Take it back—*
> *Take it back—*
> *Take it back—*

And then, with a power that seemed to split the sky:

> *Take back the Garden!*

The coyotes howled.

I could've told you, Papa. You can't kill them. They just keep coming back, again and again.

He ran until he rose from the asphalt, and then he flew with new wings.

24

Ascension

The Journal of Clifton Bonner:

The fires outside have banished the night. Whatever is coming in its place will take all my energy, all my life.

This, then, is my last entry for a long time.

A long, long time.

* * *

As the concert began, I intended to go about halfway to the stage and sit on the floor so I could be alone for whatever happened. But then Blunt Instrument began playing "Tomorrow Is the Day," and The Music pulled me to the end of the tunnel.

I found myself standing by the auxiliary sound board. On the platform to my left, Tycho pounded and flailed, and on the stage in front of him, Fug played furiously beside a towering amplifier. Far to his right, Cherry stood bent over Sullivan's bass, her fingers as dark as ebony against the silver finish.

Between them, trapped in white light, stood the Bastard Child, singing her mother's song.

All around, swarming, were the wasps, with red and yellow lights glowing among them like imprisoned fireflies. The mingled smells of smoke and sweat stung my nostrils.

Then The Music grew louder and swept away all other sensations. I felt as if I were caught in the center of a tornado of sound that I could never hope or want to escape.

393

Lieza strutted and sang with a fervor that went beyond anything I'd ever heard on her records.

I wished I could make her love me.

Joel had implied that she already did, but I knew better. He had just been trying to perform one last act of kindness before dying.

Out on the floor, the Brits were laughing and dancing as if they were at a sock hop, which surprised me. "Tomorrow Is the Day" has a driving beat that makes your muscles jump, but it isn't bubblegum. There's too much anger in it.

At the song's finish, Lieza windmilled her left arm and took the band directly into "Race You to Hell."

I'd heard the song before, of course, but had never really listened closely. This time I did, and the lyrics made me cringe. They conjured up visions of the slick wooden church pews I sat in as a kid, and of bald-headed preachers with purplish noses, railing about war and hell and welfare.

Poor Mom and Dad. They so wanted to do the right thing for me, to give me a religious background so I'd grow up to be a man of moral conviction . . .

So here's the result, I thought. *One Class A Jagoff.*

And then there's Maria. She had even more training in how to be holy than I did, and she just spent Christmas vacation humping a regiment of Gurkhas.

There I went thinking about my sweet blue-bottomed ex-lover again. That was all I needed.

> *If that's your heaven . . .*
> *If that's your heaven . . .*
> *Yeah, if this is your heaven . . .*
> *Then I'll race you to hell.*

Blunt Instrument ended the song with a series of chords so loud that I thought my skull would split.

The building shook with the audience's cries, and sparks flew up from hundreds of metal-box fires. Some of the lights set into the distant ceiling came on.

Lieza stood at the front edge of the stage with her arms limp and her head bowed. She looked even weaker than Cherry, and I was afraid she was going to fall into the mob.

Then her voice echoed all around me, telling the audience to shut up, that they were nothing but zombies, that they didn't deserve The Music.

The crowd's roar became a murmur, then a hiss.

Tycho hit a drum beat that sounded like a gunshot, and when Lieza looked at him, he shouted encouragement.

She glanced at me for a moment too, but I just stood there, a useless thing, a tumor in the body of wrack & roll.

The Bastard Child turned back to the crowd and told them that the next song wasn't for them, but for Joel.

This would be the one she had written at the hospital. My body tensed as I waited for the first note, and I looked out into the throng to see whether any of them had any idea of the magnitude of what was coming.

My gaze fell on a grinning, gum-chewing woman in the midst of the crowd on the main floor. She was jumping in excitement, her breasts and her dark blonde hair bouncing in counterpoint to the rest of her body.

The Music started again, but I hardly heard it.

The only word my mind knew was *Maria.*

* * *

I couldn't think about anything else.

Not even about you, Lieza, or what you were singing.

After all, you were only the woman I worshipped. Maria was the woman who had betrayed me.

I saw a way I could get into the crowd. With the air throbbing around me like a giant's heartbeat, I crept behind the drum platform to the left rear corner of the stage.

The wooden island was at least six-and-a-half feet higher than the main floor and was surrounded by a ring of Straight security people. I sat down on the edge, tapped the closest two Straights on opposite shoulders, and jumped down between them when they turned.

The floor was cement, and my ankles stung when I landed; but my momentum was stronger than the pain, and I dove into the crowd. Something brushed the back of my shirt—one of the security men making a grab—and then I was enclosed in a mass of leather, denim, and skin. There had been a few feet of space between each Wracker in Piccadilly Circus, but here the bodies were literally crammed against one another.

I had to duck low and squeeze past hips and legs. Three times, I jumped up to check my position, and each time I saw that I was getting closer to Maria.

On the third jump, she waved to me. She might have called out, too, but I couldn't hear her over the constant pulse of The Music.

Then, when there were only a few layers of bodies between us, I stopped. What the hell was I going to do when I reached her? Was I going to hug her and tell her I'd missed her terribly, or was I going to call her a traitorous slut and try to strangle her?

Or, more likely, was I going to stand there dumbly while she giggled and called me "Cliffie"?

Did I hate her or want her so much that I was willing to go through that again?

I pushed forward through the crowd.

And couldn't find her.

I jumped up a fourth time, and a fifth, but she was gone. If she had ever been there to begin with.

Sick with self-contempt, I turned to go back to the stage.

And there, blocking the way, was Genghis Khan.

He was dressed in khakis, with a scabbard hanging from his belt.

* * *

I should have known he would be there.

The fact that the end of the world was around the corner was irrelevant to him. He had a vendetta against me, and nothing would keep him from carrying it out. I had escaped him in the Circus, but it wouldn't happen again.

I wondered whether Maria had deliberately lured me into the crowd for him.

Genghis Khan grinned, revealing his rotten teeth, and drew a longknife from his scabbard.

Slowly, he used the sword to draw a circle in the air

above our heads, and the Wrackers around us squeezed away as if by magic. One of them looked at us and mouthed "Jesus," but the rest, after getting out of the Gurkha's reach, kept their attention focused on the stage.

Genghis and I were left alone on a spot of bare cement five feet in diameter, and I couldn't run without hitting a wall of flesh.

My enemy put the tip of the longknife on my forehead, and I heard Lieza's voice for the first time since seeing Maria in the crowd:

> He rode a dragon to the sun
> And cooked his mind insane.
> When he came back he swung the sword
> And gave us all the mark of Cain.

The sword jerked, and I felt a sharp, burning sting as the skin over my right eyebrow opened.

I couldn't hear my own cry.

Genghis pulled back the longknife and grinned again.

For a moment, as the blood started its slow trickle toward my eyes, I felt a weird kind of relief.

That's all, I thought. *He's set the mark, and now no one can harm me.*

It was a fantasy. Mark or no mark, Cain never gets a break.

The Gurkha brought the knife tip toward me again, and the insane thing inside me chose that moment to aim a punch at his throat.

Genghis sidestepped it and kicked me in the groin.

A hot wave of pain washed into my abdomen and chest. By the time it reached my head, I was on my knees.

I ought to be praying, I thought.

But I knew better.

The sword touched my cheek and nicked open the skin. As I winced away and fell onto my left side, I was submerged in a sea of bodies—and knew my dream was coming true.

Genghis grasped the longknife in both hands and raised it high.

My head would join Bill's and Joel's in the swirling current.

Then, as Genghis tensed to strike, a black man wearing a plaid shirt stepped into the circle.

He stopped just behind the Gurkha and looked down at me, frowning. His lips parted, and I saw that one of his front teeth was the color of a polished penny.

Genghis Khan's concentration faltered as he sensed the presence of the intruder.

It was Eddie Dixon. Alive.

Lieza *had* seen him in the Circus.

"Are you deaf, boy?" he asked. It was as if his voice came from inside my own head.

Genghis was turning now, and in another instant he would see who was behind him.

"Open your ears," Dixon said. "Listen close for a change."

And then The Music came in a torrent:

> *Is it right that we should burn*
> *For finding evil, trying to learn?*
> *Is it right that we should pay*
> *For knowledge that's been warped this way?*

Dixon nodded to me and stepped back into the crowd. But Lieza's song kept on:

> *We must storm the walls—*
> *Rush the fence—*
> *The demon thrives*
> *At our expense.*

I felt that she was singing directly to me, telling me that Genghis Khan had power only because I granted it.

The Gurkha, seeing that he couldn't reach Dixon, turned back and raised the longknife again.

He was strong, just as the kids at the swimming pool had been strong.

But strength isn't power.

The will to live is power. Rage is power.

The Music is power.

And I had all of those things if I chose to use them.

Lieza sang:

> *Take it back—*
> *Take it back—*
> *Take it back—*
> *Take it back—*
> *Take back the Garden!*

The longknife swept down, and I did as the Bastard Child commanded.

I thrust my feet between Genghis Khan's ankles and scissored them wide, simultaneously twisting my body to the right. The Gurkha's left hand flailed away from the sword hilt as he fell, and the blade glanced off the cement by my ear.

Still rolling, I grasped my enemy's right wrist, twisting his hand open and spinning him so that he landed on his back.

His face registered no pain; only surprise.

The longknife fell between us.

He scrabbled for it, but it was already mine.

As I rose to stand above him, I felt as though I were ascending to heaven.

* * *

The crowd had gone insane, and our circle closed as they surged forward. Something had happened that had nothing to do with me or my enemy.

Genghis Khan had no room to maneuver now, and his eyes said he was sure of what I would do next. I would thrust the point of the longknife into his throat.

I might have done it, too . . . but then I heard Lieza's call to rebellion, and felt the explosion of sound that was the Wrackers' response.

An intense vibration surged through me like electricity, and at that moment I realized that Genghis was no longer important. I turned away, leaving him there on the floor.

The first thing I saw was a falling banner, and I flung

the sword at it. The weapon speared the red-and-gold cloth in midair and stabbed down into the stage beside the Bastard Child.

She was on her knees, her arms spread wide. She was bleeding.

I don't remember fighting my way through the mob, but I remember the moment I climbed onto the stage and pushed in between Fug and Tycho to reach her.

Her eyes looked unfocused. "Pretty good, huh, Straight boy?" she said in a strange, distant voice.

"Better than that," I answered.

Daniel P. Jackson appeared beside me and said, "Better than anything."

I saw in his face, and hers, what they believe they are to each other; and I knew that I would never be the one to tell them otherwise.

Lieza's wounded hands touched the cut on my forehead, and our blood joined.

* * *

Now, sitting beside her bed while the window glows brighter and brighter, I think I've reached the truth of what has happened.

She's smiling, and I know her dreams are telling her that The Music has saved the world from itself.

But it isn't so.

The Music is only sound, a distortion of air. No matter how much energy Blunt Instrument put into her song, no matter how desperately she and her bandmates wanted it to make a difference, it would have meant nothing to the crowd or to the world if Zackman hadn't come for her.

I've written that God always requires a sacrifice if He is to answer your prayers, but I was wrong.

It isn't God who requires the sacrifice. It's everybody else.

So it wasn't Lieza Galilei's song that saved us, but the Bastard Child's blood.

No bombs have fallen yet, and if the news from Churchill-Chiang Station is true, none will. Not this time, anyway.

Lieza stirs.

"Want to go away," she murmurs. "Far away..."

Big Ben isn't ringing, but my watch says it's 12:00 A.M., January 12, 1980.

A new day.

Hysterical Perspective VI: *Without Form, and Void*

Lieza Galilei, Daniel P. Jackson, and Clifton Bonner each claimed to have seen Eddie Dixon that night. Based on the reported times and locations of the sightings, however, I must conclude that the Founder had the ability to move through crowds with the speed of an Olympic sprinter.

A Believer, on the other hand, would say that Dixon's ghost could have appeared to all three of them simultaneously.

What happened afterward is less mysterious:

The riots in London, Washington, and Peking were tremendous, but riots never change the minds of those in power. A nuclear war would have taken place regardless, were it not for what occurred on Churchill-Chiang Station.

The Station's spysat center was monitoring the various broadcasts of Blunt Instrument's concert, and someone decided that putting The Music over the public address system would be a terrific morale-booster. By the time the military commandant ordered it cut off, the Bastard Child had already sung "Take Back the Garden," had been shot, and had urged a revolution. Three strikes, you're out.

The result was that thirty-five Station residents, Wrackers all, tried to storm the Weapons Control Center. As they approached, however, overlapping steel plates irised shut and blocked the passage. The commandant's voice ordered them to disperse or face the consequences.

So they dispersed, but three of them put on EVA suits and went outside, where they removed a few access panels and cut off the Weapons Control Center's power.

"We realized that what had happened to Bitch Alice was now happening to the Bastard Child," they later said in a Declaration of Non-War. "We also realized that we were being made a party to it, and this in turn pissed us off."

(The Alliance's Moon base had a few nukes as well, and the Lunies could have tossed them wherever they wanted—but they couldn't survive without the bimonthly deliveries that were launched from the Station. So, as long as the Wrackers owned the Station, they also owned the Moon.)

The negotiations that followed, both on Earth and in space, went as might have been expected. Agreements were reached and broken; skirmishes with conventional weapons broke out in a hundred different cities; thousands of people died; and Venezuela claimed Concepcion for itself, telling both the United States and Britain to skag off. Business as usual.

But there was no nuclear war.

* * *

Inevitably, a new political party arose in both the United States and the Alliance nations. They called themselves the Rollers, and their candidate in the November 1980 U.S. Presidential election, Elizabeth "Bazz" Watson, earned a narrow victory over J.R. Fitzgerald—who might have won had he been able to appear in public without twitching.

Watson's first Presidential act was to initiate Project Barsoom, a cooperative venture between the United States and the Anglo-Chinese Alliance. Its goals were "to promote friendship between our nations and get off this scrodheap."

Winton R. Wilson was in hiding by then, because Pissant Jackson had publicly named him as the man responsible for the death of Bitch Alice. In 1982, the Big Whig's body was found in a Joplin, Missouri, hotel bathtub, and although the death was ruled a suicide, the circumstances were questionable. He had ingested three quarts of KhromeKleen.

Annabelle "the Squid" Kirk fled to Mexico after the election and lived well on cash she had embezzled from a White House slush fund. She died in 1989, cause unknown.

As for Blunt Instrument . . .

Lieza Galilei eventually recovered from her wounds,

although her guitar playing was never quite the same, and her band continued to perform until 1986. In that year, the Bastard Child began training to do something else—perhaps because she thought it was what Bitch Alice would have done.

* * *

Project Barsoom's first expedition landed the *Lowell's Mistake* near the Candor Chasma in the Valles Marineris on October 12, 1986. Pissant Jackson, who had served as liaison between NOSS and EASA since the Project's inception, lived long enough to hear voices being broadcast from Mars, and then died that evening of complications stemming from cirrhosis of the liver.

The Bastard Child arranged to have the second expedition scatter his ashes over the Tharsis plateau.

The inevitable colonization mission finally arrived in seven landers on September 2, 1994, on the site of what is now New Miami. The conversation between the first colonists to step outside is of particular interest:

DOCTOR C. BONNER: This is a goddamn desert.
STEVEN "FUG" LEWIS: [Unintelligible grunt.]
BONNER: I have a feeling . . . this place is going to kill us.

LIEZA GALILEI: Isn't it skagging wonderful?
And kill them it did . . . but on their terms.

I've taken a walk while dictating this chapter, and now I'm standing over a great slab of orange rock with four words carved into its surface:

WE TOOK IT BACK

Man, ain't it the glorious truth.

—Lorna P.N. Chicago-deSade,
A Brief, Biased History of Postwar America,
1945–1995, Complete with Nude Photographs (New Miami: Purple Press, 2019), pp. 392–96. [Flattering holographic study of the author, p. 397.]

Coda

We goin' up to Tharsis
Got a pick and got a plow.
Yeah, we goin' up to Tharsis
Got a pick and got a plow.
And then we gonna sing a song
'Cause, Lord, we sure as hell know how.

—Anonymous,
    written on a tabletop in
    a London pub, ca. 1980